BITTER FRUITS

ALICE CLARK-PLATTS

ISIS
LARGE
PRINT

First published in Great Britain 2015
by
Penguin Books

First Isis Edition
published 2016
by arrangement with
Penguin Books
Penguin Random House

A catalogue record for this book is available
from the British Library.

ISBN 978–1–78541–156–4 (hb)
ISBN 978–1–78541–162–5 (pb)

Published by
F. A. Thorpe (Publishing)
Anstey, Leicestershire

Set by Words & Graphics Ltd.
Anstey, Leicestershire
Printed and bound in Great Britain by
T. J. International Ltd., Padstow, Cornwall

This book is printed on acid-free paper

BITTER FRUITS

The murder of a first-year university student shocks the city of Durham. The victim, Emily Brabents, was from the privileged and popular set at Joyce College, a cradle for the country's future elite. As Detective Inspector Erica Martin investigates the college, she finds a close-knit community fuelled by jealousy, obsession and secrets. The very last thing she expects is an instant confession . . . The picture of Emily that begins to emerge is that of a girl wanted by everyone, but not truly known by anyone — that is, except for Daniel Shepherd: her fellow student and ever-faithful friend, and the only one who cares. The only one who would do *anything* for her . . .

SPECIAL MESSAGE TO READERS

For my mum and dad

CHAPTER
ONE

The body was found in the icy coffin of the weir. The cathedral loomed above, its shadow stretching flat across the dark waters which had played with her hair. It streamed out behind her body in the flaky current, turning this way and that. Damp tendrils stuck to her face, her eyes open, knowing. She wore a university T-shirt, purple and clinging. Tight jeans hugging her splayed legs in the lapping water; fingers teasing the weeds in which she had become entangled.

A heron plopped its foot in the water. It turned its head slowly to one side, considering. Grey-bearded clouds bumped into each other above, sagely taking on board the crime scene below. All that could be heard, aside from the swishing of the universe, was the sucking of the air pocket beneath the small of her back: *fnuck, pause; fnuck, pause; fnuck, pause.* Steady and meditative, the heron spread his wings and took flight.

Monday 22 May, 5 a.m.

A fluorescent glare from Martin's phone stabbed into the darkness of the bedroom. Awake already despite the untimely hour, she was quick to sit up and put it to her ear, murmuring softly to avoid waking the sleeping form next to her. The blue of a cold sunrise inched through the cracks in the curtains as she finished the call and swung her legs off the bed. She looked across the room to the mirror which hung above a chest of drawers, her reflection becoming clearer as more light entered the room. Her red hair was mussed, her mouth and eyes still drowsy with inaction.

"What is it?" Jim asked, stirring to life beneath the covers. His hand touched her back for a moment before being withdrawn. Martin considered this retreat for a second before she answered.

"Work," she said, twisting round to look at her husband, who had pushed himself up on to his elbows. "Could be something . . . I might not be home for a while."

Jim gave a querying look. Martin touched his hand briefly and then stood, rolling her shoulders back, setting her chin.

"A body's been found down by the weir," she said in the quiet, reaching for her clothes.

Martin found her way to the crime scene thirty minutes later. Approaching the gate on the track leading to Prebends Bridge, the car headlights swept the thick line of trees bordering the slope down to the riverbank. Darkness was lifting to reveal dank cobwebs of mist spun through the air. Martin parked her car next to the gate and jumped out, taking a pair of white rubber wellingtons from the car boot and replacing her ballet pumps with them. She pulled on a plastic raincoat,

2

shoving the arms of her parka bulkily through the polyester sleeves. She walked down past the gate and on to the bridge. From there, drifting over the water, she could see the lights of the response unit and the dayglo outline of the tent being used to house the body. The river stretched on beyond the morbidity, blackish navy and glistening, its banks sloping upwards to where last night a thousand students had caroused in bars. Martin jogged down the steep path which led to the river and flashed her card at the constable on the cordon.

"I'll take you to Doctor Walsh, ma'am," he said, turning away from her.

"Don't bother. I'll find him. You'd better stay here and watch for marauders."

"They'll all be sleeping off their hangovers, this early in the day," the constable sniffed.

Martin carried on past him and headed to the tent, briefly acknowledging the various SOCOs who stood around, waiting for the call to start the minutiae of their investigation. As she pulled on her protective shoe covers and plastic gloves, she noticed the outline of what must be a boathouse further up river, bunting flapping forlornly from its roof, detritus of some sort scattered in front of it over the dewy grass. Martin bent to open up the tent flap before peering inside.

"DI Martin?" The man who spoke was crouched over the shape of a girl. He considered Martin with a frown as she edged inside stiffly where body heat fused with the dank smell of sodden ground. "When DCI Butterworth said you'd be the SIO, I assumed he meant a man. Sorry."

3

He didn't sound sorry, Martin thought. Perhaps if she was called DI Flowers, she could prevent the continual assumption that she was male — although why her sex actually mattered, she wasn't entirely sure. She chose to ignore the stab of irritation this caused and turned to look at what faced her. The body stared upwards, her head crooked to one side and her palms spread, as if she were shrugging. She looked abandoned, Martin thought. The girl's mouth was twisted in condemnation, indelibly taken aback by what had happened to her. Her chin was high and her blonde hair, dirtied by the mud of the riverbank, coiled around her neck in wet strings. A tiny black leaf stuck to her cheek, a beauty spot gone wrong.

"Doctor Walsh," she said to the doctor, giving a curt nod. "Has she been moved?"

Walsh nodded. "Couple who found her dragged her up here. Tried to give her mouth to mouth." His eyebrows lifted at the futility.

Martin breathed deliberately, steadying her instinct to move fast, the loud clock of the crime scene ticking relentlessly within her. The scent of mildew cloyed in the enclosed space, and she could feel the beginnings of a headache as the infinite possibilities crowded her brain; those possibilities more tortuous for someone like her than an empty trail.

"Could be a baptism of fire for you," Walsh continued, gently moving the girl's hair to reveal dark wine-coloured bruises bisecting the line of her throat. "Might be drowning I suppose, but these marks are nasty."

4

Martin bent over double to ease herself further into the tent, awkwardly shuffling on her haunches up to where the body lay. She swallowed, wanting to hear her own voice, to normalize the scene.

"I wish they'd make these things bigger. They know average-sized human beings will have to work in them."

"Better ones in Newcastle, were there?" Walsh said without looking at her, shifting in his squat to the left to give her access to the body. She ignored him, looking intently into the girl's face.

"Young." She paused. "Suicide, do you think? You must get a few around exam time. Unlikely with those marks I guess."

The girl's eyes stared back at Martin. Glazed but judging. Walsh leaned forwards and closed them.

"Hard to drown yourself," he said. "Not unheard of, I suppose. As I say, we don't know yet."

"Time of death?" Martin risked.

Walsh narrowed his eyes. He backed out in as dignified a manner as possible, his head the last bit of him to leave the tent.

"I'll be in touch when the post mortem's done."

Martin bent her head again to the body and breathed softly, the sound of it a comfort in the overly warm stillness of the tent. There was a tenderness to the girl's face, a peacefulness now that her eyes were closed. Martin knew, though, that if the girl had been strangled, there would have been no serenity at the end. She would have battled. And she had lost.

Martin's eyes travelled down the girl's body. Why was she only wearing a T-shirt at this time of night? Even though it was May, the evenings were cold and the wind in the north-east was unkind to those not hardened to its charms. Martin studied the girl's limbs, which were already taking on a marble-ish sheen. She turned the girl's left arm over, and her fingers hovered over the scars running in neat horizontal lines from her wrist to her elbow. Funny to wear a T-shirt too, she thought, if you were a self-harmer. In her experience, those scars would be desperately covered up for fear of discovery.

Martin let her eyes linger on the girl's face for a last moment, knowing that she would soon be moved, that the clues to her death would be disturbed. Who was she? What had she seen before the end? Martin moved her lips, the words of a long-forgotten prayer coming to her briefly. Shaking it off, she crawled out of the morbid fug of the tent into the air and stood, stretching her back and flexing her fingers to the sky. She turned her head and lowered her arms as she saw a female figure approach.

"Morning, boss," the woman said. "DS Jones. I don't think we've been formally introduced."

Martin nodded and shook the proffered hand. Her promotion to Detective Inspector as head of the Major Crime Unit, moving here from Newcastle, had taken place only three weeks previously, and she had still to meet all the members of the force. She appraised Jones, a square sort of girl whose innate cheeriness was clearly being held in check with a frown and firm mouth, a seriousness represented further by her stolid laced-up shoes.

"Good to meet you, Jones. Have we got any ID yet?"

"Student card in the back pocket. Name's Emily Brabents. She was at Joyce College. First year."

"Joyce. That's on the Bailey?"

Jones nodded.

"Anything else on her? Phone or bag?"

"Not so far."

"We need to inform the next of kin. We'd better get ourselves up to Joyce and see the principal. Get someone to call him or her. Tell them we're on our way."

Jones spoke rapidly into her radio, and Martin indicated to the SOCOs that they could begin their work. The women turned from the tent, walking together up the slope, away from the water, their feet crunching on the wet and pebbled ground. Martin looked up at the fading crescent of the moon as they approached the stone ramparts of the bridge. "How long have you lived in Durham, Jones?" she asked.

"All my life," Jones answered, shoving her hands into her pockets.

Martin glanced across at her. "This was Regatta weekend, wasn't it?"

"Yes. It'll make initial enquiries messy," Jones commented. "The amount of people traipsing along here over the last couple of days."

Martin nodded, the eyes of the dead girl still emblazoned on her brain. She stopped and circled back for a second to look at the river as it wended its silvery way between the verdant bush of the trees framing the riverbank. As the morning mists began to clear, Martin

7

could see at last the vast, pale shape of Durham Cathedral emerge above the old mill on the right bank. Despite her short time in the city, the cathedral seemed to Martin to be ever-present, an unyielding frown buttressed by the might of its own endurance.

A sullen breeze huddled the tops of the trees, a crowd of crones bending to observe the crime scene and all its activity. The white-suited bodies of the SOCOs began to spread out along the bank, finger-tipping the ground. Martin inhaled sharply, watching them, thinking it through. "A murder of a student is bad news. Bad for tourism, university morale. Press interest."

Jones remained silent with her head down, falling in with Martin as she resumed walking.

"What's it like between the students and the locals here? Any tension?"

"Some. Nothing out of the ordinary. Friday and Saturday nights are for the local kids to come out and play. The students mainly stick to weeknights. But the Regatta's always on a Sunday." Jones looked at Martin, who seemed deep in thought. "Some of the uni lot might've been rubbing the town's faces in it." She shrugged. "It happens."

Martin nodded. "Is there CCTV along the river-bank?"

"Nah, boss." Jones shook her head. "The council won't even approve proper street lights on Prebends Bridge." She smiled a little. "Technology is seen as the devil in some parts of the city."

The women reached the car, and Martin began to take off her boots. "Do you read books, Jones?" she asked as she put her pumps back on, divesting herself of the polyester jacket. The day was brighter now, the sun clawing its way through the clouds, scaling the grey sky.

Jones was nonplussed. "Uh, yes, I suppose so, guv. I like the odd murder mystery." She watched her new boss closely. Martin seemed different from the usual lot here. She took things in her own time, it was plain. Jones was less a thinker, more a grafter. But there was something about Martin she liked. She had a certainty about her, something you could trust. "My gut's telling me this is murder, boss," she chanced, wanting to have Martin agree with something she said.

"Save your gut for the Christmas party, Jones," Martin answered. "We don't know anything yet. Stick around, though. Someone who reads murder mysteries will be good to have along." She winked at Jones and got behind the wheel.

CHAPTER
TWO

Monday 22 May, 7.30 a.m.

Martin considered the stone façade of Joyce College from the cobbles outside. Built in the nineteenth century, the college sat on the Bailey, the street which once enclosed the Norman walls of Durham Castle. Opposite it was Keats College, housed in the castle itself. These were the aristocracy of the collegiate system at Durham. Martin knew that direct paths lay to them from Eton and Harrow, from Uppingham and Benenden. Within their walls, the next editor of The *Spectator* drank in the college bar; the next Chancellor of the Exchequer lay on his bed dreaming of poetry; the next high-jumping gold medallist pounded the track circumnavigating the sports field, a few miles down the road from the ancient buildings. She shook her head a little, shaking off the pomp which seemed to bear down on her from the rooftops. It was only a building, after all.

The river mists had risen with the morning sun, but the inside of the college was still snug in comparison with the chilled air. Martin pushed through the entrance door with a show of confidence she at a stroke didn't feel, pleased to find Jones keeping pace. New to the way they did things in Durham, she would need someone on side with this investigation, an ally she could rely on. The pathologist at the riverside was right. If this was murder, it would be a baptism of fire. Martin's first case as a detective inspector, performed under the glowering stare of the university.

The interior of Joyce was a study in mahogany, with brocaded walls and a grand staircase which arced round, out of sight to the casual visitor. The carpet was a deep green, patterned with gold swirls. A vague smell of cabbage intermixed with freshly baked bread hung in the air. "God, it smells like school," Martin said, sniffing disparagingly. She looked to her right, where a cubby hole was positioned in the wall, a sign declaring it to be the reception. Martin tapped the accompanying bell and waited, shifting on her feet. Jones patrolled the opposite wall, reading the raft of notices tacked to the board there. After a moment, a middle-aged woman with short hair, dyed a vivid red, appeared at the cubby hole's window. Martin flashed her ID at her with a friendly smile.

"Oh the police," the receptionist said in reply, with a buttonholed misery. "You'll be wanting Principal Mason I expect."

"Detective Inspector Martin and Detective Sergeant Jones, Ms . . . ?"

"Mrs Earl. I'm the receptionist here. As you can see." She walked out of sight and then reappeared through a doorway along the wall. "I'll take you to him," she continued, starting up the stairs. "Don't suppose you'll tell me what's going on?"

"I'm sure there'll be an announcement at some point, Mrs Earl."

"Yes, I'm sure," the receptionist said as she made her way down a carpeted corridor along which several large doors faced a mahogany balustrade looking down on to the entrance hall. She paused outside one of the doors and seemed to steady herself before knocking.

"Come in," answered an authoritative voice within.

Mrs Earl poked her head around the door, saying, "There's police here, Phillip. I think you're expecting them?"

"Yes, of course."

Mrs Earl pushed the door wide, opening the view to a large office with a desk in front of a bay window. Phillip Mason was a man's man, Martin thought, albeit with the long, delicate fingers of a piano player. In his fifties, he had the hard physique of a tennis player, tall and lean, with a buzz cut of grey hair and cool blue eyes. His shirt was unbuttoned at the top and he wore no tie. He had a distracted air about him but stood up as the policewomen walked in.

"Detective Inspector Martin," she said again, holding out her hand as they approached the desk.

"DS Jones."

"Phillip Mason, as you know," he said, waving a hand to the chairs in front of the desk. "Thank you, Julia."

Mrs Earl left the room despondently, calling out as she left, "I'll be downstairs if you need anything . . ."

They sat. Mason placed his hands in front of him on the desk in a prayer position, the tips of his index fingers grazing his chin. A steaming mug sat on his desk, and the aroma of just-brewed coffee hung in the air. He offered them nothing. He was the type of man in a position of power she'd seen before, Martin surmised, a man who would let a door slam in the face of the person behind him because he would always be unaware that there was anyone else in the world at that moment but him. She stored that thought and looked over at Jones, who leaned forwards.

"We have a preliminary identification of a body found down at the weir past Prebends Bridge. I believe you've been informed of this . . .?"

Mason looked at Jones for a moment before moving his gaze in studied dismay to his desktop. "I was told the body of a student had been found. I haven't been told who it is."

"Her name was Emily Brabents," continued Jones.

Mason looked up, frowning. "Emily?"

"Did you know Emily?" questioned Martin.

Mason shook his head, apparently bewildered. "She's a Fresher." He stared at Martin, swallowing. "Was a Fresher. I wouldn't have expected it . . ." The principal appeared shocked. "She seemed very popular. I don't know what to say." He paused. "How awfully sad."

Martin remained silent, giving the principal the opportunity to fill the quiet.

"We have a big community spirit here. The Joyce spirit . . ." the principal floundered. It sounded as though he were reading from the college prospectus. "It was the Durham Regatta weekend," the principal looked up at Martin, "as I'm sure you know. I remember seeing Emily only yesterday, down at the boathouse. She looked like, well, she just looked very happy, and everything was, you know, normal."

"Who was she with, when you saw her at the boathouse?"

"Oh," the principal spread his hands out over the desktop. "Her usual crowd. Hard to say, there were lots of people milling about." Martin noticed a tiny twitch pulsate in the corner of Mason's left eye. "You might want to speak to the college president of Joyce. He's reading Politics here. I know he was down there for a while. He might know who she was with."

"What's his name?" Martin asked.

"Simon Rush," answered Mason. "His rooms are just down the road. In the same building where Emily lives actually," he paused uncertainly. "Uh, lived. He'll be there now, given the early hour, I expect. Shall I get Mrs Earl to bring him here? I suppose, well, I should probably be with him when he hears the news."

"Thank you, yes."

The principal picked up the phone and muttered briefly into it. "She'll go and find him," he said to the women afterwards.

"We'll need to interview all the students who knew Emily. Those on her course. Her friends. Enemies."

"Enemies?" Mason laughed. "I don't think she would have had any of those. I mean," he halted. "Why would that be relevant?"

Martin and Jones were silent.

14

"You're saying her death was an attack? Not suicide?" Mason searched the policewomen's faces for clues.

"Why would you think Emily would want to kill herself, Mr Mason?" Martin asked, but the principal looked blank as he processed what he'd heard. "We'll understand more after the post mortem," she continued eventually. "In the meantime, we have to cover all possibilities." She paused. "I should warn you that the press may come knocking on your door about this."

"My door?" Mason gave a quick frown.

"Well, the university's door," Martin replied. "A young girl has died in a public place. Whether or not it's under suspicious circumstances, there may be talk. Particularly given Durham's academic reputation." She altered her position in her chair. "I just want to prepare you for that, sir."

Mason stared at her in a continuing reverie as a knock came at the door and an extremely tall — six foot three or four — wiry-framed boy came in. He had close-cropped dark hair and vivid green eyes behind silver-framed John Lennon-style glasses. He looked fresh, as if straight from the shower, although Martin could detect an underlying aroma. What was it? It may have been the reek of self-assurance as he came forwards and stood before the principal's desk, resting both of his hands by their thumbs in the belt loops of his jeans. He wore sandy-coloured desert boots, bulky in contrast to his general leanness.

"You wanted to see me, Phillip?" he asked the principal.

Martin frowned. His attitude was overly easy towards someone with the principal's clout in the university.

"The police need to speak to you, Simon," Mason gestured to behind where the boy stood. Rush turned to look at them and gave a lopsided smile. Martin felt oddly uncomfortable being seated while he stood looking down on her. She shifted in her chair but couldn't stand without relinquishing power to him.

"Do you know Emily Brabents, Simon?" she asked.

"Yes, I know Emily well," he answered, still smiling with only one half of his mouth.

Is he smirking? Martin thought, puzzled. Something wasn't right here. She looked across at Jones, who was studying Simon Rush closely.

Mason coughed softly. "I'm afraid, Simon, that I have some bad news." He leaned forwards over his desk, as if he wanted to hug his student. His hands stretched empathetically over the leather top. "Emily has, Emily was . . ." He paused, seemingly stricken but with hard eyes. His words hung soft and close in the air. Mason's lips were dry, Martin noticed. He and Rush were locked into each other, each set of eyes clamped on the other man's.

"Emily is dead, Simon. I'm sorry." Martin broke the silence at last. Rush appeared to inhale with a faint judder, wrenching his eyes away from the principal. Then he looked at Martin and Jones steadily in turn.

"Emily is dead," the boy repeated tonelessly.

"Yes, Emily is dead." He continued to stare down at them in their chairs.

Martin could hear the tick of the clock on the mantelpiece. Something about the boy's reaction was a playact; it didn't ring true. The silence continued. "I'm sorry if this is a shock for you," she forced herself to say, trying to wade through the swamp of quiet which seemed to have engulfed the room. Her voice sounded too loud within it. *Keep calm*, she thought. *Let it unfold*.

Simon swallowed deeply, his Adam's apple shifting visibly. His face changed, and at once a noise shot from him, the scream of a laugh. Martin jerked involuntarily, her hands instinctively reaching for the arms of her chair, ready to leap up and restrain him.

"Oh, it's not a shock," he said, barking laughter for a few seconds as he saw the effect of his behaviour on the women. He snapped the smile off his face. "It's not a shock in the slightest." He tapped himself on the head violently with both hands. "It's not a shock," he repeated for the third time, now staring again at Principal Mason. He began to move his head weirdly from side to side like a caged animal. As he did, the lenses of his glasses gave the illusion of turning white, their reflection bouncing back the light in the room, leaving him for a second eyeless, with blank spaces where the windows of his soul should be. He splayed his hands towards Martin and licked his lips. "Because I'm the one who killed her." His eyes seemed to bore into Martin's. "And then I dumped her in the weir, just as she deserved."

17

CHAPTER
THREE

I came to Durham on a cold October morning, on the first train out of London. My mother had come with me to King's Cross Station to see me off and she carried on standing forlornly at the ticket barrier, long after the train had pulled out of the station. I don't know that she did this as I couldn't see her, of course. But I imagine her doing it. It's the type of thing she would do. Since my father had died of a stroke, she had whittled herself down to something constantly sad. She seemed even diminished in height, and the lines of her face cragged more heavily than ever before. She had turned-down cow eyes much of the time, often brimming with tears, which would drip into the teacup held in her lap as she watched daytime television more faithfully than any other activity she undertook in her life.

By the time the train pulled out of the station, I had put on my headphones and was being blasted by indie rock, guaranteed to quell even the smallest emergence of sympathy for Mother. I couldn't afford to be sympathetic to her any more. I had to escape. I was already a year behind my peers in starting university, thinking I would have to delay indefinitely to look after her. My sister, married with three children and living on an estate in a village twenty-five miles out of London, was no use to me or my mother. She had barely registered the sacrifice I was making when I rang her a year ago, shouting it down the phone over the rabble noise at her end. Sighing, I had put the phone down and reconciled myself to endless copies of *New!* magazine and cups of builder's tea. I considered taking up smoking, but this seemed an unnecessary expense — even for someone who wanted to pretend they lived in Paris while living in Walthamstow.

Mother and I bumbled along during that year. I took a part-time job in a local pub to make some money and contribute to housekeeping. Mother carried on watching overly tanned middle-aged men sell things for other people, and so it went on. Every Saturday, I would pop into the newsagent and put five pounds down for five lottery tickets for her. And then the unimaginable happened. She won. Two hundred and seventy-three thousand pounds on a rollover week. I was free. *I was free*.

Mother paid off the mortgage on the house, and I employed a cleaner to come every day with some shopping. Evie would pop in for a cup of tea and she would watch *Cash in the Attic* with Mother before doing a cursory swish around the house with a duster. It was the company Mother needed, and once I could see they were friends, I made the call to Student Services. They were really very good about it and said I could start that October with the new Freshers. I would be a Fresher, I said to myself while looking in the mirror one morning. It didn't seem real. I was travelling two hundred and fifty miles north of London. Away. It clenched in my stomach. Away!

The train rattled on, and I nodded off to sleep for a bit. When I woke, it was almost dark outside. It wasn't yet midday but a thick bank of cloud had built up in the sky, and the gloom pervaded the train carriage. The lights came on inside, warming us within — the calm of the carriage whistling through the wild and woolly landscape. I could see my reflection in the train window, the collar of my coat upturned, the briefest whisper of stubble on my chin. My hair was short with a sort of quiff at the front. I thought this effective.

I began to look in my backpack for my book. I was obsessed then with Graham Greene and was two-thirds through *The Power and the Glory*. While not a Catholic — in fact, my parents had abhorred any mention of religion in our house — I had always been attracted to its rituals, romanticized those who gave up their life to accept its austerity. The martyr in me, recently demonstrated by my care for my mother over and above my own needs, relished its severity. I was gripped by Greene at this time and opened the book eagerly.

It took some time, therefore, for the noise of crying to seep into my brain. It wasn't loud sobbing, more a persistent sniffing accompanied by long sighs which caught at the beginning of each fresh bout of downpour. I sat up in my seat and looked around, straining my neck to look over the seats in front of me and behind. Two rows ahead was a girl about my age. She was sat at a table and faced me. She had shoulder-length blonde hair and wide-spaced brown eyes, which gave her a look of innocence. This enhanced her attractiveness in my opinion. She was wearing a pink button-down shirt with the top two buttons undone. She had an Alice band in her hair, black velvet as I recall. Her hair was thick and curled at the ends. She sat, looking down, crumpling tissues over and over again in her hands. The table displayed the discarded tissues like a monotonous collage.

I sat back in my seat heavily. What was I to do? Should I just ignore her? I looked at my book in dismay. Yes, I would ignore her. I picked up the book. The priest was seeking refuge at Padre José's house. It was a tense moment. The girl began to cry again, slightly louder. The diminuendo had altered, rising to an agitato. I saw her looking at her mobile phone in her hands. I sighed and rose from my seat. I sidled into the seat opposite her at the table and looked at her kindly.

"I'm about to go to the buffet car. Looks like you could do with a cup of tea. Can I bring you one?"

The girl glanced up at me in surprise, her crying stifled by my interruption. Her nose was red, and her face completely wet. She pushed the back of her hand across her face in a valiant attempt to rid it of dampness. She blinked slowly at me.

"Oh, I don't know. I'm sorry . . ."

"Don't mind me. Can't bear to see a damsel in distress, you know," I said to her, somewhat awkwardly. "Tell you what, I'll get two teas and then, if you want one, you can have it. No questions asked. You just drink it on your own."

I stood up in the aisle, rocking slightly along with the movement of the train.

"I'll get you lots of sugar. Sugar's good for a shock."

I returned some time later. There had been a reasonably sized queue, and the woman behind the counter was typically moronic. I placed a polystyrene cup before the girl along with three packets of white sugar, two miniature cartons of milk and a white plastic stirrer.

"There you are. Nice and hot. That'll make you feel better."

I returned to my seat, picked up my book and tried to immerse myself back in the world of Greene. A few minutes later, however, the seat next to me shifted as the girl pulled herself in to sit beside me, holding the tea in one hand. I drew down the table tray for her, and she put the cup upon it.

"I'm Emily," she said. "Thanks for the tea."

"Daniel," I replied. "Daniel Shepherd."

She smiled at me sadly. "It isn't a shock."

I looked at her.

"Why I'm crying. It's not that I've had a shock. I'm being silly really. I'm just on my way to something new and I think . . ." She sighed again, and her body juddered with the effort of battening down the sob.

"It's all right," I said, patting her clumsily on the arm. "You don't have to say. I don't want to intrude."

"No, it's not that. I don't mind. I just feel like an idiot, that's all. It's just that I'm going to miss my home. My family."

"Ah," I said, "I understand," although of course I didn't because I had raced out of my family home with all the excitement of a spaniel about to be taken on a three-hour walk across muddy moors. Then it dawned on me.

"Are you starting at Durham?" I asked.

"Yes," she nodded miserably. "I'm going to be in Joyce College."

I knew the name of Joyce. It was one of the colleges on the Bailey, in the heart of Durham. I had trudged up it when I had visited the city for my interview. My own college was up and out of the tiny city on a hill with the other newer colleges, a much less salubrious environment. It would certainly have more state school applicants than this Emily would be meeting in her new surroundings.

"I'm at Nightingale," I offered.

She smiled broadly. "You're going to Durham too? That's awesome!" She beamed at me.

"What are you reading?" I asked.

"French and History," she grimaced. "I only really wanted to do French, but Daddy said that was just an excuse to go travelling for a year and unless I wanted to end up as a primary school teacher, I'd need a subject with backbone." Her eyes twinkled. "His words." She took a sip of her tea. "This tastes awful," she said happily. "How about you? What are you reading?"

"English." I shrugged, acknowledging the book turned face down on the table. "Anyway," I said, wanting to steer the conversation away from myself, "why are you sad? We're going to have a great time. Everyone says university is the best time of your life."

Emily looked downcast again, as if she'd forgotten the reason for her sitting next to me. "Yes, I suppose so." She paused. "Do you think it'll be awfully cold there? Mummy says the rooms won't be heated. She made me pack all kinds of thermal underwear."

I laughed again. "I'm sure you'll be fine. They definitely have central heating these days. I'm sure of it."

She smiled in response. She was pretty, I thought. Her lips were small, like a bow. I liked her, despite the fact she was nothing like me. She was the antithesis of me. She would be popular — you could see it in her bones. She would go out with the captain of the rugby team; she would start to turn her collar up instinctively; she would play some kind of team sport — lacrosse maybe.

We continued to talk until the train shunted slowly in to Durham. As the station sign came into view, I felt a mixture of excitement and apprehension, a growing knot in my stomach that would harden in me as time went on. Emily and I stood in the train corridor with our bags in our hands, our suitcases waiting to be hefted out of the luggage compartment nearest to the train doors: mine a terrible grey fabric — hers was some kind of designer label, I could tell. The train jolted to a stop beside the platform. The last of the day's early-autumn sun streamed valiantly through the grimy plastic roof overhanging the tracks. I helped Emily down out of the carriage with her luggage, and then we trundled towards the taxi queue together.

"Shall we share?" she asked me.

"Okay, if you're sure," I answered, grateful not to have to fork out the cost on my own. "We'll drop you first."

We stood for a few minutes in the queue, in the biting north-east wind, in from the sea and the salt marshes. I could smell brine on the air and a vague scent of petrol, of bitter fruits. I could smell the working classes nestled in the hills surrounding the station, hosting these young brains, funded by older money. I could smell that too.

I asked the taxi driver to drop Emily up at Joyce first and then on to Nightingale. With his reply, I had my first taste of the accent I would come to love. At that time, however, it was incomprehensible to me, and Emily and I looked at each other in cahoots as I gave a small shrug. It was a surprise to us both, then, when the taxi stopped first at the bottom of the hill, outside my new home, and not Emily's.

"Why have you stopped here?" I asked.

The driver looked steadfast out of the windscreen, refusing to attempt to communicate with us kids any more. I looked apologetically at Emily.

"Don't worry," she said kindly, patting my hand. "I'll be fine." She rooted around in the handbag on her lap. "Let me take your number and I'll give you a text later to say I've arrived."

I gave it to her and then reluctantly shifted out of the cab. The driver popped the boot and I retrieved my case before handing in some money to Emily through the passenger window. "Good luck," I said uncertainly.

She smiled bravely, her chin up in the air. "You too!"

The cab sped its tyres, off and up the hill, leaving me in its wake. Nightingale College, to my left, waited for me to enter.

CHAPTER
FOUR

Monday 22 May, 9.11 a.m.

Martin and Jones stood outside the principal's study door. "You take him in, Jones," Martin said quietly. "We'll need to get what he says down in writing before we make any kind of decision on an arrest. Get him looked at by the medical examiner. I don't want his brief chucking inadmissibility at us. I'm coming right behind but I want to have a look at Emily's room before the SOCOs crawl all over it. Call Butterworth on the way and fill him in." She looked at her sergeant for a moment. "Can't say I was expecting that."

Jones shook her head. "Nope. What do you reckon?"

Martin breathed in sharply. "Hard to tell at this stage. He certainly acts like a zoomer. If he is, we may need an appropriate adult." She turned back towards the door. "Treat him carefully. These are kids after all," she said with an apparent softness, before opening the door, "Simon? We'd like you to come with us now please. DS Jones here will accompany you to the station."

"I want to go with Simon, if that's okay," Principal Mason said from where he stood with his hand on

Rush's shoulder. The boy sat wordlessly in the chair which Martin had vacated to give to him after his outburst. His mouth hung open, his eyes glassy, staring into nothing. Jones helped Simon up and propelled him gently by a hand on his back, steering him out of the door and into the corridor.

Martin watched them descend the college stairs and head out of the building. Her thoughts were rapid, drinking in what had just taken place. This college was so different from anything she had experienced herself at school or university, the students so confident, so sure of their place in the world. Taking a breath and turning headlong into the squall of the case, she followed them down at a distance and stepped into the lobby, where Mrs Earl stood in front of mahogany panelling bathed in the flickering blue lights of the police cars outside. The receptionist looked perplexed as Rush passed her flanked by two uniformed constables.

"I'd be grateful if you could show me Emily's room," Martin said to her. Pulling herself out of her daze, Mrs Earl reached back into the reception cubby hole for a bunch of keys. She led Martin outside the main entrance of Joyce on to the Bailey, where two white police vans edged the roadside. Due to an abrupt meander in the River Wear, which encircled the city, the north and south ends of the cobbled street curled like a peninsula around the medieval hub of the castle and cathedral. The oldest university colleges, of which Joyce was one, flanked the cathedral, their buildings facing the reddish stone walls of its boundary. The sky had lightened to a pigeon-grey by this time, and the cathedral bells tolled the quarter-hour as Martin and Mrs Earl walked briskly up the road.

As the women headed past the police vans, their back doors opened and numerous white-suited figures jumped out to follow them up the narrow street. Mrs Earl gasped a little as she realized they were being tailed, but Martin guided her on with a hand on her back, after nodding to the SOCOs and asking them to wait outside when they got there. One of them threw Martin a plastic-wrapped packet, which she caught with one hand. After a minute's further walk, the receptionist stopped and punched a code into a black door set into a white stone building.

"Do all the student residences have security systems?" Martin asked.

"Yes, the main doors all have private codes, and then the students have keys for their rooms."

Mrs Earl opened the door and stepped inside. As she made to go in after her, Martin noticed a track-suited figure wearing a hoodie drawn down over their face on the other side of the street. Whoever it was ducked behind a car as soon as she noticed them. She waited for a moment, but the figure didn't reappear. Following Mrs Earl with a frown, she ascended the stairwell to the first floor, sweating in her jacket despite the cold outside. "Did you know Emily well?" she asked as they approached the door to Emily's room.

The receptionist shook her head. "Not well. Just to see around the place. It's a small college in comparison with some of them, but there are still five hundred or so students." She looked up at Martin. "You're not from the city, are you?"

Martin shook her head. "Not from Durham itself, no."

Tears sprang into Mrs Earl's eyes. "We're close to each other here," she said. "It's murder, isn't it?" She looked wide-eyed at Martin, who said nothing. "It's a terrible thing to happen in a place." She wiped her eyes disbelievingly. "To think that Simon, of all people . . ."

"Don't make assumptions," Martin said, patting her on the arm. "We don't know what's what just yet."

Mrs Earl sniffed and nodded. "Here you are, then," she said, gesturing at a door covered in stickers and posters. There was a notebook stuck on the door with a pen attached with a piece of string. There was no message, but as Martin peered closer, she could see that the last page of the notebook had been ripped off, leaving a jagged edge. A faint impression had also been left on the page underneath, a note of some sort. Martin made a mental note to tell the SOCOs to bag it.

"Thank you, Mrs Earl. You can go now if that's all right." Martin smiled at her with her back to the door. After a short pause, Mrs Earl nodded again and walked away back down the corridor. Martin opened the packet she had been thrown and carefully put on the required protective clothes. She pushed open the door slowly, a pile carpet halting its progress. She wanted a moment alone in there to try and sense who Emily was — get the nub of her — before the room was turned upside down by the SOCOs, before she became subsumed in the tunnel of the investigation.

29

She also wanted time to think through what had just happened — thoughts shuttling through her like headlights over tarmac on a dark country road. What was behind Rush's confession? Was it the truth? She wasn't sure. Why would he confess outright? Was he indeed a zoomer — insane? What was his relationship with Emily? She sighed and began to look around the room. Maybe something here could provide a clue to it all.

It was a large room yet stifling hot as the radiators appeared to have been turned up to full. The windows were covered in condensation, undrawn curtains either side of them. A sink had been drilled into the right-hand wall next to what looked like the door of a built-in cupboard. Two big windows faced the door through which Martin had entered and looked down on to the street below. She went to stand over the desk, which sat under the left-hand window. If she craned her neck, she could just see the central tower of Durham Cathedral to the left. To her right, the road curled away downhill, towards the hub of the city centre. If you squinted, you could imagine carriages and horses trotting down its streets instead of the BMWs and Range Rovers which glided noiselessly over the cobbles these days.

On the desk sat a small MacBook. Martin let her gloved fingers touch the top of it lightly. She turned away from the desk. There was a lull in time; silence heavy in the air as Martin scanned the room, her eyes resting on every item for a millisecond, considering, *was this relevant?* There appeared to be nothing out of the ordinary about the room, a space which told of a female inhabitant, a young girl. Different, though, from Martin's own room as a teenager, which had been more an obstacle course around huge stacks of books than a pretty-in-pink sanctuary.

Against the left-hand wall of the room was a single bed. A heart-shaped cushion and blue teddy bear sat on the pillow, a patchwork quilt pulled up over it and the duvet. The bedside table held a small lamp and a book, *I'm OK, You're OK*. Martin looked up at the walls over the bed: posters of people Martin could not have named and an old movie poster of *The Philadelphia Story*. She walked over to the wardrobe and looked inside. Jeans were hanging folded alongside some black cocktail dresses; a hockey kit bag sat on the floor in front of it.

Martin stood in the middle of the room and breathed, her eyes closed. *Who are you, Emily?* She could smell — what was it — Estée Lauder Beautiful? An old choice for a young girl. She half-opened one eye and was proved right as she spied a bottle of it on the dressing table next to the sink. *What else?* A feeling permeated the room, cloyed as it was with over-heating and hormones, *what was it?*

She opened her eyes wide and strode to the cupboard. It was large, and as she opened the door she could step inside, where shelves lined the walls. In there were about thirty pairs of shoes thrown carelessly in a pile at the bottom; on the shelves were heaps of crumpled T-shirts advertising some college fundraiser; suitcases and tens of handbags. That wasn't what interested Martin, though. Feeling the sting of tension in the back of her neck, she whirled round, and there, on the back of the door, was a mass of photos — tacked on the wood in a jumble, stacked on top of each other, hundreds of them. They were of parties and balls, cricket matches, picnics, a theatre trip it looked like. And all of the photographs featured one particular boy. Sometimes with Emily and sometimes not. A hundred or so photos of this boy, smiling, laughing, his arm draped over Emily's shoulders. His face looming out from the back of the door. Over and over again.

CHAPTER
FIVE

"I'll call you later," Emily breathed down the phone to me. She was whispering, hurried. I rolled over and glanced at the blinking red light of the digital clock on my bedside table. 3.18 a.m.

"Really?" I said, almost crossly. Not too askance though. I was never irritable with Emily.

"I've got to go, he's coming." She spurted the words, frothing with excitement. "I'll call you back. You won't believe the night I've had!"

I lay flat on my back again.

"I'm sure," I said, irrelevantly it turned out, as the phone was put down on me. I sighed and switched on the bedroom light. There was no hope of going back to sleep now, so I wearily picked up *My Antonia* and opened it where I had turned down a corner of a page about a third of the way through. The Americans weren't doing it for me. Hawthorne, perhaps. But James? And as for Cather. Well really, all her descriptions of making hand-crafted Christmas presents just weren't cutting the mustard. Nevertheless, I picked it up at Mr Shimerda's funeral but found I couldn't concentrate.

I knew Emily was at Nick's house. They'd all have gone there in a crowd after leaving Sixes. I hadn't been there. The idea of pushing into the barn-like room at the top of two flights of concrete steps, almost vertical in incline, ordering a concoction of tropical fruits and booze by which to get smashed, dancing to jungle beats accompanied by waving hands and screeching voices, well, let's just say I would rather have stuck with Jim Burden and Antonia. And that's saying something.

That night, I'd watched her in the Joyce College bar with the others, before they tumbled out to go to Sixes. I had taken to wandering up there on occasion and would sit, nursing a pint of Guinness, and talk to Emily when she had time for me. We had been at Durham for two months now. It seemed an eternity. Mother and home were light years away. I walked the cobbles from my room at Nightingale, over the bridge shading the River Wear below, down to the lecture halls and back, day after day. Often I'd run past the weir, my trainered feet slapping against the sludge of wet leaves which inundated the path. I could hear my breath coming hard, the sky grey with the north, geese hovering and honking. I thought about W. B. Yeats and "Ephemera".

I had been running on my third day there when I next saw Emily again after our train meeting. I was sprinting up the steps to Framwellgate Bridge and was going to take a left, past the cinema, and stop off at the newsagent's to get a bottle of water. As I emerged up from the riverside, though, I walked straight into her.

"Hi!" she had exclaimed. "How are you?"

Her voice had already changed. Although she had been well-spoken previously, her sentences were now further punctuated by the "ah" sound, the form of diction handed down in a thousand public schools across the country, swathes of their inhabitants congregating here in Durham, generally at Joyce College.

"I'm good," I said, breathing hard and bending over, my hands on my knees.

"Running," she stated the obvious. "Admirable."

I straightened up, rueing my thin frame, my gawky chest. "Yep." I controlled my breath and managed to smile. "How are you? How are you settling in?"

"Really well, thanks! I don't know what I was worried about, really. Everyone's so nice. I've made some great friends already."

I continued to smile while at the same time thinking that any friends I made in the first three days of anything would never last the distance; they would be comrades in arms, a fellow body to walk in a room with, to pretend to laugh with. But they wouldn't be friends, not really. Did Emily really think these people would be life-long compatriots? Or was her naivety genuine — a lone petal of innocence in a field of scrub?

"Which way are you going?" she asked.

I pointed towards the cinema.

"I'll walk with you. It's a beautiful day for once."

We walked together over the bridge. Emily was shorter than me, she only reached my shoulder. She had that petite frame I've always found attractive. I had some desire in me to put my arm around her or pat her on the back perhaps. A kind of contact nevertheless. I controlled it, and we walked side by side.

"What's your room like?" she asked brightly. "Are you sharing?"

I described to her the shoebox I shared with a physics student named Zack. He had already put up numerous *Doctor Who* posters, installed decks at the bottom of his bed and situated a large collection of vinyl records along the only free wall. I wasn't sure if this meant he was a pirate DJ looking for gigs or was planning a rave in our room at a later date. I had said nothing to him about it, though, and merely unpacked my box of books on to the shelves on my side of the room. My toiletries I kept in a wash bag under the bed, not wanting Zack to see my toothbrush for some reason. My only real problem was my towel, which never seemed to dry out. We had a small electric heater whose minimal effect was instantly negated by the fact that it was situated underneath the room's only window. This wasn't double-glazed and sucked the heat out of the room with all the vigour one might expect of a black hole. Zack had been at great pains to tell me, however, that the "suck" of a black hole was an extreme gravitational effect, whereas what I was describing was merely a transfer of thermal energy.

Emily laughed. "He sounds a nightmare."

"No, he's okay really. My towel, however, is growing mildew on it. Along with the bottle of milk in the downstairs kitchen which nobody wants to claim."

"I know what you mean," Emily said. "But I just give my towels to the cleaners. They wash them every day."

"Ah, yes. Well, that would be the difference between Joyce and Nightingale," I said sagely. "We don't have cleaners —"

"No cleaners?" Emily interrupted, horrified.

"No cleaners," I repeated. "Just a cupboard under the sink with a duster in it and an old aerosol of Mr Sheen."

She laughed again. It was a pretty laugh, I thought. I spied a coffee shop set back down a small alley as we passed. "Would you like to get a drink?" I asked on the spur of the moment, gesturing towards it.

Emily peered down the alleyway suspiciously.

"It looks a good place. Good coffee."

"Okay," she said making up her mind. We sat upstairs, opposite each other, in a bay window. It was one of those places that have sprung up everywhere these days. Wooden floors, chalked-up blackboards, artisan bread — whatever that means — but the smell of ground coffee has always pleased me. Even if it never tastes as good as it smells.

Emily ordered a skinny latte. I had a double espresso. She didn't even offer to pay — girls like her don't. I didn't mind, though.

"So how are you finding it?" I asked, not sure where to put my legs under the tiny table. If I bent them, the table would lift an inch off the ground. I stretched them out instead, crossing my ankles to the side of Emily's chair. The sweat which sheened my body had now cooled and dried, and I could taste salt on my lips.

"It's really good. Joyce has some nice people. A few weirdos." She smiled shyly.

"How's the course?"

"The course? Oh, you know. Boring." She played with an end of her hair, twirling it around her finger. She looked out of the window. "I joined the hockey team. Try-outs for the uni squad are on Wednesday."

I nodded, not knowing what to say to that. I liked running and occasionally watched the snooker, but that was about as far as my sporting ambitions went. Emily breathed in rapidly as if remembering where she was.

"And you? How's Nightingale apart from the weird roommate?"

"Yeah, good. Just finding my way around." The sun had made its way in through the window and now hit me in the face, leaving me squinting somewhat as I looked at her. "The food's awful but the bar's okay. Have you been? To the Nightingale bar?"

"There's a crawl on Friday. Some of us are going. I think it's in drag."

I must have looked puzzled, as she laughed.

"You know, guys as girls, girls as guys. Stupid, really, but fun, I guess."

I sighed.

"What's up?"

"Oh, it's just. Well, I find all that a bit . . ."

"A bit what?"

"Childish I suppose."

Emily straightened in her chair. "But we are children, aren't we? Isn't that what university is?" She laughed slightly nervously. "A big playground?"

"Yes," I agreed. "But I suppose I was hoping it would be more experimenting with new things. Trying things out. Not getting hammered and wearing a woman's dress around town." I coughed awkwardly — this wasn't going the way I wanted. "Don't worry, I know it's good fun and everything." I smiled at her. "You'll have a great time on Friday."

Emily relaxed somewhat. "You're right, it's stupid. But you know, everyone's doing it."

I nodded. "Yeah, well, enjoy yourself. Be careful too."

"What do you mean?"

"Oh, you know. Make sure you've got someone to walk you home at the end of the night. I'm just looking out for you. Don't want you stranded in the middle of town by yourself."

She smiled at that. I could see that she liked to be protected.

"I will." She swallowed the dregs of her latte. "Be careful, that is."

She stood up to leave, and I followed her down the stairs and back out into the street.

CHAPTER
SIX

Monday 22 May, 10.06 a.m.

Annabel watched the police and bodies dressed in white go into Emily's building. She waited for a while, as the light flicked on in Emily's room, watching the figures move across the window. She jumped a little to keep warm on the spot of her observation point, behind a van on the opposite side of the road. She looked again at her mobile phone and tapped in a number for the umpteenth time. No answer from either of them. Where were they? One of them had to pick up.

Giving up for a moment, Annabel tucked her hands under her armpits, tears glittering in her eyes as she thought about what she had seen that morning. That yellow tent on the riverbank. The police crawling everywhere. The weir frothing in front of them all, none of them knowing her, none of them caring. The sun still rising, even though Emily was gone. Gone. She shook her head. She couldn't believe it.

She'd been with her at the boathouse yesterday afternoon. They'd lain on the grass, in the late-spring sunshine, drinking plastic pints of Pimm's, listening to the band. Emily was fine. She'd rolled on to her stomach, laughing about something. Nick had been in touch. Everything was *fine*.

"It's all coming together, Belles," Emily had said with one of those hard smiles she sometimes gave.

"What is?"

"Oh, Belles. Always one step behind, my lovely. I mean, they're all falling into place. These boys. Just where I want them."

Annabel had laughed, still uncomprehending, hiding the dislike she had for Emily at those moments. Which were more and more frequent these days. Always better to hide your dislike. Until you were pushed, that is.

But things had gone too far now. She had to stop things. She'd said things she regretted and now she wanted to take them back.

The door to Emily's building opened, and Annabel shrank back behind the van as the red-headed police woman stepped out. She wasn't in uniform, but Annabel could tell she was police. She had that aura about her: nosy. The policewoman seemed to look directly at her. Annabel didn't take any chances and ducked into a doorway of a student house on the other side of the road. As she left, her fingers tapped again at the keys in a now familiar rhythm. Come on, *please*. Please pick up the phone.

Detective Chief Inspector Butterworth was already at the front of the Major Crime Unit incident room when Martin walked in. The room was packed with bodies, ostensibly lounging on chairs or looking at computers, but she could feel that crackle of energy, the buzz and urgency of the officers, the feeling you only got when there was potential homicide on the books. Butterworth stood with assurance in front of a whiteboard, in the centre of which was Emily's photo, her face displaying the innocuous smile people give in passports or student cards. Martin stood quietly for a second, considering Emily's face when it had been alive. Her features were even, her shoulder-length blonde hair curling slightly at the ends. Her brown eyes so different in expression from when Martin had last seen them, staring vacantly at her in the tent down at the weir. They were calm in the photo — wide-spaced, giving her an air of innocence, making her look younger than her years. She was pretty, Martin observed, not beautiful.

Butterworth coughed and gestured for Martin to come and stand next to him, to face the squad. She pulled her eyes from Emily's photo and moved her way through the room. She was at once aware of the volume of people there, taking comfort for the moment in Butterworth's support for her, his backing of her move to Durham. Sam Butterworth and she went further back than either of them sometimes cared to remember.

"This is Operation Limestone." Butterworth looked around the room. "As you know, DI Martin joined us a couple of weeks ago from Newcastle CID. She'll be Senior Investigating Officer on this and will be running the show here."

Martin looked at her team as of now, her heart thumping as the room settled. She knew some of their faces, but most were strangers. She noticed how some

42

of their eyes flicked to her legs. Wondered again how far her looks would take her before they realized she would rather break their balls than use what she looked like to get decent work out them. She took a breath and a step forwards, an inch past Butterworth.

"Simon Rush gave an oral statement this morning, which we've now got in writing, where he has confessed to the murder of Emily Brabents." She wouldn't do the niceties. They'd seen her around the last couple of weeks. She could play nice in the pub. "The medical examiner has seen him and said he's good to go. He's now in custody and under arrest. However," she paused with a mild expression of frustration. "Rush's dad is some hotshot criminal silk. He's on his way up here from London to represent his son, so Rush stays where he is until we can interview him with his dad. Given his odd behaviour in the college, it's probably worthwhile anyway.

"We should get the post-mortem results later today, but until then I'm treating this as a homicide. And even though we've got a confession; that might not be all there is to this sorry tale."

Martin watched herself from above as she doled out tasks to the team, interviews to be conducted, statements to be taken, the riverbank to be scoured. She needed the SOCO analysis of the crime scene, particularly the ripped-off note on the door; Emily's MacBook would be sent off to forensics. Her social media needed analysing: who was she friends with? What was her relationship with Rush? And all the time Martin spoke and instructed and ordered, a whisper drummed in her head. *Who killed Emily? Who killed Emily Brabents?* She pointed at people, allocated tasks to these people for whom she was an outsider, who didn't know her, didn't trust her.

"Forensics need to look at Rush's computer, and I'll come with the search team to Rush's room. I want to see it before I interview him," she said, aware of Butterworth smiling behind her like the politician she knew he had to be.

"What about the victim's family, boss? Should we focus on them?" Jones asked.

"It's a possibility. We certainly need to know where they were at the time of the murder. They don't live far: they've got a place in a village about an hour's drive away." Martin looked down at her notes. "So a quick trip up here last night isn't out of the question, and they need to be checked out. Then there's the boy in the photos in Emily's room." She pointed at the whiteboard, where pictures of the unknown boy were tacked next to one of Simon Rush. "Any news on that?"

"Yes. Student Admin has a photo of him on their system. Nick Oliver," Jones answered. "Second-year law student. Lives in a house down by the Viaduct."

Martin knew where that was at least. An enclave of miner's cottages now inhabited by students who moved out of the college environs in their second and third years, paying cheap rent for walls tacky with Sellotape and no central heating. "Good. So let's get busy. The more evidence we have about Emily and her mates, the more we've got to establish whether what Rush says is true." Martin exhaled loudly. "A young girl is dead. We need a good and clean result. The city won't like this, the university even less so."

"And I think it goes without saying," Butterworth interjected, "that we all need to work fully as a team with DI Martin and help her settle in to how we do things in Durham."

You're right, Martin thought, *it did go without saying*. But now that you've made a big deal of the fact I'm new and know nothing about how things are done here, let's get on with it. She flashed a quick smile at her superior and at her team before walking briskly out of the room.

CHAPTER
SEVEN

I became acquainted with Annabel soon after I met Emily. She reminded me of a bun. All curves and chest, wrapped in cashmere, soft and inviting but with a creamy ooziness about her that I found slightly off putting. She had met Emily at the hockey club, where they had both qualified for Durham's third team. Emily was bedazzled by this. "The *thirds*!" she had exclaimed to me. "And I'm only a Fresher!" Annabel was also a Fresher, at Keats. I had seen the two of them walking arm in arm around the hockey field like excitable rabbits, practically bouncing on their heels with joy at being allowed into this exclusive club.

Annabel lived in a house with another girl called Cat and two mysterious boys who I never saw in person but who were represented throughout the house by the largest shoes I had ever seen outside of a circus. Annabel was delighted to have been placed in one of the houses Keats owned in the city of Durham itself, as opposed to rooms in the college building. "You can get more in with the living-out set," she had confusingly relayed when the three of us had gone for a drink at the pub at the bottom of her road. "You know, the second and third years," she had explained in response to my perplexed expression as to what this "living-out set" consisted of.

The pub was tiny, not much more than a single room with a burning log fire and a world-weary landlord who tolerated the money of the students but would never warm to them. I sat with my back to the fire. It was a Sunday night, always quiet in Durham, the clubs shut, the pubs closing early, everyone steeling themselves for the week ahead of more drinking and revelry. I had an essay due the following morning on *The Wings of a Dove*. I had laboured over it for the whole of the previous week and was now even more fed up to the back teeth of James. I had called Emily on the off chance she felt like a drink and she had invited me along to meet up with Annabel. I suspected this friendship was as much based on Emily's good looks — and how Annabel could use those to her advantage in meeting the right type of people — as it was based on their love of hockey. Both girls drank vodka and soda — the most slimming drink, according to Emily. I had my usual Guinness. They were in raptures this evening about the possibility of a hockey social later on in the month.

"It'll probably be at The Sun," Annabel said knowingly.

The Sun was a large pub in the middle of the city which had a boutique hotel attached to it. This was the favoured choice of residence for parents coming to stay in Durham in order to celebrate graduation, and the venue had a sort of panache for that reason.

"The last social was held there, Shorty told me. It was *wild*," Annabel laughed.

Emily sipped her drink. "Do we take dates?" she asked. "Or is it just each man for himself? So to speak . . ."

"The latter, I think," replied Annabel. "We can go together, no?"

Emily nodded eagerly. "Of course." Then she looked at me, slightly uncomfortable. "Um, I hope . . ."

"Oh, don't mind me," I came to her rescue. "Couldn't imagine anything worse than standing round all evening getting drunk with a bunch of hockey players."

This may have come out harsher than I intended, as both girls looked slightly uncertain as to whether my judgement painted them in a negative light.

"What I mean is," I said somewhat more pleasantly, "I'm not offended in the slightest that you don't want me as your date to this auspicious occasion. I will just wish you a great evening and look forward to the gossip." I appeared to be turning into some sort of camp agony aunt. I swallowed my pint loudly in an attempt to appear more manly. "Who wants another? My round."

They acquiesced, and the evening wore on. The landlord eventually rang the bell for time, and we three stood, hefting our thick coats on over our shoulders. As we walked out of the door, the wind bit into our faces, and the girls involuntarily turned towards me, to shelter. This was more like it, I thought, floating my hand behind their backs, guiding them down the street. We walked Annabel to her door, and then Emily and I began the longer walk over Prebends Bridge and down the Bailey to Joyce. Emily seemed lost in thought to begin with and would occasionally let out little sighs, puffs of icy cloud which dispersed before her face in the dark of the night as we walked.

"Are you okay?" I asked after a while.

Emily turned to me and shrugged. "Yes, I'm fine, thanks."

I nodded. The more time I spent with Emily, the more I liked her. Yes, I thought she was pretty, that went without saying. But it was more than that. Something in her made me feel like I was all right, after all. I hated to admit it to myself, but being with her, talking to her and listening through her to what went on in everyone else's lives made me somehow feel as though I *belonged*. It wasn't just that I found her attractive, although of course I did, it was more that. With her, I was stronger, I was *endorsed*.

"Everything all right at Joyce? Any romance to report?" I laughed softly.

She was silent.

"There *is* something?" I questioned. "But we've only been here a couple of weeks." I gave another weak laugh, trying to disguise my disappointment.

She dug her hands further into her pockets. "It's nothing. No romance." She turned to look at me. "Honestly. It's just, there's . . ." She stopped.

"Someone you're keen on?"

"Well, yes. Sort of. Not that he'd notice me. He's a second year. Plays hockey, sometimes subs on the cricket team."

"Hmmm," I pondered, knowing exactly what sort of idiot this would be.

"He just seems *nice*, you know?"

I didn't, no.

"Oh, anyway, it's not worth bothering about. He's probably got a million girlfriends."

Indeed.

"Do you think?" She looked so sweet as she turned her face to me then. She so wanted to be reassured. I couldn't not do as she asked even though I hated the words as I said them, wanting in all honesty to crush any hope she might have. I took a breath.

"Of course he won't have. Won't have time, with all that sport he's playing. Just — just take it easy, I guess, Emily. We've only just started. You should take your time. Don't get hooked into anything you may want to get out of in the future."

She sighed again. "I know. I'm being lame."

I chuckled sadly. "No, you're not. It's perfectly normal. Here we are anyway." I looked up at the shadowed outline of the pale buildings of Joyce. We stood before the metal railings which lined the street. Emily unexpectedly gave me a hug.

"What was that for?"

"Oh, you know. Just for being there for me." She darted into the building, waving goodnight. I turned to walk back the way I'd come, up the hill to Nightingale. I beamed the whole way there.

CHAPTER
EIGHT

Monday 22 May, 10.48 a.m.

Simon Rush's room was dark and musty, filled with the ubiquitous adolescent smell of hormones and body odour. Martin strode across it and abruptly pulled open the curtains, letting light stream into the large oval-shaped space. Officers from the MCU began to fan out around the room, removing books from shelves, dusting for fingerprints.

The room had been guarded and had remained as it was when Rush had left it that morning to come to Principal Mason's office. His bed was to one side of the room, a blue duvet thrown haphazardly across it. Clothes had been abandoned on the carpet, pants at the bottom of the bed; overflowing ashtrays on the coffee table; wine bottles with candles stuck in the necks, the wax stopped in time. Stick it in a modern art museum, Martin thought, and you'd have the male Tracey Emin exhibition.

Underneath the bay window was a line of those awful chairs that seemed to be found in every publicly funded institution in the country: wide seats, MDF arms, and all covered in that grey-green rough, furry fabric that reminded Martin of an old army coat her grandfather used to wear. From the number of chairs, Rush either held college meetings in here or was having regular parties.

Martin bent down to examine an ashtray. She sniffed at it, the tang of weed still floating amidst the aroma of tobacco. Roaches fashioned of rolled-up cardboard remains of Rizla packets were scattered on the table. She carried on, making her way around the room. On a desk, no books to be seen, but Martin peered at a photo in an old silver frame: a woman with a young boy, perhaps eight years old. They stood at a garden gate, and the woman was laughing, the boy gazing up at her adoringly as the shutter clicked.

In the bathroom, there was the usual male grooming detritus. Martin looked closely at the sink and wiped her gloved finger around its flat edge. It was impossible to tell whether the white powder was cocaine, no matter what the cops in American TV shows rubbed into their gums. But, as she pulled back the shower curtain, she saw a lighter and a teaspoon lying on the edge of the bath, its shiny surface stained brown.

Calling to one of the officers to come inside and remove it, she was about to leave them to it when she noticed a small cupboard next to the bed.

"Has anyone checked this?" she asked, already moving across to it. She squatted down and rooted around the contents: some condoms, a half-drunk bottle of Bells, a girly magazine and some homosexual porn, which she passed to the exhibits officer to bag.

52

At the bottom of the cupboard was a seemingly insignificant brass plate. Martin frowned, leaned in and got a fingernail underneath. She managed to flip the plate and hook it so that the bottom of the cupboard lifted upwards, revealing a tiny space concealed within. Inside was about an eighth of Black wrapped in foil, some more weed and, sure enough, a small, sealed packet of cocaine.

Martin sat at her desk, thinking. She sighed and closed her eyes for a second before reaching forwards and checking her phone. Despite the sudden pull of this investigation, she couldn't help herself. After the row last night, still she had heard nothing from Jim.

Martin loved the way Jim looked first thing in the morning, how he'd looked that morning. His eyes were heavy-lidded, easier to look at than later, when he became wide-eyed about things. When she'd left, he would have dragged himself out of bed, creased from sleep, tugging his old university rugby shirt over his head from the back of his neck. He would have rubbed his face, as he did every morning, before he moved under the shower, as if preparing himself for the change in sensory stimulation.

Lately though, he had not been accepting of change. Jim hadn't been prepared for the move away from Newcastle. His suit and tie, the clothes of a giant striding across the world, these were not the clothes befitting an hour's commute in a car that didn't match Jim's expectations of himself. The house they had settled for, in a town outside the hub of the city, not where he had anticipated to be in his life just then.

In the last few months, since she had been told of her promotion, Martin had felt shrink-wrapped by Jim. Five years older than her, sometimes he looked at her as if the weight of his experience was a hard cross to bear, that he was waiting for her to catch up. She sighed, rubbing her temples, trying to focus. It wouldn't leave her, though, the truth of it — that the love for Jim she had first thing in the morning had generally waned by the end of the day. As if the day had grown him, or maybe her, beyond the reach of love.

Martin opened a bottle of water and took a long drink, pushing these thoughts away. She took a couple of Ibuprofen and rubbed her temples, shaking it off, as Jones walked into Martin's office precariously carrying two grande lattes and a paper bag containing, Martin hoped, an almond croissant. Jones sat at the desk opposite Martin and passed the bag to her.

"Cheers." Martin said, tearing off a large piece of the croissant and popping it in her mouth. She fired up the computer on her desk and tapped on the keyboard for a while. "Found a stash of drugs in Rush's room by the way. Not just weed. Looks like he was taking coke too."

Jones lifted her eyebrows, wearily unsurprised.

Martin took a sip of coffee. "Presumably the university has a social networking site?"

Jones flicked through her notebook. "Yes. It's linked to all the colleges' email systems. We've got the passwords already for Emily's Facebook and Twitter accounts. And some of the team will be looking at

54

Rush's." She slid the notebook across the desk to Martin.

"Let's take a look at Emily's now, then. Rush's dad won't be here until this afternoon I shouldn't think. When do the parents arrive?" Glancing down at the notebook, Martin continued to tap on the keyboard and move the mouse across the pad on the table.

"About lunchtime, I'd say. Phillip Mason's putting them up in the college. He'll meet them off the train with uniform. I'll get DC Tennant to take them to the morgue to identify Emily if you'll be in with Rush . . ."

"Fuck . . ." Martin interrupted, peering closely at the screen. "Look at this, Jones."

Jones leaned forwards over the desk. "God," she whispered as she watched Martin scroll further down. "That's Emily's Facebook page?"

Martin nodded, minimizing the screen and enlarging another. "And this is her Twitter feed. Jesus Christ . . ." She was silent for a moment, her eyes travelling rapidly over what was displayed.

Emily's social media page carried the same photo that had been tacked on to the whiteboard in the incident room. Underneath it was her tag line: *Happiness is a Choice*. Her favourite films were: *Anything with Leonardo DiCaprio; Bridesmaids; Twilight (shame LOL!)*. Music: *Bob Dylan (hippy parents:)); Taylor Swift; LOVE Bastille* . . . Books: *I Capture the Castle* and *The Other Boleyn Girl*.

Under this and links to various tweets and comments were a series of photographs of Emily in different poses: the first one was of her on her knees in front of a semi-naked male figure. Others showed her in underwear; gazing at the camera suggestively. A few of the photos had been crudely drawn over with an electronic pen, adding or enhancing Emily's body parts. In some, speech bubbles had been grafted on to Emily's mouth importing sexual phrases from her mouth to the camera.

"It looks like she's actually posing for the photos," Martin said softly.

Jones shook her head. "The comments. They're Benny Hill, but it's nasty Benny Hill," she said.

"It's just nasty, is what it is," Martin replied continuing to scan the images. "*Slut, whore. Get yourself a rampant rabbit, you sick slag.*" She glanced over at Jones. "Poor girl." She sat back in her chair, her fingers resting lightly on the desk. "Emily wouldn't post these photos herself, would she?"

"Wouldn't imagine so."

Sitting forwards again, Martin clicked on the mouse. "It looks like Emily hasn't made any status updates or whatnot since," she paused, still scanning what she was looking at, "well, since the beginning of the year. But other people have been adding comments on these photos, it seems."

"Anyone can comment on photos if they're friends with the person on Facebook. But if you wanted to post a photo yourself on someone else's page, how easy is it to hack into their account?" Jones asked.

Martin shrugged. "I'm no expert, but pretty easy I'd say. You'd only need to know Emily's username and password. It can't be that difficult. They're social media accounts, not Bletchley." She tapped again on the keyboard. "Let's see what happens if you do a search on Facebook for Emily's name. Yep, see there," she pointed at the screen. "Christ," she whispered, taking in the title of the page. "*Emily Likes It Like This*" was another spread of photos — replicas of the ones on Emily's own page — with more comments in the same vein. "This page must have been created by someone else. I can't see Emily doing it. And if that's the case, she wouldn't be able to take it down or change anything on it unless she had the password."

Martin pushed her chair back and stood up, energy pulsing through her. "Who's the boy in this photo?" She said, pointing at the screen at the photo of Emily on her knees. "Is it Nick Oliver? You can't see his face. Did he post the photos?"

"We need to speak to him," Jones said.

"Undoubtedly," Martin said quietly, almost to herself. "Emily was self-harming. I saw the scars. Was it because of this?"

"It's definitely possible." Jones said. "A lot of people have seen this, obviously. She was being trolled. Look at the comments."

"*You deserve to be raped?*" Martin shook her head in disbelief. "*Why don't you just fuck off and kill yourself?*" She shuddered, her eyes glazing a little as she digested what she'd seen. "We'll need to go through all the comments. First priority, though, is to find out who posted the photos." She paused in silence for a moment. "Is Rush's name here?" she asked abruptly, scouting the screen again.

"Kids don't have to post with their own names, though," Jones said as Martin looked in vain. "Wouldn't want to if they were trolling, would they? I'll look into it. See if any names cross-reference, if any names correlate."

"Good for you, Jones." Martin smiled at her quickly. "I wonder if Principal Mason knows about this. We need to find out." She walked to the window with her coffee and took a swig, watching the seagulls wheel and squawk outside. "So Emily was being trolled. But the question is," she turned to face Jones, "who took the photos? Was she posing for them? And, if so, why?"

Jones shifted in her chair, not knowing the answer.

"And," Martin continued, "what does Rush have to do with it?" Martin tossed her empty cup expertly into the bin and picked up her jacket. "Come on, Jones. Time waits for no woman."

CHAPTER
NINE

The night of the hockey social came around fairly soon. By this time, I had become a stalwart, really, of Emily's. I didn't ever socialize with her amongst her big group of friends at Joyce, but we would meet up, just the two of us or sometimes with Annabel tagging along. I was her sounding board, her support system, if you will.

I was bumbling along at Nightingale. We were moving on to the Romantics, and this tied in with the change in the seasons. The autumnal colours were intensifying, deepening their hues; leaves fell sadly to the ground as the natural cycle moved to a time of bareness, of stone-grey branches, slate skies and frosty roofs. The weather made for treacherous runs sometimes, but it wasn't until the night of the hockey social that the first snow fell.

I had decided to spend the evening in the library reading T. S. Eliot's essay on Byron and had made a flask of hot tea and some ham sandwiches to keep me company. As I walked through the city past Joyce to where the library sat at the very top of the hill, I let my thoughts turn to Emily. She would have been getting ready about now. I tried to ignore thoughts of her with Nick, I didn't want to think of her like that — with someone else. I focused on her as my friend. Really, my only friend since coming to Durham.

The library was unsurprisingly quiet, it being a Friday night, and so I secured my favourite seat by the window on the first floor, overlooking an expanse of lawn fringed by thick oak trees. As I read, I would occasionally glance up and look at the wind ruffling the trees. When it grew darker, my own reflection began to stare back at me.

I wondered. About me. Was I destined to always be on the outside? I was self-aware enough to know I hated large groups, much preferring the company of one or two people. But even then, why hadn't I made more friends since coming to Durham? Even my roommate Zack had seemed to attract (forgive the physics pun) a posse of like-minded dudes, hell-bent on tearing up the Nightingale common room with Brian Cox DVD nights and physics pizza parties. The others on my English course were fine but, apart from one girl who hid behind her waist-length hair in every tutorial and barely said a word, they all seemed to be from that set to which Emily belonged. They were racehorses: glossy and slick, all prancing hooves and tightly wound emotions. They looked identical, I thought. Big white teeth, rounded chins; the girls had long blonde hair, the boys had a short back and sides and wore shirts indicating some interest in sport, with their collars pulled up to the backs of their ears. They carried their course books in front of them, hugging them as if they cared.

It was their eyes, though, that I really noticed. These were discs of dissembling. Their thoughts lingered in the air before them, as visible to me as fireflies, while they considered me whenever I came into contact with them — was I a person of note, they would think to themselves. Was I worth a chat? Then the dissembling would conclude and, on the whole, they would step aside and skirt round me as if I were no more than a shadow on the footpath. I wasn't even accorded the status of an obstacle, merely a puddle to be avoided. If, perhaps, they did recognize me through my association with Emily, they would slur a greeting, their lips barely deigning to form the words. "Hiiiiii, how are you?" they'd ask, their eyes skittering behind my head as I answered, already searching out someone better, more connected, more *like them*, to talk to. Why couldn't they see that I was interesting? That I had something to give of value?

I suspected that this was why I liked Emily so much. Because she actually acknowledged my existence in the world. I sighed and looked at my watch. Ten p.m. on a Friday night. Seriously? I was pathetic.

I walked out of the library with my shoulders hunched, crunched like a piece of wastepaper. The snow began to fall, lilting on my eyelashes, blurring my vision. It sopped the path before me, a perfect sheen of white now being marred by my footprints. I looked only at the ground but found myself away from Nightingale, back down the hill, on to the Bailey and into the oldest section of the city. Here ye olde tea shoppes sat next to gift shops and ladies'-wear boutiques, which I could never imagine selling anything to anyone. I breathed in the scent of winter, the freshness of the new snow underlain with a smell of bonfires, charcoal pyres. I raised my head to inhale it more deeply and realized I had come upon The Sun, its bright lights within searing the cold pavement outside. I stood on the opposite side of the road, taking it in: the din of drunken voices, the odd shout, the muffled thump of the music. I wrapped my arms around myself, at last noticing the freezing air. The snow was by then coming down thickly, and I retrieved a beanie out of my jacket and shoved it on.

I think that's why Annabel didn't recognize me at first. She bundled out of the main entrance and rushed across the road without looking. I had turned to leave but she crashed into me blindly as I stepped off the kerb.

"Oh, sorry," I exclaimed, before noticing who it was. "Annabel? Is that you?"

Her mascara was smeared down her face, and tears spilled down her cheeks as she breathed some sort of coconut-infused alcohol on me.

She looked at me, confused. As usual, she struggled to remember my name. "Um, hello?" was all she said.

I immediately felt embarrassed to be seen as if I was stalking them at their party. "I, um, I was just out walking and, well, here I am," I finished lamely.

She was too drunk to consider this properly and nodded, accepting this lack of explanation as good enough.

"What's wrong anyway?" I asked, changing the subject.

Annabel rubbed her hand over her face, trying to stem the flow of tears. "Stupid. I'm just an idiot. Nothing." She attempted a smile. "Nothing, seriously. Just had too much to drink." She was struggling to speak and she hung on to my arm to prevent herself tottering.

"Are you heading home?" I asked. "Would you like me to walk you back?"

She nodded again, miserably, then looked up with a start and back at the pub. "Oh, my coat . . . But I can't go back in there."

I didn't want to go in either. If Emily saw me, she'd think I was following her in to a party where I hadn't been invited. "Here, take my jacket."

"Really?"

"Yes, it's fine. A bit of snow won't kill me," I said looking up into the sky as the snow rapidly multiplied itself into a blizzard. I was rather wishing I had stayed in the library at this point. I handed Annabel the jacket then shoved my hands as far into my jeans pockets as I could. She hunkered down into it and we began to walk down the hill towards the bridge at Prebends.

After a few moments silence, punctuated only by the sound of our breath in the stillness, I asked again, "What's wrong, Annabel? Why have you been crying?"

She didn't answer to begin with but walked on mutely. Annabel often did this; her mouth would harden and she'd set her face much as a toddler does during a sulk.

"Come on," I nudged her shoulder with mine. "What is it? Didn't you have a good time?"

She laughed bitterly, enunciating her words carefully — so as to get them out in the right order, I thought. "Yes, I had a great time! It's always good to be ditched by your best friend at a party." Then she clamped her lips together as if she'd spoken in error.

"What do you mean?" I questioned. "Where did Emily go?"

"Ask her," Annabel shrugged, bitterness sparking off her so that I could almost smell the phosphorus. She looked at me side-on, seeming to debate something. "She was at the party but then she . . . left."

"Left? Why? To go home?"

Annabel sighed. "Just ask her, why don't you? I can't be bothered to think about it any more. It makes me feel sick."

I could see that she had turned a pale shade of green. "Are you going to be sick?" I asked, worried. I didn't want the dry-cleaning bill, if I'm honest.

Annabel shook her head. "No, don't worry. I just feel it. I don't like it. What she's done." She was almost muttering to herself now. "It's wrong, that's what it is. Just plain wrong. Call yourself a friend." She grabbed my arm abruptly, pulled me round to face her. I could see then how drunk she was. She looked vaguely wild, her eyelashes clumped with the black of her streaked *Clockwork Orange*-esque mascara, grey stains on her cheeks revealing the path of her tears. "Don't you think?" she asked almost desperately. "Don't you think it's just *wrong?*"

I didn't know how to respond, and Annabel's eyes glazed over. She retreated for the rest of the walk and let herself into her front door with barely a word. I hefted off, back up the hill again at last to Nightingale, puzzling over what had happened. I was to find out in a few hours.

CHAPTER
TEN

Monday 22 May, 11.35 a.m.

"Nick Oliver's at a lecture at the moment," Jones said. "Should we see him there so publicly?"

"We're not arresting him, just having a bit of a chat. Anyway, a bit of police publicity around the student population never did us any harm. Let's see how he reacts to a little spotlight on him."

Martin and Jones rounded the corridor to face the station exit which lead on to the street. "Bugger . . ." Martin exclaimed as they saw that the pavement was filled with half a dozen people, lounging on the brick walls of the building, smoking cigarettes and drinking coffee. "Bloody press. They've got wind of this quickly. We'd better take the other door."

They turned on their heels and headed in the opposite direction. Pushing through the back exit, Martin eyed benign clouds as they got outside. "Thank God it's a nice day for once. I could do with some refreshing after what we've just seen online."

Jones assented.

The police station was almost opposite the university lecture theatres on the main street of the city, New

Elvet. This was the newer part of Durham, the River Wear twisting along its boundary, circling around the medieval heart of the city, creating a peninsula. This had the effect of creating a separate land mass, linked to the bulk of the city by bridges bisecting the river. As she walked, Martin thought of this as symbolic, the further emphasis of the ancient and the great entrenched together through time.

"The town kids must hate these students lording it up with their money and privilege," she remarked as they got within sight of the lecture theatre. "So much more opportunity for the kids from out of town. This is your home and you're stifled by it."

"Not always," Jones mumbled.

Martin shot her a look. "Ah, I didn't mean that, Jones." She flushed a little. "I'm from round here myself. Just up the coast, in Seaham." She took a breath and looked about her. "I certainly felt stifled enough where I came from. It's just *different*, you know? What's that Plath line — you know, about trying to die after they buried you? Not exactly on point, but you get my drift?"

Jones looked at Martin, startled. She had no idea what Martin was talking about.

"Nah, what I mean is," Martin shook her head and carried on, "cities like this, have a lot of emotions bubbling away under the surface. You know, Jones?"

Jones made a noise which could have been an agreement, or may have not, depending on how you heard it.

"Lots of people trying to fit into something they're not anyway," Martin finished her treatise, looking up and squinting into the burgeoning sunlight.

They weaved past the students milling about in the road, leaving and entering the main lecture building. When they finally made their way inside, Jones looked at a piece of paper in her hand. "Second level, lecture theatre F5, apparently. He should be in there for another hour."

"What do we know about Nick?" Martin asked as they walked up the stairs, students giving them looks through the white balustrade, curious as to these adults in their midst.

"Calls himself a hockey-playing legend on his Twitter feed and Facebook page," Jones answered wryly, shrugging. "What information is there to get from these things? I dunno. His favourite film is *The Shaw-shank Redemption*. Doesn't appear to have ever read a book."

They reached the double doors of the lecture theatre.

"That's the one with Morgan Freeman, isn't it?" Martin said. "I quite liked that." She pushed the doors open into a muted, dark space. Images on a large screen at the front flashed in the darkness. The sound of a microphoned voice droned, as the women walked down the stairs to the stage at the bottom.

"Sorry, what's going on?" A suited man behind the lectern at the front asked immediately, breaking his exposition on the finer aspects of equity law.

Martin showed her ID and turned to face the students.

"Is there a Nick Oliver here? Please raise your hand."

The students murmured, turning heads to find someone out. A hand rose vertically, nervously.

"Here," the boy said uncertainly.

"DI Martin and DS Jones from the Major Crime Unit in Durham. We'd like you to come with us now, please, Nick."

Whispers rippled around the auditorium as Nick got to his feet and shrugged his rucksack on to one shoulder. He shifted, red-faced, past the others in his row to the end of it, where Martin and Jones waited for him. They bookended him either side, walking back up the stairs to the doors out of the lecture theatre. Once outside, Martin turned to face him. As she did, the boy stood taller, as if remembering where he came from.

"Is this about Emily? Why have you dragged me out of my lecture in front of everyone?" he asked, the force of his embarrassment shunting his words out. He appeared fractious, not as a friend in mourning, Martin observed. She smiled and gestured towards a wooden bench which sat opposite the doors to the lecture room. "Shall we? Let's just have a chat."

Nick stared at her and then made up his mind. He went and slumped down on the bench, put his rucksack between his legs, dangling between his fingers. He had an insouciant charm about him, a tan from some recent holiday. Martin had seen his type a million times before. Brown eyes, confident hair, headed to the City with eyes faced forwards at all times. His hands were strong, she noted, big and rough, probably from hours spent outside throwing a ball to his teammates. He would be good at sports, Martin surmised. He would drink lager on the whole, perhaps Guinness on Sundays, Flaming Sambuca shots on a Friday night in the student nightclub Sixes.

"This is about Emily, right?" Nick said again, pre-empting Martin.

"What do you know about Emily?" Martin asked, sitting down next to him. Until Emily's parents got to Durham and formally identified her body, there would be no official announcement about her death.

"Well, she's, uh, dead, isn't she? Everyone knows." Nick swallowed. "I thought everyone knew."

Martin sat straighter on the bench. "How do you know, Nick? Where have you got that information from?"

Jones sat down on the other side of Nick, flanking him. Nick moved his head between the women, a mild panic in his eyes. He licked his lips, trying to assemble his thoughts. "Uh . . . well. Someone called me this morning. Said there were police down by the weir. Police in Emily's room."

"Who called you?" *Would he grass,* Martin wondered, throwing a mental coin up in the air. *Tails, he does.*

"Annabel. Annabel Smith."

Tails.

"Annabel Smith called you this morning to inform you that Emily was dead, is that what you're saying?"

"Yes."

"And Annabel Smith is . . .?" Martin asked, knowing the answer. All of Emily's known acquaintances were being preliminarily interviewed to establish the closeness of their relations with Emily and garner their whereabouts in the last forty-eight hours. Martin then would assess who she needed to speak to personally.

"Emily's friend," Nick muttered.

"And you'd be happy for us to ask Annabel this, maybe check your phone records?"

"Uh, I don't know. Yes, I suppose."

"You were also friends with Emily?" Jones asked.

"Yes," Nick replied, clearing his throat now that he was on surer ground. "She was part of a crowd of us at college." He looked at them both, dipping his eyes. "It's a tragedy. We're all pretty shaken up by it."

Martin waited, wondering if he would expand on his grief. When he failed to do so, she continued, leaning forwards with her hands clasped together. "How well did you know Emily? Was she a girlfriend of yours?"

Nick ran his hand through his hair, shifted on the bench. "Well, I wouldn't call her a girlfriend exactly. She was a friend." He couldn't help the dimple which appeared in his left cheek. "A good friend."

"Were you sleeping with her?" asked Jones.

Nick coughed, sheepish. He wanted to laugh, Martin could tell. *These kids*, she thought. Experimenting with life decisions like a Collie plays with a ball on the beach.

"Um, well, I suppose I *have* done. I'm not sure you'd call it *sleeping* as in the present continuous — it was more of an occasional thing, you know?"

Martin sighed, "Yes, Nick, I do sadly. How did Emily feel about that relationship?"

70

"Was she cool about it, do you mean?" He paused. "Yes, I think so. She never told me she wasn't."

"When did you last see her?" Jones asked.

"Before she died?"

"Yes, before she died," Jones answered patiently.

"It would have been at the Regatta. Down at the boathouse." He shifted imperceptibly. "I barely saw her though. I saw her a few days before as well. There was a big hockey tournament on the Thursday down at Maiden Castle. A few of my mates were playing, Emily was playing. We went down about three in the afternoon and, when the tournament finished, ended up having a few beers in the bar."

Martin looked over at Jones.

"The one which overlooks the sports field?" Jones asked.

"Yeah. Emily was there, I'm pretty sure. Had a few cheeky ones and then headed home. Quite early. I've got a nine a.m. every Friday morning, which is a pain." He seemed to wilt then, rubbing his hand over his face.

"Are you okay, Nick?" Jones asked softly.

"Yeah. I mean, no. It's a bit of a shock I suppose." His hands were trembling, Martin noticed. "You didn't speak to Emily then, at Maiden Castle?" she persisted gently. "Just saw her there with others?"

"I think so. Might have said hello or something." He directed this at Jones, seeming to prefer her easier audience. "Loads of people there to see, you know?"

"At the Regatta, do you remember who Emily might have been with? Who were her friends?" Jones asked.

"Um, Annabel was there, I think. Emily didn't live with anyone, though, you know, like in a house share. So, she was friends with lots of different people. I don't know them all." Nick rubbed his knees and gave a loud sigh. "Look, is this going to take much longer? If I'm missing this lecture, I at least want to make hockey practice at lunchtime."

Martin looked at him. A boy who had heard about the death of his sometime girlfriend only this morning and yet came to his lecture anyway, played hockey at lunchtime as if it were a normal day. A boy who said he'd heard about the death before anyone else, before any official announcement had been made. Another poker chip of possibility spun into the pile, resting in a corner of Martin's mind.

"Where were you, Nick? On Sunday night?"

Nick looked at the women. "Seriously?"

Martin nodded.

"I was there. At the Regatta. Ask anyone. Loads of people saw me. I left about 7.30p.m. and walked down the river back to the college bar. Had a drink and had an early night."

"You walked along the river? Which way did you go?" Martin asked.

"Down to Prebends and then turned left up to Joyce." Nick's voice cracked in the middle of this sentence. He nodded as if to convince himself.

"You didn't see Emily on your way home?"

"No."

"Sure about that?"

Nick met her eyes with his. "Yes."

"Is there anything you want to tell us, Nick? Anything at all, anything out of the ordinary?"

There was the smallest of hesitations before the boy shook his head. "No, nothing," he said.

"Do you know Simon Rush?"

Nick looked startled. "Yes. He's the college president. Why?"

"Was he friends with Emily, do you know?"

He shrugged. "Not especially. He's a third year. Has his own crowd." He looked at them intently. "Is he involved in this? Do you think he's involved?"

"Do you have a Facebook account?" Martin asked, ignoring the question.

Nick looked puzzled for a moment. "Yes, of course," he answered as if Martin had asked him if the sky was blue.

"Twitter? The Durham Media account?"

Nick nodded. "Yes and yes."

"Anything you want to tell us about that? About Emily's Facebook account, for example?"

Martin noticed a scarlet tinge begin to creep across the boy's face.

"No," he said, less certainly.

"Sure? No photographs of you and Emily you think might be in any way relevant to this case?"

There was silence. Martin could suddenly see the stress Nick was under, the pulse point on the line of his jawbone jumping like a bean. He gave a nervous laugh. "Well, there's no point denying it, is there? You must have seen it."

"Seen what, Nick?" Martin asked quietly.

"The photo Shorty put online. The one I took of Emily at the Christmas Ball."

"Shorty?"

"Uh, Chris Wells is his name. Mate of mine."

"Tell me about the photo, Nick."

Nick was chewing his lip, staring at his hands. "It was just a joke, right? For the lads. Emily was cool about it. Everyone does it. Everyone knows. You send texts, you email things. It's just a *joke*."

Martin said nothing. She waited.

Nick stood up all of a sudden. "Look, I've had enough of this. If you want to ask me anything else, I want a lawyer." He paused. "And my father."

Martin looked into Nick's eyes for a moment, then seemed to weigh something up. "I think we're done then, Nick. Don't leave town, though," she said.

"Are you kidding?"

"Not in the slightest. We may well need to talk to you again in the coming days."

Nick got to his feet and hoisted his backpack on to his shoulder. "Right. Well, no plans to escape at the moment. Keep me posted."

Martin nodded as if to dismiss him, and he walked off towards the staircase without a backwards glance.

"What do you think?" Jones said quietly in the empty corridor as Nick disappeared down the stairs.

"I think I want to get in the interview room with Rush," Martin said abruptly. She looked over at Jones, who met her gaze calmly. She took a breath. "Nick's scared. He doesn't know how much we know." She exhaled loudly. "Not that we know a huge amount right now." She paused, thinking. "Presumably he doesn't know about the photos Emily had of him hidden in her bedroom cupboard."

"Emily had a crush on him. So what? What can he add in the light of a full confession from Rush?"

Martin rolled her shoulders and moved her neck side to side to loosen it. "We don't have a time of death yet. Nick admits he was there at the boathouse so he would have seen Emily. Why couldn't he have followed her to the bridge, dumped her in the weir?"

"The confession . . ." Jones said again.

"The confession bothers me," Martin said. "Still, we're stuck with it until we can interview him, unfortunately." Her mobile phone beeped noisily, and she put it to her ear, looking at Jones as she listened. "Thanks, we'll be right there." Martin snapped the phone shut.

At once, a shrill bell rang out, and the lecture doors sprang open. Martin and Jones were surrounded by a cacophony, dozens of bodies, talking, jostling past them. The women faced each other, island-like in a moving sea.

"Thank the Lord, Rush's dad has finally arrived," Martin said over the rabble noise. "But Emily's parents have also got here. Tennant's taking them to the mortuary. We'll have to meet them there before we can see Rush."

CHAPTER
ELEVEN

Emily started sleeping with Nick the night of the hockey formal. I knew this because she texted me in the early hours, after I had left Annabel, to tell me she was at his house. I had no illusions as to what that meant and tried to ignore it, staring up into the blackness of the night, trying to get back to sleep. She had obviously abandoned Annabel alone at the party — female betrayal always the result of attention from a prince.

This became a pattern of sorts. Emily going out and me sometimes meeting her first for a drink. Then she would go on to join Nick and his cronies, and I would be relegated to a lonely latter part of the evening, sitting in a pub, drinking a pint and reading. I would eventually go back to my room and, Zack's presence depending, hit the sack until the early hours, when I would get some sort of update from Emily.

It's odd but I didn't really think this was a strange or pathetic way of life. I just accepted it as my lot. The rest of my life, which went on without her, was filled with daydreams and ideas: novels lacking cohesive plots, travel plans lacking cohesive funds. I studied and read and ran. That was my life. And when I did see Emily, everything was okay. I didn't articulate it at the time, what I wanted from her. I couldn't. It was as though, if I said it out loud, it would dissipate what I had with her — it would evaporate like the mists hanging over the river that I ran through every morning. But I would dream as I ran along the bank, ducking through those wisps of wet cloud. I could be anyone I wanted in those mornings. I could pretend, quietly to myself, that it would be on *that* day that Emily would realize that she loved me.

But always the run would end, and I would stalk up the steps on to Framwellgate and back into the land of the living. I would return from the run as Emily's friend once more. Her *amici*, I thought sometimes, with a sneer. But I allowed it. I took what I could and to some extent I lived through her. Which was peculiar, because so much of what she did I thoroughly disagreed with.

Emily had a steely side, she had ambition. As much as her vulnerability brought out the best in me, made me feel useful, I have to admit that I liked this other aspect. It made me think that if I stuck with her, she would stop me sinking into obscurity, reducing into nothing more than a human encyclopedia of twentieth-century literature and running routes on the north-east coast.

As I say, though, often my views completely diverged from hers. Sometimes I even took Annabel's part — Annabel, who was the more obviously conservative of the two. She had seemingly forgiven Emily for dumping her at the hockey social but looked at her with a cat's eyes now, I could tell, slyly weighing her up, working out which side of her to butter up so that she could get some benefit from the relationship. Whether this was Nick too, I couldn't tell — God knows what girls saw in that cretin. Both girls looked similar, they wore strands of pearls, curled their blonde hair to their shoulders and had a liking for cashmere jumpers, which made their bosoms look more mumsy than sexual. But Emily had it in her, I could tell, to rip the cashmere off, revealing a black lacy bra. And, as it turns out, that is indeed what she wore underneath.

That quiet proclivity of hers became clear at another drink the three of us were having on a listless Sunday night. This time Annabel had driven us a little way out of the city, to a pub on the outskirts of Durham. Both girls were *depressed*, they'd said, emphasizing the word in their timbre as if the word on its own didn't have the necessary effect. This was a common trait in the university. Language was considered almost an aside to the convoluted facial expressions and expressive body language used by my fellow students; as if a statement had no meaning unless accompanied by the actions of an Italianate clown.

Anyway, there we were, out of town *at last*, Annabel had said, waving her hands as if to dispel a cloud of flies. I bought them both the ubiquitous vodka and sodas as well as my own familiar pint of Guinness. Emily was antsy and kept checking her mobile phone, which sat in front of her on the table.

"There's this game," Annabel said at one point. I looked at her while Emily continued tapping away on the screen of the phone. "Everyone puts their phone in the middle of the table. Whoever reaches for theirs first has to get the bill." I smiled at her, a shared acknowledgement of Emily's distance; she hadn't even heard Annabel's joke.

Annabel raised her eyebrows and gave me a weary glance when Emily went to the ladies at one point.

"She's obsessed," she said.

"With Nick?" I asked, knowing the answer.

Annabel nodded. "He pissed her off today. Him and Shorty and some of the other hockey players were looking at these magazines in the JCR. Girly mags."

"And?" I said. This news didn't surprise me.

"Oh, you know," Annabel took a sip of her drink, wincing a little at the cold of the ice as she swallowed. "Laughing about all the tits. They had a section called 'Assess My Breasts', or some such awfulness. You couldn't even see the women's faces. Just hundreds of boobs all over the page. It was disgusting."

"And Emily was disgusted too?"

At that point, Emily came back to the table, smiling a little, holding on to her phone. "What was I disgusted by?"

"Nick looking at that magazine today. When he said your boobs would be too small to get in something like that."

"He said that?" I asked.

"Oh," Emily shook her hair back from her face. "He didn't mean it. They're not anyway," She winked at Annabel before lifting her glass.

"That's not what you said earlier," Annabel said, apparently in a huff now that her gossip had been undermined.

Emily gestured to her phone. "He's just texted to tell me." She curled her lips in a sly sort of grin. "Thinks mine would be the best of the lot."

I said nothing, flummoxed as to how to respond to this. I could feel my cheeks reddening as I gulped down some stout.

"Well, who would want to do such a thing anyway?" Annabel said finally.

"I don't see anything wrong in it," Emily answered. "It's my body. I can do what I want with it."

"Making money by getting naked?" Annabel spluttered.

This is what I mean. Annabel and I were actually more in line with our views. But there was something about the brazenness of Emily. I must admit, I found it attractive. She was blooming at Durham, seemed to be coming into her own. Even though this might diminish my role as her protector of sorts, I had to admire it. I never thought, of course, that any of her views would actually be tested.

CHAPTER
TWELVE

Monday 22 May, 2.05 p.m.

Doctor Brian Walsh looked up from his desk as Martin entered. He handed her a file of papers as she sat down. "I've emailed the report to you as well. Death caused by manual asphyxia. Some petechiae and contusion of the anterior neck," he said, as Martin scanned the report. "Her skin was drying out by the time the body was found, yet the contusions were dark, as you saw. I'd put time of death on that basis between eight p.m. and midnight."

Martin looked up. "Fast work, thanks. Anything else?"

Walsh leaned back in his chair. "Her hyoid bone was shattered. That's a small bone in the throat," he explained. "It's very unusual to see that damage in someone as young as her."

Martin raised her eyebrows in a query.

"Means whoever did it was a nasty bastard," Walsh continued. "Used a great deal of force."

Martin thought about this, remembering the peacefulness on Emily's face as she lay with her eyes closed, the waters of the weir gurgling next to her. She shivered. "You were right about that baptism of fire, Doc."

Walsh nodded. "Looks that way. Hard for the city. For the kids to deal with something like this."

Martin got to her feet with a sigh. "Is she ready? Her parents are downstairs?"

"She is. We've kept her eyes shut to hide the haemorrhaging, and her neck's covered. Best they don't see her up close, though. We've put her next to the observation room."

Martin picked up her bag and made to leave. "Thanks, Doctor Walsh."

"Fight the good fight, Inspector Martin," Walsh said, swinging his chair back to his computer.

Martin smiled briefly and nodded before closing the door behind her.

Rebecca Brabents sat staring into space, tissues poking through the crevices of her tightly curled hands. Her husband was next to her, his chair pointing slightly towards hers, his hands reaching for her but failing to make it beyond a slight scrabbling at his knees. Phillip Mason sat with them in the morgue waiting room, his body turned towards them, a study in empathy, his brows knit together, an expression of physical pain on his face.

Only Mason's head lifted as Martin entered the room with Jones. She hated these places. The mushroom-coloured walls and *Reader's Digest* magazines provided no comfort here. The sole reason a person would be in this room was for the acknowledgement of death. The incessant drip and hum of the coffee vending machine the only vague life rhythm the place had to offer. Why was Mason still there? Presumably he'd met them at Joyce when they arrived in Durham. They would be staying there for the foreseeable future. But why had he come to the morgue? She would get rid of him; it wasn't appropriate that he was here.

Martin cleared her throat, and the Brabents looked across at her as if they were deep-sea divers, their eyes clouded by a hundred gallons of seawater. She made the introductions and then indicated that Michael Brabents should accompany her. At this, Rebecca Brabents, now twisting a piece of tissue into a tightly wadded snake, whipped her head around to face her husband. "I'm coming too. I want to see her."

Michael Brabents nodded, closing his eyes for a second as if to steady himself. They were an attractive couple, Martin observed. Rebecca had a boyish frame, wore skinny jeans and a furry gilet and had expertly highlighted hair which curled just short of her chin, appropriate for a woman of older years. He was wearing jeans too, with a pale-blue V-neck jumper and white T-shirt underneath. Michael Brabents gave the appearance of being relaxed, albeit grief-stricken, although a muscle twitched incessantly in his left temple. He had a nervous energy about him, Martin felt. He couldn't remain still, some part of him seemed always to be tapping or jerking. She searched her brain for the apt word: he was *taut*.

The sorry party moved out of the waiting room, leaving Mason behind with Jones. Martin led them down a white corridor. Nobody spoke. The whole scenario felt faintly surreal, Martin thought, a claustrophobic hush pulsating through the air. This was the worst part of the job. The forced stillness of acceptance before activity could resume.

"Here we are," she said as they reached the appropriate door. Martin paused, resting her fingers on the handle. "Take your time," she said before pushing the door open. They walked into a fairly large room with a glass partition separating one side from the other. Beige curtains hung across the glass. As they entered the viewing space, the curtains rolled slowly open to reveal Emily's body lying on a bed in the middle of the next room.

Rebecca turned to Martin, confused. "Won't I be able to touch her, to hold her?" she asked.

Martin shook her head. "It's not allowed, I'm sorry."

"She looks so cold," Rebecca said, her voice rising faintly. "She needs a blanket over that sheet."

Martin said nothing, not knowing how to reply. This clinical room held such humanity, such *life*, despite its stillness and its silence. Where did it go, all that love and hate and grief and anger? Into these bland walls, into thin air? She shuddered a little. One thing was clear: there was nothing left in the body on the table. Whatever had been the essence of Emily Brabents, whatever had spurred her on, brought people into her life, made her laugh and made her cry — all of that was gone.

Rebecca stood still, transfixed by her daughter's shape. Michael was beside her, his knee jiggling as his eyes travelled the scene before him. Emily's blonde hair was swept back from her forehead, a white sheet pulled up to her chin hiding the marks which showed where her life had been squeezed out. Rebecca made a sound without breath, a guttural cry, as she put her hand to the glass, tracing the outline of Emily's head. She leaned her own forehead to the pane, crushing her face on it as if to get nearer to her baby, the cry turning to sobs. Michael moved closer, turning her into his arms, bending her head into his chest. He turned to Martin with dead eyes.

"It's her," he said. "It's our daughter, Emily Brabents."

Martin nodded. "I'll give you some time," she said quietly before leaving them alone in the room. As she waited outside in the corridor, the keening of Rebecca Brabents soared into the silence, accompanied only by the sound of a rhythmic thud. It was a moment before Martin realized that this must be Michael Brabents steadily knocking his head against the glass of the observation pane.

Back in the waiting room, Mason and Jones looked at each other, Jones giving a quick smile before turning her attention to her BlackBerry. She wanted to get back to the station and start looking through all of the Facebook comments. And Annabel Smith still needed interviewing.

"Sergeant Jones," Mason said, breaking the silence. "Simon Rush. Um, well, how is he?"

Jones looked up, surprised. "He's fine," she answered. "He's in custody. We're waiting for his father to arrive."

"He's not considered a minor, is he? Why is his father here?" Mason seemed to have turned pale.

Jones shook her head. "No, sir, not a minor. He's twenty years old. His father is a criminal barrister, so he's asked for him to represent him." She gave a small shrug. "It's allowed."

"Good. Uh, good idea." Mason seemed to be struggling with something. He shot a glance at the door, as if expecting the Brabents to reappear at any second.

"I, uh, I don't want to — what I mean is, are you sure this is right, Sergeant? Are we *sure* Rush is our man?"

Jones studied the principal for a second before replying. "He's confessed to the murder of Emily, sir. You heard it yourself. That's all I can tell you at this time."

"And is that possible?" Mason coughed a little. "I mean, do all the facts add up?"

"Is there something you want to tell me, sir?"

Mason flexed his hands, jacked himself up a little straighter. "No, no. I just want to be sure things are solid. I'm the college principal, a guardian *ad litem* if you will. I just want to check that Simon is being looked after."

Jones nodded. "Don't worry about that, sir. You leave Simon Rush to us. He's in safe hands." She looked at him again. "By the way, sir. Rush as the college president — how does that work? Is he voted in by the other students?"

Mason shifted perceptibly on his seat. "Uh, yes. Normally that would be the case."

"Normally? What was the case here?" Jones asked patiently.

"Well, the vote was a tie, a draw. So, a casting vote had to be made."

Jones was silent for a second. "And who gets to make that casting vote, sir?"

"Uh, I do," Mason answered hoarsely.

The door opened, and Mason sat back quickly, folding his hands in his lap. Martin remained outside as the Brabents came in to the waiting room, following them in afterwards. They looked like ghosts, sitting down in despair on the waiting room chairs. Martin stayed standing, looking over at the principal as she spoke, "Mr Mason, I'd be grateful if you could give us a moment alone with Mr and Mrs Brabents," she said.

Mason raised his eyebrows in surprise before giving a thin smile. "I'll be waiting outside," he directed to the Brabents before sidling out of the room.

"First let me offer you our deepest condolences," Martin said after he had left, knowing as she did so how ineffectual the words were. "I must tell you, now that we have a formal identification, that we are treating Emily's death as a homicide." She paused. "I'm afraid the post mortem revealed that she was strangled."

Jones looked up at Martin at that and then back down at her lap, her thumbs crossed over themselves. Michael Brabents lifted his head, his mouth twisting as if in pain. "So when are we going to get the fucker who did this?" Spittle dotted the corners of his mouth, a red flush spread across his cheeks. His grief had turned hot.

Martin paused before speaking and, when she did, it was in a firm voice. "We will get the fucker, Mr Brabents. I can promise you that." She looked him in the eye, a beacon of certainty. "To do that, though, we need your help. Both of you." She looked across at Rebecca until Emily's mother lifted her head to return her gaze. "We need you both on side, helping us to work out what was going on in Emily's life before she died."

Jones took a breath and moved forwards, leaning her elbows on her knees. "Mr and Mrs Brabents, we need to paint a picture of Emily. Find out what her interests were, who she hung out with, who she had a crush on."

Michael spoke, "She didn't have a boyfriend, if that's what you mean,"

"Well, that's what we need to discover. She may have had relationships with people that you didn't know about. Did Emily mention any names at all? Romantic or not."

"Did Emily talk about anyone called Simon Rush?" Martin asked.

Michael shook his head. "I don't know him. No, not really. She didn't really mention anyone."

"We didn't listen," Rebecca said, turning angry, jabbing her finger at her husband, her sodden tissues falling to the floor. "*You* didn't listen, as usual. That's the truth of it."

Michael shifted his eyes to Rebecca and then back to his lap as if she hadn't spoken. "We spoke to Emily a lot. In fact, I talked to her just last week. She said she might come down next weekend. That was the last time we spoke to her . . ."

"I had bought a chicken," Rebecca said, dull now and staring out of the viewless window. "I was going to roast it. We hadn't seen each other for a month, I was so excited."

"You hadn't seen her since the Easter holidays?" Martin interjected. "How did she seem then? Happy or sad? Did she talk about her friends, her course?

"She never mentioned her course. Hardly ever. I don't think she was very interested in it. The subject was Michael's choice." Rebecca smiled sarcastically. She drew in a breath, a shudder spilling from her, the effort of keeping herself together all too visible to Martin. "I know some names. I spoke to my daughter, and *listened*," she hissed towards Michael before taking another breath, calming herself. "She had lots of friends, people who wanted to be with her. But she was close friends with Annabel. There was a boy called Nick I thought she might have liked. He played hockey, and she was forever going to matches to watch." She paused slightly, thinking. "There was someone else, though, I think. I got the impression they were friends, but she never said his name."

"*His* name?" Martin asked, sitting forwards.

"Actually," Rebecca answered, wiping her eyes, which had begun to seep more tears, "he came to Kit's gig, remember?" She looked at her husband. "At Christmas? I think that was the same boy."

"You don't know his name?" Martin said again.

Rebecca shook her head, frowning. "Our son, Christopher — Kit — he plays in a band, and they had a gig in Hammersmith over Christmas. It was a busy night, we had lots of friends there. I remember Emily saying someone had turned up from university, but we just didn't pay any attention . . ."

"Do you remember anything more about this boy, Mr and Mrs Brabents?" Jones asked. "It's very important we know all the people that Emily was associating with. Can you recall anything about him at all?"

Rebecca looked again at her husband, who continued to stare at his knees. "We didn't ask. Did we, Michael?"

Brabents ran his hands over his face then, mumbling. "We should have done. Oh God," he said in anguish, looking round the room as if realizing where he was. "Why didn't we ask?"

"Please don't beat yourselves up," Martin said quietly. "I know this is very hard for you. Details can be hard to remember after time's passed."

Rebecca nodded, wiping at her eyes again. "At Easter, though, you're right. She was, um — she was subdued, I suppose you'd call it. Distant. We went to France for a week, and she was quiet. She read a lot. We took walks. I thought, you know, perhaps she'd had a fight with someone. But when I asked her, she wouldn't say. She said it didn't matter, that everything was fine. We — I — just let her be. So *stupid* of us."

Martin shook her head. "No, Mrs Brabents, it's not stupid." She paused. "Did Emily ever mention any problems she might have been having online? On the internet?"

The Brabents looked baffled. "What do you mean?" Michael Brabents asked. "What kind of problems?"

"It seems as though — and this is somewhat delicate . . ." Martin shifted in her chair. "Emily had been in some kind of a relationship. And the boy she was seeing had taken photographs of her. Posted them online."

"What boy?" Rebecca said. "We told you, she didn't have a boyfriend."

"Well, it may not have been a formal relationship," Jones said. "Someone she saw on a casual basis."

"No," Michael shook his head firmly. "Emily wouldn't do that. She wouldn't dream of it. She must have been forced into it."

"Sometimes children do things that we aren't always aware of," Martin said. "Things we might not even agree with."

"Do you have children?" Rebecca asked sharply.

"No," Martin acknowledged.

Rebecca turned her palms to the sky, a pearl of a tear in the corner of her eye. Martin felt her judgement as a sharp edge, a woman with no kids investigating the murder *of a child*. She pushed the paranoia down, ignored it with an effort.

"These photos," Michael asked roughly. "Are they still online? Can anyone see them?" His eyes moved rapidly between Martin and Jones. "Where are they?

Bloody Facebook, I expect." He looked at Rebecca in disgust. "Vile thing that it is."

"Yes," Martin said. "Some of the photos are on Emily's Facebook page."

"You're on it enough. Why didn't you see anything?" Michael spat at his wife, his mouth curling down dangerously. He turned to the policewomen. "She's on it every bloody minute of every bloody day. Tap, tap, tap. You can barely get her to look you in the face."

"And of course it's not the same when you're on your BlackBerry, is it?" Rebecca's voice was cutting. "No, of course not. Because that's *work*, isn't it? *Highly* important of course. God forbid you should be dragged away from it and forced to participate in your own family's life."

"*Did* you see anything on Emily's Facebook page, Mrs Brabents?" Martin asked, her hackles rising at this interchange. Clearly all was not well in the Brabents' household.

"No, nothing," she shook her head. "But, contrary to what my dear husband says, I'm *not* on it all the time. I just go on it when he's away. He runs events — parties — down in London. When he's gone, it's lonely, you know?" She looked at them with miserable eyes. "Especially now the children aren't at home."

"What kind of events, Mr Brabents?"

"I run a PR agency," he answered. "Often we have launches of various products."

"You get skinny models prancing around for no good reason, you mean." Rebecca's voice and accompanying smile were bitter.

"This isn't relevant, Becca," Michael said brusquely. "The point is, are these vile photos still online?"

"We've shut down the pages," Jones answered. "They can't be seen by the public, but obviously we're scrutinizing them as part of the investigation."

"And did the university know about it?" Michael asked, his disbelief audible.

"We don't know yet, I'm sorry," Martin answered. She watched them closely as they retreated from anger back into their grief. Michael Brabents began to rake his fingers up and down his legs as if digging the ground, searching for answers.

"We can never second-guess the extent of evil," Martin found herself saying, wanting to reach out to them. Jones looked over at her in surprise. *Too much*, Martin thought, annoyed with herself. She coughed and resumed. "I don't suppose you have any photos of your family home, do you?"

"Yes, I'm sure we do. Why?"

"Sorry to ask. It just helps me build up a picture. Helps me try and understand what's happened."

Michael Brabents calmed the motion of his fingers and found his voice. "We'll do anything we can to help, of course. I'll have someone from the office email something over."

Martin stood. "Many thanks then. We'll be in touch. I gather you'll be staying at Joyce College?" She looked over at Jones, who nodded.

"But when?" The words burst out of Rebecca Brabents' mouth. "When can we have Emily back?"

"Ah yes," Martin shifted on her feet. "I'm afraid we need to keep Emily here until our investigation is concluded." How could she say it? That Emily's body was the only evidence they had at the moment? That they needed to keep her to ensure they could form a case against her killer? "I'm very sorry. I know you'll be wanting to organize the funeral."

"Yes, yes," Rebecca began sobbing freely now, the sound of it spilling out from her hands, which covered her face.

"Perhaps something could be organized in the meantime?" Jones suggested gently. "A memorial . . . or . . .?"

Martin stood awkwardly, not knowing what to do. "Our deepest condolences," she said again eventually. They stood and exited the room, Martin exhaling the tension as she leaned back against the door. To her left, though, she saw Mason lurking in the corridor, where he had been waiting outside. "One question, Principal Mason, if you don't mind," Martin said, turning to face him. "Does the university or Joyce College have any kind of counsellor on campus? Anyone who the students can see if they're struggling with things?"

Mason gave a short cough, twisting his lips into an odd shape. "Yes indeed. We have a comprehensive moral outreach programme at the university. Our guidance counsellor, Stephanie Suleiman, is particularly excellent in her dealings with the students."

"I'd be grateful if you could check if Emily was seeing Ms Suleiman. If she was, we'll need to see her right away."

"Of course." Mason adopted a pose of agreeable fatherly compassion before moving to re-enter the room where the Brabents remained. It made Martin shudder for some reason.

"Someone walk over your grave?" Jones asked, getting the car keys out of her handbag as they exited the building and reached the car outside.

"Hmm," Martin answered. "What do we think about Mason?"

"I had a very odd conversation with him while you were with the parents," Jones said. "He seems very concerned about Rush's well-being. A bit too concerned, if you know what I mean."

Martin gestured for Jones to throw her the car keys. Catching them, she got into the car and turned her head to reverse out of the parking space. "Yep, something's odd." She turned the steering wheel. "And who is the friend of Emily's down in London I wonder?"

"Rush?" Jones answered.

"Maybe. Maybe someone else. How's the cross-referencing of the trolling, the social media, going by the way?" Martin said, glancing in the rear-view mirror as the car made its way through the streets of Durham.

Jones gave a wry grin. "I'm going to see Annabel Smith and then I'm on it as soon as we get back. Why did you ask for a photo of their home?" she asked, after a while.

Martin sighed and tapped the wheel as she pulled up before a red light. "I'm not sure in all honesty," she said. "I just feel like something could have happened there which might give us . . . something . . ." Her voice tailed off as she remembered the feeling she had had in Emily's room. Something tugged at the back of her brain, as yet undeciphered. "Emily Brabents, what did you think of all these people in your life?" she murmured as the car pulled forwards into the building traffic.

CHAPTER
THIRTEEN

And then came the university Christmas Ball. This was an extravagant affair held in Conzie Castle, owned by some mortgaged-to-the-hilt aristocratic family who flogged time shares in their ancestral home for the readies needed to pay the utilities bills. It was a thirty-minute drive out of the city, and buses had been laid on to transport us party-goers to and from it. It will astonish you, no doubt, to hear that I was *actually attending* this auspicious event. Zack had taken pity on me and invited me along with his physics pals. Knowing that Emily would also be in attendance, I swallowed my dismay at the cost of a ticket and decided to throw caution to the winter wind.

On the night itself, the buses pulled up a distance away from the castle entrance, so we had to walk the last bit, up a path where flaming torches burned either side of the entrance doors set in the middle of its sandstone walls. A bagpiper stood at the entry, piercing the winter night with his wails.

The sky was heavy with snow, casting that frozen, faraway blueish light over everything, emphasizing the dark outline of the castle against it. I couldn't help myself, I was impressed. Zack had told me where to rent my dinner jacket, and I didn't think I looked out of place. I resolved to make the most of the evening and, I promised myself, I would not spend the majority of it looking around the room for Emily.

I walked in with Zack and a mate of his named Jay. The physics group had all shortened their names in a hopeful expression of cool, hiding the true geekiness of the Zachariahs and Justins that they had actually been christened. If I'd have been part of their group, no doubt I would have called myself Dan. As it was, we entered the large hall where the ball was to be held to a particularly penetrating strain of the bagpipes. It was enough of an assault on the senses to ensure a number of people looked over in our direction as we came over the threshold.

I saw Emily straight away. We caught eyes, and she gave me a half-smile, before turning towards Nick and his ever-present acolyte, another hockey player called Shorty. She looked exquisite in a floor-length midnight-blue velvet dress. *She walks in beauty, like the night, of cloudless climes, and starry skies*. But I put Byron out of my mind and deliberately moved in the opposite direction and made my way to the makeshift bar by the floor-to-ceiling windows shrouded in deep red curtains.

The overhead lights were dim, yielding attention to the garish disco lights dancing across the parquet floor. I ordered a bottle of lager and stationed myself by a selection of green baize tables proclaiming to be a casino and a bored-looking guy who appeared to be permitted to paste body-art tattoos on to giggling girls' arms. The music was anachronistic, the stuff we had listened to as children; now, here we were, pretending to be so adult that we even knew how to feel nostalgia. We danced in a sort of mockery of ourselves, so cool that even as we were dancing we took the piss before anyone else could do it to us. The unspoken agreement was that no one would actually dance *seriously* or with any kind of *true passion*.

Passion doesn't exist in places like Durham. It has been replaced by a knowingness, an all-seeing self-irony. I blame the American teen television series of the 1990s personally. Since them, we have become so emotionally articulate that the expression of any sentiment has actually become pointless; such is our *"me too"* culture that the only way you can really draw attention to yourself is if you can successfully ridicule anything you are genuinely feeling. There's a weird sagaciousness to this when you think about it: through ridicule you can control what you're feeling and it won't scare you. It means ultimately, though, that everything has become banal. We are being subsumed by our banality. I thought about this as I stood watching my peers, pogoing in a whirl of postmodern irony around the dance floor. I finished my lager and got another one.

There was a buffet table in another room, and I wandered through to have a look at it. I was quite hungry by this time. I remained unconvinced by the battered prawns and chicken satay, however, so took some bread and cheese on a paper plate and went to stand, again at the side of the festivities, to eat and observe. I smiled at a chap I thought I recognized from Nightingale standing not too far away from me, wondering if he felt just as out of place as I did. He nodded back, and I turned an inch towards him to offer a friendlier greeting when a girl appeared out of the shadows and took his arm, leading him on to the dance floor. I covered up my mistake by shifting a bit more on my feet before realizing that this might look as if I were dancing on my own. I stopped moving immediately, stock-still with awkwardness.

There I was, as Annabel came in with Shorty and I think her housemate Cat. They were drunk, heads together. I nodded at her, but she ignored me as usual, whispering something instead to Shorty, who laughed at her answer, and I felt a flush on my cheeks, as if all the spotlights in the room had spun around to illuminate me: *the one on his own*. I put my plate down and walked off, pretending to look for the gents. I left the main ballroom and found myself in a corridor near the cloakrooms where the girls at the ball had all left their coats. Boys weren't supposed to wear coats; we were hard men, inured to the biting wind and snow.

I stood at a loss in this hallway. I walked this way and that, debating: should I go back in and find Zack? At least there was another body to which I could attach myself. I felt sick in all honesty, a fake and a fraud. I should never have come to this disaster of a social occasion. I decided to abandon it, to walk down to the nearest road and try to get a cab back to college. Maybe I could even persuade one of the bus drivers to give me a lift for some cash. As I made up my mind, I heard soft giggling coming from the rack of coats.

I recognized Emily's voice immediately.

"Sssssh!" she whispered, a laugh in her throat. "Someone will hear us!"

There was a pause, a fumbling.

"Come on," I heard Nick's voice. "Just a little bit. It'll be nice."

"Nick . . ." Emily's pleading sounded tenuous, a pit-stop on the way to submission. "We shouldn't. Let's go back in."

He moaned gently. "What are you doing to me, Emily? Look, feel this . . ."

I banged through the nearest exit doors I could find into the fresh, cold air. I inhaled oxygen as if I'd soared from the plunging depths of a suffocating free-dive. I held on to a stone pillar and continued to breathe. I shuddered, sick to my stomach, turning back to look through the glass doors from which I'd stumbled. As I did, I noticed a flash, a spurt of white light shoot through the hallway where I had been standing. It didn't really impinge on my thoughts then, although it would later. All I could think was that I had been a voyeur. I was disgusted: with myself but more than that, with Emily. I expected no more of Nick, this was his stomping ground, and he frolicked in it with all the subtlety of a water buffalo in mating season. I had thought more of Emily, though, to be so public with her — *sexing*. I wiped my mouth with the back of my hand, wanted to spit it out, this foul taste I had now.

I lurched away, my back to the castle. I managed to find the buses and one of the drivers took pity on my shaken demeanour. He drove me back to Nightingale. When I got into bed, I looked at my watch. It was only nine p.m.

CHAPTER
FOURTEEN

Monday 22 May, 5.12 p.m.

Stephanie Suleiman woke up with a start. She had fallen asleep at her desk again, and now a silvery trail of dribble had pooled from the corner of her mouth on to a letter from a student's parents requesting that they Skype her on Wednesday for a conversation regarding his recreational drug use. Stephanie wondered about the term "recreational" drug use. What did it mean? That you could separate forms of drug-taking? Ah yes, you might say: I use marijuana in my work, but when I snort coke on a weekend, that's just a hobby.

Stephanie wiped one hand across her mouth, removing the spittle, and looked at her watch on the other hand. She really needed to go home. She swivelled around in her chair and opened up a filing cabinet behind her desk. Stephanie put the Brabents file in front of her and opened it at the same time as picking up a half-eaten Daim bar and finishing it off. Emily Brabents. A sweet girl who reminded Stephanie of her own daughter in many ways. Rosena was as naive, possibly as sexually precocious — although Stephanie would never say this out loud to her husband

— and had an essence of Emily, a quality which had the effect of ensuring other girls hated her.

Stephanie sighed: why was it that girls turned on each other in this way? It never happened with boys. They could eke out their frustrations on a football or in a boxing ring. Girls found solace in coming top of the pile, it seemed. Rosena had had to be homeschooled for a time, the bullying had been so bad. And then there was Emily. Stephanie swung around in her chair, thinking about the last time she had seen her. They had been having regular sessions for the whole of the Epiphany term. Emily had come to her distraught one afternoon after a hockey match. She had been sitting outside Stephanie's office door, quietly weeping, and had told her carefully and with no malice in her voice, merely a bewildered self-pity, that her life had become a living nightmare.

The last time they had seen each other had been only two weeks ago. Stephanie had felt confident that the cutting had waned, if not stopped entirely. Emily had told her about the self-harming just before the Easter holidays. She had been wearing a shirt with long sleeves but had reached up to push her hair off her face, and Stephanie had noticed the marks, raw and red down by her wrists.

"Shall we talk about that, Emily?" she had asked, gesturing towards the scars.

Tears had flooded from Emily's eyes. "I can't," she had sobbed. Stephanie had said nothing. Eventually the crying had ceased, and Emily had sniffed loudly, her tissue a sodden ball in her hand. She had taken a deep breath.

"I do it because I deserve it," she had said.

"Why do you deserve it?"

A shudder had passed through Emily, and she struggled to keep control.

"Because of what I've done. With the photos. Bringing all this disgust on myself."

Stephanie had remained silent.

"I know, I know. I haven't really brought this on myself." She had scoffed. "Whatever. I *have*, though, because I did it. I'm the one who's responsible."

"And Nick?" Stephanie had asked quietly, after a pause.

Emily had shifted in her seat, pulled her sleeves down further.

"Yeah, yeah. I *know* he's responsible too, But they don't care about him. It's all right for boys. If I had just kept control, I wouldn't be in this mess. I wish I was just normal. A normal girl who'd never slept with anyone."

"Is that what normal girls do? Not sleep with people?"

"It's not just that, though, is it?" Emily had said. "It's like, it's not enough, you know? To have them talk to me. To know they like me, or they fancy me or whatever . . ."

Stephanie had spun her pen slowly between her fingers, waiting for more, as Emily's brown eyes had flittered from the counsellor to the window, trying to pin down the meaning of it all. Then Emily had looked closely at her hands, at her nails. She had spoken in a near whisper.

"If they don't like me, then I'm nothing. If I can't get them to want me. And . . ." Her eyes lurched violently to Stephanie's, seeking a lifebelt which the counsellor refused to toss. At bay, Emily had continued, forcing the words out. "And that's why I cut." She had swallowed. "Because I'm so disgusted at my neediness." Swallowed again. "You know Annabel, right?"

Stephanie had inclined her head. Annabel Smith was also a student she saw regularly. A prim girl with a closed mouth which she prised open once every two weeks to spit angry words inside this office because she couldn't bring herself to direct them to the people she claimed to hate. Stephanie had said nothing of this to Emily; knowing that one of the targets of Annabel's vitriol was Emily herself.

"She's supposed to be my best friend, right? But I know she's slagging me off behind my back. They all do. On Twitter or Facebook or whatever. They hide behind the screen like it's a fucking . . . a . . . a . . . ?"

"Shield?"

"Yeah, right, a shield. 'Cause they know they won't get caught. Annabel pretends to be on my side and be my friend, but if Nick clicked his fingers, she'd be getting off with him before you could blink twice."

"And how does that make you feel?"

"How do you think it makes me feel?" Emily had sobbed. "It makes me feel like shit. Like I can't trust anyone, can't rely on anyone apart from myself. Nick says he likes me, or whatever, and then he sits around looking at porn on the net, laughing at women. It's frigging disgusting."

The image of that had hung in the air, causing Stephanie to shudder a little. She had pulled her shawl tighter around her shoulders.

"But then . . .?"

Emily had looked at her. "Then why did I take the photos?"

The counsellor had said nothing.

"Because I knew it would get his attention." Emily had given a smile older than her years. "Because I'm a fucking idiot." At once, she had seemed to shake it off, had given a silly giggle as if she were speaking in front of her friends in the college bar — she'd been too serious and said too much. Emily had become mute and stared silently into space, through the window, where a vista of trees and spring-green leaves danced in the wind.

Stephanie had seen the time and called it, and Emily had gone home for the holidays. When she'd returned, she'd seemed better, more sure of herself. And yet . . .

Now Emily was dead. Stephanie shivered. A vague notion of guilt lay within her. Could she have done more? She glanced down at her mobile phone. She had had a missed call from Annabel that very morning, which she had yet to return. These students were spinning around her like a cloud of electrons encircling a nucleus. The police would want to talk to her. And she certainly didn't want that to happen. What was she going to say? Yes, the poor child was being bullied. Yes, she cut her arms to ribbons as a plea for help. No, she

106

didn't know who had murdered her, but maybe it was one of the bastard phantoms who were telling her to kill herself on a daily basis online.

No matter what anyone says, hurt comes with words; that was the truth. In a way, it didn't matter who was saying it. Those words represented the world's view of Emily Brabents. Which was that she was a slut.

She rose to her feet and looked at the Picasso poster on her wall. Innocuous primary colours put in a space either to soothe or to lull into a state of distraction — better for winkling out of their shell their thoughts and their fears. The police were bound to look at her in judgement. She had let Emily down.

Stephanie had come to Durham after a three-year spell in Hong Kong, where she had followed her husband and his fund managing, training as a counsellor to quell the need for — what? For *something* at least. Her husband's company had relocated him to the north-east, and so she had applied for a job here. She had thought it cosy, undemanding; a place where she could stretch her wings and find out what the job meant. It had been nothing of the sort. Stephanie had been bombarded with cases from the moment she set foot over the threshold of the university eighteen months ago. She was based in the main administrative building down on New Elvet and would watch the students stream along the pavements day in, day out and wonder, in God's name, when would it all end?

She dealt with anorexia, bulimia, alcoholism, self-harming, drug addiction, failing in all subjects, criminal assault, theft — for pity's sake, she had students who had *stolen*. Nothing was off limits. It was a cornucopia of debauchery, a Pompeii for our times. The problem was, she thought to herself as she sat at her desk, that nobody was relishing their freedom. They were, in fact, abhorring it. They turned in on themselves to destroy it, destroy themselves. Sometimes Stephanie thought that segregation was better. Let's be truthful and let the elite have their time. Let the men rule the roost. Bring women — girls — into the mix and there's a confusion. You'll have sex and messy sex at that. And the girls will think they have a right to something, which of course they'll learn in the real world means nothing, and the boys will resent them for strutting around, tossing their hair like ponies, spouting nonsense about their so-called rights. It was no good, thought Stephanie. No good at all.

Ah, it was the end of a long day. She switched off her computer and picked up her bag. A late burst of spring sunshine burned valiantly at the window, as if putting her into a spotlight. She would go home and forget about this for now. She would try to put all of these nightmares outside of her mind.

THE *DURHAM CHRONICLE* NEWS WEBSITE "PURPLE PROSE": THE SOCIAL COMMENT COLUMN BY SEAN EGAN MONDAY 22 MAY

Pop band Bastille have it right in their song "Pompeii": the walls have come tumbling down.

There is a violent disease sweeping the student community. And it's not something you get after a drunken liaison in the alleyway behind Sixes.

The disease is fame, and the cure is the internet.

Anyone can get it — it's remarkably easy to catch. If you're eighteen or nineteen, chances are, you already have. All you need to do is switch on a variety of ON buttons — on your TV, your computer or iPhone — and the disease could steal into your brain.

Tragic victim Emily Brabents (18) had it. She had been parading herself online for months before her senseless death. She craved attention, was desperate to be popular. So she put photos online of her in sexual poses I suspect her mother would have been ashamed to see. In doing so, she became the latest victim of a culture of abuse and trolling that our children are all too familiar with these days.

The police are struggling to solve this *dreadful crime* which has terrified our community. It will prove a hard task — not just because they haven't got a clue how it happened, but because of the sheer volume of online abuse Emily was suffering at the time of her death. In reality, if the cause of death is revealed to be murder, the perpetrator could have been any one of those trolls.

A culture has been growing for too long, its mould seeps up the walls of the oldest, most respected colleges here in the university. It degrades, not only female students, but boys too. It involves nude pictures online; videos of sexual liaisons and, perhaps the worst aspect of all, an ethos of students anonymously abusing each other.

A source who wishes to hide their identity told me, "It's the law of the jungle. If you don't join in, you're seen as boring or weak. Basically, you might as well not exist."

I think back to my university days (yes, Ed, I did go!), where we drank coffee until 3 a.m., listening to jazz. It all seemed so simple then.

"If *you* don't troll, they'll get in first," my source said. "I've got a stash of material on tons of people — I don't want to say who — but it could blow the roof off the place."

These are interesting times, readers. Be aware of it. The world is different from the one my generation grew up in — it's a battleground. And not just globally, but here, under our noses, under our skin. Clearly there will be more to come, more will be said. But in the meantime, *the tragedy of Emily Brabents remains*.

Speaking of which, it will be interesting to see how the new detective inspector takes to the challenge of solving things for the community. Particularly, so I hear, when (Ssssh! Allegations only of course!) it seems an old romance may be lurking backstage . . .

For details of the proposed memorial service for Emily, please see the website at www.durhamchronicle.co.uk.

For any information regarding the above, tweet or email me at @seganjourno or segan@durham-chronicle.co.uk.

CHAPTER
FIFTEEN

Monday 22 May, 5.15 p.m.

Jones met Annabel Smith in the small, overheated room at Joyce College which the MCU had been given for the task of interviewing the students. Annabel was a rounded girl; demure, Jones thought. Bottle-green cords and a cream cashmere jumper, she had thick caramel-coloured hair pulled into a low ponytail, tiny pearls in her earlobes and brown heeled boots pushed as far back as she could manage against the base of the leather club chair on which she sat. She looked as if she were posing for a school photograph, albeit one where she had red-rimmed eyes and a constant sniffle. From outside, signs of continuing college life from the nearby refectory trickled into the room: the clank of plates being stacked; the smell of peppers frying; the low rumble of voices.

"Annabel," Jones said gently, "I know this is hard for you, but we need to find out as much as we can about Emily's life, who she was mates with, what she did. You were friends with her, right?"

Annabel sniffed. "Well, I, um, I don't know if you'd describe us as *best* friends. We were friends, yes. But

I've got lots of those." She tossed her head imperceptibly. "Emily was one of them. We hang around in a group, you know?"

Jones looked down at the notes she held in her lap. "I do. But it seems from what other people say, what we've seen online, that you and Emily spent a lot of time together."

Annabel brought her hand to her mouth and began chewing on a nail. A deep frown appeared between her eyes, and she pulled her knees closer to each other. There was something childish in the movement, Jones observed. "What do you mean, what you've seen online?" Annabel asked.

"What we've seen on Facebook, Twitter. All of it."

"So, you've seen . . .?"

"The photos? Yes we have." Jones leaned towards the girl. "Why don't you tell me about that, Annabel?"

Tears began to drop from Annabel's eyes. She shook her head, squeezing them tight, clasping her hands on her lap. "Of course you would," she muttered. "Fuck . . ."

"What's upsetting you about that, Annabel? You didn't have anything to do with the photos, did you?"

"No!" She opened her eyes at once before fixing her mouth into a flat line, a mulish stripe of obstinacy. Something in her had retreated behind high walls. Jones tried a different tack.

"Okay, tell me about Joyce, then. What's it like being here?"

Annabel gave a miserable laugh. "It's all right."

"Only all right?"

Annabel moved her eyes away from Jones and fixed them on her lap, twisting a silver and turquoise ring on her middle finger. An internal debate flickered across her face.

"What it is . . ." she began.

"Yes?"

She lifted her chin. "You don't know what it's like. It's hard, you know? Being a Fresher. Everyone expects so much of you. You need to fit it all in."

Jones made a sympathetic face: *I get it*, and the girl seemed to loosen up. She unclasped her hands and rolled her eyes. "I know — First World problems, right? But sometimes . . ." her hands now fluttered in the air, searching for the words, "it's hard to be yourself, you know?"

Jones opened her mouth to speak, but Annabel was on a roll. "Like, online, right? I mean, like what you say on Twitter, for example, or what you might email someone, well, perhaps what I say isn't *necessarily* what I mean. But people take it as gospel, you know? And then it gets churned out and said back to you as if you're the only person who's got a view. And then someone might think that those things were coming *from* you. When all along, you're only saying what everyone else is . . . because, you know, it's like, that's what you do here."

Jones took a breath. They would need to check out Annabel's online output. But she seemed to be implying something else. It hung in the room like a bat with open eyes but firmly closed wings. Jones thought fast.

114

"So, right. Are you saying that you've said something online has been taken out of context?"

"Well, not exactly. Nothing I can completely point to," Annabel said, dipping her eyes. "But, you know, there's been some press. And I wouldn't want you to think that I'd been *talking* to anyone. Certainly not in the press," she said quickly.

Meaning, Jones thought, *that she had indeed been talking to a journalist.*

"Okay, Annabel. Well, moving on. Just a few more questions. Did you see Emily down at the boathouse on Sunday? Were you with her?"

"Yes. We were drinking Pimm's on the grass for a few hours. Then Emily headed off after seven."

"Do you remember the exact time?"

"Twenty past? Something like that?"

"And did you see anyone go with her? Had she arranged to meet anyone on the way home?"

Tears sprang again into Annabel's eyes, and her face crumpled as she shook her head. "I tried to call her later, but she didn't answer."

"So she definitely had her phone with her when she was at the boathouse?" Jones asked, making a note.

Annabel nodded miserably. "Yes. We were taking selfies with it. She emailed me some, and I posted them that night. I can't bring myself to look at Facebook now, though."

"Was Emily dating Nick Oliver? What was going on there? Having seen the photos with him . . ."

Annabel wiped her face. "He's just a wanker. Emily . . . well, I don't know what she was doing. But he took

115

advantage of her. Oh, I don't know." She looked exasperated. "It's so confused. One minute I think it was him that was playing her and the next I think she was the one playing everyone." She began to cry openly. "I just can't understand why she's dead."

"I know. I'm really sorry, Annabel. Just one more thing, though, and then you can go."

Annabel was sniffing repeatedly, her face brackish with tears.

"Do you know Simon Rush, the college president? I know he's a third year, but have you had many dealings with him?"

Annabel chewed her lip and looked down at her lap. "No." She shrugged. "I mean, I know him by sight. Everyone does." She gave a self-conscious giggle. "He's gorgeous, right? And everyone likes him. Emily was always flirting with him. We had a drink with him once, ages ago. But, no. I don't know him as a friend." She glanced up at Jones. "Why do you ask?"

Jones straightened in her chair and gave a brief smile. "Thank you, Annabel. That's all. We'll be in touch if we need anything else."

Martin looked at her wristwatch as she scrolled down Emily's Facebook page again on her computer. She had got back to the station after giving a short, prepared statement to the press. No questions or information about the murder or Rush's confession: just an appeal for witnesses.

Jones had returned from interviewing Annabel and was tucked in, next door in the incident room, coordinating the cross-referencing task she was so keen on getting stuck into. Looking at the scope of the comments, it would be a hard task. And now Jones seemed to think that Annabel had been talking to the press about life at the university.

Mervyn Rush, Simon's father, had asked to see her before the interview took place. And after it, she would need to brief Butterworth. With every step of this investigation, she felt she was getting further and further away from Rush. It was as if she were in one of those dreams where you were running through treacle, obstacles popping up preventing you from getting to where you must go. She had to drown out everything else. *Who was Rush? Had he been the one to murder Emily?*

Martin let her mind wander around the kids she had met so far, the university staff. The place was a study in hierarchy. Mason hovering at the top — the college principals of Durham were emperors of this particular universe. And then the pecking order of the students themselves. Rush as college president lording it over the new blood. Was that why the first years were called Freshers, Martin wondered? Fresh meat for the rest of the student body? She shuddered. Something dark lurked here. She couldn't put a name to it, but she felt it. The absence of something, or the . . . what was it? She'd noticed whatever it was in the interchange between Rush and Principal Mason. Something had jerked in her brain, made her skin prickle. What was it? Something that would show that Rush was a murderer?

Martin looked again at her watch and then at the old postcard of an Emily Brontë poem propped up on her desk, given to her many years ago, the only piece of personal paraphernalia she had brought into this new office. She bit her lip, Jim's face coming unasked into her thoughts. She batted it away; she would call him later, after the interview. She reached down to get her handbag to pull a brush through her hair as Jones hustled in to the room.

"Anything?" Martin asked.

"Might be something. That note on Emily's door? Where you saw the impression of some writing?"

"What about it?"

"Well, all the witness statements are correlating with Emily leaving the boathouse at 7.30p.m. or thereabouts. And the impression left on the pad seems to say something along the lines of *Meet you at the bridge later — D.*"

Martin's head whipped up. "D?"

Jones nodded. "Seems to be. Not S or N, that's for sure, anyway."

"So, who's D?"

"Dunno, boss. And nothing's come up on Rush's computer or social media. Just the usual. He was friends with Emily on Facebook, but that's it. A fan of Beethoven though, apparently." Jones looked baffled by this. "And liked Seamus Heaney, whoever he is."

"Irish poet," Martin muttered, tossing her brush back in the bag.

Jones gave one of her cheery grins. "Anyway, just wanted to wish you good luck. I'll walk you out."

118

Martin nodded, more touched by that than she could say. The women stopped at a vending machine in the lobby, where the lifts would take Martin down to the cells. "Want anything?" Martin asked as she put in the coins required for a Crunchie.

"On a diet," Jones said, pressing the button for a lift.

"Yeah, me too," Martin answered, unwrapping the chocolate bar which had popped out with a clunk. "We shall see what we shall see, Jones," she said as she went into the lift. As the doors closed behind her, the word she had been scrabbling for came to her — the way to sum up the atmosphere of the university, which had eluded her since early that morning. It wasn't insouciance, she thought, it was *carelessness*. None of the people she had met so far had shown any care for their surroundings, their peers or even themselves.

Mervyn Rush stood outside the interview room where his son had been brought from his cell. He was an imposing man, and had a few inches with which to try to intimidate Martin. He wore a black suit with thick white pinstripes over a pink shirt. His hair was akin to a clown's — two bushels of black curls sticking out either side of his head. His face was not that of a clown, although his nose was red. Martin attributed that to the revelries of the Bar. *Networking*, she suspected Mervyn Rush would've called it. She disliked him on sight.

"You've got nothing." Rush spoke with a low voice, a conspiratorial cloth draped over a Samurai's sword.

"Why did you want to see me, Mr Rush?" Martin parried. She leaned against the corridor wall, on the face of it relaxed but with the feeling in the stomach she used to have as a kid when someone made a dare. She would always take it. She could play this game as well as him.

Rush looked at her as if appraising an artefact. He seemed to decide something before speaking. "Are you aware of Simon's history?" He released a smile from his cheeks as if making a stab with a knife, before sucking his mouth back into its usual purse. He was a cold fish, Martin thought. Red cheeks, cold heart. She didn't answer but waited for Rush to continue.

"He saw his mother drown when he was ten years old," Rush whispered, his lips moist. "She walked into the sea at Brighton in front of him. He's been seeing the university counsellor about it. Tell me, Inspector, what effect will the knowledge of *that* have on this so-called confession do you think?"

Martin frowned a little. So he would be angling for diminished responsibility. She sighed. "Mr Rush, can we stop playing Perry Mason out in the hallway please? At the moment, we only have a statement from your son. I have been waiting, *very patiently* I might add, for you to arrive. I would now like the opportunity to interview Simon and see if we can work out what's happened here. Would that be all right with you?"

Rush nodded briefly before turning his back and entering the room. After a beat, Martin followed him in.

As soon as Martin entered, she saw it had been a mistake to allow Mervyn Rush to represent his son. All

120

the cockiness of Simon, so visible in Principal Mason's office, had shrunk into a horrible emptiness. He seemed undone, unravelled, splayed in the plastic chair in the interview room like an unwanted toy. His body language reeked of fear, his shoulders twisted away from his father. Only his chin let him down, which tilted up in a sad sort of way, his mouth down-turned: the chin of a small boy trying to make the best of it.

A high narrow window on the back wall let in the only natural light in a room which was otherwise blank with the glare of a fluorescent tube and claustrophobic in its dimensions. Martin studied Rush. He had a quality about him, although now his face was pale, blanched by the strip-lighting above. He had one of those faces that pulled you into its wake. Despite his current lacklustre stare at the greasy Formica table, he had something appealing; Martin could imagine people voting for him, wanting to be around him.

Martin sat opposite Simon at the tiny table, her legs tucked under her chair so as not to bump his. Mervyn Rush was next to his son, a pad of paper in front of him. He didn't look at Simon once, merely unscrewed a gold fountain pen and sat still as stone, pen poised to strike. Martin bit her lip. She would need to be careful here; the dynamic teetered on a knife edge. Which way would Simon veer? To his father? Or to the truth? Martin flicked her eyes quickly to the CCTV camera in the corner, where she knew Butterworth and the team would be watching. She swallowed. It was time.

She leaned forwards, speaking in a gentle voice. "Simon, I've got the statement that you made to DS

Jones when you arrived here and which you've signed . . ."

"We'll be arguing that that statement is wholly inadmissible, DI Martin," Mervyn Rush interjected. "Why you thought it wise to get it without a lawyer present is beyond me." He finished with a nasty smile.

"Let's not pretend we're in court now, Mr Rush. As you well know, we needed something in writing after an oral statement was made of such significance, so that admissibility isn't in fact an issue. Your client now has the opportunity to deal with the substance of the confession and my questions, with his lawyer in the room — who will undoubtedly provide the best advice." Martin smiled back and continued. "I'm going to turn on the tape so that this interview is recorded. It's now 6.23p.m. on the twenty-second of May and I'm going to re-caution you. You do not have to say anything during this interview. But it may harm your defence if you do not mention when questioned something which you later rely on in court. Anything you do say may be given in evidence." She tried to make eye contact. "Is that clear? Do you understand?"

Simon refused to look at her but nodded.

Martin smiled at him. "Mr Rush has nodded, for the benefit of the tape." She paused. "Quite a speech you gave this morning in Phillip Mason's office. Quite a claim."

Simon skimmed a quick look at his father, who remained silent, then moved his eyes back to the table.

"Big words, Simon," Martin continued. "Hard to take back once they're made." She leaned back in her chair. "I just want to be sure. I want *you* to be sure that what you've said is entirely accurate."

There was another bout of silence. Mervyn Rush narrowed his eyes, the nib of his pen millimetres above his pad. He had, as yet, written nothing.

"Maybe the best thing is to go through your statement, Simon. Might be easier to get things rolling that way. Let's see . . ." Martin picked up a sheaf of papers from the table, scanned their contents. "So it says here that you met Emily on the first day of this academic year. Is that right?"

Simon cleared his throat. He gave another sidelong look to his father, who nodded briefly. "Yes," he said at last. "She'd got the train up from London I remember. She'd been staying with friends." His voice was hoarse, his throat dry. Martin poured him a glass of water from the jug on the table and passed it to him. Simon took the glass, looking for the first time at Martin as he did so. His eyes flashed wild for a second, and then the shutters came down again.

"You're a third year, though — that's right, isn't it? Emily must've been impressed to meet you." Martin smiled. "I know when I was a Fresher, third years were like gods."

Simon's lips twitched at that but he said nothing. Martin sighed and spread her hands on the table between them as a kind of entreaty. "Listen to me, Simon, I can't help you if you don't talk to me. You've admitted to doing a terrible thing. We need to sort it out, see if we can make things right. You want to do that, don't you?"

Nothing. Martin tried another tack. "Did you like Emily? Did you fancy her? She was a pretty girl." She looked down again at the statement. "You said to Sergeant Jones, *before your dad arrived*," she looked up at Mervyn then, to see him smirking — the emphasis wasn't lost on him. "You said that you had a good friendship with Emily. That she was different from your other friends. Tell me about that. What was different about her?"

Simon let out a long, soft breath and folded his arms across his chest. His sleeves were rolled up, and Martin could see the strength in his forearms. Seeing her glance, he widened his eyes and looked at her directly. "I loved her," he said with a small smile.

Mervyn at once scribbled something on his pad. Simon noticed and jerked back slightly, as if he had made a mistake. Martin threw another glance at the CCTV camera. This was like getting blood out of a stone. At this rate, they would have Simon's statement made without legal representation and nothing else. She felt the pressure rising. It had become hot in the small room.

"So let's talk about the night of the Regatta. Sunday night. You were down at the boathouse. Who else was there?"

Mervyn seemed to nod again, and so Simon spoke. "Everyone from college. All the Freshers, Emily and her friends."

"You say in your statement that you followed Emily when she left the boathouse. Can you tell me why? Did you want to see her alone?"

124

Rush gave a lethargic blink and moved his tongue across his teeth. He spoke like an automaton. "I followed Emily from the Regatta. I walked behind her all along the riverbank. All the way down to the bridge."

"Which bridge was that?"

"Prebends."

"And?"

"We spoke for a while."

"What about?"

Simon gave a short laugh before putting his hand over his mouth as if to stuff it back in. "Things. How she'd ignored me down at the boathouse. She'd been drinking again." He pulled the lapels of his black coat up around his neck as if wanting to hunker down, to try to be invisible.

"Did Emily know about your feelings for her?" Martin asked, going for a punt. "Was she aware of how you felt?"

"I don't know. She should've been. I made it pretty plain," Simon mumbled, speaking into his chest. Mervyn shifted in his chair, put his pen carefully down on the desk. He flexed his fingers while staring, bug-eyed, at Martin.

"I can't hear you, Simon. You'll have to speak up. Look at me, please."

"I've had enough of this," Mervyn spoke up angrily, jabbing his finger at Martin. "You have the confession. Simon isn't required to answer these questions. He's clearly been coerced. This whole business is absolute bullshit."

Martin remained silent.

"Do you have a prima facie case to charge him or not?" Mervyn continued in the same vein before stopping and taking a breath to control himself. Martin watched him unclench his fingers from the tight ball in which they had been curled, paste a disdainful look on to his face. He gave a nauseating smile before speaking, calmer now, quietly, with the poise of an arching, venomous snake. "If you need a motive then you should find one. You know," he sneered, "investigate."

Martin smiled at him, unperturbed. Moving her eyes back to Simon, she continued to address him directly, ignoring his father. "Simon?" She waited for a second. "I think you want to tell me. I think you want to tell me how it was. Let's go back a bit. How often would you see Emily? Every day? Once a week?"

Simon closed his eyes. He sank even further down into his chair, his arms a barrier across his chest. "All the time," he said, shaking his head at the memory of it.

"And would you always see her in person? Or did you email each other? Chat on Facebook, that sort of thing?"

Simon became very still.

"We've seen the photographs, Simon." Martin continued, noticing his stillness. "We've seen what was happening to Emily. How she was being bullied. It was awful, what was happening to her, wasn't it? Really terrible for Emily."

Simon had begun to visibly sweat. *Come on*, Martin thought, *come to me, Simon.* "Did you comment on Emily's Facebook page, Simon? The names attached to

126

the comments aren't real, are they? They're made-up identities, pseudonyms. What was yours?"

Simon sat up an inch and began to flick his index fingers with his thumbs on both hands in a rapid manner.

"So awful for Emily, what was happening to her. Why would anyone want to treat another human being like that? Say those sorts of despicable things to her? I can't understand it. I really can't. Especially not to a *friend*. What kind of friend would do something like that?"

The breeze-blocked walls in the room seemed very close to Martin then, pushing in on the three of them, squeezing all of their thoughts and strategies up into a jumbled cloud near the ceiling. She could feel a trickle of sweat make its way down the centre of her back. *Come to me, Simon. Come on.*

"I can't say," Simon said after a pause, finally unfolding, extending his hands out over the desk between them. He slid his eyes back to his father. "I can't say exactly why."

"What do you mean? Explain it to me."

Simon reached about him with his fingers. "It's a feeling, you know. An expression or a — a *quality* . . ."

Martin felt the hot air in the room pulse. She waited, she would get it. *No coward soul is mine.*

Simon looked at her then, his eyes bulging in earnest. "The quality Emily had. What I mean is . . ." He swallowed, still searching for the words. "I've been under a lot of pressure."

"Is this part of your confession, Simon? Something to get you out of the mess you're in?" Martin banged her hand on to the table unexpectedly, and his head snapped up. "Tell me!"

Simon shut his eyes. "I was sending Emily messages. I admit it."

"What kind of messages?"

"Nasty ones. Ones about the photos she put up."

"*She* put up?"

He shrugged. "Whatever." He shook his head. "She wanted it. Look at the photos. Anyone who acts like that. Poses like that. They want it."

"What do they want, Simon?"

He leaned forwards, over his splayed hands on the table, and said calmly. "They want to be fucked."

A silence filled the room. Her cheeks hot, Martin swallowed to gain control of herself after the violence of this remark. She looked down at her notes, her mind spinning, annoyed at herself for reacting. Feeling his eyes upon her, Martin looked up to meet Mervyn's cool gaze. They faced each other, gunslingers over the table. A knock interrupted the tableau. Martin walked to the door to find Jones outside.

"You're wanted, boss," Jones said quietly. "It's urgent."

Martin stared at her, amazed. Jones nodded, flicked her head towards the corridor, and they stepped outside, closing the door behind them.

"What the fuck, Jones?"

"It's Principal Mason," Jones said. "He's downstairs with Tennant. He says he was with Simon the night Emily was murdered. That he can't have killed her."

Martin rubbed her hands over her face.

"Shit," she looked at the metal of the door in disbelief. "He's given him an alibi."

Martin re-entered the interview room with Jones close behind.

"What's going on?" Mervyn Rush said loudly. "Who's she? Are you going to charge Simon or what?" he asked, talking across his son.

"Daddy?" Simon whimpered.

"I'm sorry about the interruption," Martin said calmly. "We need to take a short break. Won't take long. Simon, you'll be taken back to your cell."

"This is out of order," Mervyn protested.

"I'm sorry," Martin replied, "but it can't be avoided."

Simon made a small moan. Martin looked at him. He seemed to be at the beginnings of a panic attack. He breathed heavily, gulping down air; his hands clawing at his knees as he began to rock his head from side to side.

"Son, are you all right?" Mervyn asked, finally deigning to look at his son, taking one of his hands. Simon pulled it away roughly. He began to move his upper body backwards and forwards in a rhythmic fashion, groaning at the same time.

"Do you need a doctor, Simon?" Jones asked.

"Daddy," Simon moaned again, his hands now tearing at his hair, his mouth curled downwards, his eyes vacant. Without warning, he stopped still. His eyes were rheumy, unfocused; his mouth hung open.

Mervyn leaned towards his son. "Simon, talk to me. Are you okay? What's going on?"

Simon's face crumpled as he looked at his father and he began to cry. "It's not good enough," he mumbled. "It's just not good enough." He sat quietly sobbing for a few seconds, shaking his head in disbelief. He lurched his head up without warning and banged his fist on the table. "It's not fucking good enough, is it?" he screamed at his father.

Mervyn Rush stared in bewilderment for a moment before pulling himself together and speaking with authority. "This interview needs to be terminated. My son is clearly in no fit state to be questioned. He needs medical attention right away."

Martin stared hard at Simon as Jones muttered into the tape machine hastily before turning it off. She glanced at Martin, who nodded imperceptibly. "Yep, okay, interview suspended. We'll call the Force Medical Examiner to come and see Simon in his cell."

Martin gathered up her papers, still looking at Simon, as Jones opened the door to leave. Simon began a high-pitched giggle. "Cornetto, please, Mum. The one with the strawberry sauce. Wait!" Moving to the door, Martin turned back to find Simon's eyes locked wide on her in a stare. A feeling of sudden coldness stole through her; his eyes were like ice. "Don't leave me . . . please. Mum! Please don't go," he yelled. Martin closed the door behind them as Jones jogged down the corridor to get the Custody Officer. Standing outside, Martin felt the thump of her heart in her throat,

130

hearing Simon's cries morphing into the keening of an abandoned child.

What had just happened there? What was Principal Mason doing giving Simon an alibi when the boy had confessed? Martin walked slowly away from the room, away from the cries resounding in the hallways, bouncing off the dark-grey ceilings of the police station. She shivered involuntarily, remembering the stare Simon had given her in the room, which pulled against the weight of the alibi, now stuck to the case like a limpet on the underside of a hull.

There was something in that stare. Something wrong about it. But the truth remained that if the alibi was good, then who had been the one on the riverbank that night? Who had been the one to strangle Emily Brabents?

CHAPTER
SIXTEEN

I saw the photo the week after the Christmas Ball. I had kept my head down since then. There were only two weeks or so until the end of term. I would be going home to Mother, of course, for Christmas and I was dreading it. For most of my childhood, I can remember only about two happy days in Walthamstow, and on both of those the sun was shining. The idea of going back to my mother's little house with the gas fires blazing and winter darkness descending every day on the dot at four o'clock was almost too much to bear. My bedroom was cold; the duvet cover matched the curtains. Even living with Zack was preferable to staring at pebble-dash houses across the street from my tiny double-glazed window.

I put it out of my head most of the time and carried on. My essay on James had been reasonably well received; I was now concentrating on Byron for my swansong essay before the holidays. It was only when I was leaving the library after working on this the following week that I first knew anything about the photograph.

The main library doors opened on to a small terrace, which sat at the top of a large flight of stone steps leading down to a grassy mound. People would mill around on this terrace, smoking and chatting, procrastinating, avoiding going into the library, where they would have to face the reality of work.

I was standing outside, taking a break with a polystyrene cup of stewed tea, breathing in some air and thinking about light and darkness and the *Hebrew Melodies*. Perfection was a tricky concept. Even in the few people I had loved, it tripped around the edges of them; I supposed it was their imperfections which emphasized the good in them, was that what Byron was saying?

I leaned over the railings at the edge of the terrace and looked down, dangling my now-empty cup between my fingers. Below me on a patch of grass sat Shorty, Nick's friend. He was with another sporting type; they had kit bags between their legs, which were splayed on the ground — yet more display of their cock-a-hoop confidence. I could hear them laughing as I hovered above them.

"Seriously, she was loving it. That's what he says anyway." Shorty was holding his phone, it's screen flat in his palm, so I could see what was on it.

The other boy spoke, "She looks like she's loving it." He snorted. "Nick's such a cunt, though. Does she know about the photo?"

"Nah, don't think so. He texted it to me on the way home."

"Didn't she stay with him?"

Shorty laughed, "That's the hilarious thing. He didn't even take her home. Shagged her in the cloakroom, and then the bus took her back along with everyone else."

"Jesus, he's got some nerve."

Shorty got to his feet. "Yup. That's why we love him, dude."

They both stood and began to move off. I didn't hear much else, I didn't want to anyway. I was frozen there. I couldn't believe my ears. I was so angry, I'd never felt that rush before, a swinging sensation inside of me. A palpitation of rage so pounding it drowned out the crowd noise of the idiots around me. My knuckles flexed involuntarily as I realized I wanted to hit something. I hoisted my rucksack on to my shoulders and, tossing my cup into a dustbin at the bottom of the stairs, I ran. Down the hill, burning my lungs, singeing them with a lack of oxygen, sucking in air too infrequently for it to be called breathing. My feet slapped over the cobbles, I was winged; at once I was Pegasus. I flew through the streets, hard now over the tarmac. And then I was at the bottom. Deep and dark, the sun had gone cold; I was at the bottom by Nightingale, my college, my alma mater. I stopped, taking in the air I had missed. I leaned over, my hands on my knees.

"Hello?"

Again, Emily had found me post-run, at bay with physical exertion. I raised my hand weakly, managed a half smile as I continued drawing down air. Emily laughed gently. "Running again? Why are you always in such a hurry?"

I straightened and arched my back slightly. I didn't know what to say. The photograph had left a negative on my brain. Looking at Emily, all I could see was her body, curled over Nick's; long legs, open, inviting, *disgusting*. I shivered, my eyes dipping away from her.

Emily's head dropped. "You've seen the photo," she said, a statement.

"How do you know . . .?"

"Everyone knows. Someone's put it on Facebook. Fraped, they call it." She grimaced, a tiny frown on her forehead. "Raped by Facebook. Nice, isn't it?"

"Can't you take it off? Delete it?"

134

Hey eyes were dull. She shook her head and put her hands in her pockets. "They've created a separate page. I can't even get access to it except to comment and what am I going to say?" She gave a bitter laugh.

I looked up the street where we were standing. "Look, let's go to the pub. We could do with a drink."

Emily shrugged, and we turned to walk away from the bottom of the hill. We went into the first pub we came to, The Marlowe, a tiny pub not often inhabited by students due to its serving of real ale as opposed to fluorescent drinks in bottles. I bought Emily a Baileys and I had a pint. We sat in the back room, opposite each other in a booth. Our knees touched under the table. We sat in silence for a moment.

"Are you all right?" I asked in the end.

She nodded, turning her glass around in her hands.

"Have you spoken to Nick about this? What he's done?"

Emily looked up. "Have you seen it?" she asked.

"Seen what?"

"The page. What people are saying?"

I shook my head.

Tears fell then on to a cardboard coaster on the table advertising Harp lager. I fumbled in my back-pack and found a tissue, which I handed to her.

"It's disgusting. You can't imagine what it's like. It's so humiliating."

"But why would he do such a thing? Why would he take a photo in the first place?"

I didn't ask the question which blazed inside me: *why were you having sex with him in a cloakroom at a ball?*

"I don't know. He said it was just a joke. But," Emily swallowed, "it's got out of hand." She reached into her bag for her iPhone and scrolled down until she found what she was looking for. She passed it to me over the table. I glanced at the screen, not wanting to see what was there. Thankfully, she'd passed by the actual photo but had stopped at the comments underneath. *How can you live with yourself, you slut?* said one, *You deserve to be tied up and gang banged.*

I gulped down about a third of my pint. My cheeks were flushed. *Why don't you just commit suicide and save us all the bother?*

I stared at Emily. "Who's writing these things?"

"I don't know. I don't recognize the names. People must make fake accounts." She gave a sad smile. "They can't really be called Princess87 or Thunder-pants. Ugh. It makes me feel sick." She looked around the pub as if she were caged or trapped.

"Me too, Emily. This is crazy. Have you shown Nick? What does he say about this?"

She looked down at her drink. "It's not his fault. He didn't post the photo. It was Shorty, I think."

"He took it."

"I know. But — you know, I was stupid."

Yes, you were, I wanted to say but didn't.

"You need to tell someone. Why don't you go to the police?"

Emily shuddered. "I can't. It's too humiliating. I just want to forget about it."

"What about the principal of Joyce? Mason, is that his name?"

"Him? You must be joking. What's he going to do?"

"He can get this stuff taken down off the web. This is — this is abuse. He can tell the police if you don't want to do it."

136

"No. I don't want that. Nick would get in trouble."

"Seriously? Why are you protecting him? The guy's a dickhead."

Emily finished her drink, swirls of cream clinging to the sides of the glass before reaching fingers of dregs down to the bottom.

"I'm tired, you know? I'm really tired."

I couldn't think of anything else to say, so I just sat there. Useless. It wasn't a feeling I liked. "You know what?" Emily finally said. "I think I might just go to bed."

She left me there, sitting in the pub. Sitting there alone because I didn't know what to say to make her feel better.

CHAPTER
SEVENTEEN

Monday 22 May, 8.05 p.m.

Principal Mason was waiting for Martin in the small room adjacent to the police station's main reception area. This served as an interview room for those who walked in off the street asking to talk to the police in private. Martin looked in through the glass window of the door, watching him before she entered. He sat with his head bowed, a puzzled expression on his face, as if finding his previous confidence leeched from him, hiding beneath his feet on the linoleum floor. As Martin walked into the room, though, he snapped his head up, mustered a look of pure authority on his face.

Martin pulled the chair out opposite him and sat down without saying anything. There was silence for a minute or so, before Mason let out a short puff of air from pursed lips.

"Can you keep this confidential?" he asked.

Martin shook her head. "You're going to have to make a statement. You're giving him an alibi. It needs to be seen and digested if we're going to let him go. If we're going to disregard his confession and not charge him." She leaned forwards. "What you're doing here?

It's big. You're saying that Simon is lying and that Emily's murderer is still out there."

Mason had the decency to swallow nervously, Martin thought. She wanted to ramp this up with him. Make him see the consequences. She sat back in her chair, put her hands in her lap. "Let's take this one step at a time," she said. "Where did you see Simon and when?"

"He was on New Elvet. It was about seven-thirty."

"Why were you there?"

"I was supposed to have a meeting in Churchill Hall. You can check with Julia Earl, it's in my diary. I was due to meet with members of the administrative board. I walked all the way there from Joyce but when I got there, it turned out the meeting was cancelled. The message hadn't got through to me."

Martin gave a questioning look.

"It's true. So I left Churchill and was walking back towards Elvet Bridge when I saw him. He was sitting smoking on the wall outside the main lecture theatre."

"Did you speak to him?"

The principal shook his head slowly. "No."

"So you only saw him for a short while. He could easily have walked down to the river from Elvet. He could have got there in minutes."

"No. It didn't happen."

"What do you mean? How do you know?"

"I know because I followed him." Mason looked Martin dead in the eye. "I followed him," he repeated. Martin could see a film of sweat shining across his forehead. She realized she was kneading her fingers

139

tightly into the top part of her thighs. She stopped it and took a breath.

"Why were you following Simon, Principal Mason?" she asked.

Mason closed his eyes before answering. "I was interested in him. He, uh, interested me."

"Sexually?"

"I suppose so." His eyes opened again. "But you must believe me. Nothing had happened."

"You liked him from afar?" Martin clarified.

The principal nodded.

"Does anyone else know about this interest?"

Mason shook his head. "I would be grateful . . ." He paused, letting the implication hang.

Martin pinched her nose with her fingers. It was at these moments when she loved her job, the adrenaline coursing through her. She was very aware of her body, of her movements, of the need to control her genuine reaction. She could feel it bubbling inside of her — she almost wanted to laugh. "So, where did he go?"

Mason looked puzzled.

"Rush. When you followed him. Where did he go?"

"Oh, nowhere really. He finished his cigarette and wandered up to the city centre for a while. Looked at the cinema and then walked back to college."

"For how long?"

"An hour? Forty-five minutes?"

"And when he got back to the college?"

"He went to his room."

"You saw him enter."

140

"Well, I saw him enter the building. I didn't follow him to his room. That would have been odd."

Martin smiled. "Indeed."

Mason shifted, acknowledging something. "I didn't ask for this," he said finally. He found something of his old veneer, plastered it on his face. He would be believed because of who he was. He gave Martin a smile which rested on the fringes of patronizing.

"Easy for you, isn't it?" he said.

Martin looked at him levelly, saying nothing.

"Sitting in judgement of people." Mason scoffed quietly. "As if you know anything."

Martin continued to stare at him. Her heart pounded in her chest. She tried to breathe deeply without Mason noticing her need to calm herself. Someone walked past the room outside in the corridor, and the sound of their voice dropped into the room, breaking the moment.

"I know that a young girl has been murdered," she said at last. "I know that her parents will never be the same. And," she leaned forwards again, "I can see that there were some kids here who were chasing their tails, driving themselves crazy with sordid photos and texts. With nobody to guide them, nobody to reassure them that they didn't have to behave like that. Nobody. Quite the opposite in fact. Just a sad old man who wanted to get his rocks off on a child half his age."

Mason inclined his head. "You think it matters? A tramp like Emily getting her comeuppance? She asked for it. I've seen the photos." He smiled. "They showed me them, the boys. We looked at them and we laughed." He tilted back in his chair sticking his feet out in front of him, crossing his legs at the ankles. Martin noticed he was wearing yellow socks. Mason bent his head forwards as if imparting a confidence. "Between you and me," he whispered, "she would have spread her legs for anyone who asked."

He sat back like a man who has played his last ace. Martin bent her head to one side, considering him. When she spoke, her voice was a velvet cloak on a bed of nails. "Why would Simon lie?"

The principal coughed as if what he'd just said had never taken place. "I don't know, Inspector," he said wearily. "He's had some issues this year. He's under a lot of pressure with his studies."

Martin kept silent.

"He's expected to get a double first. His father anticipates great things from him."

"He'd confess to a murder he didn't do?"

Mason sat up straight, curling his mouth in anger. "I don't know! I'm just telling you what I saw."

Martin stood up, adjusting her suit jacket as she did so. "Thank you, Mr Mason. What you've said has been most revealing. I'm going to send in Detective Constable Tennant now to take a statement." She nodded briskly and turned to leave the room. Stopping at the door, she moved back to look again at Mason, who was gazing up at the ceiling. The words sat on her tongue like bullets, ready to spit, ready to maim. She dug her fingernails into the palms of her hands and left the room.

Oh, Emily, she thought as she walked down the corridors in the bowels of the police station to find

142

Tennant. *Who did you have to help you? Who had been your friend?*

Jones sat at her computer. Facebook was an absolute waste of a life, she thought. That and Twitter. What on earth was the point of it? Nothing anybody had to impart was remotely interesting. To *anyone*, Jones would have thought, puzzled by the whole concept. Emily's page in particular was filled with utter inanity. She "liked" numerous things, including several awful bands, in Jones' opinion, along with Joyce College itself, the Durham hockey team, Sixes nightclub and a society calling itself the Chunky Carrots, which Jones had absolutely no intention of investigating further if she could help it.

She scrolled down the six hundred or so friends that Emily had on her page. Many of them were based outside of Durham's confines, it was going to be a hard task to go through them all. Jones debated passing the job over to one of the DCs but then steeled herself to it. She wanted to contribute to this investigation. She wanted to impress Martin.

Jones focused first on Emily's friends from the university. She recognized some names, certain of which popped up again and again. Most of these friends had made comments on the statuses Emily had put up on the site, although she had stopped doing this after the sexual photos had appeared. Emily had become mute on Facebook since then. Those photos had their own appalling comments and "likes". Jones concentrated on the statuses before then, looking for a constant online presence. It was a punt, but it seemed likely that this mysterious friend whom Emily had seen in London would be online.

Jones looked back to the beginning of the university year and began again, trawling through the activities Emily had thought worthy of public consumption. Many of her statuses described events at the hockey club, and she often tagged Annabel Smith in them. Those two appeared to be best buddies.

Moving the screen down again, Jones saw a status entry at the end of October. It was a check-in, describing where Emily was at that time: *Quiet drink at The Prince Bishop with Annabel Smith*. Somebody called Daniel Shepherd had liked this post. Daniel Shepherd. The name rang a bell. Jones leaned back in her chair and scratched her elbow. Leaning forwards, she moved the cursor back up to the beginning of the year, when Emily had come to Durham. Now she saw why the name had triggered something. Jones scrolled down through all of Emily's status updates. Daniel Shepherd had "liked" every single one of them.

CHAPTER
EIGHTEEN

Monday 22 May, 9.45 p.m.

Sam Butterworth sat in the dark at his desk, the only light a spot from the antique anglepoise lamp he had bought himself for his fortieth birthday. Butterworth liked to sit at his desk like this, in the dark, perhaps with a short glass of whisky at his elbow. The scenario gave him gravitas, he felt, a little Chandleresque. Tonight, however, the set-up was not having the desired effect. The Durham bigwigs had been on him since the early morning, insisting on the need for this murder to be *shut down*. What they meant was, it was May. Next month, the tourist season would start in earnest. And what was Butterworth doing putting Martin in charge? A copper who'd been in the city for less than a month, someone who knew nothing of its ways or, let's be honest, Butterworth thought, its politics. Added to which, she was a woman. Assistant Chief Constable Worthing had already given him an earload this afternoon.

Butterworth had persuaded him to give her a chance. It wasn't even twenty-four hours since the body had been found. Worthing had been assuaged by the news of the confession; Butterworth had convinced him that everyone just needed to relax. Martin was an excellent copper, woman or not. She had proven herself beyond compare in Newcastle and she would do so again here. Butterworth sighed, pulling a paperclip apart and sticking it in his mouth. He wished he could start smoking again.

Outside the door, Martin had her head resting against the door frame. She breathed slowly, in and out. She had to pull it together. Even though her head was pounding and she was desperate for a drink. When she opened the door at Butterworth's call, however, she saw she might at least get the latter part of her needs met.

Butterworth pushed a glass over to her side of the desk as she sat down. She raised it in a mock cheers and took a big gulp of whisky. She sat back, and they looked at each other for a second. Butterworth gave a short smile.

"So."

"So," Martin replied, returning the smile.

Butterworth shifted and sighed. "We have a slight problem."

Martin looked at him. *Go on.*

"Rush is up at the university hospital under observation. But he's withdrawn his confession. His father called an hour ago."

Martin shook her head. "We should never have waited for him to come up. He's got a hold over Rush. He's controlling him." She moved in her chair, exasperated. "Fuck! I don't know what the Medical Examiner was playing at, saying he could be

146

interviewed. Why didn't he pick up on the fact he's obviously a complete fruit loop?"

Butterworth sat back in his chair, still playing with the paperclip. "Well, he's out of custody now; at least the time pressure of detention's off. If we get a healthy report back from the psych team, we can bring him back in then."

"And then they'll chuck diminished responsibility at us."

"You've got the problem of Mason's alibi anyway."

"*I've* got the problem?"

Butterworth shifted in his seat. "We have."

Martin raised her eyebrows. "Mason fancied him. I don't think the alibi is worth much. The confession means more."

"If he did it."

Martin looked at him, chewing her lip. "Hmmm," she said at last. "You saw the interview?"

Butterworth nodded.

"He didn't mention strangling, and we haven't released that to the press. So . . . I don't know. He seemed as though he was on another planet, calling for his mum. She committed suicide in front of him when he was ten, so his dad says." Martin grimaced and took another sip of whisky. "I'm going to do some digging into Mason. He was interested in Rush and he talked about 'the boys' tonight." She made the sign for inverted commas. "Doesn't give a very good impression. What with that and all the stuff about Emily on the web, Joyce is not coming out of this thing well."

Butterworth sighed again and topped up their glasses.

"You getting it in the neck?" Martin asked.

"Yup." He moved forwards and turned his computer screen around to face Martin. "This hasn't helped."

Martin leaned across the desk to see the website of the local newspaper. The photograph of Emily stuck on the board in the incident room stared out at her now from the screen: "PURPLE PROSE": THE SOCIAL COMMENT COLUMN BY SEAN EGAN. Martin skim-read the beginning of it before giving up in exasperation.

"The main article on the actual murder is on the front page. It won't take long before that's picked up nationally," Butterworth said quietly. "Talks about a lack of CCTV, lighting on the bridge, police presence in the city, et cetera. But this is more dangerous. Where is he getting his information from?"

"Knee-jerk journalism. For a start, they're running with murder before they even know that's the case."

Martin sighed. "We should take them up on that. It'll probably only get worse."

"It talks about you," Butterworth said. "And me."

Martin stared at him.

"Makes reference to an old romance. I'm presuming Newcastle. Whether things there . . ." His voice trailed away.

"They mean whether I'm up to the job. Whether I actually slept my way into this position?" Martin asked sharply.

Butterworth inclined his head.

148

Martin sank back into her chair, her glass dangling between her fingers. "Top brass?" she asked eventually.

"I've reassured them," Butterworth answered. "But it means you don't have much time to play with."

And it means my team will look at me differently now, Martin thought with frustration. "Fuck," she said again. She leaned forwards to peer at the screen, see the name of the author of the article. "I'm not going to be a scapegoat here, Sam. I won't be bullied. If I rush, things will get done wrong. They'll have to wait." She swallowed. "I'll get them their result. You can be sure of it."

Butterworth was looking at her intently. "How's Jim?"

"Good," Martin lied. "Busy," she shrugged.

"How's the move been? Is he okay with it?"

"Sam . . ." Martin put her glass down on the desk. "Let's not talk about Jim, all right?"

They sat in silence for a while, and then the moment passed. Martin stood up. "I said I'd pop in for last orders with the lads, so I should go."

"Okay." Butterworth cleared his throat and looked down at the papers before him. "Don't speak to Mason again without clearing it with me, Erica," Butterworth said as Martin turned to leave. "That's an imperative."

"Aye aye, Cap'n," Martin saluted as she opened the door. Butterworth didn't look up, his head framed by the spotlight as he considered what was on his desk.

Embarrassed, Martin closed the door behind her and leaned her head back on the doorframe. Sam Butterworth. Consummate politician and yet something in him tugged at her. He moved through the world like a basking shark, achievements coming to him as readily as plankton. But his eyes weren't the dead black of a shark, they were warm, and a fear glinted in them, some kind of insecurity that Martin liked, she could relate to it. They had never slept together — in Newcastle or anywhere else. But that didn't stop people acting as if they had. And Sam championed her, put her on a pedestal for some reason. Or maybe she felt the reason but wouldn't admit it.

She knew the time without looking at her watch. She knew she was due at the pub. And she knew that, despite her self-bargaining earlier in the day, she had finished the interview with Rush and still not telephoned Jim.

"Daniel Shepherd is the mystery friend," Jones said with excitement as she stood at the bar with a bottle of Budweiser in her hand. Martin ordered a Talisker with ice. A few members of the team sat at a small table in the corner, and she and Jones joined them. "At least, I'm pretty sure he is," Jones continued. "He's all over Emily's Facebook page. He literally likes every single thing she says or does."

"Do we know anything more about him?" Martin asked, taking a drink. No more booze after this, she was already feeling spaced from the whisky in Butterworth's room, and her head was still pounding.

"Nothing more than what's on his social media page. *Reader, Writer, Runner. Just me.*" Jones quoted. "And he's a big fan of Graham Greene. And likes French

150

films. At least, I think they're French — *Subway? Jean de* something . . .? Anyway, I'll get on to Student Admin tomorrow when they open and see which college he's at."

"Might be worth checking with Annabel Smith? She must have known him if he was such good mates with Emily."

"Good plan," Jones said, opening a packet of peanuts and leaning back on her stool. "So what do you reckon to Durham, boss? Liking it?"

Martin nodded, turning her glass around on the tabletop. She realized that the table had grown silent, waiting for her reply. "It's a good place." She looked at them all, staring at her. She felt she could hear their thoughts and wonderings, a garble of the judgements and opinions and labels they would be putting on her. And that was before they read what was on the newspaper's website. She ran her hand through her hair self-consciously. It was cold from the ice in her glass and eased her head a little. She was no good at this stuff, hanging out with the other coppers. She wanted to be back in the incident room, drawing charts and making lists, organizing all those possibilities which still crowded in her head, passengers on a platform, jostling to get on the train of thought which would lead her to Emily's killer.

Martin was saved by her mobile vibrating and jumping on the table. She answered it, making a face of apology to the others. She walked out of the pub, tipsy enough to talk to Jim, sober enough to drive, she thought. She walked back to the station to her car, talking softly to him as she went, hoping that the fresh of the night air through the open car window would combine with the whisky to make sure she slept through the night for once.

CHAPTER
NINETEEN

The last chapter of the Christmas term was Eliot and *The Wasteland*. We were racing through it. Literature spun around me, letting me glance quickly in through narrow, swirling windows — a zoetrope of words and ideas. I liked Eliot. I liked that he wrote this majestic work while on the tipping point of a breakdown. What adventures you can have there, what things you can see when you are at rock bottom. I once tried to tell Emily this, but she just stared at me vacantly.

Eliot was wrong about one thing, though. April is not the cruellest month. It is December. The washed-out face of Emily sank without trace into the pigeon-grey skies. She floated through the streets like a shrivelled ghost, sucked into herself. My stream of consciousness used to trail after her, through those streets, like stars. I was the Milky Way of her sadness, a twinkling mass of gathered miseries. I blew them across the cityscape, the blackened chimneys in the night, trying to disperse them for her, letting her wretchedness run through my hands like water. It didn't work.

It was a few weeks after the photograph had been posted online that things began to change for me. I met someone who changed things for me. I had gone to a poetry reading in a small bookshop down one of the tiny streets which sprout from the hub of Durham. I liked going there, browsing through the books. There is nothing like a book, in my view. Something tangible to hold, a key to a door. Most of my Durham peers, if they read at all, did so on electronic devices, pancakes of technology they could spin on the palm of their hand like a plate. Where was the excitement in that? Compared to the absolute joy of looking at the cover of a book and wondering, *what is inside?* Anyway, I had strolled along to the bookshop on yet another cold evening, my scarf over my face, thinking of those lines of Eliot. *The river's tent is broken: the last fingers of leaf, clutch and sink into the wet bank*. It made me think of Emily, broken and reducing. Where had her strength gone?

I pushed open the bell-topped door of the shop and entered into its warm confines, unwrapping my scarf as I did so. It wasn't very full. The local poet who was giving a reading had clearly struggled to rouse much interest. But there was a table with some mulled cider and even a pre-Christmas mince pie, so I took one of each and went to study the shelves before the reading began.

It was then that I saw him. Simon Rush. I had noticed him several times before at the bar in Joyce — he was the president there. I had always been envious of his confidence, how louche he was, how he would dangle an arm over a pal, his easy way with those in authority. He was standing next to a bookcase filled with political biographies, his finger tracing the titles of the books about halfway down.

My instinct was to turn and run, walk quickly out of the shop before he saw me. I don't know why I had this reaction, it just reared up in me. I sensed something from him, that once I let him in, things would change irrevocably. Someone like him would really rule the world. His was the *chuckle spread from ear to ear* that I woke with a start in the night about, my heart pounding my chest like an angry baboon.

I tried to move, to make my escape, but was hindered by my plastic cup of cider and the blasted mince pie. As I hovered, desperately trying to find a suitable place to deposit them, he lifted his head and noticed me floundering ridiculously at the end of the aisle. He smiled at me and nodded. I was mystified. *Was he wanting to speak to me?* By then, you see, I was so inured to my loneliness that I took persuading that anyone would. Particularly someone as — well, as attractive as him. How sad does that sound? I nodded back, feigning relaxation and sipped at my cup.

Simon came over, gesturing to my scarf. "Nightingale, are you?" he asked.

"Yes," I replied, my mind racing, my words tripping over themselves in my head.

"Should be good, tonight. I've heard he's excellent." He grazed his hand against my elbow, implying I should turn around, take a seat with him. I was gob-smacked. I nodded again, desperate to find my real voice. We took a seat next to each other on two plastic folding chairs, our legs touching somewhat as the seats were very close together. He looked pleased with himself as the poet came on the small stage the shop had fashioned at the front.

As we listened, I felt his warmth next to me. I could see the pulse spasm in his wrist. It made me realize that he was alive. Just like me. As the cider burned pleasantly in my stomach, I began to truly relax. I began to feel that maybe the winds would change, that I would make more friends in this cold place. That I would no longer be alone.

155

After that evening, I continued to see him. It gave me confidence with Emily. Despite the photos, she continued to moon after Nick much in the manner of an abused wife who clings to her fist-brandishing husband. I would see her in the bar as I sat, nursing my pint of Guinness, and I would remember my secret friend.

I had begun to hate the Joyce bar. The countless times I had sat there, waiting for Emily to condescend to speak to me — occasions that were becoming more sporadic the more hooked she became on Nick. My loneliness, painted so brightly through the sky for everyone to see since the Christmas Ball, was swathed through the place as a putrid scent. Often, before I entered, I would pause a second before pushing through the swing door, relishing the silence before the assault on my senses came, of hops and yeast and stale tobacco, the clamour of voices, ringing laughter, generic music. I couldn't think in there, couldn't get things clear. The whole world was a war zone. And Emily was part of this. She stood in the middle of them all like a water nymph, gurgling under the violet waters in which she let herself drown.

I rolled over in my bed, thinking all this through, that last day of the first term. And I felt I needed a break. From the Durham world and those who ruled it. Even though I dreaded the thought of it, I knew it was time to go home for a while. The taxi driver summed it up as he dropped me at the station in the dark and freezing fog of the late afternoon: "Best get yourself home, boy," he said with a wink. "You look like you've been in some tangled webs, my lad."

CHAPTER
TWENTY

Tuesday 23 May, 6.45 a.m.

The smell of bacon woke Martin before her alarm clock. By the time she'd got out of the shower and into her suit, Jim was sitting on the bed with a bacon sandwich for them both and a pot of tea.

"What have I done to deserve this?" Martin said with a smile.

He shrugged. "Thought you could do with some sustenance. It'll be a long day."

Martin sat on the bed next to him and took a bite of the sandwich. "True enough," she said with her mouth full as Jim swigged from his mug.

"Are we okay?" she said eventually when she'd swallowed. She moved her hand between them. "You know. Okay?"

Jim leaned back on the pillows, resting his mug on his stomach. "Yes, of course. We're just tired at the moment. It's like that sometimes."

They looked at each other in silence.

"Tell you what," he said, sitting up. "How about we get a takeaway tonight? You can tell me what's been going on, and we'll have a couple of beers."

157

A flash of irritation passed through Martin. As much as she would have loved to do this, Jim always seemed to forget what her job entailed. He just didn't get it. In the middle of a murder, to act as if everything was normal, as if life just carried on. *Nothing* would carry on normally for Martin until Emily Brabents' murderer was safely locked up in Durham Prison. She said nothing, her eyes moving down to her plate. She didn't feel hungry any more.

Jim sighed. "Well, if you can. I know things will be hectic for you."

Martin took his hand and squeezed it. This was the problem with them. A moment of carelessness, a moment of anger and then always the remorse. The house was full of it — seeping out from him and then her and then back to him again.

"I'll do my best," she said eventually as he lay back, putting his mug softly on the bedside table. "Really, I will," she said, leaning in to him. He nodded, a resigned look on his face.

"Thanks for the sandwich," she said, standing up as her alarm clock finally began its relentless tolling.

Martin walked up the North Bailey with a takeaway coffee in hand, looking up at the cathedral towers as they appeared between buildings. The slow rising sun had made a peach melba of the sky, and Martin breathed the crisp air in through her nose, enjoying the feel of the cold on her skin. Durham was beautiful, and empty, at this time of the morning. On a whim, she saw the cobbled alleyway up to the cathedral and wandered

158

up it, reaching Palace Green at the top, where her shoes were gradually dampened by the dew-stained ground.

A voice called out to her as she neared the main entrance to the cathedral, still locked shut given the untimely hour. She turned to see a man approaching her over the grass. The man slowed, his gait easy. He was wearing biker's leathers, his blond hair flattened — presumably by his helmet. He nodded at Martin, holding out his hand. "Sean Egan," he said with a friendly smile. "Good to meet you."

Martin looked at him blankly for a second before the name flared in her brain. *Press*. He was the little shit of an author of the website article she'd read last night in Butterworth's office. She raised her eyebrows and shook his hand reluctantly, wondering how to play it.

"How are you finding Durham?" Egan asked.

"Great," Martin replied, wondering idly when people would stop asking her that question. "What can I do for you, Mr Egan?"

"It's more like what can we do for each other," Egan said with a smile, putting his hands in pockets. "It's in your interest too, isn't it — to get the truth across? We're your best bet for that. So tell me, what's going on here? With the students?"

Martin could hear the bolts of the cathedral door sliding across. The mechanism of the clock tower began to grind. Once the doors opened, she could escape from this conversation. She exhaled then took a slow sip of her coffee. "You know I can't say anything about an ongoing investigation. You will have heard my statement yesterday, no doubt." She couldn't help

159

herself and gave a condescending smile. "Even despite that, you seem to have a lot of ideas about it."

"Ah, you've read my article I see," Egan shrugged. "I've seen what's on the internet," he continued. "The photos of Emily."

Martin's lips wavered for an instant on the rim of her cup. Had Egan seen the evidence of the trolling of Emily *before* it was taken down by the team or afterwards? If the latter, how had he managed it? And if before, why had he been trawling the university social media?

"It's a great story, Martin. You know it. Trading sex photos online. Obsessed love amongst the students," Egan smiled again. "Murder." He rubbed his thumb against the corner of his mouth. "People want a result. Young girl killed in plain view." He clicked his tongue disapprovingly. "Time's ticking on."

The cathedral bell boomed out its first of eight chimes as the entrance doors creaked open slowly. A maroon-dressed verger peeked out, squinting into the bright of the sunlight. Martin took her chance and turned rapidly away from Egan and headed across the grass towards the building. "Be careful, Mr Egan," she threw over her shoulder at him as she went. "Get your facts straight before you print."

"And what about the principal?" Egan called out over the noise of the bell. "What about his relationship with the students?"

Martin paused, imperceptibly she hoped, before she recovered and quickly entered through the large oak doors, into the sanctuary within. She didn't turn back to see if Egan was following but a moment later she heard the roar of a motorcycle engine spark into life and then fade into the distance.

She paced to the west end of the cathedral, to the slender columns of the Galilee chapel. Here, the building hovered over the precipitous gorge down into the River Wear, near the spot where the weir funnelled its waters. She sat heavily, running her mind over what had just taken place. She thought about what Mason had said yesterday — talking about *the boys*. Whatever the situation was there, was it common knowledge in the university? How did Egan know about it?

The sound of the cathedral organ barrelled its way through the previous quiet, making Martin jump. She looked at her watch, she needed to get going. She headed through the cloisters, which stretched off into the distance ahead, leading down to the nave and the famed stained glass at the eastern end of the building. The window depicted the Annunciation, where Mary towered, bejewelled in coloured glass, shrouded in blue and gold, stars in her hair. Her hands, in supplication and crossed over her body, reminded Martin of how Emily had lain similarly, almost in state, in the police tent down on the riverside.

Several tourists were already making their way quietly along the route which Martin had just taken, stopping now and again to study the fresco murals and statues which lined the walls. *Who was Emily?* Martin wondered as she walked past Mary, the sun streaming through now, illuminating the gaudiness of the glass, reminding Martin of cellophane sweet wrappers.

161

According to what they'd found out about her in the last twenty-four hours, Emily seemed a typical upper-middle-class girl from a normal family. She'd come here to Durham in the way that most kids did these days. No real hankering to learn, no massive desire for education — just because that's what was done. University was a given for someone like her. To *not* have come would have been a rebellion.

Conversely, Martin's university education had been an anomaly. Her parents had never understood how it signified her escape from Seaham, the small place where she'd grown up. She'd gone to Northumbria University in Newcastle to study English Literature and Psychology, where a dearth of grants coupled with an explosion of tuition fees meant she'd had to live at home her whole time there, studying alone at the small desk in her bedroom. She remembered the puzzled looks her mother would give her as she brought her cups of tea, pausing on the threshold of the room to stare at her daughter in small wonder at what she was packing into her head from all those books.

Martin reached the exit, at once surrounded by a host of tourists despatched from a coach. The selfish hustle of life, no patience given to the dead, it seemed. Everyone wanted a result and they wanted it quickly. Emily's murderer needed to be found, and then they could all get on with their lives again. A bird squawked as Martin emerged into the morning light. She would take her time, though. She had to be slow, deliberative. She wouldn't hurry Emily. Emily still had her story to tell.

Twenty minutes later and Martin considered Stephanie Suleiman as they sat in her office. She wasn't your average-looking counsellor: she wore a sari, she looked demure, sedate, shockable. Not someone who, Martin knew, would be dealing with the students' lives in dirty, minute detail.

"Thank you for seeing me, Ms Suleiman," Martin began.

Stephanie shrugged.

That was the other thing, Martin thought. She didn't act like a demure woman either. She seemed positively ballsy. Martin internally flexed her muscles and got down to business.

"I know we've received copies of your files on Emily, but obviously I wanted to talk to you in person about her. A picture is emerging of Emily as someone who was suffering a large amount of bullying. I believe also, in confidence, that she was self-harming. Do you know anything about that?"

Stephanie glanced down at the papers on her desk and then pushed them away slightly from her. She looked up to face Martin. "If you know already, then . . ." She shrugged again. "Yes, she was self-harming. She'd been cutting her arms since Easter. At least, that's when she told me, when we talked about it. Look, Miss . . .?"

"Detective Inspector Martin."

"Miss Martin. A lot of students come to me with issues, you know."

"Yes," Martin acknowledged. "But I want to talk to you about Emily — about *her* issues. Why was she doing this? What had happened just before Easter to make her want to do this to herself?"

"She had got involved with a boy. The boy wasn't that interested. She slept with him to keep his interest. He took a photo of her in some kind of compromising position." She frowned and opened her hands wide. "Somehow it got on to the internet, was passed around by the students who thought that gave them free rein to torture the girl."

There was silence.

"That's it?"

The counsellor stared at Martin. She turned her palms flat on the desk. "What more is there?"

"Who posted the photo? When did it happen?" Martin continued.

"I'm not sure. I think it was just before Christmas, but I wasn't seeing Emily then. She had experienced these attacks for some time before she came to me."

"She came to you for help."

"Yes."

"And did you help her?"

"Yes."

"How, may I ask?"

"I gave her a space where she could talk, get things off her chest. She could talk to me about the cutting. About her feelings, her emotions."

"And did she?"

"Did she what?"

"Share her emotions? What did she say about it, Ms Suleiman?" Martin looked at her, vaguely exasperated. "This is a murder investigation. We need to know

164

everything we can about Emily and what she was going through. Everything."

Stephanie stood and walked to the window. "There is no everything," she said with her back to Martin. "There is only what I heard. Gestures I saw. A feeling in the room." She turned to face her. "These are not 'everything'. They can give you an impression, a picture, but you will never know everything, Miss Martin. You will always be in the dark to a certain extent."

For fuck's sake, Martin thought to herself. "Thank you, Ms Suleiman, for pointing this out. I realize we can't know everything from every angle." She took in a slow breath. *Patience please*. "But what I'm asking, then, is what *your* impression was. What did you think was happening to Emily?"

The counsellor inhaled and brought her hands together in a prayer underneath her chin; she was in shadow as the sun shone in behind her through the window. "Miss Martin. I see how it works here, you know? I see everything. Men and women think about sex in different ways. It's an illusion to think otherwise. Once girls believe they're equal to boys, that's when the trouble starts. They can never be the same. Ever."

Martin looked at her, frowning. "You really believe that? That they can never be equal?"

The counsellor sighed and spoke patiently. "Women don't want sex in the same way as men. It's a biological fact. If they pretend they do, that they like it indiscriminately with no strings, then that is when the irony occurs. Because in handing it out on a plate, like

165

food, they may think they're strong but they are in actuality giving out what is desired by the men." She upturned her palms with a beam on her face. "Sex with no strings! The men don't care whether the women want to do it or not. All they care about is the prize, the upshot." She looked at Martin. "The orgasm."

Martin shifted in her chair. She didn't buy this. "That's saying that all men would rape, though, given the opportunity — and we know that can't be true."

Stephanie tutted loudly, apparently misunderstood. "Not rape, Inspector. No, no. But in a situation where a girl is just as promiscuous as a man it cannot be the same."

"Why not?" Martin demanded. "Why wouldn't a woman want sex just as much as a man?"

The counsellor was silent, her eyebrows high.

"That's not how it's presented here anyway," Martin continued. "The photos, the trolling. There's more to it than that. It's hard and aggressive but, when it comes down to it, isn't all of it just peer pressure? Which is why Emily was so upset. Because she was so judged and maligned for what she did. It was unfair. She played the game and then got ostracized."

"You still have a choice, though, do you not? If she was so strong, as a woman, why would she bow to that? She liked to think she was beating her own drum, she was carving the way for other girls . . ."

Happiness is a choice: the tagline on Emily's social media pages flashed into Martin's brain, and she suddenly felt desperately sad for these girls who walked

166

a tightrope between what they believed about themselves and what life presented them with.

"I don't know, Ms Suleiman," Martin said. "Maybe Emily really did enjoy it. The sex, I mean. And the thing that made her unhappy was everyone's reaction to that." She stopped for a second, thinking. "And if that's true, then what choice is there really? For the girls? Until things change in the wider world." Martin mentally shook her head: this interview was becoming an exposition. "All I can see is a girl who wanted to get a guy and be in with the popular crowd. You and I might go about it differently, but," she smiled, "that's what makes us all unique."

"Emily was like this, she convinced herself she was inured to it. But the truth?" Stephanie paused, thinking. "The truth is that Emily — or any woman in fact — can't give herself up sexually without feeling. Whether they're a first-year student or a pornographic star. My impression of Emily? Emily was acting out something foreign to her. And not in a nice way." She nodded as if corroborating it to herself. "Emily was not something I understood, really." She stared at Martin good-naturedly. "We cannot know everything, I believe. What Emily was — well, I don't think she even knew herself."

Martin left the counsellor's office, frustrated by the lack of concrete answers she'd provided and yet annoyed by what she had said. Maybe everything couldn't be known — or *shouldn't* be known — but that was what Martin fought against in her job every day. The not knowing. She would conquer it — that feeling — she would not be beaten by it. She would work Emily out, discover who she was and find out what had happened to her.

She walked back in the direction of the station, breathing in the spring air deeply, deciding to make a quick detour along the riverside to see if anything was happening at the Joyce boathouse. She shoved her hands in her pockets as she trotted down the bank to the weir. Within the police cordon, the luminous yellow tent remained over the ground where Emily's body had lain, protecting the earth which might yet hold clues to her death. Further up the river, Martin could see the red roof of the boathouse, bunting still fluttering in the breeze — a continuing reminder of the day of the murder.

As she headed in that direction, the gurgling river to her left, she thought about what the counsellor had said. Did she mean Emily was acting out something by posing in the photos? Or in the self-harming? This was the problem. Why couldn't the woman just answer a question? Why had Emily agreed to pose for Nick? Had she known he, or his mate Shorty, would post them for everyone to see? Why would she want to be seen like that? Despite what she had said to the counsellor, Martin couldn't imagine ever wanting to be viewed in that way.

She reached the boathouse, ducking under the cordon, nodding to the lone PC who was left there, waiting to interview intermittent passers-by. Flowers had been left along the nearest stretch of the bank leading up to the boathouse. Martin bent her head to read some of the messages attached to the bouquets. A few intransigent observers of the crime scene persisted, huddling under nearby trees. Martin watched them watching her. That ghoulishness of the public, the fascination with actions which went beyond the pale. She could understand it. It was why she did her job.

A seagull squawked above her, the noise of it bringing her back to reality. She breathed in deeply and turned away, deciding to time the walk from the boathouse to Prebends Bridge. She strolled along the riverside, looking up at the bending tops of the trees, putting herself in Emily's place on that night, the night she died. Why had she left the boathouse when she did? Had she planned to meet someone? Or was she just pissed and tired and wanting to get back to her room in the college?

What would Emily get out of the photos online? Viewing it from every angle, Martin couldn't see the advantage. Thoughts flocked into Martin's head, making her shake it a little, try to settle them down. Emily was using her sexuality. At first to get Nick and then . . . why? Martin thought back to last night with Butterworth, to the thoughts she'd inadvertently had about the male members of her team and how they might view her. She exhaled swiftly, feeling uncomfortable all at once. Was this what women still did? Used their sexuality to get ahead? She thought back to what the counsellor had said, about the simple lack of equality.

Martin arrived at the bridge and looked at her watch. It had taken her less than fifteen minutes to get there. Were the photos actually just a red herring? Were they connected to Emily's murder at all or something entirely separate? Martin walked up to the centre of the bridge and looked down on to the weir, the green, clear waters dashing over the stones on the river bed. She lifted her head to look up the length of the river, which curled around and out of sight, banked by the bush of the trees, the cathedral towers rising above. Emily had started self-harming at Easter, so the counsellor had said. But the trolling had started before then, after Christmas. What had happened at Easter to change things in Emily's mind?

Martin headed back to the bridge to return to the station. Nick had said the photos were a joke, and it seemed from the mass of comments and contributions online from the other students that the use of the internet to take the piss and bring people down was prolific. Was the university in control of this, Martin wondered? Maybe Emily had accepted the trolling up to a point, but at Easter it had all got too much.

Martin reached the stone steps which led up from the river to Framwellgate and climbed them to the top. Was this all part of what that journalist Egan had been saying? That, basically, sex was a commodity here. And if that were the case, Martin thought, reaching the entrance to the station, was Principal Mason a part of that culture?

THE *DURHAM CHRONICLE*
NEWS WEBSITE
"PURPLE PROSE": THE SOCIAL
COMMENT COLUMN BY SEAN EGAN
TUESDAY 23 MAY

So, new whispers swirl that someone *very high up*, in quarters not so very far away, is more than a *little close to one of the students* at a certain reputable college . . .

Far be it from me to stir the pot, but my little birds have also told me that the tragic murder of Emily Brabents, announced yesterday, is being investigated with only one person in mind.

Tweet on, little birds. It's what you're good at.

Remember, *nothing strengthens authority so much as silence* . . .

CHAPTER
TWENTY-ONE

I spoke to Emily a couple of times over the Christmas holidays. She was downcast. She had gone back to her family home. Her parents were arguing a lot, she mentioned. Emily had an older brother, Christopher, although everyone called him Kit, she said. He was away a lot as a drummer in an indie group, and they were all very excited because the group had just got a recording contract. They were heading down to London between Christmas and New Year to watch them play a gig in Hammersmith. Even with this news, though, Emily sounded distant. She said she was dreading coming back to Durham in January.

I didn't know what to say. I scanned the Facebook page daily, along with the other Durham social media sites people posted on to. I didn't know why, really. Everything on it was horrible. The remarks people made were truly some of the most atrocious things I had ever read. Names I recognized, people in Joyce. It didn't seem to stop either. It carried on mercilessly. I couldn't stop looking at it, it became a kind of compulsion. The jokes and links to porn sites. It was appalling.

On Christmas Day, I sat in the front room with Mother, watching a sitcom about a family nothing like ours, but which we were supposed to find funny because it was so similar to us, or so different, I couldn't tell. Mother had a cup of tea, and I had my second bottle of lager between my feet on the carpet. My sister hadn't been able to come, she'd told us, frazzled, on Christmas Eve, because the second child had chickenpox and the husband was going away on business the day after Boxing Day. Mother and I didn't care really. Those children were a pain, and we knew what we liked on Christmas Day. Now that we had a bit of money, Mother could afford to get a free-range chicken (turkey was too big for just the two of us), and I had bought double cream and made dauphinoise potatoes. Mother had laughed at this, said I was getting hoity-toity (her words) now I was at university. But they were delicious, and we toasted each other with a glass of wine, the bottle of which now sat half-drunk with the cork in it, in the fridge. Mother would probably throw it out before the New Year began.

As we watched TV, I was flicking through my phone and checking my email account. I had a message from someone whose name I didn't recognize. They seemed to have sent it to themselves, which made me think I wasn't the only recipient, that I had been blind copied. The email itself was blank but there was an attachment. It looked like a video. Who had sent me this? Who else had been sent it? I excused myself to Mother and ran up the stairs to my bedroom. I pressed the triangle in the middle of the picture, and the video began to play.

Emily and Nick were in a bedroom I didn't recognize. It wasn't hers, so I imagined it must have been his. She was sitting up in the bed, resting against the pillows. She was naked, I could see her breasts. She laughed, tossing her hair. Nick came into view. He was wearing jeans with the fly unzipped. The camera seemed to be at the end of the bed, slightly raised, and the right corner of the vision was hidden by something, the duvet perhaps. He said something to her that I couldn't catch and then she crawled over the covers to him on all fours. She reached for him at his waist and — I turned it off. I couldn't watch.

I knew, you see. That was what disgusted me. It wasn't that she was seemingly about to give him oral sex or that I had now seen her naked — seen her so intimately that I could see she had a mole at the top of her left thigh. No, it wasn't that. It was in the last movement I had watched her make as she crept towards Nick, her hips in the air. The camera had been close on her head, her lips fashioned into a tight smile. Right before I switched the whole thing off, she had turned her face to the camera and done it. She'd given a slow wink. Her face was buttoned up and closed but her right eyelid had come down and then up. That was what was so upsetting.

Emily was doing this after she had been so distraught about the photograph that Shorty had posted on the Facebook page. The date in the corner of the screen showed that she had made this video with Nick afterwards. I didn't understand it. How could she parade herself like this? She knew she was being filmed, that was bad enough. But more than that, Emily was acting in this video. Nick was filming her like some kind of porno. And she was letting him.

CHAPTER
TWENTY-TWO

Tuesday 23 May, 10.00 a.m.

The trouble with secrets, thought Stephanie as she drove out of the city, is that there are never any water-tight ones; they drip like jelly through muslin. After Martin had left her earlier, she had reached under her desk to where a small tape recorder was taped to the underside of it. She didn't know why she had concealed it from Martin and the police. It was a matter of instinct, she told herself, and she was good at instinct, at feelings of the gut.

Hers was cast iron, a product of her south Indian heritage, good and spicy Keralan cuisine. This situation with Emily was a little like that. A green peas masala: simple ingredients, peas and onions and coconut milk in a stew. But throw in ginger, turmeric, fennel, coriander, chilli, garlic and look at what you had. A soup of yellow velvet dotted with emerald balls which burst in your mouth: a harmony of spices, an orchestra of culinary elements. This was the problem here. You had Emily and Nick and whatever his stupid friend was called — the one that posted the photo on the internet; all fine and manageable. But then here appears

Annabel, out of joint with the recipe, a jealousy berry pie. Then, and more crucially, here comes Daniel. Daniel Shepherd was the spice. Without him, Stephanie suspected, all you'd have was a pretty bland Durham gravy.

She carried on driving. It was one of those early summer days when you want to open the window and blast music out at the countryside. She zoomed past hedgerows, all so very English. Even the unreliable weather — sparkling sunshine bouncing off the rape in fields but, in the distance, purple clouds circling, honing in on their prey — this was quintessentially English: one moment, all smiles and welcome to our country; the next, bugger off, it's pissing down with rain and the picnic's off. Stephanie tightened her grip on the steering wheel. There was something about it she liked, though, she had to admit, despite all of this.

When Louis had suggested the move back to his native continent, she'd cried for weeks. She would be taken away from their beautiful apartment in Repulse Bay, watching the junks smoothing around the water; Rosena would lose her tennis lessons and weekends playing beach volleyball; their ama would be packed off, back to the Philippines. They would live in a spiky city of mirrored glass and rubbish swirling on the streets: a *burgeoning city, up and coming in Europe,* Louis had said, persuasion in his voice. But Stephanie had known that that wouldn't affect them, sitting in their cosy lounge with the curtains drawn from four in the afternoon. Whatever the economics, they would be transported from turquoise waters, holidays in tropical Indonesian islands, fresh papaya and pineapple every morning — to this.

But still, she liked the people for the most part. No bullshit about them, that was for sure. She was probably more accepted here than in the expat landscape. Here, she was termed *quirky*; there, she was just thought of as a bit weird. Here, she could work with her maiden name unjudged; more to the point, here she could *work*. She tapped her fingers in time to the music and adjusted the sun visor. The road ahead was a Roman roller coaster: straight as a die, bending meticulously over an abundance of hills. After about half an hour, she indicated right and turned into a smaller lane. She followed it for about a mile before turning off again, on to a wooded track, which eventually ended in front of a detached stone cottage on the edge of a wood.

Stephanie got out and stretched her back. They lived only about twenty miles out of Durham, but it felt like another world. She lifted up the hem of her sari as she walked to the front door and let herself in. She sat at her desk, having made a cup of fennel tea, and switched on her computer. Rosena was at school. Louis was at work. She found it easier sometimes to concentrate, here in the quiet, without the bustle of students outside her window.

She tapped on the keyboard and inserted a memory stick. She wanted absolute peace to read what was on the screen. Having spoken to that policewoman, she had several ideas about things. About Emily.

A document appeared, and Stephanie leaned forwards in her seat to peer closely at its contents. After a while, she minimized the screen and sat back, sunlight streaming in through the window. She knew she would have to mention him to the police. The boy who had been writing to her throughout the year, a boy whose emails gave full and intimate details about the last few months of Emily Brabents' life.

She extracted the thumb drive and placed it carefully in front of her, next to a small tape she had removed from the machine hidden under her desk in the office in Durham. The tape was of Emily, recorded by Stephanie during her last few sessions, speaking from the dead. And, here, she tapped the thumb drive thoughtfully, here was Daniel Shepherd. Stephanie smiled to herself, her heart bumping more loudly than she was used to, despite the calm of the tea.

Here they were together. Daniel and Emily. Together at last.

CHAPTER
TWENTY-THREE

Tuesday 23 May 10.40 a.m.

Martin sat in the incident room at a computer, looking at the whiteboard on which were stuck the photos of Emily, Simon and Nick. She added one of Annabel Smith, drawing a line between her and Emily. Above them all, she had written "Daniel Shepherd??".

Butterworth put his head round the door. "Still nothing on the psych report from the hospital, Martin. They're still assessing Rush." He looked around. "Where is everyone?"

Martin leaned back in her chair, still looking at the board. "There's a massive culture of trolling going on here, Sam. All the students are doing it. They're thick with it," she murmured.

Butterworth sat on the edge of Martin's desk. He passed over a manila envelope. "It's the photograph of the Brabents' house which you requested." He gave a puzzled shake of his head. "Any reason why?"

"Hard rage disguising fair natures," Martin said quietly, her eyes glazing over as she stared off into space. "Or the other way around?" she whispered.

"Eh?"

Martin sighed and focused on Butterworth. "I need to talk to Mason again. I bumped into that journalist this morning." She turned the computer monitor around so that Sam could see the screen. "Another little gem of an article from him this morning, by the way."

Sam read it quickly. "Who's the person high up he mentions? Mason?"

Martin rubbed her nose. "Seems likely. This Egan guy knows about the trolling, knows about the photos of Emily. Jones reckoned Annabel Smith had been talking to someone in the press. He seems to think he's the next Carl Bernstein about to uncover Trollgate or something . . ." Martin's voice was rich with disdain. "Whatever. But the trolling was tolerated, it would seem."

"I want you to tread carefully with Mason. I don't need to tell you that he wields a lot of power in the university."

Martin shrugged.

"Yes, Martin. Tread carefully," Butterworth repeated. "It's in your own best interests." He glanced up at the board, folding his arms. "Who is Daniel Shepherd?"

"I don't know," Martin answered, opening up the envelope and taking out the photograph. The Brabents' house was impressive. Tudor, she guessed. Ecru and black with a thatched roof, casement windows, a magnolia curling up its walls. To the front was a typical country garden but to the side lay an expanse of lawn. Martin's eyes moved to that section of the photo. The grass sloped downwards; the edge of the photo indicated that its boundary met rolling fields. A football net sat in its middle; there was a shed, it seemed, at the very bottom.

"What do you think?" she asked Butterworth, pushing the photo over to him. He had good hands, she thought absent-mindedly as he took it. His nails were square and clean.

"Nice house," he shrugged. "I'm still not sure why you're bothered by it though."

"I'm bothered by it because we need to know where Emily came from, what kind of person she was. This is a middle-class house; her parents are well-to-do." Martin sat back in her chair. "So I still don't have a reason for what prompted her to come to Durham, a bastion of tradition, and get her kit off for the lads."

"I don't know," Butterworth acknowledged. "I can't understand it myself. If my daughter behaved like that," he sighed. "I'd lock her up for the rest of her life."

They both sat silent for a moment before the telephone bombed into their thoughts with a yell. Martin snatched up the handset. "What is it?" She paused, listening, looking at Butterworth as she did. "Fuck a duck," she said softly as she put the phone down gently. "Fuck a fucking duck."

"What is it?"

Martin stared at him.

"Come on, Martin, what? You look like you've seen a ghost."

She shook her head, swallowing. "That was Jones. The response car called her on route."

"On route to where?"

"Joyce College. Emily's mum — Rebecca Brabents?" Martin hesitated. "She's been found dead." She looked at Butterworth. "Hanging from the rafters in one of the college guest bedrooms."

Jones was waiting for Martin outside Joyce. The women exchanged glances as they crossed the threshold of the college but said nothing. Julia Earl stood in the lobby, waiting for them. "Principal Mason is with Mr Brabents." Her voice shook. "It's a terrible thing. We're all very upset as you can imagine."

Martin nodded. "She's upstairs?"

"Yes. Some of your lot are there with the doctor. They were staying in one of our visitor rooms. We have them free for guest speakers, VIPs and the like." She twisted her wedding ring in a reverie, snapping out of it as Martin cleared her throat. "Oh, sorry. I'll take you up."

Martin and Jones followed Mrs Earl up the stairs to the corridor where Principal Mason's office was situated. Beyond that door, around a corner, led another flight of stairs, and they continued up until Martin could hear the voice of Brian Walsh. He was just leaving the room as they reached it; a uniformed bobby stood outside as sentry.

"Martin," he acknowledged her arrival.

"How are you, Dr Walsh? What have we got here?"

"Looks like suicide by hanging, I'm afraid. Can't say for sure obviously until after the post mortem. Have a look yourselves, she's certainly hanging. No other marks on her except on the neck." He looked at

182

Martin. "There's no sign of a struggle. I'll try and get the report to you in the next twenty-four hours anyway." He inclined his head as if to tip a hat and made his way past the policewomen to leave, his black bag dangling uselessly in his grip.

Mrs Earl gestured towards the room's interior in a limp fashion. She moved backwards down the corridor as if unable to turn away as Martin and Jones spent some seconds putting on their protective suits.

The room was filled with the silence of the dead. Rebecca Brabents' body swung from a thick wooden beam which crossed the high ceiling over a bed covered with a thick crimson bedspread. Her head lolled forwards at an angle. Martin walked under the body, trying to see her face; her eyes bulged, purple spiny veins standing out from her eyeballs, pupils dilated into black discs. Martin peered closer; she had used what looked like a golden rope to wrap around the beam and then her neck. Martin scanned the room and saw that a thick, brocaded curtain tie was missing from one of the windows. It cut into her flesh, red raw marks visible beneath it. Her hands swung at her side, her toes pointing down to where a three-legged teak stool had been kicked over. A cool breeze permeated the room, and the body swayed a little in its thrall.

Rebecca's arms were bare, and Martin studied them. "No other marks apart from the neck," she said quietly. "Walsh is right. Doesn't look like a struggle." She looked around the room. It was overstuffed and overly decorated. The furniture was dark and cumbersome, the soft furnishings all in various shades of red. Martin shook her hair back from her head. It was a room of nightmares, a red room of death. They would need a new SIO to handle this, alongside the investigation into Emily's death. Martin could already hear the scream of the newspaper headlines, ramping up the heat which already emanated from the university.

"Any note?" she asked as Jones, too, scouted the room.

"Not yet. Except . . ." She reached under the bed, where the handle of a bag could be seen poking out. "Here's her handbag." She put it on top of the bed and looked carefully inside. She pulled out a cream envelope. "A letter addressed to Michael." She handed it over to Martin, who opened the envelope quickly. She scanned its contents then looked back at Jones.

"This case just gets more fucked up with each hour," she said softly.

CHAPTER
TWENTY-FOUR

I texted Emily immediately after I'd watched the video. I didn't mention I'd seen it, I just pretended it would be good to catch up when she was down in London. She texted back almost at once and invited me to her brother's gig. I should say I was excited about this. I would have been looking forward to seeing Emily anyway, but the idea of going to see a proper band, where I almost knew the drummer, was pretty thrilling.

The gig was on the Wednesday in between Christmas and New Year. I told Mum I was meeting a friend from university and ignored the raised eyebrows that this information produced. I wore jeans and a black T-shirt, completely innocuous, I thought. I wrapped my Nightingale scarf round my neck and over my jacket before stepping out into the cold London air. The tube was busy from Walthamstow to Hammersmith. The Christmas party season was in full swing and I had to barge my way out on to the platform at my destination. I picked up one of those trashy free newspapers as a defence mechanism as I was still quite early. It annoys me that I am so incapable of being late. I am always fascinated by those people who can never get anywhere on time. What are they thinking? How can they forget that they are supposed to be somewhere — is life so all-consuming, exciting or stressf for them that the time disappears from their consciousness? Arrangements I make with others never leave the front of my brain. They stay there as markers to hold on to, that I am actually part of society, not merely its ironic observer.

I had a pint in the pub next to the Apollo before going in. I had arranged to meet Emily in the lobby. Of course, she was late. I stood there with my paper, looking at posters of upcoming gigs. It all seemed so apart from me, so disparate from what fired my soul. But still I was intrigued by it. I observed its glitter with the stealth of a magpie, trying to find a way to steal a prize. A prize I didn't really know if I wanted. Emily was part of that. She was my connection to that world, the bridge I could take to it, my only way in. But then I remembered, Emily was lost at the moment. She, who had been accepted so easily by the realm which spun separately from me — that realm was a dark and desperate place for her nowadays.

"It's so good to see you. Thanks for coming." She rushed at me, dabbing at both my cheeks with her lips, a child pretending to be a grown-up. I felt as if I were at a cocktail party and not standing in a dingy pseudo-Victorian lobby surrounded by gothic-clothed teenagers carrying supersized cups of Coke. Emily's family were making their way into the auditorium. They didn't bother to greet me, naturally accepting my presence as a hanger-on. Emily seemed buoyed by my company, though. She linked arms with me as we walked into the dark of the concert hall. We walked past the needless red velvet seats, all pointing upwards as their occupants stood, bunched in, fated to move restrictedly, in rows of stilted dancing. The Brabents family and I moved on past them to a doorway in a corridor off the main space. We would be watching the gig from a box at the side of the stage.

We stood there, a crowd of shadowy shapes in the dim light off-stage. Emily's dad (I presumed) opened some bottles of champagne, and we remained there in the half-light, holding plastic glasses of warm fizz. Emily and I were towards the back of this small group, near the door to the corridor. She was in front of me as I leaned my back into the wall, but we could hardly hear each other over the noise of the kids jamming in to the theatre, the heat rising in proportion to the squashed masses.

"How have you been?" I semi-shouted over the din.

More friends of the Brabents crammed into the box. I removed my scarf awkwardly, looping it over the arm which held my plastic cup. Emily shrugged.

"Okay."

"How was Christmas?"

"Fine." She jutted her chin towards her parents standing at the balustrade, looking down at the stage. "They've been a bit of a nightmare." Mrs Brabents was wearing a spaghetti-strapped top with skinny jeans, and her face was thick with make-up. She looked less a mother, more a secretary on a night out.

"How so?"

"Oh, you know, just . . ." She looked over at them. Mr Brabents had his back to his wife, talking to another man in jeans. We were all wearing the same clothes, I noticed, and I sighed.

"What's wrong?" Emily looked up at me, her eyes shining in the golden light of the stage. I smiled ruefully.

"Nothing." I took her hand. "Thanks for asking me tonight."

She patted my hand. "That's okay. I know you don't have many friends at Durham."

I grimaced internally. The waiting instruments on the stage took on a frustrated quality. Why wouldn't somebody just get on and play them? I sipped from my cup.

"And you?" Emily said brightly, oblivious to my discomfort. "Christmas good?"

The elephant in the room was practically sashaying down the aisles at this point. Could I tell Emily about the video? "Yes," I decided to persist with this inane conversation. "Fine."

Emily nodded. She turned to look at the stage and then at her watch, an expensive circle of silver on her slim wrist. I finished my drink and pretended to look at the stage too. Seriously, it was interminable. When would they start? The crowd were also restless. People had begun to spill into the aisles, out of their seats, edging closer to the stage.

"I'm going to get a beer," I said suddenly.

"Oh, but there's more wine . . ." Emily gestured ineffectually towards her father. I smiled. "Don't worry. I'd rather have a beer. Do you want anything?" She shook her head as I left the box and headed back down the velvet-swathed corridor. The Victorians really did know how to make a meal of their décor, I thought as I headed back to the lobby. I couldn't help but think of brothels: the richness of opulence so in your face, it made a mockery of its supposed class. Carpetbaggers, I thought. A bit like the company I was keeping. I felt anger rise to the back of my throat as I walked off. It was a rank taste in my mouth.

188

I stood in line at the small bar near the entrance. This was not how I'd planned this evening to go. I was on the verge of leaving, when Emily appeared at my elbow. "I'm sorry," she said softly. "This isn't much fun, is it?"

I looked up at her from where I'd been staring at the floor, lifted my eyebrows a bit, part puppy dog, part James Dean, I hoped. "Not really," I admitted.

"I'm sorry," she whispered, touching my arm gently. "I do like you, you know. Even if I'm a bit rubbish at saying it." She licked her pretty pink lips with the tip of her tongue, her eyes meeting mine for a second too long.

The queue moved, and I went with it, reaching the bar and leaning on it, turning my head towards her. For once in my life, I think I looked cool.

"Beer?" I said with a slight smile.

CHAPTER
TWENTY-FIVE

Tuesday 23 May, 2.36 p.m.

Butterworth leaned over his desk. He was frowning, his white shirt pulled tight across his chest, pearls of perspiration dotting his forehead. It had turned into one of those hot afternoons that stab incongruously into the season, catching people unawares, hurriedly ripping off their jumpers, debating bunking off work to make the most of it, larking around in fountains, a holiday atmosphere. Not here, Martin observed quietly. She looked at Butterworth. He was on the cusp of anger, she could tell, his eyes dark with annoyance.

Butterworth finished reading the note left by Rebecca Brabents, placed it on his desk and looked up at Martin and Jones. He rubbed the back of his neck. "Fucking air conditioning," he murmured. "What's the point of it, if it doesn't work on the hottest afternoon of the year?" He sighed, adjusting to the new development at hand. "So, talk to me. What are your thoughts?"

"We're waiting for the post mortem results, obviously. But it seems pretty uncontroversial to state that Rebecca Brabents hanged herself. We've had a look t her phone. You can see the video on it. Looks like someone emailed it to her from an anonymous account. It must have been horrendous for her to see Emily like that. And looking at this," Martin gestured to the letter, "she had some serious issues with Michael Brabents."

"This video," Butterworth asked, "we're sure it's genuine?"

Martin nodded. "Certainly looks that way. We'll need to get Nick Oliver in for a formal interview. He's quite obviously the boy in it, and Emily's face can be clearly seen."

Butterworth sat back in his chair, looking perplexed. "So Emily was making pornos . . . ?"

"Not necessarily, sir," Martin interjected. "This could've been another private thing between the two of them. She might not have known it would be uploaded online for everyone to see."

"Why the wink, then?" Jones asked quietly.

Martin looked at her for a moment. "I don't know," she said at last.

"Who sent the mother the video?" Butterworth asked.

"Someone who wanted to provoke a reaction," Martin answered, her mind spinning through the possibilities and coming up with her own conclusion. "Look, something was happening in this family that we haven't got to the bottom of yet," she carried on. "Rebecca Brabents appears to be accusing her husband of abuse. Violence towards her and the family. It's not set out in so many words but . . ." Martin read from the note which Butterworth passed to her. "*I can't go on with life as it is now. What you've done. You've wrung* everything out of me. All of us have been affected, there's nothing left of us now. Kit barely sees us because of you. And now Emily has gone."

"You take that as meaning abuse, do you?" Butterworth asked.

"*Your anger and temper are too much for me. I can't take it any more,*" Martin read out loud and looked up again at him. He was testing her, she was thrown back to her English class at school. Her interpretation of a book versus her teacher's. She didn't like it. "Rush mentioned something about it, if I remember rightly. She'd come up on the train from London at the beginning of the year. She'd been staying with a friend then, not with her parents. If they'd been having problems, if Emily came from this sort of a background, and then is thrown into a culture of sexual bullying, she may have thought she had to join in. Survival of the fittest in a way."

"That's a leap, Martin."

Martin shrugged. She knew that was the case. She was beginning to see Emily.

Butterworth gave a loud sigh and stood up, moved to the window. Martin shifted uncomfortably in her seat. Humid air hung in folds across the room, a bad-tempered shroud. She knew he was under pressure, and the pot looked like it was about to boil over. "How many fucking potentials are we looking at in this case, eh?" he said with his back to them. "It's been over twenty-four hours now, and we've got a confession from Charlie Manson on speed, we've got Dirk fucking Diggler on film with the victim and now we've got — oh guess who?" Butterworth gave a sardonic laugh. "The father!"

Jones stepped up to the plate. "We couldn't have foreseen this development, sir. Mrs Brabents' suicide was an unexpected incident. Obviously, now, this is a big lead, and we'll run with it."

Butterworth turned to focus on Jones. "Thank you very much, DS Jones, for that stunning piece of summary and logistical planning." He moved to come round the desk. Standing over them both, he folded his arms, his height and build overshadowing them. *Here it comes*, Martin thought.

"This is a fucking shambles!"

Martin stood too. She had had enough of this from him. Standing, she equalled Butterworth, eyeballed him, unbowed. "I need to go down to see where the Brabents lived," she said firmly. Butterworth looked as though he might protest, but she cut him off. "What was going on in that family?" she asked. "We haven't understood Emily yet and we need to." She nodded. "Michael Brabents is being watched discreetly in the rooms at the college. He's not going anywhere. He'll wait for the post mortem results of his wife."

"They've organized a memorial service for Emily tomorrow. The university thought it would be good for the kids. He'll be here for that," Jones pointed out.

"Right. So I'll go down this afternoon. It's not far — an hour or so in the car. We can take a decision then on our next steps."

"I'm not sure that's a good idea, Martin. I need you here, solving this murder, not off on your fucking summer holidays." Butterworth unfolded his arms, put his hands in his pockets. He sat back on the desk, retreating. A sign, Martin hoped, that he knew he was out of line.

"I'll be a few hours," Martin said calmly. "In the meantime, Jones can be looking for Daniel Shepherd while we wait for the psych report on Rush. Then we've got all the information. Then I can interview Brabents."

Butterworth's pupils dilated into dark swirling planets.

"Trust me, Sam," Martin said with conviction. Butterworth seemed to exhale.

"All right. Get out of here before I change my mind," he said in a softer tone, looking at Martin. Jones glanced from one to the other, narrowing her eyes. Martin turned and walked out, Jones following swiftly behind.

CHAPTER
TWENTY-SIX

Stephanie walked through the woods near the cottage, the sunlight dappling through the trees as she went. She thought back to when she'd first had anything to do with Daniel Shepherd. It was just after the Christmas holidays, and all the students were back up at Durham. Emily had left her office after a particularly upsetting session, and Stephanie had been writing up her notes carefully, worrying about her. But what could she do in reality, she remembered thinking. In the course of that session she had actually advised Emily to go to the police about the Facebook comments and the threats, but Emily had looked at her as if she were mad and had left, tears still wet on her face.

Stephanie wrote her notes, turning over in her mind whether she should go to see the principal of Joyce College about the situation when an email had arrived in her inbox. It was from a non-university account, but Daniel was a student, he said. She skimmed his email. There was nothing unusual about a student messaging her out of the blue, and they often did it from their personal accounts, worried about prying eyes, many of them needing someone to talk to confidentially. The email was brief, but she liked his tone.

Daniel said that he was worried about Emily, that he was her good friend. He understood that Stephanie would be unable to talk to him about Emily directly, but he asked her just to keep him informed, let him know if there was any way he could help. He wanted to be there for Emily. What she was going through was so awful, and she didn't have anybody else watching out for her. He had sounded so defeated — even the principal of Joyce, he wrote, wouldn't listen to him, although he had tried to contact him to let him know. Stephanie had printed off Daniel's email and filed it and then, later, maybe because of it, given up the idea of contacting the college.

Stephanie hadn't broken Emily's confidence, but she had kept in touch with Daniel. He had begun emailing her regularly. A shadow lurked on her conscience about this. In all honesty, she didn't know why she had reciprocated. Maybe it was because they'd never actually met. She had suggested it once, wondered whether he was in actual fact crying out for help for some reason of his own. They had arranged a time one evening, and she had waited for him for over an hour. Eventually, he had sent an email apologizing but he had an essay due on Samuel Beckett and was battling the deadline. She hadn't proposed another meeting until recently. Somehow it was easier talking to him without seeing his face. In this way, she had persuaded herself that these emails were a brief respite; that it was okay. It was so easy to get bogged down by it all, her job, trawling through the detritus-laden waters of these kids' ives.

Stephanie stopped for a while in a small clearing. That's why they called it trolling, Stephanie remembered, breathing in the smell of hay bales drifting in from the surrounding fields. It was a loaded hook, trawling through the sea from a fishing boat. Trying to get a rise out of someone, tempting them to take the bait. Stephanie was lured on a daily basis, listening to their stories, hearing their sorry tales. But Daniel was different, he seemed somehow *above it all*. He cared about Emily, he cared about himself. He even seemed to care about Stephanie. She knew the university authorities would find it odd. But these weren't children. They were considered adults by society. If she wanted to have a friendship with one of them, really, where was the harm in it? It was like writing to a younger brother in many ways. Her younger brother, Ajay, whom she hadn't seen for so many years.

Daniel wrote to her constantly about Emily, about his relationship with her. Stephanie told herself that this was good, that it would mean she could help Emily. She could see from his emails that Daniel was falling in love with Emily and that this was not reciprocated. She felt sorry for Daniel, he was so vulnerable, so sincere in his dealings with her. She had almost cried when she had read his last email to her. How he had gone away for Easter. How dreadful things had become with Emily. She had replied, asking him to meet her. But he had refused, and since then she had heard nothing.

Stephanie began walking again, heading out of the wood towards the open fields, rounding a corner to see a carpet of brilliant blue Gentian flowers spread before her along her path. She knew the legend that if the flowers were brought into the house you could be struck by lightning. That's how she thought of Daniel. An innocent boy, struck by lightning. Caught up in the seediness of this world, this university world, where everyone was out for each other, where they fought to scramble up the popularity mountain, never caring about the heads and hearts of the people they were standing upon.

Maybe that was it. Maybe Daniel had been struck by lightning. And, if she were truthful to herself, as her profession demanded, maybe she felt a little the same. Stephanie made a noise of assent, gazing at the flowers as they dazzled, a sparkling azure sea in the sunshine.

CHAPTER
TWENTY-SEVEN

Tuesday 23 May, 4.00 p.m.

The drive to Great Whittington was picturesque. Winding burrows of roads, delving deeper into countryside where hedgerows got higher and higher, brambly tunnels of a journey. It was a softer landscape inland than Martin was used to from her upbringing on the coast. Here, mellow fruitfulness was in abundance, despite the earliness of the season. She turned off the radio, opened the window and enjoyed the drive in wind-rushed silence.

The hire car's satnav predictably faltered as she drove through a series of tiny villages, hamlets really, leading to her destination. She spotted a local garage on the outskirts of the community and pulled into the forecourt to ask directions to the Brabents' house. A sun-beaten man, wearing a faded red Diet Coke baseball cap, sat on a stool next to the pumps. As she got out of the car, he said something to her, but she ignored him and went straight into the shop. It was tiny and empty, selling not much more than a few shammy leathers and some de-icer.

Martin emerged from the shop. The man was still sitting on the stool. He gestured to her car, and she realized he was the only employee in the place. He wanted to fill her car. She felt a town-mouse fool and went back towards him, asked him to top up the already nearly full tank. She smiled at him as he began to do so.

"Do you know where the Old Orchard is?" she asked casually.

The man nodded, taking off the fuel cap.

"Two miles down the road. Take a left towards Scratcher's Farm, signposted for Crowley. You'll see it on the bend in the road there by the river."

She shifted, put her hands in her pockets.

"Do you know the Brabents?" she asked.

The man nodded again.

"Moved to Whittington a few years ago. Started coming down on weekends." He looked at her from under the peak of his cap. "Get a lot of them. Empty in the week. No business for us."

She smiled encouragingly, jingled her keys in her hand.

"Must be annoying," she said. "But they moved here full time?"

"As I say." The man wiped the nozzle of the petrol pump with an old rag and replaced the cap. "Got a couple of kids I think." He looked at her side-on. "Bit odd, if you must know."

"Odd? In what way?" Martin leaned against the car, n expression of relaxation.

The man shrugged. "Keep themselves to themselves. They've had some parties there. Loud. Disturbs the village." He sniffed. "City types, I shouldn't bet. That'll be five pounds fifty."

Martin reached into the car for her handbag. "But that's quite normal, isn't it? Having parties? You said odd. What does that mean?" she asked, handing over the money. "Don't worry about the change."

The man's eyes narrowed. "Who are you anyway? Friends with them, are you? Then you should know."

Martin took out her ID, showed it to the man.

"What do you mean? Odd?" she repeated.

Barely reacting to the ID, the man pocketed the money and sat back on his stool, stretching his legs in front of him.

"Talk to Nerys. She cleaned for them. Lives up in the village. They'll point you in the right direction at the post office. She'll tell you."

Martin walked round to the other side of the car and opened the door. "Thank you," she said, before getting in and pointing the car in the direction the man had indicated. She looked in the rear-view mirror as she drove off, the man watching her leave all the way along the road until she was out of sight.

Nerys Hopkins was a cottage loaf of a woman. Her neck rolled into her ample bosom, which rolled into her larger stomach, hooping into a wide skirt, narrowing off slightly into chubby calves and ankles. Her feet were crossed over each other. *Prissy*, thought Martin. They were sitting in Nerys' front room, as she called it, beckoning Martin back in there from the kitchen after she'd made a pot of tea and put some digestives on a plate.

"I wouldn't say they were odd." She put her head on to one side, half-closing her eyes, a biscuit halfway to her mouth, its journey halted by the weight of thought. She opened her eyes to look at Martin. "Towny." Her biscuit-free hand scrabbled in the air for the words. "They were . . . *towny*."

Martin knew what she meant. The Brabents were that stereotypical breed which had marched into the countryside of late, looking for the perfect country pile, searching for the perfect vintage cushion fabric, home-grown tomatoes for chutney to be put in dinky little jars, boozy lunches on striped tablecloths under lemon trees — a photo shoot of glamour, while at the same time pretending to be ever so ordinary. Towny or not, Martin could see how they would have seemed out of place in this little village which still ran on wind-up clock time, where you had to flag down an approaching train at the station.

"Did you like them?" she asked, leaning forwards to help herself to a biscuit.

Nerys shrugged. "Like or dislike. Don't mean nothing to me. I'll clean anyways."

Martin smiled. "I'm sure, Mrs Hopkins. But, what I mean is, were they decent people? Was there anything about them you didn't like? Thought peculiar, or unlikeable?"

"Not peculiar," she mumbled, crumbs escaping on to her bottom lip as she spoke. "She was nice, Mrs

202

Brabents." She chewed some more as she considered. "Once, though, I remember. I turned up on the Tuesday morning as normal. Nine a.m. sharp it is." The way she looked at Martin made her think Nerys' timekeeping must often be doubtful.

"And?" she prompted.

"And there'd been a kerfuffle, I'd say."

"A kerfuffle?"

"You know," her hands scrabbled again, word-searching. "A ding-dong. Used to have them with Bob. They hang in the air. You can smell them."

"So you sensed there'd been an argument in the Brabents' house?"

"More than that, really. There was some broken china in the kitchen on the floor. But it was more that . . ." She paused.

"What?"

"Well," Nerys coughed slightly. "I'm sure there was blood in the kitchen sink. And then Mrs Brabents, well, she wouldn't see me that day. No one was around. Normally she lets me in, makes me a cup. We have a chat, you know. But that day she stayed in her bedroom. Said I didn't have to clean it, she'd change the bed linen."

"Was there anything else you can think of? Any other incidents?"

Nerys looked uncomfortable. "Well . . ." She faltered.

Martin waited, patient.

"They had a party once, a year or so ago. Not too big, just a few friends over for lunch in the garden.

203

They asked me to work, to help with the washing up, there was a few of them, you see. Beautiful day it was. We put the table out on the lawn. Not a cloud in the sky." Nerys stared off in a reverie. Martin coughed to get her attention.

"And?" she prompted.

"And, it wasn't nothing much, but you're asking me for any kind of incident . . ."

"Something happened that day?"

Nerys nodded. "It was after lunch, everyone was lounging round in the garden, reading the papers in deckchairs. Boiling hot, it was. Mrs Brabents suggested putting on the sprinkler, you know so the children could run through the water. Everyone laughed, and Mr Brabents said they were too old for that, that was for little 'uns. But by that time, Emily and a girlfriend of hers had run upstairs to get changed, they didn't hear him say no." Nerys looked at Martin.

"They should have listened?"

The cleaner rubbed her eyes sadly. "Her and her friend came down in their bathing costumes. Bikinis or whatnot. And he went mad. Threw his glass on the ground so it smashed. Stormed off into the house and came back with a couple of towels. Grabbed Emily's arm and threw them at the girls, told them to cover themselves up. They were awful embarrassed. Emily shouted out how she hated her dad, and they went off back into the house."

"And what did Mrs Brabents do?"

"I was in the kitchen, at the sink, watching it through the window. Mrs Brabents, she sort of sank down into one of the deckchairs. So heavy, like, that it ripped right through. She ended up on the grass, awful embarrassed, and Mr Brabents, he shouted at her."

"What did he say?"

"Well," Nerys sniffed. "I don't like to use the language, but it was something like she was too effing fat and should watch what she ate." Nerys shook her head. "Made a right atmosphere it did. After that, everyone sort of dribbled off home."

"But he wasn't violent?" Martin asked. "Just shouted?"

"That's right," Nerys nodded. "But I always felt something was . . . something was . . ."

"Something was . . .?" Martin encouraged.

"Something was wrong. More than wrong. I felt something in that house. It wasn't fear. I can smell that too." She stared at Martin, daring her to argue. Martin said nothing. "No. It wasn't fear. It was —" she picked at her skirt, fat fingers twisting the material — "*rage*. It was rage."

CHAPTER
TWENTY-EIGHT

I didn't want Emily to see my house. Mother had made some good improvements to it since she'd got the money but, still, I didn't think Emily would have been impressed. Mum may have been pleased with the new John Lewis curtains and she still couldn't get over the excitement of the dishwasher, but Emily came from a class apart from this. I imagined her often, over those Christmas holidays. Not just after seeing the video, but in her house in the countryside, sitting around a big pine table with her family, drinking freshly ground coffee, laughing at something Kit had said, her mum lifting a steaming casserole out of the Aga, her dad pouring glasses of Burgundy for everyone.

Seeing them in Hammersmith had altered this image in an uncomfortable way for me. I liked the countryside image. But now I had the one of Mr Brabents pouring fizzy wine into plastic glasses, of Mrs Brabents leaning over the balustrade of the auditorium, her breasts hanging slightly out of a too-revealing top. It sort of made me shudder. I tried to ignore it as much as possible and just focused on Emily, on her being lost. This would be the key, I thought. The key to something good for me.

The next time I saw Emily was at a bar in west London. She was staying with a family friend and had texted me to meet for a drink. Once again, I traversed east to west on the tube and, once again, I was early, standing at the bar with my newspaper when she walked in. She looked different somehow. I compared her in my mind's eye to our first meeting on the train up to Durham, when, even though she had been crying, she had been something of herself. Now, she seemed a vapour; a fragment of what she had been before.

I bought her a gin and tonic and I had another pint of bitter. We went and sat at a table by the window, a floodlit darkness outside making a film set of the streets. They had an unreal quality about them, I thought. The pub was one of those soulless chains, nothing to it despite the jaunty writing on the mirrors behind the bar and the whitewashed floorboards that would soon be skimmed with detritus from the repulsive footfall within. Emily and I looked at each other across the table. It was weird, but since the gig in Hammersmith, I had felt emboldened with Emily. I knew now that I could ask her about the video. She appeared to me as a vessel, something empty which I could pour into. What I would pour, I didn't know. I didn't know.

"I've seen it," I said. I leaned back in my chair and smiled a little. My hands encircled my pint glass.

Emily went red and looked down at her own glass, where condensation dribbled down it, wetting her fingers.

"What were you thinking?" I asked, a headmasterly question.

She glanced up at me, then looked out of the window, pushing her hair back behind her ears. She had lovely ears. Small with tiny pearl earrings in the lobes.

"I didn't know what else to do," she said quietly. "He told me it was fine. That everyone was doing this kind of thing."

I laughed in a nasty way. "Well, he would say that, wouldn't he?"

"But it's true," she said in earnest. "They have these competitions. Even in Sixes. You've seen it, haven't you?"

I shook my head.

"Well, you must have missed them. They get girls up on the stage. In T-shirts. And they spray beer at them until . . ." She coloured again. "Until you can see through their tops."

I looked at her.

"You get points, they give you points . . ." Her voice tailed off.

"What else?" I asked. Something in me was enjoying this. A hint of a devil twisted a knife in my stomach, the feeling you get when the car you're travelling in takes a fast dip in the road. I have to admit I was excited by it. Watching her mouth describe it.

"Then there's the website," she said dully. "It's called something stupid like *Hot or Not*." She looked down at her fingernails, chewed on one of them. It made her look like a beaver. For want of a better word. "People have to vote. Girls and boys." She glanced up at me, as if this made it better. "They vote on photos. If you get a thousand 'likes'," here, she made the sign of inverted commas, "you might get spotted. You never know," she said, lifting her chin with a flash of her old spirit.

I shifted in my seat and coughed slightly. "I'm sorry. What are you saying?" I wiped my mouth with my thumb and then sipped my drink slowly, letting the liquid calm my burning throat, calm all I wanted to say. "You're saying there's a website where girls can put up photos of themselves and people — girls and boys . . ." I inclined my head towards Emily in acknowledgement of her comfort in this fact, "vote on whether the girl is hot or not." I laughed, amazed. "And girls actually volunteer for this?"

"It's about reclaiming our sexuality," Emily said as if she was reading from the latest edition of some ridiculous magazine. "We're proud of our bodies. We're empowered." A tear glistened in the corner of her right eye. "We are," she said more firmly.

I tipped my pint glass to a forty-five-degree angle, watched the brown dregs of the bitter lurch and then settle. I put it down carefully on the table and then leaned forwards, my hands empty now.

"Let me get this straight," I said. "You think that by doing these, these competitions, you're being *feminist?*" I couldn't believe my ears. I had been right all along. The world was nothing like me.

Emily had begun to silently sob.

"Jesus, Emily," I stood up angrily. "Is this how you use your vote? To decide on the *hotness* of other women?" I stalked off to the bar and ordered another round, although I don't think Emily had touched hers. She sat there, as I waited to be served, staring at her hands on the table. I turned back and looked at myself in the mirror which ran the length of the wall. There I was, tall, not bad-looking, clever. The barmaid handed me my change without a glance. I existed in the world like a cipher. I wasn't noticed. I could pass through this life without anybody giving a damn. *I had something to give*! And in the meantime these disgusting people who were abusing Emily and girls like her were striding across the globe like giants, swinging their dicks in their hands like gods. It made me sick.

I sat down again opposite Emily and pushed another gin and tonic towards her. She half-smiled and looked at her first drink, intact.

"It's just the way it is," she said sadly. "You have to be like them or they don't see you. We pretend we don't care, that our bodies are just that — bodies. We can be naked, flaunt them, shove them in your face," she smiled wryly. "And none of it matters because we're the ones in control. We decide to do it. We're not forced, we're not," she swallowed, "raped. We just live in a tough world." She looked up at me then. "You've got to be in it to win it." She giggled slightly, putting her first glass to her lips and taking a long drink.

I thought about this. But what about me? I didn't play sports, I didn't even join in the ridiculousness of the physics club with Zack. I rued my status as an outsider but I didn't appear to need to change myself to fit in. *Why not*, I wondered?

"It's like being a member of a club," Emily explained, her tongue loosened slightly by the first swallow of gin. "If you're in it, you feel secure. And who doesn't want attention?" she asked me, wide-eyed.

I didn't know how to answer that except to think to myself, *I don't*.

"It's like being famous, you're acknowledged, you're kind of *honoured*."

"Because of your tits," I said crassly, causing another blush to creep up Emily's neck. I leaned forwards, desperate for her to understand, desperate for this devil inside me to be culled. "They make you think it's your choice, but it's not. It's the

210

baying of the crowd, nothing more than that. They're getting titillated by you, for free. And the best part? They don't even have to feel guilty or ashamed about it, because, according to everyone in that room, or on that website, you've done it freely, you have chosen to do it. But why, Emily? Ask yourself why. Why do you need that attention? Why do you need to be liked? By them of all people?"

Emily stared at me, tears fringing her eyelashes, giving her a startled look, adding to her vulnerability. I could see it. I could see why they wanted to hunt her down, capture her for their own. A shadow passed across her face. "You're just the same," she snapped. "Why do you hang around me? You want to be in it too. Isn't it better to be *in* something — rather than outside, on your own?"

I bit my lip. Was that right? Even if what you would be accepted into was abhorrent?

Emily's face softened. "I thought you'd understand," she said finally. "I thought you would get it."

I looked out of the window at the commuters walking past, the news stand, the red postbox, the chocolate wrapper flitting through the gutters, the sleeping man in the doorway, the reflection of the streetlamps in the oil-slicked puddles, the utter meaninglessness of it all. And I thought, *I do. I do get it*.

I turned back to Emily and smiled. I picked up her hand, stroking her thumb with mine. I wanted her so much. I wanted to keep her here, in this private place — away from everyone and everything to do with university. But I couldn't do that, I sighed softly to myself. Emily was out there now. She had spread herself wide open. I looked at her. I wasn't disgusted by her, and the realization surprised me.

I loved her.

I knew it suddenly like a heat-tipped sabre boring relentlessly into the middle of me. *Ah, do not mourn*, I thought to myself. I knew it then as I'd known it when I first met her. *Our souls are love, and a continual farewell.*

CHAPTER
TWENTY-NINE

Tuesday 23 May, 5.35 p.m.

Martin walked into a little country pub she had noticed on her drive into the village of Great Whittington. She walked in and leaned against the bar, waiting for the jowly man behind the counter to finish wiping a pint glass with a towel before ambling over to take her order. After he'd done so, she moved to a small table underneath one of the windows. The pub was on the main road which weaved its way through the village, and the sound of the odd passing car filtered in, breaking the otherwise emptiness of the saloon bar. She was the only punter as yet, and so after the landlord had shouted to whoever was in the kitchen out the back with her order, he stood cordially at the bar, continuing to wipe along its top and anything else which came in its path.

"Holidaying round here, are you?"

She shrugged and took a sip of her drink. "Something like that. Looking up some old friends."

"Oh yeah? Who are they, then?"

"The Brabents? Do you know them?"

The landlord nodded. "Yup. Live down the road. Haven't seen them for a while, though, now you come to mention it."

Martin was silent.

"Nice family," he continued. "Not like some of them from the city. Join in with things. Down here for the quiz night a fair bit. And Mike Brabents has played village cricket a few times. Nice chap." He paused. "Not around, though, now, I don't think. Were you planning on visiting?"

"Mmmm," she assented. "Just driving through and thought I'd look them up."

The landlord glanced up from his wiping and considered her.

"Is that right?" he said after a while, as her sandwich arrived through the kitchen hatch. He walked round the bar and placed it on her table before standing there, looking down at her, winding his tea towel in his hands.

"I'm ex-army, me," he said.

"Really?"

"Yeah." He smiled. "So I know a copper when I see one. Why'd do you want to know about the Brabents? Something happened, has it?"

Martin wiped her mouth with a paper napkin and looked closely at the landlord. "You may have read about it in the papers. I'm here as part of a murder investigation."

"Murder?" The landlord was nonplussed. "Who?"

"I'm afraid Emily Brabents was murdered at her university."

The landlord went pale in the face and slumped down into the chair opposite her. "Emily? I haven't

214

seen anything about it. I can't believe it." He stared off into the middle distance, shaking his head. "Surely not. How are the parents taking it?"

"I'm afraid Mrs Brabents has also passed away," Martin said gently. "It looks as though she couldn't take the strain of her daughter's death."

"Blimey," the landlord said quietly. "And you haven't caught the bloke, then?" he continued. "But hang on . . ." He leaned forwards on to the table. "You don't think Mike had anything to do with it, do you?"

"Why do you ask?" Martin said.

"You're here, aren't you? And — well, why would you be here if you weren't investigating someone?"

"Do you know Michael Brabents well?" Martin asked.

"Well, as I said, he used to come down here sometimes. Not all the time, but fairly regular. I played cricket with him a few times. He'd come in with his missus and have a pint. Nothing heavy."

"What was his relationship like with his wife? Did they get on?"

The landlord looked up at her, indecision passing across his face. "Well, uh. You know. I don't know about that."

"This is important. Please, Mr . . .?"

"Robbie, I'm Robbie."

"It's important, Robbie. They may well have been a nice family. But all families have their problems, don't they?" Martin said. "How can you get anyone into trouble if you tell the truth?"

Robbie gave a laugh. "Quite easily, if you don't mind me saying. Me mam always taught me to keep a still tongue in my head."

Martin waited.

"Look, I'm not saying anything that no one else will have seen, right? It's a shame 'cause he was one our best batsmen." He glanced down at his cloth and flexed his knuckles, taking a breath. "I did see them argue, right? It didn't seem that bad, but you never can tell, can you? What goes on behind closed doors, I mean. I thought . . . I thought the wife looked like a wet weekend most times she came in here . . ."

Martin said nothing. She had that feeling when you accelerate to overtake a car and get into that sweet gear when the speed's just right and you soar past them, feeling the engine purr.

"He had a temper on him, that's for sure."

"Did you ever see him lose his temper?"

"A couple of times. It wasn't too much, you know." He looked at her anxiously. "Just after a few jars. One time I saw him push her. The wife, I mean. I had to step in. But, you know, it was Christmas. These things happen." The barman's face turned apologetically red on behalf of either Michael Brabents or mankind, Martin couldn't tell which.

"Did you ever speak to them about it?"

Robbie looked as if he would more likely have swum the Channel.

"Did the children ever come in here?"

"The boy never. He's basically left home. Emily, not much. She came to watch the cricket. She seemed . . ." He paused.

"Seemed, what?"

"Ah, I don't know. I don't know if it was her or him or . . ."

"What is it?" Martin asked patiently. "What are you trying to say?"

Robbie coughed and continued to move the cloth over the surface of the table. "Ah, I don't know."

"No one's getting in trouble here unless they are in trouble already."

"Well, it just seemed as though the girl and her dad were very close. I wouldn't have noticed it, said anything about it but I just remember one time . . ."

"What is it, Robbie? What do you remember?"

"He got a century once, Michael. You know, at cricket. It was quite a big deal as we were second in the league, needed a win. Anyway, we don't get many centuries on the village green," Robbie smiled ruefully. "When he came off, he got a round of applause, as you would, you know. He would've got a drink on the house. But . . ." He looked at Martin, the pub windows rattling as a truck sped past on the road outside. "The weird thing was, when he came off the pitch, he ran straight to Emily. Didn't look at his wife once. Him and Emily went off together, arm in arm as if . . ."

"As if?" Martin prompted.

"As if they were the couple, not him and his wife."

The house looked as it had in the photograph. Martin parked her car as near into the hedgerow as she could on a bend on the same side of the road, hoping as she did that no one would zoom around the corner and crash into it. She walked up to the gate and walked through. The air was still and quiet, although she could hear the vague rumblings of a road in the distance. Some kind of bird beeped and shrilled as Martin made her way up the path to the front door. She knocked at it and then turned around, looking back down the path. Nothing. The stillness was ominous. Martin felt sweat trickle down her back as she stood at the door in the last burst of sunlight before the evening would fall. A bee buzzed somewhere nearby.

She walked round the house, looking in the windows as she went. The pause button had been pressed on family life here, presumably when the Brabents had received the call about Emily. At the large kitchen, Martin peered in and could see washing-up sitting in the sink, half-drunk coffee cups on the table. A desk sat by the window in another room, covered in mussed-up papers.

Martin rounded the house and, walking through a gate topped by what looked like the upper half of a wishing well, she came into the garden, the edges of which she had seen in the photograph. A large fenced-in trampoline was at one end of the garden, leaves scattered across its stretched tarpaulin, doubtless unused for some time, given the ages of Emily and her brother. The football net she had noticed in the photo sat next to it on the grass.

Martin's phone suddenly beeped, the peal of a clanging bell in the still of the garden causing her heart to stop for a second. Calming her breathing, she peered at the message in the glare of the sun and frowned. Looking up from it, she noticed the shed. She remembered it from the picture just as a gust of wind puffed past, and the shed door rolled slowly open.

Martin glanced around and walked quickly across the grass to it. She didn't have a warrant, Butterworth had scoffed at the prospect of this on the evidence they had. She wanted to see where the Brabents had lived. Who were they as a family? Was Michael a bully to his wife and children? Why had Rebecca been scared of him? If she went inside, the evidence could be inadmissible, depending on what she could get at interview. But the door was open. It was too much of a temptation with no one around. Martin moved quickly inside the shed.

The shed's interior was orderly. An old dresser lined its back wall, its shelves filled with spray bottles and pesticides. Garden tools hung neatly from hooks and a lawn mower, its electric lead wrapped tidily up, rested from a large hook to the left of the door. There was a small rug on the floor and a camping stool with a stack of old newspapers at its feet. A sign on the wall read "Dad's Shed". She ran her fingers along the top of the dresser. No dust. Whoever was in charge of the gardening kept this place spotless. She opened one of the dresser drawers. Seed packets and some old gardening magazines. The next drawer was locked.

Martin rested her hands on the dresser top, considering. She looked up and took one of the tools from the wall. It was a thin metal spade-like thing, the purpose of which Martin had no idea. She jemmied it into the top of the drawer and yanked. It wouldn't budge. She tried again, hefting her weight against the

219

handle of the metal spade. The noise made in this effort was an explosion in the stagnant country air. She paused again, looked behind her out of the misty shed window to the garden. Nobody there. She gave herself one last chance and wrenched the spade handle downwards and towards her. The lock splintered, giving way and exposing the inside of the drawer through a small jagged hole where the catch had once been.

Martin pulled the drawer open and stood for a while, looking down at its contents, thinking carefully. Her thoughts hummed on the periphery of her brain like tinnitus, teasing her until she thought she'd go mad. She was getting Emily, she thought. The puzzle was clearing. It certainly looked as though Michael Brabents had been physically abusing his wife. Did that explain her suicide? Other than the fact that Martin was fairly sure that the journalist Sean Egan had emailed her the video anonymously. She stored that thought. She would need to find out where he'd got a copy of it but she was certain it was him — trying to provoke Emily's parents into a reaction to their daughter's behaviour, something to stoke the fires of the potential sexual-bullying scandal surrounding the university since Emily's death.

Now Kit had left home and Emily was gone, what had Rebecca got left, Martin wondered? A life spent alone with a man who hit her down the pub when he'd had a few too many jars.

But more than that, she thought as she looked down at the drawer. Had Rebecca Brabents known about this? Had she known what her husband had felt about his own daughter? Had she had any inkling or knowledge at all that, at the bottom of her garden, in the shed, was a drawer. And in that secret place were hundreds of photographs of Emily, stuffed out of sight, put there for Michael Brabents' eyes only.

CHAPTER
THIRTY

January was an icy plinth in the academic year. It stood proud, guarding the entrance to what was to come. I felt it as soon as I got off the train at Durham. London had been cold, but here the weather was bitter. The sweet snow of December now seemed girlish, replaced by a brittle hoar frost, the city transformed into a treacherous skating pond.

The first people I saw were a crowd of girls from Joyce; one of them was on my English course. She had been sitting in one of the carriages further up the train and I only recognized her at the ticket barrier as she struggled to heft her bag through the ridiculously small gates. As I made to help her, she flicked her hair in order to glance at me, a smile on her lips. This disappeared when she saw the identity of her gallant aide.

"Oh, hi," she said disappointedly.

"Hi, there. Good Christmas?"

She smiled a thin smile which failed to reach her eyes. "Yes thank you. You?"

"Great," I said positively, dragging this conversation forwards by a sheer force of will. "Let me help you with your bag to the taxi."

"Oh, it's fine, seriously. Really, I'm fine." She lifted up her bag on to her shoulder and turned her back to me, heading towards the taxi rank to join her friends. "See you around," she called over her shoulder.

I remained there in her wake, standing alone. My lips were chapped from the cold, and I chewed on them, staring after her. *They were bitches*, I thought. *What absolute bitches*. I swung my rucksack on to my back and followed them out of the station to the line of people waiting in the cold. The dark of our coats against the white of the frost, the smoke of the buildings from the bottom of the hill reminded me of a Lowry painting. I laughed to myself. Those bitches wouldn't even know who Lowry was.

I did, though. In the midst of all this shit these people kept throwing at me, I knew of myself that I was better than them. My brain was better, it would keep one step ahead of them. I breathed out, clouding the air in front of me. And they didn't know yet, all the cretins at Joyce and Keats and everywhere else. I hugged it, as a secret to myself. They didn't know that I had been the victor in the holidays. That Emily and I were closer than ever.

The start of the Epiphany term was sluggish for most people, I thought. Classes plodded on, climbing that interminable curve up to the middle of term when without warning we would find ourselves hurtling downhill towards the prospect of next term's exams. Zack and the physics crew were getting overexcited about a firework display planned for the Palace Green in a few weeks' time. Zack was in charge of The Rockets, the committee responsible for, yes, you've guessed it . . . I refrained from voicing to him my concern that a bunch of geeks should be in charge of setting off explosives in a public place *that they themselves had designed*. But so be it.

The university authorities clearly thought it good for morale, and our bedroom thus became a den of balsa wood and some very worrying brownish bottles which I suspected contained a chemical no one in their right mind wanted to sleep next to. As usual, however, I kept my head down and ignored things.

I was, in actual fact, going through something of my own personal epiphany at that time. We had started looking at the Irish writers in class. I was battling with Joyce, falling in love with Yeats and hating Beckett. If you want to know the truth, my main reason for hating Beckett was that a comprehension of his work remained as distant to me as the Moroccan sands. But it was more than that. I taped a picture of him in his black polo neck jumper above my desk. His long face with the blue eyes, quiff of striped grey hair, crags in his face meandering like the sides of a vase being pulled slowly out of a potter's wheel. He was a lesson to me, Beckett. He talked of non-knowing, the subtraction of things.

I knew this was wrong. I didn't like it. I was positive that it was only through knowledge that we could own things, that we could possess them. I couldn't let things slip away like that, let them go as leaves floating down the green waters of the weir. Every time I thought about this, I would get hot in the face. I would strap my trainers on hurriedly and run down the banks of it, checking constantly with my eyes that things were just as they should be, that nothing had stolen away.

The first time I saw Emily that term, I was, once again, out running. She was part of my second epiphany. She was dawdling along the path of the riverbank, halos of breath resting in her hair before disappearing into the winter sky. I pulled up short in front of her, but she side-stepped me, unseeing. After a cold stab of disappointment, I saw she had her headphones in so I patted her on her elbow. She looked up, startled, and then smiled. A rush of warmth entered the iciness suffusing my body at that. I knew I wasn't as alone any more.

"Hi, Emily," I said heavily, catching my breath.

"Running again."

I nodded, wiping the sweat off my forehead with my wrist. "How are you? Annabel says your dad drove you up."

I fell in beside her, and we carried on, ambling along the riverbank. A heron swooped down next to us and landed on the muddy slope to the water, but I barely noticed it. I shivered slightly as the sweat began to freeze on my bare arms. It was another glacial day.

"Yes. He wanted to make up for the fighting in the holidays, I guess." She shrugged. "It was fine. He turned around and drove straight back." She looked up at me. "How are you, anyway? How's things at Nightingale?"

"Oh, you know. Same. Working. Not doing much else." I looked about me, albeit I was completely unaware of my surroundings as we walked. "So . . ." I floundered a little bit then. How to approach it? "Have you seen Nick since you've been back?"

"It's only been a couple of days," she said. Did I discern a melancholy in that remark? She seemed to brighten then, though. "I love this weather, don't you? It's so fresh, galvanizing really!"

"Yes, I suppose so." I thought she sounded fake, cheerleading her way through her life. I thought for a moment and found a topic she'd be interested in: "Are you going to Sixes on Friday?"

Emily wrapped her arms around herself and nodded. "'Sposed to. Annabel wants to go. I guess Nick and that lot will be there. I don't know . . ."

"Don't know what?"

"I don't know if I want to do it any more. After I saw you in the holidays . . ." She looked up and smiled at me again. "I just feel like last term was a bit of a nightmare, you know? Maybe I should just put it all behind me, start again afresh." She laughed ironically. "Actually do some work?"

I stared at her as we walked. Emily tottered somewhat on a patch of icy leaf mulch and reached out for my arm, which I gave to her. I needed to think about this. Emily starting afresh was not something I had considered. An Emily without Nick. Without Annabel. Available to be my friend without any of the trappings of the rest of the bollocks. I stopped and turned her to face me.

"Yes, Emily! That's exactly what you need to do. Start anew. Ignore them all, leave them to it. We can work together. I can help you." I could feel the earnestness of my face reaching epic proportions. I tried to rein it in. "Tell you what. How about we both go to Sixes on Friday? You come with me. We'll have a few drinks, nothing crazy. Then you can have a good time and you're not dependent on them. You can leave when you want and just go home." What I was saying was, *Look, I'm fun too! We can have fun together! I'm not just about boring old work and slog. I can let my hair down like the best of them. But I also know when to stop — I'm good like that!*

Emily looked disconcerted, but — I knew her so well — I could see the peaks of her deepest worries lurch across her face. She was scared that maybe I was now her only friend.

226

"All right," she said uncertainly. "Let's do it." We'd reached Prebends Bridge by that stage. I will always remember her standing at the end of it, framed by the stone archway that marked the beginning of the climb up the Bailey to Joyce. She had a pink beret on, one side of which covered her left ear. Her cheeks were rosy from the walk, and she wore big white mittens. She looked like a child. She seemed to cling on to me then with her eyes. I saw it. I was her anchor. She waved and ran in the other direction to me, up the slope to where the vultures awaited her.

CHAPTER
THIRTY-ONE

Tuesday 23 May, 9.46 p.m.

Stephanie was still in her office. It was late and she checked her phone. Three texts from Rosena. She sighed and picked up the phone, still standing.

"Hi, darling. Yes, I'm sorry. Something came up." She frowned as she listened to her daughter's complaints. "Didn't you find the spaghetti bolognese in the fridge? What? Yes, I meant for you to just heat it up in a bowl in the microwave." She twisted the telephone wire across her desk so she could sit down and did so, planting her feet up on the desk. "I'll be about another hour. I'm sorry, Rosie." She nodded and listened some more, frowning a little. "I'll be as quick as I can, I promise," she paused. "I love you," she said finally, before replacing the handset.

Stephanie took her feet down and reached for her bag. She withdrew the tape and opened a drawer in her desk, taking out a small Dictaphone recorder. Putting the tape in, she leaned back in her chair and massaged her eyes with her fingers. It had been a long day. *What to do about Daniel*, she thought. She was risking serious opprobrium from the police in concealing her knowledge of him, if not a criminal charge. Stephanie leaned forwards and pressed play. A loud hiss of static filled the room, and she quickly moved to turn down the volume. As the balance settled, she could hear her own voice. She shivered slightly before pulling a purple shawl draped over the back of her chair around herself. She closed her eyes and listened.

"How are you feeling, Emily? Okay? If at any time, you want me to turn this off, I can. If you get uncomfortable with it."

The sound of a creaking chair.

"I want to record you in this session because it will help me in my analysis of you. Sometimes, things are said which are missed, and I don't want that with you. Okay? Okay. Now. Tell me. How are you feeling today? What's this week been like?"

A pause, then: "Awful. Dreadful. I don't know what's happening any more."

Sound of quiet sobbing.

"Yes?"

"I'm doing things I would never . . ."

Silence apart from soft crying.

"What things, Emily? What things are you doing that are upsetting you so much?"

A sniff.

"I can't seem to stop myself. He says if I stop, people will think less of me. That I don't have the balls."

"And what do you think?"

"I think he's right. It's gone too far now. The way people look at me."

Sound of hiccuping.

"Would you like a tissue? Here."

Pause.

"Emily, I want you to think back. I know it's hard. But think back to when this first started. What did you feel then?"

"Ha, what did I feel? I don't know. Embarrassed? Ashamed?"

"This was the first photo with Nick, in the beginning?"

"Yeah."

Sound of short laugh.

"I thought I was in love with him. I thought he liked me. So I wanted to please him. Keep him with me. I would have done anything."

"And so that's how it started. And has it stayed like that? Or have things changed? Have you changed?"

Sound of water being poured.

"I didn't ask to be a girl. It's shit being a girl. Always on the outside. Even if you're on the inside. Do you know what I mean?"

"Tell me."

"Uh, it's like — you can never be in on it. The joke. They're always one step ahead of you. You try and be like a boy, laugh at sex, drink loads, get your tits out like you don't care. And then . . ."

Pause.

"I can understand how that would be very hard, Emily. That's a lot of pressure."

Sound of sniffing.

"Yes, it is. But it doesn't work. They look at you, and you're still a girl. Nothing more than a walking shag. I tell them — I get on better with boys than girls. They pretend they agree, that they like it. But until . . ."

Pause.

"Yes?"

"Until I can play sports and fuck girls, I'll never be one of them."

"Why do you need to be one of them?"

Sound of sighing.

"Because they run it. The boys." Pause. "Girls like Annabel. She doesn't care. She's happy to be their hanger-on. But I want to be as good as them. I want to be them. I need them to like me, I guess. The more attention they give me, the more they must like me." Sound of faint laughter. "God, I'm pathetic."

"I think you're doing really good work here. I think you're dealing with all of this really well."

"Yeah. Well . . . Sometimes I wonder, you know. What my life would be like here if I hadn't done it. Hadn't decided to take those photos."

"The first one wasn't your fault."

"I know. But the others . . . If I hadn't thought it was a good thing."

"Why did you, Emily? Why did you think it was a good thing?"

"I see them looking at magazines. Once I was with them — in the JCR — and they were passing one round. And it was like . . . it was like I wasn't even there. They were looking at these women's bodies as if it had nothing to do with me. As if I wasn't a woman.

That, essentially, they were ogling at what I look like underneath my clothes. And they just didn't get it. It was like that body was *their* property . . . But for that moment, all they were thinking about was *her*. Nobody else . . . And I wanted to be that . . . My dad does these events. These girls, they wear bikinis; they stand there. They get paid for doing nothing. It's easy. I see the way men look at them. And, really, what's the difference between a photo I didn't know was being taken and one which I did?"

Pause.

"What is the difference, Emily?"

"At least I chose. It was my choice."

"Do you feel like it was really your choice?"

Sound of sighing.

"If I hadn't have done it, I would have always been that girl who Nick ripped off. The loser who everyone laughed at."

"And who are you now?" Pause. "Emily? Are you okay? Look, let's take a break."

"No, I don't need a break. You want to know who I am now? I'm fucking known." Pause. "They know me. They don't like me. They want to fuck me but they don't like me. But at least they fucking know who I am."

Martin let herself into the redbrick 1980s terraced house she shared with Jim in Chester-le-Street, a market town not far from Durham where rents were cheaper and the atmosphere was less cloistered: less world heritage site than the university city.

In the kitchen, a note sat on the marble-topped island. She read it and murmured something to herself before pinging on the microwave without checking what was inside it. After two minutes, she eased the plate out with a tea towel and stood up at the counter, fork in hand, staring off in to the middle distance as she shovelled leftover pad thai into her mouth. She jumped as Jim appeared in the doorway.

He blinked at her, hitching up his pyjama bottoms. "What time is it?"

"Late." Martin turned to put the plate in the sink. "Sorry."

Jim opened a cupboard and took a glass down. "Water?"

"Thanks."

He filled the glasses and handed one to her. "How's it going?"

Martin put her glass down and hoisted herself on to the island, her legs dangling. "Getting there, I think," she said, taking a sip of water.

"The bloke who confessed?"

"Maybe." She put the glass down again carefully and reached for her husband. "I'm not sure yet."

Jim took Martin's hands and came to stand between her legs. He rubbed his stubble where water had dribbled and then took hold of her waist.

"How was work?" she asked.

He shrugged. "Good. Interesting."

"Found the cure for cancer yet?"

"When are you going to learn what it actually is I do for a living, Erica?"

Martin gave a weak smile. "I know what you do, you idiot." She nuzzled into his neck, wanting some contact. "I'm tired."

Jim stroked her back. "I know," he said. "Long days."

"I'm sorry I didn't get back earlier."

No answer came from Jim, just the warmth of his breath on her head.

"Shall we have sex?" Martin said into his hairline, not able to look him in the eye to hear the rejection.

"Honestly? Not really," Jim said sadly. "It's late, and I've got to be up at six to get in for seven."

Martin nodded, mute, as Jim straightened. "Rain check?" he asked, kissing her lightly on the lips.

She stifled a yawn. "Yep. No problem."

Martin jumped down and followed him to the kitchen door, looking back for a while at the island where they'd been standing. Jim had already gone upstairs by the time she switched off the light.

CHAPTER
THIRTY-TWO

Wednesday 24 May, 8.43 a.m.

Martin looked over at Jones. "Is that what you're wearing?"

"What do you mean?" Jones replied as she sipped at a cappuccino. She and Martin were in the cafe three doors down from the Durham police station.

"To the memorial?"

Jones was wearing a black T-shirt and trousers with a denim jacket. "Suit's back at the station, boss. I'll get changed when I get back from getting the forensics report."

Martin nodded. "Good. Can't say I'm looking forward to the memorial. Especially after what I saw yesterday." She sighed, toying with her toast. "It looks like Michael Brabents was the violent sort. The cleaner says there had been arguments. There'd been blood in the house, and apparently they'd been having fights down the pub; he was seen pushing Rebecca. Pub landlord says Brabents and Emily were unnaturally close. The main thing, though," she said as she considered her empty mug on the table, "is the photos I found in the garden shed."

"Christ. What?" Jones asked.

Martin shook her head. "Not porno. Just loads of Emily. Stacks of them. All fully clothed, nothing particularly untoward. But the question is," she said, dusting her palms of toast crumbs, "why would you hide photos of your own child in the garden shed? In a locked drawer?" She stood up, hoisting her handbag over her shoulder. "Doesn't make sense. You could just pop into the study and look through photo albums, couldn't you? Why keep them under lock and key?"

"Unless . . ." Jones said as she pushed back her chair and gave a wave to the waitress.

"Unless you wanted to look at them by yourself. In private." Martin finished for her.

"Exactly," Jones agreed as they walked out into a warm and bright morning. "Makes him look like a pervert."

"The landlord says Michael and Emily had a weirdly close relationship too. But we'd get annihilated in court based on that alone. We need more." The women headed in the direction of the station. "We'll need to get a warrant for the house. We need proper evidence of the abuse, the secret perversion. Speaking of which . . ."

Jones thought fast, keeping up. "Mason?"

"Mmmm," Martin said, looking about as the noise of a metal shop shutter being flung up screeched into the quiet of the morning. "I'm going to go and see him now. We still haven't got to the bottom of that yet. There's still Nick to see about the video and I want to talk to Annabel Smith myself."

"So when we will get Brabents in for questioning?" Jones queried.

"Depending on what Mason says, straight after the memorial," Martin answered. "In the meantime, let's knock this mysterious friend on the head. Can you head to Student Admin, get to the bottom of Daniel Shepherd?"

"I'm having problems with Daniel Shepherd," Jones said. "I can't find him. He's disappeared off the planet."

"Really? I got a weird text from someone when I was in Whittington, asking me to meet them. I'm wondering whether that was Daniel." Martin paused. "Apart from Facebook, though, how do we connect him to Emily? What do her friends say?"

Jones shrugged. "Not a lot."

"So we've got him making comments online and we think that he might be the friend down at the gig in London with Emily. We've got the mysterious 'D' on the note on Emily's door, which seems likely to be him — as opposed to anyone else — and that he arranged to meet her on the day of the murder. But there was no time on the note so it could have been any time that day." Martin raised her eyebrows. "But there's nothing concrete, is there?"

"Nope," Jones replied as they reached the building. "The other thing about Shepherd . . ."

"What?"

"I've already been to Student Admin. I went yesterday afternoon, when you were in Whittington."

"And?"

Jones shook her head, a puzzled look on her face. "They don't know him. I mean," she swallowed, "I should clarify . . ."

Martin stood on the steps outside the station and turned to face Jones. "Clarify what, Jones? Spit it out."

"There is no student called Daniel Shepherd at Durham."

Martin looked at her.

"Whoever he is," Jones said, "he isn't a student here. He might be a local lad, might be a friend of Emily's out of town, but he isn't a student. They were quite sure about it. Daniel Shepherd is not at the university here."

Martin left Jones at the station while she made her way on foot up the Bailey to Joyce. She breathed in the morning air, sunlight hitting the rooftops of the Durham colleges, the majority of which were set next to each other higgledy-piggledy, in a Victorian jigsaw all the way to the top. This city was beautiful, she thought as she walked. She was getting used to its hills and its greens, the viaduct stretching across it all like a rainbow, a constant reminder of the divide between the red roofs of the townsfolk and the ivory towers of the university. Martin liked that juxtaposition. Something in her understood it. The battle between the old and the new, between gravitas and frivolity. She reached Joyce, looked up again at its stern exterior, the imposing portico straining to batten down the mulch of humanity which writhed within it.

238

Mrs Earl was again in her cubby hole and nodded in a friendly manner to Martin as she entered the Joyce reception.

"He's expecting me," Martin called as she took the stairs two at a time, denying Mrs Earl a chance to stop her. She strode down the corridor, reached Mason's door and knocked briefly before walking in without waiting for a response.

Mason was on the phone, which he put back in its handset quickly as Martin plonked herself down in the chair in front of his desk. Struggling to rearrange his features, he quickly composed himself and put his hands in their usual position of a prayer on the desktop.

"To what do I owe this unexpected pleasure, Martin?" Mason asked in a controlled voice.

Martin smiled, relaxed. "Something's bothering me, Mr Mason, I must admit. We all know what's being said about Joyce. Sexual bullying rife between the students, a culture of online harassment." She leaned forwards towards the principal. "And we know, of course, from your own statement, about your unhealthy interest in Simon Rush."

Mason moved his head to one side, considering her.

"But there's something I'm not sure about. Maybe you can help me with it?"

There was a pause. A vague tapping could be heard from outside the window. A gardener banging his rake against a wall.

"You do realize, don't you, sir, that the alibi you've given Simon is undermined by your interest in him?"

Mason shifted.

"Bear with me," she continued. "Let's say you and Simon were married." She gave a wide smile. "Now then, in some circumstances, we couldn't compel you to be a witness against your own husband," Martin waved her hands as Mason frowned, "so to speak. And the reason we couldn't is, well, of course, it's the law. But it's also because we'd *expect* a person with an interest in a criminal to lie for them. It's sort of boring, you know?" She gave a short laugh. "Never ask a mother or a wife to testify against their son or husband. They'll only say he's either holier than thou or covered in shit." She waited. "Do you see?"

Mason wrinkled his nose. "What is your point, Martin?"

"My point is that Simon is still very much in our sights as a person of interest in Emily's murder. Alibi or not."

Mason sighed and leaned back in his chair, placing his hands on his knees. "You said there was something you didn't understand, Martin. Can we get to the point? I've got a lot on today."

"Ah, yes. Emily's memorial. I'll see you there," Martin smiled at him. "What I don't understand is a comment you made at the police station the other day. You said you'd seen the photos of Emily and you'd laughed at them. You said you'd been shown them by the boys." Martin waited a second. "Who were the boys, sir? I'd like you to help me with the names of those boys."

Mason creaked his chair back further and put his hands behind his head. "I can't remember."

240

"Mmmmm. Okay. But I wonder if you will remember when you're asked in court about it by a barrister and in front of a judge. Court cases are funny things, Principal Mason. They're like a big, fat salacious book that falls open in front of everyone — the community, the parents, the press . . . Whoever is tried for the murder of Emily — and that will happen — whatever's taken place prior to her death is going to be looked at in minute detail. So that we can figure out why this has happened. Do you understand?"

Martin looked at him squarely as the sound of the rake scraping along the flagstones in the garden outside continued. "By the end of this process, we will know *everything*. Believe me. So it's up to you. Tell me now, and we can try and help with some damage limitation." She shrugged. "Leave it until the last possible moment, and I can't help you."

Mason looked at her, surreptitiously running his tongue along his dry lips. He gave a quick nod. "Okay," he said eventually. "Okay."

The shadow of the cathedral loomed large over the lawn which bordered it. Black-suited mourners gathered in pockets across the grass, huddling in patches of sunlight which escaped through gaps in the building. Martin walked slowly around the lawn on a concrete path, squinting whenever the sun managed to find her face. She scanned the crowd, looking at the people gathered there. Would the mysterious Daniel Shepherd pitch up, she wondered.

241

Michael Brabents was near the cathedral entrance. Martin stared at him, thinking of the hidden photos. He looked done in, as though he were being physically supported by the tall thin boy, in his twenties, who stood next to him. Martin surmised that this must be Emily's older brother, Kit. In another puddle of people, some obvious Durham students stood, dragging their toes into the grass. Despite their height and bulk, they looked like schoolboys, an identical expression of earnest seriousness on their faces: crinkled eyebrows, chewing gum. Martin could see Annabel near to them. She was tapping something on her mobile phone. What was she doing? Checking her presence at the funeral in on Facebook perhaps? Martin wondered, cringing inwardly at the thought.

Martin watched the great and the good of Durham band together. The gold-chained mayor, the university principals, all with furrowed brows, none of them under sixty, most of them male. What did they have to do with Emily, Martin thought. They were supposed to have been her guardians but they hadn't been: they had let her down. The dean of the cathedral had given special permission to the Brabents family to hold Emily's memorial service here, so Butterworth had told her. In the absence of a funeral, this was the only place Emily's family and friends could project their grief and loss. Maybe it was because of the grandeur of the cathedral, Martin thought, but it all seemed so removed from who Emily was. She felt chilled by it; it just seemed meaningless.

242

The bell in the cathedral tower chimed, and the throng began to move in slowly through the great oak doors of the entrance. Martin stayed where she was, watching the crowd filter in, looking for a loner, a boy on his own. A cloud passed over the sun, putting them all in shade for a moment. She saw Jones jogging over the grass to meet her, and they walked together to the cathedral entrance doors.

"How did it go with Mason?" Jones asked quietly.

"I've got a list of names of boys that Rush used to hang out with."

"Is Shepherd on it?"

Martin shook her head.

They entered the cathedral to the sound of some music Martin didn't know. She and Jones sat at the back. Bowed heads multiplied before them, a few hushed voices which silenced as a choirboy stood in the stalls and Emily's family began their procession down the aisle. Martin thought of the wedding Emily would never have now and a burn started in her chest. *So fucking unfair, this life.* She kneaded her hands together as the clear notes of "Pie Jesu" reached the height of the stone arches buttressing the nave. Martin did know this tune, her mother being the world's biggest Lloyd Webber fan.

An enlarged photograph of Emily's face, now so familiar to Martin, stood on a stand in front of the altar. She was frozen in time, her head turned to one side, the black velvet hairband holding her blonde hair away from her head. The smile she gave haunted Martin at every minute of the day. A smile of someone

243

who knew she had her whole life ahead of her. Martin forced herself to keep looking at the crowd as she remembered that Kit Brabents would also be going to his mother's funeral before the month was out.

The service progressed slowly. Emily's father sat with his head in his hands for much of it. Martin kept her eyes straight ahead. The college principals were bunched in a line together towards the front, the mayor in the middle of them as if the centrepiece of a bouquet. Soon she would have to take part in the bit of her work that she dreaded — walking outside and going to commiserate with the family. This job was a nightmare, really, Martin thought to herself. She looked over at Jones, standing next to her, unsuccessfully mouthing the words to the hymn they were supposed to be singing. *Peace, perfect peace, by thronging duties pressed*. Indeed, Martin thought, as Kit Brabents stood and walked to the lectern to give the eulogy as the last bars of the hymn were played. *Death shadowing us and ours*.

Kit began to speak of his sister. As he did so, a shaft of light hit his face from the door opening at one side of the cathedral. Martin snapped her head around and saw a shadow in the doorway, the merest impression of the dark of a negative. She stood quickly and sidled her way out of the pew. Trying not to draw attention to herself, she half jogged, half walked towards the cathedral doors. As she exited, she whipped her head round to the right and saw a figure disappearing around the back of the cathedral. Following quickly, she found herself in the small graveyard attached to the

244

back of the building, unused in recent times now the need for greater space saw bodies shuttled off to a cemetery outside the city. She weaved in and out of the headstones, trying to catch up with whoever it was. Why had they come to the cathedral and then run away? Was this Daniel Shepherd?

"Hey!" Martin called after the shape. "Stop! Why are you running?" She chased after him, but the figure went too quickly for her. It was a boy, she was sure of it. "Hey. Daniel? I just want to speak to you. Come back!" Worn down by her own unfitness, Martin slowed to a halt, watching the back of the boy disappear, running expertly over the wet leaves of the undergrowth, down the winding path to where the bank met the swirling waters of the weir.

THE *DURHAM CHRONICLE*
NEWS WEBSITE
"PURPLE PROSE": THE SOCIAL
COMMENT COLUMN BY SEAN EGAN
WEDNESDAY 24 MAY

A sad day for the city today, as friends and family gathered on Palace Green to say goodbye to Emily Brabents. It was a moving and fitting tribute to the girl who seemed to have it all: a boyfriend in the university hockey team, *rich parents* who met her every whim and friends in all the right places.

Perhaps it was this good fortune that drove her killer to attack?

Yesterday came the shocking news of *more unbelievable tragedy* to strike the Brabents family with the *untimely death* of Emily's mother, Rebecca Brabents.

As usual, we have been given no further information on this from the police other than to express their condolences . . . (:-0)

One thing certain in this mire of confusion is that Durham's own Detective Inspector Erica Martin is failing to answer the hard questions posed by this case. Described as a rising star in the police force, she seems to be floundering in this humble column's opinion. When is she going to get to grips with it?

My little birds are tweeting again that the university will soon be clamping down on her conduct in this matter. *Too junior*, they say. And

246

where is DCI Butterworth? Why isn't he Senior Investigating Officer on one of the biggest murder inquiries to occur of late in the city?

Tut, tut, DI Martin. Scurry on, now. The people of the city are waiting to feel safe in our beds. *And the family of Emily Brabents demands justice for their little girl.*

Any comments on the above, tweet or email me at @ seganjourno or segan@durhamchronicle.co.uk.

CHAPTER
THIRTY-THREE

Sam Butterworth looked as if he could do with a drink. Martin had refused a seat and stood before his desk, wanting some kind of stature to deal with Butterworth's take on things, how he thought that this case appeared to be unravelling.

"It's only Wednesday," Martin had reasoned.

"It may as well be Christmas," Butterworth barked, as usual unable to meet her eye when he bollocked her. "You entered Brabents' property illegally, Martin. I mean, what the . . ." He waved his hands at her in despair.

"It won't make the photos inadmissible, you know that as well as I do. The evidence is too important to the case."

"You're not a fucking lawyer, Martin. You're an inspector." He glared at her. "Act like one." He exhaled, sitting back in his chair as if defeated.

"It's a massive lead," Martin said. "You know it. We've got to get him in and ask him about the photos." She waited a beat. "We got the forensics back from the crime scene. Nothing. Traces of skin on Emily's neck,

248

but they were from her own fingers where she tried to prise the assailant off." Martin paused, letting that sink in. "Otherwise nothing. No DNA, some fibres on her clothes but they could be from anyone. She'd been rolling around in the grass at the boathouse all day." Martin leaned forwards, putting her hands on the desk. "We need something, Sam. We need something to break," she said in earnest.

Butterworth sighed and rubbed his eyes, his elbows on the desk. "I've put my neck on the fucking line for you, Martin. The fucking line."

Martin dropped down into the chair opposite him. "I know," she said softly.

"These bloody articles aren't helping." He gestured at his computer screen. "This idiot journalist has got you in his sights. It's adding to the pressure. You must see that."

Martin shook her head, wanting to dispel the memory of the latest article by Egan. He was still digging into the principal of Joyce and the relationship he had with his students but he'd also got Mason quoted as being concerned that the police investigation wasn't *quite up to scratch*. Martin had been named and shamed.

"He's pissed off because I avoided him the other day." Martin sighed before giving a wan smile. "It doesn't matter. It's only my reputation he's damaging."

Butterworth put his hands behind his head and leaned back, looking at Martin, anger dissipating from him in a long exhale. "Have dinner with me," he said.

Martin breathed in, her stomach lurching. She looked down at her fingers, her wedding ring bold as brass glinting up at her. "That's the last thing we need," she said eventually. She lifted her head to meet Butterworth's eyes. "But I will solve this case for you, Sam." She nodded. "I swear it."

Butterworth hesitated before giving a rueful smile. "Ah, you swear it. Well then . . ."

"Let me bring in Brabents. We've still got the report to come in from Emily's MacBook. The medical report on Rush is due back this afternoon. If he's fit, we'll get him back in too." She stood up. "This case is far from over. Quite the opposite, in fact."

She walked to the door before turning back to him. His eyes were harder now. He and she had lost something in the moment, both of them.

"Get on with it, then," Butterworth said at last. "But you've not got long."

Martin was heading back from Sam's office to the incident room when her phone beeped with a message. Glancing at it, she saw the same number come up which had appeared in the garden of the house in Great Whittington. *Cum and c me*, the message said. *Im outsde frnt of station*. Martin felt a pulse of adrenaline. Was this finally Daniel Shepherd ready to reveal himself? She turned on her heel and jogged down the stairs to the ground floor.

CHAPTER
THIRTY-FOUR

I sat in the back row of the Student Union theatre, on the end of it, my feet planted across the black steps leading down to the stage. I love the smell of theatres. The carpentry dust, the fear. The production was doing its best to recreate sounds and sweet airs and had lodged Miranda centre-stage with an apricot spotlight bolting down on to her. I sighed, waiting for the ubiquitously turquoise Ariel to swoop in from somewhere above us. I closed my eyes. This wasn't working. I couldn't concentrate. I still couldn't trust my recollection of what had taken place last night. It had been so upsetting that I had stayed in bed the whole day — only emerging, vampire-like, once the sun began its descent and I could scurry here to secrete myself amidst a throng of theatregoers.

The evening in question had started well. Emily and I had gone to her choice of a small Italian restaurant under the railway bridge near the station. I pushed the thought out of my mind that she'd picked a place where no one would see us. Despite the length of the menu, we had been conservative in our tastes. I had ordered a Hawaiian pizza and Emily had chosen a carbonara. We shared a bottle of the house white wine. We didn't talk much. Emily seemed distracted. I kept looking over at her and smiling. She would look back, twirl her spaghetti around her fork, nibble at it daintily before sighing somewhat, putting her fork down and sipping at her wine. She drank more than me.

The owner of the restaurant bumbled over once we had finished our food. The place wasn't even half full so, deprived of a bigger audience, he was clearly keen to demonstrate his largesse. He produced a dusty bottle of lemon grappa with a flourish and poured us both thimble-sized glasses. I smiled at him while frowning, indicating that he should buzz off. But Emily downed her shot quickly and then looked up at him with playful eyes, wanting more. Luigi, for that was his name, it transpired, obliged her, and she tipped the thick yellow liquid down her throat like medicine.

"Your girlfriend likes the grappa, no?" Luigi said to me with a laugh.

I was about to nod and acquiesce when Emily interrupted, "I'm not his girlfriend. We're just friends."

And that was when the evening started to go awry.

After the meal we wandered out into yet another cold night. There are times when winter murders you with its relentlessness. I pulled my coat further in around me, and then Emily took my arm. She was stumbling a little due to the grappa I noticed.

"Shall we go to Joyce for a drink?" she asked.

I looked down at her. She was an eager puppy now that some alcohol sloshed inside of her. She seemed to have forgotten our decision the other day to start afresh, be together and forget everyone at Joyce.

"Oh, let's not, Emily," I said casually. "It's pretty boring there. Tell you what," I said, my mind racing with options. "How about we go to The Sun? Come on. My treat. I'll get a bottle of sparkling wine. We can pretend we're celebrating."

"Celebrating what?" Emily said, unsure, although she was tempted by the wine and the venue, I knew. I could feel her thoughts pulsating through the chilly air. I am shark-like, sometimes, in my ability to sense the waves of other people's meditations. Emily didn't want to go with me but she couldn't resist the opportunity to tell her idiotic friends that she had been to The Sun and had drunk champagne — so she would tell the story. Of course, she wouldn't admit she had been there with me. But she could brush that off — a drink with a mysterious stranger. I could see it all now, racing through her brain like a movie. Nick would be intrigued, he would question her, then get bored of the questioning, but the curiosity would have been piqued, and he would follow her on to the dance floor at Sixes. He would have been caught.

Before I knew it, we were tramping through the streets, past Joyce and round the bend to where the lights of The Sun gleamed brightly. I was reminded of that evening last term when I had followed Emily here on the night of the hockey social. It seemed a millennium ago. And look at me now. Here with her. Alone.

I opened the door for her and she walked in ahead of me. As we entered, I saw immediately it had been a mistake. Nick and Shorty and two other girls were sitting at a table in the middle of the dining room. The boys were wearing chinos and ties, their sports jackets on the back of their chairs. The girls wore pastel-coloured dresses, a single line of pearls dangling across their throats. They looked identical. Emily stood stock-still, a frightened rabbit. She gripped my arm. "Let's go," she murmured. "Now."

Shorty noticed us then. He said something to Nick, who looked over, a red flush seeping across his skin like a rash. Shorty laughed and brought his wine glass to his lips, mimicking a *cheers* to Emily.

"Come on," Emily whispered urgently, moon walking backwards towards the door we had come in. I couldn't seem to move though. I stood my ground as Nick pushed back his chair. He said something to the table and then meandered through the dining room to where Emily and I stood.

"Hi, Emily," Nick said sheepishly.

She looked at him, her eyes limpid, her mouth slightly open, the effects of the grappa evident by the smudging of her mascara at the edges of her eyes. She swallowed. "Hi, Nick. How are you?"

He smiled and flicked his head back in the direction of his table. "Good, thanks. Shorty's cousin's in town so we got dragged into taking her and a friend out for dinner."

I wanted to laugh. I glanced over at Emily, expecting her to scoff, raise her eyebrows in disbelief, but she was still standing motionless, filled with as much emotion as a jellyfish. Her face was pale with an unhealthy sheen to it. A tiny bubble of spittle rested at the corner of her mouth.

"Come on, Emily, let's get out of here," I said to break the silence. I gave Nick a brief nod then took Emily's arm and moved her around towards the door. As we walked out, she twisted her head round to look back at Nick, but he was already returning to the table. We made our way outside into the air, and the shock of its chill seemed to sting Emily, galvanize her into speaking at last.

"What a stupid idea. I can't believe we just did that."

"Did what? What did we do?"

254

"We looked so stupid. Standing there like a couple of losers. What must they have thought?"

I faced her, feeling angrier by the minute. "What must they have thought? Maybe that they shouldn't be having dinner with other girls when one of them's been sleeping with you."

Emily narrowed her eyes.

"All that rubbish about his cousin . . ." I continued, before trailing off lamely in the spotlight of Emily's glare.

"You don't know what you're talking about," Emily spat at me before making to walk away.

"Emily!" I yelled after her. "Emily — wait!" She stalked off, refusing to look back. I carried on after her, pleading with her. I was pathetic. "Emily, please. I'm sorry. I'm just trying to look after you. Can't you see? I just want to be your friend."

"No, you don't. That's rubbish. It's too much. You're all over me, all of the time. I can't breathe! I just want you to leave me alone. Seriously, it's too much."

I saw it spinning away from me, this evening. There it went, rolling down the hill in front of me. All of my plans, my hopes and wishes. My expectations. All dashed to hell. I breathed in deeply. I couldn't let that happen.

"Okay, okay. You're right. I like you, all right? I mean, you know that. But that's okay, isn't it? I don't expect anything. I swear. Emily. I really and truly just want to be your friend."

Emily was silent, so I took the chance she was at least listening and continued. "Let me help you. I can help you. Think about it. You want Nick. I know you do. But you're going about it wrong. Let me help you. I can. I swear."

Emily paused. We were midway over Elvet Bridge by this time. The bass thump of Sixes had started already, wending its way through the frozen night, the din of its thunderous hooves of the drink-sodden apocalypse that would rent a thousand brains before the night was over. Her head was turned towards it, as she thought about what I'd said. I willed her silently, urged her to take me on, not to abandon me to the cold Durham streets alone. She raised her head, her ponytail flicking against the back of her shoulders, presumably whisking away her doubts as her fingers beckoned down by her thighs.

"Come on then," she said, resigned. "Let's go to Sixes."

We walked up the interminable flights of concrete steps in the club as dry ice from inside drifted out to shake hands with the fog of our freezing breath. Emily walked straight to the bar and, after shouting at the barman, handed me a plastic pint glass filled with a greenish liquid.

"Blastaway," I think she said. It was the first drink she had ever bought me. I sipped it cautiously, but it was actually quite nice, it tasted of pineapple. Emily's eyes were skipping around the small room we were stood in. All the occupants were doused in an ultra-violet light which flashed and popped irregularly. Emily's eyes lit up as she saw someone she knew. She motioned to the dance floor and moved off, sucked into the crowd of dancers that swarmed in the semi-darkness. As she left me, her shape was silhouetted for a second with smoke-filled blue light behind her, flashes of green lasers caught in her hair. She was a goddess, really, I thought, as she was sucked into the pod.

I turned back to the bar and leaned against it. The barman, a local guy, gave me a look which meant *you're just as out of place here as me*. I ignored him and turned back to the dance floor. I could no longer see Emily. I looked at the door of the club just as Nick and Shorty came in. They didn't see me, of course, and went round to the other side of the bar, which jutted into the dance floor like the prow of a ship. There they stood, hips stuck out, cocks on parade, the irritating grins they always seemed to wear plastered on their faces. They appeared to have lost the "cousins".

I was feeling slightly drunk. This pineapple drink was obviously more potent than I had thought. I didn't know what to do. Emily had disappeared, it seemed, and the pitter-patter of panic was starting its rhythm again. She just would *not* be pinned down. I threw my hand in the air at the barman and he plonked a pint of lager in front of me. "Thought you'd prefer it," he said with a raised eyebrow. He was right. I swigged at it, trying to sober myself up with the familiar taste of hops. Now I was pissed off and pissed, it seemed. I edged away from the security of the bar, craning my neck to try and spot Emily in the crowd. The people on the dance floor had bloomed into a sort of flower shape, pulsing in and out, a circle of bodies, holding hands, a shape in the middle of them doing an ironic dance. In the blur of faces, I suddenly saw Emily. She was next to Nick, they were standing close, together.

I lost it. I pushed my way through the circle until I was the one in the middle. Now the crowd were clapping in time, stomping their feet as I stood there, frozen in the lights. I shook my head, trying to clear it of that pineapple.

"Come on!" a girl in a tight dress screamed at me. Her face leered in as a guitar chord twanged over and over again. I spun around, trying to find Emily as the circle moved faster around me, a spinning dream machine under the lights. I thought I saw her and moved to grab her, lurching dizzily forwards. I tripped and that would have been it — any last vestige of dignity I had, eradicated by a fall in the middle of the dance floor at Sixes. But she caught me. Emily caught me by the elbow, hauled me back up to standing. To the tanked-up minds of the throng, it could have looked like a sardonic dance move. She pushed me towards the door and out to the top of the steps. The bottom of them loomed up at me vertiginously.

"What was in that drink?" I managed to slur.

"A double vodka," Emily snapped. "I thought you needed loosening up."

I leaned against the wall as the door swung to a close, muffling somewhat the din within. I shut my eyes, feeling the first clutches of nausea deep in my gut.

"Oh, just leave, will you? You don't belong here."

I opened my eyes and looked at her. She had a hard look on her face, her lips pinched, hands on her hips, a Dickensian madam with an inappropriately short skirt.

"You're nothing but a tart," I mumbled.

"Fuck off."

We stared at each other. I knew she cared, though. I could see it in the pulse which throbbed in her temple. She exhaled then as if she were a balloon, wrinkling sadly at the end of a birthday party.

"Oh, it's hopeless."

"If you're hot, he'll want you." I didn't know where that came from. I found myself continuing, "If you show him that others want you, he'll follow. He won't be able to resist."

She looked into my eyes then. My Emily. We didn't know what we were doing, what we were playing with. We stared at each other with pupils dilated from booze as a couple of rugby players burst out of the club doors, barging past us,

258

smoke and noise trailing after them as they stumbled acrobatically down the stairs.

"Is it your choice?" I asked her. She knew what I meant. Was it her decision to take the photo, to be in the video? "Is it really yours? Or is it Nick's — or," I shook my head, couldn't get my thoughts organized. "Is it everyone here? You know, like . . ."

She thrust her hand on my arm to stop me rambling over the din inside. "I'm like them," she slurred before nodding as if to convince herself. "I am. It is my choice. I want to do it."

"Why?" I asked, despairing, reality dropping like a sober stone into the lake of my sodden stomach. "Why in God's name do you want to do it?"

Emily's eyes dipped then, and she swayed on her feet. "Because otherwise I'm nothing," she murmured. "Who am I otherwise?" she seemed to ask herself. "Nobody, that's who."

I saw the tears spark on her lashes as she lifted her head to look at me. I knew, even in my drunken haze, I knew. There was no turning back. Whatever she wanted, I would give it to her.

CHAPTER
THIRTY-FIVE

Wednesday 24 May, 3.05 p.m.

Flinging open the entrance doors to the police station, Martin stepped out into the afternoon. Sean Egan stood on the pavement, breathing out cigarette smoke into the road, where a traffic jam was beginning to build.

"Egan?" Martin exclaimed.

"Martin," he replied with a grin. "So you got my message?"

"You sent that text just now?" She frowned. "And the one yesterday?"

"I did indeed. Thought we should have another one of our chats."

Martin exhaled, cold disappointment sliding out from her pores. She glared at Egan. "I'm busy. I don't have time to feed your sick brain."

"Come on, Martin. You know I'm just doing my job."

"You're not, though, are you? You're making things up and stirring trouble. You could actually be helping this investigation, trying to get accurate information out to the public."

"But you don't have any information. Or do you, Martin? Come on. We're old friends now, aren't we?" Egan said with a glimmer of malice.

"No comment," she replied wearily. "Have you got anything of use to tell me or are you just here to waste my time?"

Egan ground his cigarette out on the pavement and folded his arms. "Ask yourself where I've been getting my information, Martin. It's not from Mason, that's for sure."

She stared him down like a cat until he gave another grin. "One boy, one girl. Think about it," he said before walking away from her up the street towards The Sun.

Martin shook her head, a thought emerging in the back of her brain.

The little shit.

Martin sat in her car on the boundary of the sports ground at Maiden Castle. The weather had turned once more, and a May squall was sitting low in the sky, waiting to shed its load. She got out of the car and pulled her jacket round her. Sean Egan's taunts of a secret source had prompted her to come and seek it out: it was time to speak to Annabel Smith.

Martin had initially gone to the girl's house but she had been informed by a seemingly stoned and inarticulate housemate that Annabel had gone for a run.

Martin drove there in less than ten minutes. The track was deserted apart from a tracksuited figure hauling itself around the running track. Annabel had a

261

hood over her head and something about her was familiar to Martin, although she couldn't place it. Eventually the girl noticed she was being observed and came to a stop at the finishing line, where Martin stood with her hands under her armpits to try and keep them warm.

"You should have joined me," Annabel puffed. "Would help with the cold."

Martin raised her eyebrows but ignored the sass, looking at Annabel in silence. The girl began chewing at her fingernail, disconcerted. "What? What do you want?"

"Detective Inspector Martin." She gave an easy smile.

"I know who you are," Annabel answered in a flat voice.

"I wanted to talk to you about Emily," Martin continued. "I think you've already spoken to my sergeant about your movements on the day of the Regatta?"

Annabel nodded, still chewing.

"I need some more information. About what was going on with Emily online."

Annabel dragged her foot along the asphalt of the track. She pushed the hood back off her face, and the wind lifted her hair, revealing a broad forehead, shining with perspiration. She had plucked her eyebrows badly, Martin observed.

"What stuff online?" she said lamely.

"Well, let's see. Shall we take a short walk?" Without waiting for an answer, Martin began to stroll slowly around the track. After a pause, Annabel fell in with her.

"Do you know who killed Emily?" Martin asked, light as air.

Annabel looked at her sharply then gave a loud sigh, something approaching a sob attached to the end of it. She swallowed to control it and shook her hands to warm them up. She was quiet for a while before shaking her head. "No. No I don't."

Martin looked over at the girl as they continued walking. "What was she like? Emily? You were friends, right?"

Annabel said nothing, her eyes turned to the clouds. Jones had said she was childish.

"We know she had something going on with Nick Oliver," Martin persisted. "How about you? Did you fancy Nick too?"

A puff of air escaped from Annabel's mouth. "Nick's a friend, that's all."

"So you were happy for Emily, that she'd started a relationship with him?"

A laugh escaped from Annabel before she recovered, putting her hand over her mouth to prevent further fugitive emotions.

"Why the laugh?" asked Martin. "What's funny about that question?"

"Relationship?" Annabel said. "If that's what you want to call it, I was fine about it." She didn't sound fine. Her face was a study in petulance. "No one's close to anyone here, and you're an idiot if you think they are." Annabel gave another affected laugh. "It's a dog-eat-dog world here, Inspector. And don't I know it."

Martin winced. She sounded like a kid from one of those American television shows they show on Sunday mornings — earnest yet entirely disingenuous. "Tell me about it then, Annabel. What's so awful about this world? Looks pretty good from where I'm standing, I have to say."

"Really?" Annabel tossed her head and then stopped abruptly and faced Martin, her arms folded. "You think it's good to have your life documented and spread out and dissected on the internet and iPhones for all the world to see? Never knowing what's going to show up next. Not being able to trust anyone." Her eyes filled with genuine tears. "Ever?"

Martin was silent, taken aback by this outburst. She put her hand on Annabel's arm. "That sounds like the stuff I've been reading in the press. Have you been talking to journalists, Annabel?" she asked the girl gently. Annabel pulled her hood back up defensively, and Martin had a flash of where she'd seen her before. "You were watching me, weren't you?" she asked. "When I went into Emily's room? You were on the other side of the road."

Annabel nodded, and tears began to fall down her cheeks. "I saw her. Emily, I mean. I was running that morning. I saw her when the police arrived." She stared at Martin in utter distress. Gone was the articulacy of a dispossessed teenager, Martin thought. Here instead was a grieving and confused young girl. Jones was right: she *was* just a child.

"I didn't want to talk to him, that Egan guy." Annabel cried. "But he read what I'd been saying online. Before Emily was . . . you know. And I thought it would be fun. To be interviewed by a paper. In a scandal type thing . . ."

Martin sighed internally.

"But as soon as I knew that Emily had . . . had died. I tried to stop him. I texted him that morning and told him not to print it. But he didn't listen."

Martin cleared her throat, waiting a moment for Annabel to compose herself before continuing. "This stuff on the internet . . . Tell me more about it. How often does it go on?"

"All the time," Annabel replied in a tired voice, turning to walk again. "Every single fucking day somebody will do something."

"And is there anyone you can talk to about it? Any adult?"

"Stephanie Suleiman, I suppose. She's the counsellor. Yeah, right." Her laugh was filled with disdain. "Call her as many times as you like, but she never even picks up the phone."

They turned a corner of the track, walking into the rising wind. Martin's words bumped into themselves as she caught her breath against it. "Right. But the photos . . . Emily seems to have consented to them. Why would she do that?"

Annabel rubbed her hand over her nose and sniffed loudly. "She wanted to be like them, I think."

"Like *them?*"

"The boys."

Martin bent her head, thinking this through.

"But she couldn't be like them. It doesn't work that way," Annabel continued, giving a sarcastic smile. "Obviously. It just meant that all the girls hated her and all the guys wanted to fuck her." She stared at Martin in provocation.

Martin made a face: *not impressed*. "So there's a culture of trolling and spying and people using information against each other. I can see how that would be stressful. No escape from it, really." She gave a thin smile. "How far up did it go? Was it just the Freshers? Or are the older years involved?"

"All of them."

"Simon Rush?"

Annabel narrowed her eyes. "Maybe."

"Do you like Simon?"

Annabel gave a small sigh. "The whole thing's toppling down, isn't it?"

"What is?"

"The whole fucking thing. It's hit the fan." She shook her head, giving a short laugh.

Martin waited a while. "What's that got to do with Simon Rush?"

Annabel looked sidelong at Martin. "Everyone knew he had something going with Mason. He was on a trip."

"A trip?"

"A power trip. He'd got the presidency. He . . ." She stopped again, uncertain.

"Tell me, Annabel. Please. You know this is really important." Martin put her hand on the girl's shoulder, her breath fogging the air in front of them. "You can trust me," she said.

"I don't know, really," Annabel said eventually. "I never went in there. I'm only a Fresher. But Simon would have parties in his room. Members only."

"Members of what?"

The girl shrugged. "Of their stupid gang. I don't know the details, really I don't. We just knew."

"Who knew?"

"Everyone. Everyone in my year. Nick and Emily, Shorty. We used to laugh about it. It seemed crazy."

"What would happen at these parties? Did you know about that?"

Annabel rubbed her lips together, shaking her head.

"So what was wrong with it, then? Why did anyone care? It's not unusual for students to have parties in their room."

Annabel stopped walking and looked down at her feet. "I'm not sure, I don't want to get anyone into trouble."

"That doesn't matter now, Annabel. We need to work, out the truth of it. Whatever happened in Simon's room — maybe it's relevant, maybe not. But we need to know about it."

Annabel was silent for a long moment, then she exhaled, as if making a decision. "It was the principal. We saw him once, at one of the parties."

"Who saw him?" Martin's heart thumped loudly in her chest at this.

Annabel nodded. "Me and Emily. He left Simon's room at about four in the morning. We were going to her room, just coming home from Sixes." She blinked rapidly at Martin. "Please don't tell him I told you, though."

"You're sure it was Principal Mason?"

Annabel nodded firmly.

"Did Emily tell Simon she knew about this?"

"I think so. I'm not sure. Simon . . ."

"What?"

"He had a bit of a thing for Emily, I think. Who didn't, right? Emily knew so many people. Especially after the photos. It was hard to keep up sometimes."

"Did she reciprocate with Rush?"

"I think she was flattered. He turned up to see her in London once, she thought it was funny. But, you know, she was so obsessed with Nick."

"Does anyone else know about Mason going to that party?" Martin asked after a short while.

"I don't think so. I haven't said anything." Annabel paused. "I don't think he liked it. Simon, I mean. I saw the way he looked. He looked trapped sometimes, I could tell. I felt sorry for him. But . . ."

"But, what?"

"But he got something out of it," she shrugged.

Martin looked up at the sky for a moment, her mind whirring as raindrops began to spatter down, hitting her face. They began walking again, reaching the other side of the track, continuing to trace it round to where they had started. *Rush and Mason*. How stupid of the principal to have been caught out, though.

"And what about Daniel Shepherd?" Martin asked as they rounded the last bend, the rain coming down heavier now.

"Who?"

"Daniel Shepherd? He's another one of Emily's Facebook friends."

Annabel pulled the sleeves of her tracksuit top down as the rain began to pelt. "I don't know him," she shrugged.

Martin frowned. "Are you sure, Annabel? This is really important. Are you saying you don't know of a friend of Emily's called Daniel Shepherd?"

Annabel jumped up and down on the spot. "Yes, that's what I'm saying. Can I go now? I'm getting fucking freezing here."

Martin nodded, distractedly. She watched Annabel as she jogged away. Annabel was Emily's closest friend, whatever she said. So if she didn't know who Daniel Shepherd was, who did?

CHAPTER
THIRTY-SIX

I stood outside in the corridor for a long time before I finally plucked up the courage to knock at the door. I had been listening to them from my position there, the grumble of their voices within, speared occasionally by an aggressive laugh which jolted me, cemented my fear of entering. I had my dad's old hip flask with me, which I'd filled with the Jack Daniel's I'd found in Zack's cupboard at the end of his bed. I took a few swallows, felt the buzz warming my insides and tapped lightly at the same time as pushing the door open.

They sat by the window in the circular room, the Oval Office, as it was called. Simon Rush had invited me. He was wearing a black undergraduate gown, the kind the Joyce students would wear to the weekly formal dinner in the refectory. The low table in front of him was covered in candles, wax dripping on to the Formica top. Bottles of wine were stacked together along with overfilled ashtrays and half-used Rizla packets. The candlelight shone upwards, bathing his face in a soft glow. He smiled at me as I came in, the circle around him shifting their eyes in order to follow his lead. They all grinned then, a pack of drunken wolves.

There were no girls. Simon patted the seat next to him, and I shuffled in, past the knees and feet of the others as they budged along to let me squeeze beside him. He threw his arm around my shoulders, as was his way. "Darlings, this is the gorgeous Daniel. Isn't he a treat?"

The wolves nodded. I didn't recognize any of them by name, although I'd seen them around the bar in Joyce, grouped together always, a solidity in numbers. I must have been wide-eyed, my sobriety at that moment outplaying my desire to fit in. Someone handed me a glass filled with red wine and another put a rolled-up cigarette in my hand. I inhaled deeply from it, knowing what it contained. I needed it. I needed to be shielded from this assault on my nerves, my senses.

One of the wolves at the other end of the circle had a computer in his lap. The cool blue light of the screen shone into his face, hitting his glasses, hiding his eyes from me. I couldn't see what he was silently watching but I could tell that the person next to him had his hand underneath the computer, in the boy's lap. He was moving his hand up and down, as the boy blinked slowly, shapes on the computer flickering in front of his hidden eyes.

Simon sighed as if sated by a feast, rubbing his thumb along my collar bone. "Daniel, it's so good to have you finally come."

I heard a snigger from somewhere else in the room.

He leaned back a little, his shirt opening further. I could see the white skin of his chest, a silver dagger dangling from a chain around his neck. He took a drag of his cigarette and turned to me, his face close to mine. "How do you like my party?" he asked.

I nodded, taking another sip of wine. "I like it," I answered.

He breathed softly, the smell of wine reaching into my nostrils. I could feel every part of my body at that moment, every hair on my arm, every joint in my bones. I licked my lips, and his eyes watched me do it. The energy was shifting in the room. It mounted like a rising breeze, touching us all as it passed. The gowns of the boys rustled as they huddled closer together like blackened birds.

It was as if I was lurching over a cliff top. After what had happened with Emily, there was no turning back for me. I was kamikaze. Maybe it was the booze and the puff or maybe I wanted to destroy something, or tempt it — God, I don't know. Right then, I just felt that I could press the button. The one that would blast us entirely to smithereens. And I would be part of it all. At last.

I would be shattered into tiny pieces of refracted glass, fragments of the clear skies of my old self caught up by, and spinning through, the dancing wind. Those countless pieces, as they separated in the cold column of the approaching Mistral, would become some new kind of wonderful whole. Good-fucking-bye. The wind was changing. The Mistral would come.

I pulled again on the cigarette I had been given. As the grass hit my brain, I succumbed. Simon took my hand, and, I am ashamed to say this now, I let him.

CHAPTER
THIRTY-SEVEN

Wednesday 24 May, 5.35 p.m.

Michael Brabents would have been attractive, Martin thought. Very attractive, if it weren't for the thinness of his lips and the closeness of the tip of his nose to his mouth. It changed his face from open and engaging to something rat-like, something hard-bitten and scrunched up, resentful of the world. He was again in jeans with a pale-blue checked shirt, the top few buttons opened; a layer of brown stubble grazed across his face. Dark circles rimmed his eyes, and his left eye seemed barely open; a greasy film of green gunk travelled along his eyelashes. He gestured to it as Martin walked in.

"Sorry about the eye. Conjunctivitis." He shrugged. "Doc says brought on by stress."

Martin sat down opposite him. She was alone other than the tape recorder. This interview would be tricky. With nothing to charge him with yet, Martin didn't want a harassment charge on a man currently grieving for his wife and child. But she wanted the formality of the interview room and the protection of a taped interview. Jones and Butterworth were watching them both via the closed-circuit video feed. Martin had to play this exactly by the book — particularly given the maverick nature of her shed investigation. As she looked at Emily's father, though, he seemed a broken man. She was finding it hard to reconcile that image with the violent, obsessive father she suspected Michael Brabents actually was.

"I can only imagine, sir," she said, turning on the tape recorder. "Now, I'm just going to use this as a precaution." She smiled. "Protection for us both. For the benefit of the tape, I will state that you have declined to instruct a lawyer for this meeting."

Brabents didn't look as though he was listening. He was staring off into the middle distance at something behind Martin. "I can't believe they're gone," he said eventually. "That I'll never see them again. Either of them." He gave a short laugh. "I think it's more than I can bear actually."

Martin looked down at her hands, giving a pause to this statement. Judging the moment had passed, she spoke.

"You may not be aware but I travelled across to Great Whittington yesterday. I went to your house. Spoke to your cleaner and some others in the village."

He looked up, surprised. "Why?" he asked.

"This is a murder investigation, Mr Brabents. I wanted to see where Emily had lived. What environment she came from. I need to know who she was. Then, I hope, I can work out what happened to her."

He nodded. "And what did you find?"

274

She leaned forwards, frowning. "I found a beautiful, idyllic house. A family who were slightly on the outside of the village. A family that had its rows . . ." She paused again.

"It's no secret Rebecca and I were going through a rough patch."

"How rough?"

"It wouldn't have led to anything. We weren't splitting up. We were just arguing a lot."

"Enough that Emily hadn't been staying with you before she started here at Durham?"

He shrugged. "She wanted to stay for a while with a cousin of hers in London. More fun down there. We saw no harm in it."

She cleared her throat. This was the difficult bit. "Was there anything that would have led you to suspect your wife wanted to commit suicide?"

He shook his head forcefully. "Absolutely not. Well — apart from Emily obviously . . ." His voice trailed off.

"Of course. But, before that. The arguments? The fights? Was Rebecca depressed by it?"

"No. Not at all. We were just like any normal couple. I can't understand it. I can only think that Emily's murder tipped her over the edge . . ."

She nodded. "I'm sure. It must be unimaginably stressful." She waited a beat. "Are you a violent man, Mr Brabents?"

"Me?"

She looked at him.

He leaned back in his chair and gently fingered his bad eye. "No," he said finally, shaking his head again. "I would never hit my children."

"What about your wife?"

"No," he answered again. Too quickly, Martin thought.

"What kind of father were you? *Are* you?" Martin grimaced a touch, acknowledging the faux pas.

"A good one, I think. I'm always there for them, they can talk to me about anything."

"And do they?"

"Sometimes, it depends. I saw less of Emily since she moved here, obviously. Kit and I have always been close. They're good kids."

She shifted in her chair, crossing her legs. "Would you say you got on better with Emily?"

He shrugged. "Maybe. She was, perhaps, a daddy's girl." He rubbed his nose. A tell? Martin wondered. He fiddled with his face a great deal, it was annoying.

"A daddy's girl. So, would you be strict with her? With boyfriends?"

He seemed to think about this. "Emily didn't really have any boyfriends. I'm not sure about here but at home — she was a good girl, you know? Concentrated on her studies. She was bright. We had high expectations for her, her mother and me." His voice cracked slightly.

Martin looked up at the ceiling, let the silence continue after Brabents had stopped speaking. It went on uncomfortably until he took the bait. "I mean, sometimes I was a bit strict. What father isn't with his only daughter?"

Plenty, thought Martin.

"Sometimes, you know, I would get angry if Emily was out too late on a school night or wasn't concentrating."

She raised her eyebrows at him. *Go on.*

"Sometimes Emily could be . . ." he searched for the words, "flighty. Maybe. She could get a little distracted. I often felt I had to rein her in a bit. Corral her."

"She could be a bit wild?"

"No, not wild. Just beyond the realms of what I thought . . ."

"What you thought acceptable?"

"Yes."

"And how would you demonstrate this to Emily?"

"We'd have rows, I suppose. Her mother would always take her side." He paused. "But that was Rebecca. She was always a girl's girl." He smiled to himself.

It was time, thought Martin.

"When I visited your house, Mr Brabents, I saw something out of the ordinary there."

"What?"

"Perhaps not so much out of the ordinary as strange because of where I saw it."

He looked puzzled.

"Do you own a shed, Mr Brabents?"

He looked at her steadily. She could see a vague flush spreading underneath the stubble as the realization grew. He blinked slowly and then narrowed his eyes. "Did you enter my shed, Detective Martin?"

"Detective Inspector. Yes I did, Mr Brabents."

"And did you have a warrant to do so?"

Not an idiot then, Martin thought. She punted. Once his lawyer got wind that there was no warrant, he would answer nothing.

"Yes I did."

A startled flicker spun across his eyes for a milli-second before disappearing. He ran his hand through his hair, the epitome of casualness.

"And what did you find?"

She smiled. "I found photos, Mr Brabents. Hundreds of photos, I would say. And all of them of your daughter — none of your son. Or your wife." She continued to look at him, still smiling. The silence mustered in the room, the air fusty. Martin could smell Brabents' body odour as he began to spark a sweat.

"The strange thing about those photos, though," she leaned forwards towards him, "the strange thing is that you had locked those photos in a drawer in a shed at the bottom of the garden." She sat back. "A shed. Dad's shed. A sign said so on the wall. A place you could be by yourself." She spread her hands out to him in an entreaty. "Why would you want to look at photos of your daughter alone, Mr Brabents?"

"Storage . . ." he answered quickly.

"But why locked up, Mr Brabents? In a place where you would go to be alone?"

He stared at her, saying nothing. His eyes wavered, but he seemed unable to blink.

She sat forwards and folded her hands on the desk. "I'll tell you what I think, Michael," she said conspiratorially. "I think you were obsessed with your little girl."

He remained silent.

"I'm right, aren't I?" She looked at him. "Your little girl. Daddy's little girl." She gave him another quick smile. "But little girls grow up, don't they? They get bigger, more attractive. Problem is, though," she snapped the smile off her face, "other people find them attractive too, don't they? And that you couldn't bear."

Tears began to stream from Brabents' good eye as the gunk in the other one seeped more. He wiped his hands over his face as he spoke. "Stop it. Stop talking."

"You couldn't touch her, have her in the way you wanted," she said. "But you didn't want anyone else to either, did you? You couldn't stomach it. People looking at her. At her body. Feasting their eyes."

He gave a moan and moved back and forth in his chair. When he finally raised his head, his face was one of absolute disgust.

"It's true, isn't it? You wanted to keep her in a bell jar like a beautiful bird. You would never let her go, would you? You stashed the photos away in a drawer so nobody else could see them. Where only you had the key. Where she could be yours for ever. What did you do when you looked at the photos, Michael? What were you thinking as you looked at them one after another?"

Brabents had turned pale. "I'm going to be sick."

"And then she came here," she said, relentless. "And you knew what would happen. She would meet boys. Do things with them. Did you see the online photos,

Mr Brabents?" She lowered her voice to a whisper. "Did you?"

He stared at her, appalled.

"Did you see what your daughter was doing here? Your beautiful daughter. Was that what made you snap?"

He shook his head. "No. Please . . ." He sobbed quietly, murmuring to himself. She had to lean forwards to hear him. "Please, I loved her," he wept. "God, how I loved her. She was everything to me . . ." He dragged his hands down, mixing gunk with snot and tears, his face in anguish. "I know it was wrong, but it didn't harm anyone. It was just my own little . . ."

Martin shook her head in revulsion. Nothing was said. Brabents' irregular sniffs the only sound.

"Mr Brabents," she said, breaking the silence eventually. "Did you drive across to Durham last Sunday night and arrange to meet your daughter at Prebends Bridge?"

He cleared his throat, his eyes downcast. "No."

"Did you?" she hissed. "Did you stand there with her and look into her eyes one last time? Before you held her close and put your hands around her neck, taking her life?"

Brabents cleared his throat loudly and pulled his focus back to the room. He became calm, wiping his face and staring at Martin full on. "I'd like to see my lawyer now, if that's all right."

She nodded and handed him a box of tissues from the windowsill before quietly leaving the room. Closing the door behind her, she leaned back on it.

"*Fuck*," she said to herself.

280

CHAPTER
THIRTY-EIGHT

Wednesday 24 May, 7.05 p.m.

"We'll need to get thirty-six hours," Martin said facing the team in the incident room. "We've got reasonable grounds for an arrest."

"Does the timing work? Brabents had an alibi, didn't he?" Butterworth asked from the back of the room, where he stood leaning against the wall.

"An alibi provided by his wife," Jones said. "Who has since committed suicide."

"The Brabents family were fucked up," Martin said. "They argued and fought, and it seems as though he physically abused Rebecca, even if not the children. They came across as cool and trendy and however else you want to call it, but underneath he was running the show like a traditional old-fashioned bully." She swung on her chair, turning it towards the window, thinking, surprised to see the sky was getting dark outside. Where had the day gone? She looked at her watch. "Have we got Emily's MacBook back yet?" she asked.

"Yep," Jones replied, reaching over her desk and getting hold of a file. "Here's the report."

Martin scooted forwards on her chair to take it and scanned the contents. She narrowed her eyes and pushed herself back to the table where she'd been and flipped open a pad, looked through it for a second.

"What is it, boss?" Jones asked.

Martin shook her head. She glanced up as if noticing the team for the first time, noticing their tired eyes — they been working round the clock. "Brabents' brief will be here in a while, so let's take the opportunity to have a break while we wait." She stood up and walked across the room as if to leave. Jones settled back into her chair, opening a can of Diet Coke.

"Come on, Jones," Martin called as she reached the door of the incident room. "You can bring your Coke with you."

The women signed themselves into the evidence room, and Martin headed where she had been directed by the uniformed constable at the guarded door. The room existed as a crime-scene library, tall stacks of shelves forming long, narrow aisles, crammed with neatly labelled boxes and bags.

"What are we looking for?" Jones asked, following behind.

"Emily's MacBook," Martin answered, scouting the shelves for a while before reaching up and bringing down a computer wrapped in a plastic evidence bag. She carried it to a table at the end of one of the aisles and took it out of its wrapping. "Grab a chair, Jones. Make yourself at home," she said vaguely as she turned on the power and waited for the machine to fire up.

282

They sat in front of the screen, the white apple sign appearing first, followed by the other icons pinging into place. Martin touched the mousepad and opened up Emily's email account.

"The report listed that Emily had sent herself an email on the afternoon of the Regatta. Thought I'd check it out. She must have sent it from her iPhone."

"She didn't have a phone on her when she was found."

"Right. Nor in her room or anywhere in the crime scene. But she did have one — Annabel said so in her interview with you. So, whoever killed her chucked it away, I'd guess. We need to think about getting clearance to dredge the river. 'Cause that's where I'd have thrown it if I was the murderer."

Emily's email account appeared on the screen, and Martin looked towards the top of it. In the three days since her murder, Emily's account had received over a hundred emails from junk sites, advertisements, university notices. Yet more evidence of the relentless continuum of life as death knelt in its midst. Martin looked further down the page to the date of Emily's murder, where a message from "Me" had arrived at 6.13p.m. Martin clicked it open. The message contained nothing but the jpeg of a photograph. Her eyes fixed on the screen, Martin pressed the photograph icon, and as the image came into view, both Martin and Jones sat back in their chairs. Jones glanced over at Martin, who still stared at the picture, frowning.

"What are you thinking, boss?" Jones asked.

Martin hesitated before speaking softly, musing out loud. "I'm thinking that there was only one reason why Emily would email this photo to herself."

Jones waited.

"Security," Martin said at last. "She knew what this photo was worth and she wanted to back it up somewhere. Somewhere other than her phone. And . . ." She stood up and paced down the nearest aisle a way before turning back and facing Jones. "Let's hypothesize that the people in this photo knew that she had it, had discovered she had it, what would they do?"

"They'd be frightened she'd show it," Jones said.

"Frightened?" Martin asked. "Or angry?"

Jones shrugged. "Yep."

"Angry enough to arrange to meet Emily and try to get her phone off her?"

"Perhaps."

"Indeed. Perhaps." Martin sat again, moving her head nearer to the screen, peering at the image that remained there. The photo showed the back wall of a pale building.

"Looks like the garden behind Joyce College," Martin said. "I remember looking at it from Mason's office." The wall was partly obscured by foliage, and thick bushes blocked total vision, leaving a large part of the wall in shadow. Simon Rush stood with his back against the building, his head in an expression of relaxation, turned to one side in an almost coquettish manner. Standing in front of him was the principal of Joyce. His hips were jutted forward and one thumb

284

rested in his pocket. His head was bent close to Rush's, a soft smile on his lips.

"Look at Mason's hand," Martin whispered.

Jones nodded in silence. Mason's other hand was spread out, his fingers resting on Rush's waistline. His thumb clearly up and underneath Simon's shirt.

CHAPTER
THIRTY-NINE

Wednesday 24 May, 7.05 p.m.

Stephanie sat in her kitchen, an incongruous bowl of cereal in front of her, given the lateness of the day. She had returned from taking Rosena to gymnastics practice, and the house was now resettling into the quiet stillness of the absence of inhabitants. Stephanie liked it like this. She could hear the hum of the tumble dryer, a tiny drip from the cloakroom tap, the tock of the clock in the sitting room down the hall.

Stephanie bent her head to the table and let it come, what she had had to keep hidden from her daughter as she had sat in front of her, eating her tea and chattering about school. The sobs shuttled through her like a train, tears pooling underneath her cheeks. She clutched at the table edges, her knuckles white with desperation. This blackness, this blackness was coming again. It hadn't visited for almost a year but now it was tiptoeing into her psyche; she could feel it like the edges of a blanket. The words to the Lord's Prayer came to her all of a sudden. She hadn't thought of them for decades, since her convent school days. The words repeated in her like a mantra, over and over again, and

286

as they washed over her, the cries subsided. She hiccuped a breath and found a calm. She raised her head and wiped her face. *What was happening to her?*

Stephanie looked at the blackboard menu stuck on to the kitchen wall with the list of things to do: *Tues @ 5.30, dentist; R — netball skirt; milk and cucumber.* She had yet to do the shopping, and, she realized, they had missed the dentist appointment. She shook her head slightly, sighing loudly and then inhaling oxygen like a drug. She had to pull it together. She eyed the blackboard again. Chores.

What was she doing? The realization had hit her this morning in the shower. She had been engrossed in the routine of the ablution, thinking nothing, meditative in her actions. And then she had stepped out, goose-bumps spreading across her skin. She had caught a glimpse of her reflection through the condensation. Her hands were curled up in front of her face as she reached for a towel, and something in the movement reminded her of a creep, a skulking, stealthy motion, a move to grab, to attain. She was naked and suddenly she was ashamed.

The box of her deceit yawned open with a pin-headed screech. *Her own stupid self-importance.* To know others' secrets, to know things others did not. This had been keeping her going in these lonely days since coming to this country. But now it was as if she had awoken from a dream. She put her head in her hands. *What was she doing?*

She swallowed. She knew what had to be done.

She thought about Daniel, the way he wrote, how his voice had drawn her in. But then the emails just before Easter — the tone had changed. Stephanie had known it was wrong, deep down. He seemed to be going beyond the pale. And Emily . . . the manipulation. Stephanie pushed herself to standing and left the kitchen to stand before the hallway mirror with her handbag and tried to rectify her swollen face with her powder puff.

She looked at her reflection. *Well, it was better than nothing*. She put on a bright-pink lipstick and rubbed her lips together. It was time now. Time for everything to be said. Looking back wistfully at the sanctuary of her kitchen, she made herself walk to the front door, put on her jacket and leave the house.

CHAPTER
FORTY

Something was changing in me, I could feel it. There was a runaway train inside my head, speeding away, pulling my centre of gravity towards something from which I could never return. I did try to rein it in, I did. But I kept looking at those websites. The internet became a fruit machine of porn for me. Videos and pictures, ordinary women sitting in chairs in their kitchens with their legs open. Men — and women I was amazed to see — debating whether a woman in a photo would be a good fuck, what her pussy would taste like. They were vile scabs of things, crusting over the detritus of humanity, the disgusting use of language to describe raw, untamed emotions, things which should be kept hidden, should be controlled. When had it become acceptable to spill these things outside of yourself? The idea that you could talk about fucking and tits and pussies, images oozing out of a computer screen like an infected discharge. It repulsed me. But once I started, I couldn't restrain myself, I started to read about it, learn from it; think about it in the same terms as these cretins.

This was the problem with the internet. People with barely a grain of literacy were allowed to tell the world about their thoughts, in cavemen terms. Dickens had described for us the effects of the Industrial Revolution on the poor, but at least he had had the decency to write it on behalf of the peasants, leaving the world with a gift instead of us having to hear their own dishevelled and angry ramblings. This is what we were subjected to now. And the irony was that the people who benefitted from it, the Nicks and Shortys of this world, contributed nothing. They merely sniggered and feasted their eyes on the spoils like some weird rugby-playing pair of Madame Defarges at the gallows.

I didn't know how to keep Emily. I saw her as a kite, drifting away from me, leaving me grasping at her tail. I was pathetic. Once, I remember, the thought reared up in me, screamed in my head, that she would never come to me. She would keep going back to Nick; he would always be her conqueror. That's what gave me the idea, actually. It's a reverse psychology if you like. My mother used to do it with me all the time, even when I was a teenager.

Watch the child by the lapping water on the beach. Watch how he looks at the waves, how he wants to swim into the deep water. He turns back and sees his mother on her beach towel. She's lying there, her sunglasses atop her head, a red-and-white striped swimsuit on. The child puts one foot into the foam of the waves. The mother has to make a decision. She does nothing, raises her eyebrows, inclines her head. *Do it*, she seems to be saying. The child hesitates. Slowly he withdraws his foot. He has tested her, and she has won. She pushed him to reach the fulfilment of his fears, and in the end he retreats. Why? Because what he thinks he wants, he doesn't. And the mother knows it. Just like I know Emily.

She would do it anyway. That's what I told myself. She would do it, and the more I told her not to, the more she would pull away from me. So I would let her go to Nick. Stupid Nick. And she would go and sully herself with him and then, when she was broken and cold and alone, she would come back to me.

I sat back in the chair in which I had positioned myself in the library and gazed out of the window. Yes, then she would come back to me.

"It'll be fine," I said to Emily. I was in her bedroom after letting myself in. Emily had given me the code to her building ages ago. She'd been pacing the room when I entered and continued to do so as I sat on her bed, feet on the floor, hands on my knees. I looked relaxed, although I didn't feel it, if I'm honest. Nick had taken a couple more photos of Emily, and she had all of a sudden got cold feet, frightened by what people would say, what he was going to do with them. I couldn't bear to think of it either, but something in me was pushing her, propelling her to see this disaster through to its terrible conclusion. Where I would be waiting for her.

"Think of the way guys will look at you. They'll *awe* you. I know they do because I'm a guy, right?"

She nodded, listening carefully.

"So these photos Nick took. What's he done with them?"

She shrugged. "They're on his computer, I think. He couldn't believe his luck. That I would do it. That I was his, sort of — plaything." She looked down at her feet, her hair falling over her face. I wanted to hold her, to tell her that it would all be okay.

"Emily, look at me." She moved her head upwards, her eyes staring into mine. "It's going to be fine. Really. This is what you wanted. Nick is in the palm of your hand now."

"But isn't he just going to think I'm a slag? That I'm easy?"

I wanted to scream at her and say *yes, of course he is*. But I had to wait. I had to bide my time. She would learn. "Not if you're the one who's in control, Emily. That's the way it works. Girls who give it away indiscriminately, they're the whores. Guys know they love it. Even Annabel's coming round to the idea now, isn't she?"

Emily considered this. It was true to an extent. Annabel's wardrobe had shortened and tightened since Emily had begun her online posturing. Even she could see the benefit of boys buzzing round the honey pot of sex on show.

"Just imagine." I straightened my back, even I was getting excited by this idea. "Imagine a girl who will do anything you ask in the bedroom but she's, like, your best friend. She's basically like a guy but who looks like a fuckable girl."

Something in the back of my brain clicked. A cold sweat began to creep across my forehead. I was in the rapids now, hurtling over the tops of the white water, my wings skimming treacherous rocks like a bird. There was no stopping me now. *A fuckable girl*. I couldn't get the phrase out of my head. It played over again like the interminable din of the ice cream van coming down the street, a sing-song chime: *a fuckable girl, a fuckable girl*.

Emily coughed, and I brought myself back to her room. She had her chin in her hands, looking at me. She knew what the truth was, I was positive. She belied a vulnerability so that sometimes I wondered whether it even existed within her. Her eyes could change in an instant from meres of marshmallow to tarns of ice. Now they were dark, unreadable. Unreadable, unfuckable. To me, at least.

"Listen, Emily," I said, searching my mind for how to persuade her. And then I had it. I remembered our drink in London over Christmas. "Remember what you told me once?" She looked at me carefully as I continued. "You said it was empowering, doing what you want with your body. It's *your right* to do it. Think about it." I spread my hands as an entreaty. "You don't care, do you? Your body's just a thing, right? You can do whatever you like with it." Emily's eyes were wide now. She looked like a girl who says she wants to sleep with the light off but then craves the comfort of a nightlight. "What *you wish*," I said, to reinforce the point, "is to be with Nick *and* be looked up to. Not be someone who can just be walked over. Laughed at. Right?"

"But everyone will just think I'm a slut. Those comments online . . ."

"It's already done, Emily!" I couldn't help it, I was raising my voice. "He's already played you. The photo and the video — he's done it already. So, either you act like a victim and you'll lose him, or . . ."

"I pretend I don't care, and he'll think I'm cool," she finished off.

I stared at her. "But you *don't* care, do you? I mean — that's what you said. At Christmas."

Emily smiled shakily. "Sure. Yeah. I don't care. Like, who cares about a pair of tits, right? Everyone's getting them out at Sixes anyway. There's this girl in Murdoch College — she got in *FHM* last month."

Something inside me slithered and twisted, a snake of disgust. "Who was it?"

"Carrie someone. She does English Lit actually, do you know her? She's in the third year."

I did know her. Of her anyway — she was well known in the department. She was predicted to get a first. I shook my head as the snake coiled down in me to rest.

"It's not long till Easter, Emily." Five long weeks of holiday when I would be without her.

Emily nodded sadly. "Nick's planning a trip to Africa over the break." This was typical of Nick and his ilk. They journeyed to exotic destinations as if taking a weekend trip to a Butlin's holiday camp.

"Hmmm." I let it pass. "Well, you're going to the Formal together, right?"

She nodded again.

"So there's nothing to worry about, is there? Trust me. After this, he'll be unable to resist."

I'm ashamed to say, I was getting a bit turned on, thinking about all of this. This is what happens, you see, when you live in the lion's lair. I shifted on the bed and adjusted myself. I thought of my mother, and the moment passed. "Well, we'll talk about that some more, later. In the meantime, the best thing is to concentrate on the Epiphany Formal. Can you do that?"

Emily nodded, seemingly reassured, although, really, I couldn't think why.

"Thank you. I know you're only thinking of me."

I smiled at her. "No worries. Shall we go down to town now and get a coffee?"

We walked down through the cold streets together. It was the fourth afternoon in a row I had spent alone with her.

That night I drank too much on my own in The Marlowe. I couldn't turn off that thing which had clicked in my brain

294

when I had been sitting in Emily's room. It buzzed inside, a frayed electric wire, shooting a current through me that I could only hope to deaden with alcohol. Why was she doing what I said? Was I really that persuasive?

"It's what she wants," I kept telling myself. "It's what she wants, and so she'll have it, and I'll be there to pick up the pieces." I'd laughed a hard laugh then, and a few people had looked over at me. I shook my head and tried to think about something else.

An older version of me seemed to sit at another table in the pub. My eyes were finding it difficult to focus, and I could see my shape, watching me, out of the corner of my eye. I kept snapping my head around, as if to catch me, but I would always be gone by the time I looked round. The old me seemed to get up at one point, just before the landlord turfed me out on to the street. *It's not even last orders*, I remember slurring at him as he bundled us out of the door. But, just before that, the old me had said something which I remember very clearly when I made it back to my room.

Zack was out. I stood at the sink in our room and despite the white toothpaste crusts trickling down the mirror, I could see my reflection. I mouthed what my old self had said to me as if I couldn't say it out loud, as if doing so would crack a thunderbolt in the sky, a pinprick of evil, spotted in a drooling mouth, yawning open, revealing jagged and sharpened teeth. I was on this trajectory now, and that was that. My education from Greene had taught me that at least.

I said it out loud at last and afterwards I vowed that I would never think of it or the old me again. I ripped the picture of Beckett off the wall by my desk and tossed it into the bin by the door. I'd stuck it up there days ago to taunt me almost. Make me *feel* what it was he was trying to teach. But it was too late now. I knew, I knew, I knew, so *fuck you, Beckett*. The words I mouthed were these:

Emily doesn't want it. Emily only thinks she's fuckable because of people like you.

I stared into my eyes.

Me. People like me. I was just like them. The Nicks and the Shortys. I had vaulted myself to lofty heights, I was the ironic observer. But the truth? I saw my mouth form the words. As soon as I was sexually excited by her, I was just like them.

I was just like them.

CHAPTER
FORTY-ONE

Wednesday 24 May, 8.30 p.m.

Stephanie sat in a turquoise sari in the small reception of the Durham police station, curled into herself, an injured tropical bird, shrunken by the drab and grey which surrounded her. Martin had come straight from the evidence room once she had been told the counsellor had turned up, wanting to see her. She looked at her through the glass in the door before going through. What secrets did this woman know?

"Ms Suleiman?" she said, moving to stand in front of her.

Stephanie looked up and smiled. "Ah," she said softly. "You have dashed to see me."

Martin shifted on her feet, confused. "I was told *you* wanted to see *me*," she said.

Stephanie nodded. "Yes, but you came fast. You know I may have something to say." Martin gestured for Stephanie to follow her, vaguely irritated by the woman's mysterious circus act routine. They walked into the cheerless interview room off the main reception area, and Martin offered Stephanie a seat.

"Actually, Ms Suleiman, you've saved me a trip, as I had wanted to ask you something quickly."

Stephanie nodded. "Yes?"

"We've been told that you had been seeing Simon Rush for some sessions, earlier in the year. Is that right?"

"Yes. I saw him for about four months of last year and then at the beginning of this one."

"And why did those sessions stop?"

Stephanie shrugged. "He just stopped coming. I can't force students to come."

Martin looked at her. "Did you try and persuade him to come back?"

"I think I sent him an email, but he never replied."

"Ah," Martin said, thinking this through, "and what was your impression of Simon? Why had he come to see you in the first place?"

"I'm not sure I'm at liberty to discuss that with you, Inspector Martin," Stephanie answered. "He is not on trial, is he?"

Martin nodded. "Sure." She paused. "But you can tell me your professional opinion, right? Was Simon suffering from any apparent disorders?"

Stephanie sighed and folded her arms. "Simon was under some pressure, yes. But I don't think you would call it a disorder as such, though, no."

Martin was quiet for a moment, digesting this. "Thank you," she said. "Now, what can I do for you?"

Stephanie reached into her handbag and pushed a tape across the table towards Martin, who picked it up and studied it.

298

"What's this?"

"A tape of my interviews with Emily leading up to just before we broke up for the Easter holidays."

Martin looked at Stephanie's face closely. Her lips trembled slightly. "A tape? Of Emily speaking?" Stephanie nodded her head. "Talking to you about what was going on in her life literally weeks before she was murdered?" Martin continued, her words hanging in the air in the clouds of a glowering storm. She swallowed, trying to control herself. Why hadn't this woman given them this before now? Clenching her fists open and shut, she spoke carefully.

"Can you explain to me, Ms Suleiman, why you have concealed this evidence until now?"

Stephanie shook her head sadly. "It is something outside myself." She shrugged. "I cannot explain it."

Martin bit her lip. "Has anyone else heard what's on the tape?"

"No."

"You didn't think this might be crucial evidence perhaps? Something which the police would like to hear?"

Stephanie looked down at her hands. "Yes, I did. But . . ." She paused, gathering her thoughts. "I wanted to get things straight in my head. I wanted to think things through."

"What did you need to think through?"

Stephanie looked at Martin, clear-eyed. "This is only half of the story."

"What is?"

Stephanie patted the table. "This tape. What Emily says."

Martin waited a moment before speaking. "Who has the other half of the story?" She put her head on one side, thinking, looking at the counsellor. "Nick?"

Stephanie smiled. "I told you before, we cannot know everything." She was silent for a second. They faced each other. Martin could hear the other woman's slow breath, the sparkle of the unsaid words on her tongue like water running over stones, the dazzle of them, what they would bring. *Come to me*, she thought for the first time since the interview with Rush. *Make the puzzle fit*.

"Emily did not tell me everything. On this tape, there is merely her version of events. What she felt, what happened to her."

"That's the key, Ms Suleiman," Martin said slowly. "That is it. What we're looking for. Emily's version of events."

"There is another version. Something further which may help you. I have been wrong to hide it . . ." Martin waited, her nerves tingling, knowing the words before they even left the counsellor's mouth. She almost spoke them with her.

"Daniel Shepherd," Stephanie said, her eyes drifting to the wall, unable to look at Martin, who nodded once. "Yes, the other version is Daniel Shepherd's."

CHAPTER
FORTY-TWO

I woke up the morning afterwards with a hangover but a fresh mind. I put the thoughts I'd been having before to one side. I was going to win Emily. I would fix it so that everything she loved about Nick would come crashing down on her like the concertina of a collapsing skyscraper, leaving her scrabbling on her back in the dust. The Epiphany Formal dinner was just around the corner, the Easter holidays looming like some awful cut-off point when I would be separated from Emily. I had to win her before then.

Emily had told me Nick had more photos of the two of them, that she was scared he would be showing them around. I didn't think he had done anything with them yet but I wanted him to. That would show Emily one last time the kind of person he was. If she was going to come to me, to be mine, everyone had to see them.

They called it *liquor* sometimes at Durham. That sluttishness. It was the label of being desired. Guys would stare at particular girls and say she gave good liquor. It conjured up images of sweets and candy, skirts like belts, rolling tongues and perfumed necks. That was what Emily had thought she wanted, what she had pretended to be with Nick, and I was going to give it to her. She didn't realize that, by becoming that girl, she would lose something of herself.

The boys might love her, but only for a fuck, a masturbation aid. She did know, though, that the girls would hate her, and that was why she was now afraid about the photos Nick had. Emily wasn't half as strong as she gave out.

I knew the real Emily — the wholesome girl I'd met on the train. The one who reflected that part of me that I liked, that I knew I could be. Once I'd broken the wild horse of the liquor, I'd have her back, begging to be *with me*. I was her Rasputin. She would come to me for everything: advice, counsel, succour. It would seem as innocuous as friendship, but it was more than that. By the time I had finished with my plan, she would be able to do nothing without me.

I followed Nick one afternoon. I happened to see him walking across Elvet Bridge and seized the opportunity to shadow him, tailing him all the way up to the library. I must admit to being surprised that he would go there of all places but I figured, if he was going to land the inevitable job in a law firm, he would need at least passable grades in the upcoming exams. I waited outside for him. He wasn't in there long.

I sipped from a lukewarm coffee and leaned over the balustrade where I had seen Shorty with the first photo of Emily. I thought back to that time and how innocent I was about it all then. Something tugged in my brain about all this research I was doing. It was sullying me. The more I read and the more images I saw, the more indelibly I felt their influence on the way I looked at the world. When I saw girls walking along these days, I immediately graded them into "Hot or Not". I couldn't help myself.

I would find myself gazing at their behinds, absently wondering whether they were wearing thongs or panties. I would notice their cleavage, give it a mark out often for bigness, for pertness, without thinking about it. I had stopped looking at women's faces, I noticed only their bodies, undulating hills of invitation. As I stood there, with my coffee in hand, the aroma reminding me of my reading in coffee shops, the simple pleasure of a good book and a comfy chair, I felt disgusted with myself. I felt, not turned on, but as if I had been turned.

These thoughts snapped shut like switching off a television set as soon as I saw Nick emerge, however. He walked out of the entrance doors and shifted his shoulders somewhat, as if releasing a burden. Or shaking off the dust of the analytical interior from which he had come. I straightened at my post at the balustrade and fell in with him as he jogged down the stone steps.

"Hi, Nick," I said casually, as if it were only mere chance that I had seen him there.

He looked to his side, recognized me and then looked straight ahead again. I was about his height but I used to feel smaller when I was in his vicinity. Now I towered above him, my power transcending his physical stature. He had said nothing in reply to my greeting.

"I wanted to talk to you," I persisted. "I need to talk to you about Emily."

He looked at me at that. "Emily?" he asked, bemused, as if I should have anything to do with her. Foolish. "What about her?"

"I wanted to ask you what you were going to do with the photos."

Nick stopped then and turned to face me. "What are you talking about?"

I looked him direct in the face. We were like titans. Sea-gods crouching in swirling under-waters, sea-weed dripping off our crowns. Or lions, perhaps, on the savannah, hind legs curled, ready to pounce.

"I know about the new photos, Nick."

He folded his arms, a gesture designed to deflect attention from the surprise which skimmed across his face. God forbid he should ever be anything other than cool. He laughed faintly. "*You* do?" he said, disbelieving. I nodded, smiling.

"I do. So . . ."

"So, what?"

"So — what are you going to do with them? You can't keep them to yourself."

Nick shifted. I almost felt sorry for him. He didn't have a clue how to deal with this.

"It's not fair," I continued. "They're hot, right?"

He couldn't help himself, he smirked.

"So you should do the civilized thing and post them. Let everyone get a look. Emily won't mind."

Some sort of decency flitted across Nick's brain, I could tell. For a moment at least. "Hang on, dude. Let me get this straight. You're telling me you know about the latest photos? How?"

"Emily told me," I said. "She tells me everything."

Nick bit his lip. "And now you're saying Emily won't mind if I spread them around? Show them to people? Everyone?"

I nodded again. "Think about it, Nick. Think of the kudos. Everyone will fucking *love* it." I saw this, too, skip across his thoughts. The slaps on the back, the hilarity in Joyce bar, how awesome everyone would think he was. He was still

304

confused, though. Maybe he wasn't such a dickhead as I'd thought.

"If I do it, though, are you sure she won't get angry? I still want a shag at the Formal." He grinned at me like a retard.

Maybe not. Dickhead central.

I shook my head, put my index finger to my lips.

"She's all yours, dude, you know it." I wanted to puke as the words left my mouth. "She'll still go with you to the Formal, she can't resist you. Parade her around. Show everyone what a nice piece of pussy you've got for yourself."

Nick smiled, almost to himself. His eyes glazed a little as he dreamed the whole scenario. He held out his hand, and I shook it. We both had dry palms, calm as we were in our machinations.

"Nice one, dude. Good stuff." He strode off without looking back. I stood there just beyond the library stairs, watching him walk away. A lump burned in my throat as I thought about what this meant. What it meant for Emily. How she didn't understand that I was doing this all for her own good. I swallowed hard, down into the darkness of my gut. I would not cry. Crying was for losers.

CHAPTER
FORTY-THREE

Wednesday 24 May, 9.11 p.m.

Having moved Stephanie into an interview room after she had arranged care of her daughter, Martin had informed Michael Brabents' lawyer that Emily's father would be spending a night in the cells while they collated more evidence.

She turned off the tape of Emily speaking as Stephanie Suleiman looked at her across the table. The interview tape, on the other hand, kept rolling. "So the night of the Epiphany Formal back in March was when Emily started self-harming? Because more photos were passed around of her with Nick then?"

Stephanie nodded. "I think so, yes."

"What did you think about it? What Emily had said? Didn't it concern you?"

Stephanie sat straighter in her chair. She looked around the room. "May I have some water?"

Martin got to her feet and opened the door, asking the custody officer to bring some. She returned to her seat and gestured towards Stephanie. "Please . . ."

"The thing is, Detective Martin —"

"Detective Inspector."

"I was frustrated with Emily. I felt that . . ." She paused, incessantly twirling her long plait around her wrist. "I felt that she wasn't making as much progress as I would have liked."

The counsellor paused as a knock came at the door and Jones walked in carrying a jug of water and two plastic glasses. She placed them on the table in between the women, and Martin poured some into a glass before passing it across to Stephanie.

Jones sat herself down at the table, next to Martin. "I'm Detective Sergeant Jones, I work with the DI," she introduced herself.

Stephanie sipped at her water. "Less than I had hoped, I mean. Look, let me be plain."

"Please," Martin said again.

"Emily had certain ideas about things. Many of the girls her age do. It's to do with their culture. They have thoughts about the place of women in society, how they can work within it, that sort of thing."

"And . . .?"

"It's frustrating for me. It was hard to keep going with her, you know? Sometimes, I felt as if I was banging my head against a brick door . . ."

"Wall."

Stephanie looked at her.

"It doesn't matter. Carry on," Martin muttered.

"I couldn't seem to get through to her. A lot of the upset she was suffering was down to her own actions. She seemed masochistic in this way."

Martin sat up in her chair. "Forgive me, but what is your job if it's not to help people who are harming themselves? By definition people don't go to therapy if they're A-okay and coping brilliantly with things, surely? Emily needed your help."

Stephanie shook her head. "I did my best, Detective Martin."

Jones glanced sideways at her boss. "What sort of things?" she asked, turning back to Stephanie. "What was Emily doing that you disapproved of?"

Stephanie sighed and flicked her plait off her shoulder. "Not disapproved of, so much. These girls. They think they have it in them to bargain, you know? With their bodies? They think it's currency. I'll sleep with you, and then you'll be my boyfriend. They don't understand . . ."

"That it's not like that?" Jones asked.

"Things aren't so different, Ms Suleiman, surely, from when we were growing up?" Martin interrupted. "It's always been the same. Once you put out, you're damaged goods."

Stephanie looked at Martin patiently. "That's what I'm trying to say. You and I . . ." she waved her hand between herself and Martin, "we know that. It's how we were brought up. But *these* girls. They seem to have missed that lesson. Emily was convinced she could have it all. That she could parade herself like one of those . . . those *bunnies*."

"Playboy bunnies?" Jones questioned.

"Yes, like that. She could prance and dance, and it would lure them in."

"Them?" Martin asked, leaning forwards.

The counsellor looked sad. "Nick." She wrung her hands together, a panoply of worry. "She already had Daniel, I fear."

"What do you mean, she had Daniel? Tell me about that. How did Emily know him?"

"Emily was self-destructing. Nothing would stop her. Daniel tried to help her in actual fact. He wrote to me, to ask if he could help."

"Wrote to you?"

"Yes, by email."

"Did you discuss Emily with Daniel?" Martin asked.

Stephanie shook her head emphatically. "No, of course not. But I knew he was her friend. Perhaps her only true one. Daniel himself had issues. He was being given a hard time by the fellow students. They ostracized him, made him feel alone. He was a victim too. Daniel was very alone . . ." her voice tailed off as she looked down at the table.

"Who is Daniel Shepherd, Stephanie?" Martin asked abruptly.

Stephanie seemed confused. "Well, he's, uh, he's a student here in Durham."

Martin looked at her for a second. "How do you know that? Did Daniel's emails come from a student account?"

"No they didn't. But, he said he was a student. At Nightingale College."

Martin looked down at her lap. "Do you have a copy of these emails, Ms Suleiman?" she asked softly.

Stephanie took a breath before nodding. "Yes, yes I do." Reaching into her bag, she passed some papers over the table to Martin, who bent her head to study them. She read rapidly: "*I came to Durham on a cold October morning, on the first train out of London. My mother had come with me to King's Cross station to see me off, and she carried on standing forlornly at the ticket barrier, long after the train had pulled out of the station . . .*"

"This is Daniel's first email to you?" she asked, looking up briefly.

Stephanie shook her head. "No. The first was about how he wanted to help Emily. This was the second. All of them . . . well, they followed on from this. How he met Emily, how their friendship grew."

Martin nodded without looking up, her hands moving through the papers, drinking in the words like water.

CHAPTER
FORTY-FOUR

The Epiphany Formal was always held in the Joyce refectory. So Emily had said. I had never been to one before, obviously, and, with my current status at Durham thus, was about as likely to go in the future as I was to walk on the moon. Emily had got me a ticket before she'd changed her mind about the whole thing. She had shoved it, crumpled up, into my pigeonhole; it had looked like a piece of junk mail which I had very nearly thrown away. When I smoothed it out, though, I saw a picture of a boy and a girl in one of those pseudo-vintage black and white photos that you find on the front of birthday cards in the *humorous* section in shops. The couple were dancing, the girl being thrown back in some kind of adventurous dance move. "Let's screw again like we did last summer!" the girl was saying to the boy, her lipsticked mouth open in a batshit crazy sort of laugh. The boy looked bored, his eyes on something in the middle distance. He wasn't answering the girl but he had a thought bubble over his head. "I think she means the twist," he appeared to be thinking. The details for the dinner and dance followed on. I sighed and, for a moment, leaned my head against the wooden rows of cubby holes. This is what my life had come down to. I had actively got myself invited to something like this.

I had the same thought as I stood outside Joyce on the night of the Formal, holding the ticket by my fingertips. If I could've held it at arm's length without being considered odd, I would have done it. I was sweating from my walk up the hill despite the cold. This was the trouble with Durham. The weather was always freezing, but you arrived everywhere boiling hot from the exertion of hauling yourself up and down the blasted hills. I was wearing a dinner jacket with a black tie. My second time of doing so in six months. It was unheard of.

I looked at the door into the college and swallowed. This was going to be hard for me. I had no one inside as an ally. I knew Emily was coming with Nick. After I'd spoken to him outside the library, Nick had emailed me to tell me he'd bumped into Emily in town and, with his usual romantic panache, had asked her to tag along with him. I couldn't get over the use of the phrase *tag along*. The guy was a dick. Nevertheless, they would be there together, and with no Emily to rely on, I had no one to help me out, prop me up socially.

I breathed out, hating myself for my timidity. I looked back down the hill to where I had come from and thought about jacking the whole thing in. I could go home now, take this monkey suit off and spend the evening reading *Gravity's Rainbow*. I looked back again at the Joyce door, hearing the hum of voices behind it, the clink of glasses. The room would be filled by now with a hundred boys who looked superficially like me and a hundred girls with saucer eyes and moistened lips, clinging on to vessels of sparkly wine, giggling, swirling the liquid around in their glasses before dashing it into their mouths. How on earth could I go into this?

312

Just then, the door opened, and there was Zack, my room-mate, standing silhouetted in the archway. He smiled at me.

"Hello, old sport," he said in some kind of Gatsby-esque imitation.

"What are you doing here, old chap?" I returned, the irony splodging from my tongue on to the cold pavement.

"Mate of mine here needed help with the sound system. This one's on its last legs." Zack looked at me with something approaching a twinkle in his eye. "They ignore the geeks until something breaks and then they're all over us, treating us like Steve fucking Jobs." He shrugged. "Said I'd help him out if he got me pissed for free." He let the door bang behind him as he came and stood next to me on my pavement-hell. "Saw you lurking outside from out the window. Here to snag that posh totty of yours, are you?"

I smiled, inclined my head slightly.

Zack nodded. "Well, stick with me, Danny boy. I'll see you right. Cal's got a bottle of Dalwhinnie behind the decks, and you can sit with us during dinner if you like."

My smile turned genuine, and I felt a rush of affection for this boy who zoomed in and out of our shared room with such energy and lust for the life he was living. I was suddenly and sharply jealous of him and his certainty about himself. He was nobody other than Zack the physics geek and sometime DJ. He knew it and he was happy with it. And, as it turned out, he was also pretty generous and friendly to wankers like me who only cared about posh totty. I slapped him on the back and we went into Joyce together. I needed a drink.

I could see them. They wittered and twittered like birds. Hunching over their phones, vultures over a kill, picking over

313

Emily's bones, over and over. She looked terrified, clutching on to her gin and tonic with white knuckles. She gave a panicked sideways smile to Annabel, who stood next to her, glowering. She shifted on her feet, back and forth, a little lonely do-si-do. Nick was standing a way off, his thumbs in his pockets. He was surveying his kingdom, a half-grin on his chiselled, handsome face. How I hated him.

I leaned on the DJ booth Zack and his mate had fabricated in the dining room. They were busy playing the decks inside it as I slunk into its shadows, watching. I saw Emily go up to Nick, her eyebrows drawn together, a glint of a tear in the corner of one eye. He seemed to laugh, made to touch her face with his hand. She shook her head away.

You see? This is what I knew. I had given her what she wanted on a plate. And she would be sick with it. She would see that this wasn't it at all. She had given Nick what he salivated over; she thought she was fishing — hooking him with the pretty azure feathers on her fly, dancing over the dappled water, sunlight in her hair. She thought she could reel in him, toss her head, open her legs and that would make him desire her enough to stay. I could see it.

Two people, hundreds of people really, who thought they knew what they wanted, who thought they knew what they were. They wanted to feed their urges — of sex and drink and popularity. But deep down, the need was actually to destroy, to hurt and to maim — to become the sole survivor of those who were fit and strong and unconquerable. They didn't have the brains to articulate this so they snickered over others' mistakes, their need to annihilate sneaking up on them in bursts, expressing itself through their fingers on keyboards, rage erupting in intermittent surges, at one remove from whoever they were making their victim because they were just typing it and, anyway, it was *just a laugh*, wasn't it? Some people just couldn't *take a joke*.

Emily had that desire to destroy in her too, I knew it. She wanted to be the strongest of them all, the queen to Nick's king. I didn't mind that. But she had deluded herself in her methods. She had no faith in her real abilities. She had convinced herself that it was *her* right to use her body to garner attention. Nobody was forcing her, she was an independent young woman. But it was obvious to me that her body was nothing but the equivalent of the new hashtag on Twitter, the latest download on YouTube, a hot gig in Newcastle. Once it had been looked at, digested and belched over, it had no value. It was as meaningless as the King James Bible at an atheists' convention.

I wandered into the middle of the dance floor on my way out of the door, and turned back to look at Emily, who was standing almost behind Nick now, shielding herself from the disgust of others. Emily was a victim even though she thought she was a warrior. She was a victim because she didn't realize that her so-called right to show her body off, her hot buttery body — well, that right didn't come from her. We had made her think that. So clever of us. We made her think it was her decision, but where had she got that idea from? The notion that it was an expression of *strength* to take your clothes off and spread your legs? We were malevolence personified. I almost laughed as I watched her cower in the traffic lights of the dance floor. She would come running to me now.

I had made my way out of the dining room, into the JCR, a low-ceilinged room containing a couple of dozen stumpy chairs covered in a rough green material which matched the cabbage-patterned carpet. If Joyce was anything like Nightingale, on normal days people would wait here for the dining room doors to open, slumped in these chairs, occasionally reading the free newspapers left lying around but on the whole gossiping, picking their noses and generally loafing. Now, though, they were dressed up but pissed. Mascara streaks down their faces, untied bows dangling on to white shirts, dinner jackets discarded on the floor. A couple were practically copulating in one of the corners. I wanted to get out of there.

"Mate . . ."

It was Nick. He had followed me out. The fact that he called me his mate made me heave. I rolled round on my heels to face him.

"All right?"

I nodded.

"Worked like a charm. Everyone thinks it's wicked." He sniggered through his nose, snorting a little. "She's not that happy but . . ." He shrugged. He couldn't have cared less. He rubbed his hand over the back of his neck. A drum beat pulsed through the dining room doors and then a wave of melody as the doors opened as someone came out. Nick swayed slightly on his feet; his eyes were a tad glazed. I had still said nothing.

"Well . . ." He faltered, confused. "Well done, anyway, mate. Nice one." He gave the loud laugh that makes an appearance in an embarrassed silence. He slapped me on the shoulder and bumbled past. Presumably to the gents, where he would fumble to get his dick out, prop himself up at the urinal with one raised arm, the other trying to control his piss,

316

which would spill out over the floor, drops splashing on to his expensive suit trousers.

I continued to stand in the same position, looking at the empty space where he had been standing. And then there she was in front of me. It had been her who had opened the dining room doors. Smoke seemed to rise from her. I could imagine snakes tumbling from her hair, frozen jade in her eyes turning me to stone.

"It was Nick," I managed to say.

Emily came up to me. Her breasts grazed my shirt. She raised her chin so that her lips were millimetres away from mine. "He told me you spoke to him, that you told him to put them online."

I could feel her breath on my mouth. She smelled of the quinine in tonic water. I wanted to push my hands into her hair, kiss her; feel her tongue on mine. I wanted her so much. I wanted to devour her.

"It's Easter now," she whispered. "Fuck off back to wherever it is you live." Her voice shook. "Fuck *off*. Do not contact me. Get this," she moved on to her tiptoes, her eye for my eye. "I want nothing to do with you ever again." She paused and then moved her mouth to my ear. "Stay away from me, understand?" she hissed before pushing me to one side and banging through the common room doors towards the exit to the street.

I collapsed on to one of the green chairs. I could hear . . . Billy Joel I think, singing in the dining room about being a backstreet guy. I laughed to myself, looking at my hands on my knees. Then I rubbed my hands across my face and realized that I was crying.

CHAPTER
FORTY-FIVE

Wednesday 24 May, 10.07 p.m.

Martin sat in the incident room with Jones opposite her. They sat in silence, thinking, as the night-time traffic noise drifted in through the half-open window. A pigeon landed unabashed on the windowsill, and Martin stared at it without seeing until it ruffled its feathers and flew off.

"The fact is," Martin said, mid thought-stream, "Emily voluntarily offered herself up to Nick again, and those photos he spread around on the night of the Formal. I mean, that's what she says on the tape, right?" She took a swig from the bottle of water on her desk.

Jones nodded.

"But the emails from Daniel up until that point seem to imply that he was the one orchestrating things. That he persuaded Emily to pose for Nick in the hope that Nick would like her. And then Nick would run true to form, show the photos to everyone, and Daniel would be there to pick up the pieces." Martin paused. "Why did Daniel stop emailing Stephanie Suleiman after the Easter holidays? She had one last one from him about the fight at the Formal and him mooning over Emily down in Brighton and then nothing. And these emails in any case," she continued, "if he was emailing Stephanie Suleiman an account of his days like a modern-day equivalent of Anne fucking Frank," she wiped her bottom lip with her thumb, "then who else was he talking to?" She snapped her fingers. "What about the Zack he talks about in them — his room-mate? Can we find him? Maybe Daniel's using an alias or something in his emails? Maybe he wanted to hide his identity from Stephanie Suleiman. But if we find Zack, we can track him down at Nightingale."

"Will do ASAP," Jones chewed her lip. "With Emily, though, it's not as simple as that, I don't think," she said, tracing a finger around the lip of her Coke bottle.

"Tell me."

"It's like with dogs . . ."

Martin frowned at her.

"Bear with me. I can't remember the guy that did it, but it's like training. Put a bowl of steak down next to a bowl of shit, beat the dog enough when he goes for the steak and praise him when he goes for the shit. Soon he'll be eating shit of his own accord."

Martin stared at Jones.

"Doesn't mean the dog likes shit," Jones finished.

"Pavlov."

"What's that, boss?"

"Pavlov was the guy with the dogs — whose experiment you've so eloquently described, Jones."

"Right. Well, you know what I mean. Emily got attention for sleeping with Nick. She did it voluntarily.

Doesn't mean she wanted pictures of it being tweeted all over the internet."

"I don't know . . ."

Jones waited. A car beeped in the street outside as the sound of grinding lorry brakes interrupted the silence. Martin was lost in thought.

"Boss?"

Ignoring her, Martin smacked her hand on the table. "But who the fuck is Daniel Shepherd?"

"We've sent the thumb drive with the emails on it to Forensics. They may be able to trace the account. But, look here . . ." Jones passed a sheaf of papers to Martin. "We finally got the psych report back on Rush."

Martin riffled through the paper. "What does it say in a nutshell?" she asked impatiently.

"Nothing untoward. Depression, they say. Anxiety brought on by stress of the college presidency and exams."

Martin whipped her head up to look at Jones, amazed. "He's not a zoomer?"

Jones shook her head. "Not according to this."

"Do they mention anything to do with his mum's death?" Martin asked quietly, flicking through the report.

"Maybe it was all an act?" Jones said.

"But then why confess in the first place?" Martin asked, thinking. She swung her chair round in a circle, her arms behind her head.

"He confesses, pulls a fruit-loop act, then withdraws the confession, meaning we've got nothing on him. Boom — he gets himself out of college to recover from stress and gets Daddy's attention at last?" Jones said, thinking out loud. She glanced at Martin to see if she was agreeing.

"Daddy's attention I can buy. But have we really got nothing on him without the confession, Jones? We've got the photo Emily took of him and Mason and emailed to herself the day she was killed. What would happen if Daddy saw that? Saw his son flirting with Mason. It's a small step to then finding out about the parties. If Mervyn Rush is the bully I think he is, Simon would want to do anything to avoid having to face his reaction to that. Does that include confessing?" Martin sighed. "We've still got Brabents on ice." She looked at her watch before rubbing her hands over her face. "Brabents, Rush, Shepherd, Nick Oliver," she mumbled. "One of those fuckers did it."

Jones waited for more, but nothing came. "Boss . . ."

"Yep," Martin answered, her head down, glancing back through the papers.

"Speaking of Nick Oliver, I think we should get him in now. Talk to him with a spotlight in his face. He admits himself he was down at the boathouse the night Emily was murdered. He says he left not long after her. Also, we haven't got to the bottom of that video of him with Emily. He's lied to us already about the level of his involvement with her, it might . . ."

Martin jumped up from her seat and turned to head towards the door. "Jones, you are a friggin' genius!"

"What, boss? I'm sorry, I . . ."

"Come with me."

"Where are we going?"

"We'll get Nick in first thing in the morning and we can start the process of getting Rush back in for a chat. No reason not to now. So let's get to the evidence room, go through it all again. The photos, the video." She turned back to look at Jones, who was rapidly following her along the corridor. "And while you're doing that," Martin grinned. "I'm going to have a wee dram with that journalist, Sean Egan."

CHAPTER
FORTY-SIX

I borrowed Mother's car most days, during the Easter break. It was the coldest Easter that had ever been known in a zillion years, so they said. And it *was* cold. Milder down in the south than the bitter rub of Durham, but the sharpness of the wind matched the ice in my spine. I wanted to see my breath in the air; I needed to remember that I did actually exist.

I drove down to Brighton a great deal. I've always thought the beach unattractive there but I needed ugliness, and the water is greenish so I could relate to it, my gills were the same. I was accompanied on these trips by waves of nausea that never seemed to leave me. I couldn't eat. I would have to hold my nose and breath as I walked past the few hot dog stands open on the promenade, the smell of frying onions pulling bile through me like a digestive magnet.

Despite the cold weather, Brighton is always full. I needed people. I would put my headphones on and walk the beach, watching my feet pound the shingle in a cocoon of sound. I didn't read a single book in four weeks.

I imagined Nick in Africa. Bouncing along in a jeep, laughing loudly, holding a rifle, pinning a gazelle to the ground with his bare hands. His skin would be tanned, his hair lightened by the sun, flopping into his face. He would wear white T-shirts and khaki shorts. Drink Tusker beer out of bottles, play pool in the safari camp as giraffes bent their elegant necks to the watering hole in the distance. As I thought about him, I would find myself running. I couldn't help myself. All the hatred I felt towards him would rush upwards in me, a fountain of loathing frothing at my mouth. I would have to spit bitter phlegm out on to the beach pebbles and run on them, pounding them, tearing my ankle ligaments to shreds.

Often I would stand and look at the fragments of the West Pier, its burned-out shell. Everything about Brighton reminded me of myself. I would imagine flying through the breaks in the wooden frame, swooping down on to the blistered struts, running my hands over the scars of the flames. She would come into my head then. Her face, swimming above the water in the clouds. Her beautiful face with the kind eyes. My eyes would burn at the injustice of it all. To be so shut out.

Fuck off. I want nothing to do with you ever again, understand?

Over and over again, interminable waves crashing on to the shore, no chord change ever again. I would scrape and scrape at it, whittling it down inside my head, sometimes lifting my face and opening my palms to the beach in bafflement. *How could this have happened? How could I have got it so wrong?* My tears of self-pity could fill up another five fucking oceans. I disgusted myself.

My mother would look up at me from the kitchen table when I would eventually bang back into the house. She would put cups of tea in front me that remained untouched. It broke my heart a little bit more, those cold cups of tea.

The utter rejection of them, which I did, knowingly. After a while, she would pick the cup up and tip its contents down the plug-hole in the kitchen sink. I would watch her do it.

We didn't speak, really. I couldn't think where to start, and she didn't have the necessary words. There were no words in reality, so I can't blame her. She would have had to climb down into the mining shaft of my brain, scout around in the blackness without a torch, decipher the cave drawings on the walls, translate the foreign images into something she could understand before she could find the right words. I needed to do the same. Except I had no energy for it. I lay listless on my bed after my drives to the sea. I strummed imaginary chords on my stomach. Remembering.

It was a clear Wednesday morning when I sat up abruptly in bed. For some reason an old Chinese saying that my dad used to mutter to himself on grey Saturday mornings when he'd have to leave the house for an emergency call-out came into my mind: *when events develop to the extreme, the trend will be reversed*. He was always a bit of a hackneyed philosopher, my dad. My bedroom curtains were drawn, and I jumped out of bed to open them. Light doused the room, and for the first time in weeks I felt invigorated.

I clapped my hands together and sat at my desk, lifted the lid of my laptop. I opened up the chat website I knew most of Durham belonged to. I paused, my fingers delicate over the keyboard; light shone from their tips. I picked a pseudonym and created an account within five seconds. I found Emily's profile easily. It was then that I paused for a second, seeing her face; her hair was wind-tousled in the picture. She was so pretty. But then a beat pulsated through me, a confident

325

cadence at last. I typed five words as a comment under her profile photo and pressed send without thinking any more about it. I buzzed. Finally, I was doing something.

CHAPTER
FORTY-SEVEN

Wednesday 24 May, 10.42 p.m.

Egan was one of only three people still in The Royal Oak, already sitting at the bar on a stool when Martin got there. The barman frowned at the lateness of the hour as the pub door opened but, recognizing Martin, he gave her a nod as she headed to the bar and rested her foot on the brass rail which ran along the bottom of it.

"Bottle of Bud, please," she said to the barman before turning to Egan. He tilted his whisky glass in her direction before taking a drink. "Cheers."

She slid a fiver along the top of the bar and took a lug from the bottle in front of her. She sighed appreciatively. "Ah, I needed that," she said, with a smile.

"What can I do for you, Martin?" Egan asked. "Seen so much of you lately, anyone would think you were stalking me."

She inclined her head. "Whatever, Egan. I just wanted a quick chat after our little talk earlier — iron out a few things. Our relationship," she swung her hand between the two of them, "reminds me of that kids' story. You know, the one about the tortoise and the hare?"

Egan looked at her, his hand still cradling his glass.

"There you are," she said, "bounding along, fast as anything, dashing this way and that. And then there's me. Slow and steady. Taking it all in. Thinking things over, working out everyone's rightful place in this little drama."

Egan gave a surprised laugh. "Little drama?" he said. "It's not little, Martin. The stuff happening at Joyce amongst the students is big. It's blowing up big time. I've got recorded interviews with people. Kids are coming forward, talking about what was going on. The bullying. Sexual bullying. People other than the Brabents girl were victims of it."

"But how do you know all of that, Egan?" she asked lightly. "Where have you been digging? Seems to me, you've raced yourself up a storm here. A storm in a teacup." She smiled at him. "Where's your evidence for all of this?"

He smirked, shifted confidently on his seat. "I have evidence. As I said."

She nodded and took another pull of her beer. "It makes me wonder."

"What does it make you wonder?"

"Where you appeared from, out of the blue. How you knew so much, so early." She shrugged. "Makes me suspicious. After all," she put her chin in her hand, "that's my job, right? To wonder about things?"

Egan took another sip of his drink, keeping eye contact with her.

328

"So there are three things that I think are definite possibilities in this case," Martin continued. "The first is that you've been trying to wheedle your way into the lives of a few of the students here for quite a while now — Annabel Smith for one. I think you got some information from her about the trolling, the parties. And then she texted you the morning Emily's body was found, making you race out of your hole and into the fray like a little rat.

"Second, I think it was you who sent an anonymous email to Rebecca Brabents attaching the video of her daughter in a, shall we say, compromising position."

Egan said nothing.

"I'm almost certain that that was you, and I have no doubt we can prove the technology of it. But if that is the case, the question remains, how did you get access to the video? We'd already closed down the student media site, Emily's social media. We were the only ones with access to that information." She carefully put her beer down on the bar top and leaned forwards, closer to Egan. "Which leads me to my final conclusion."

Egan's eyes darted away from Martin, to his glass and then to the mirror behind the bar. She looked up and met his eyes in the reflection, her head still bent to his. "That conclusion, Egan," she whispered, "is that you have been in contact with someone who has a copy of that video and that that contact was made before any recent events took place. In other words," Martin's lips grazed Egan's earlobes, "before Emily was murdered."

Egan retreated, leaning back and glancing down, away from Martin. She looked at him calmly with a cool smile before finishing off her beer and putting it back on the bar.

"I think it's your round, Egan," she said, gesturing to the barman.

Egan got his wallet out of his back pocket reluctantly. Put a note down on the counter. "I was sent it by a student about a month ago," he said.

"And . . .?"

"He got in touch with me. Said he had a story about what was going on here. Kids were out of control. Fucking each other, posting stuff online. He said he could show me. The thing is, Martin," Egan said, turning to her, mustering some confidence. "Durham's old school, right? The blue-rinse brigade love to come here, have a little look round the colleges, go to the cathedral, watch the young and the beautiful walking in and out of their ivory towers." He took a sip of his drink. "Doesn't match up with the image, does it? If what's really going on is a bunch of animals copulating in their own shit."

Martin waited, knowing he would continue. He loved the sound of his own voice too much.

"Especially not if it's condoned." He nodded his head. "You know what I mean. This whole thing's been swept under the carpet, and why? Because it suits the people at the top. People like Principal Mason. You know it as well as I do." He shrugged. "So don't give me a hard time about it. I'm just trying to get the truth across."

"Oh, Egan," she sighed, folding her arms. "You wouldn't know what the truth was if it gave you a lap dance." She paused. "What was the name of the student?" Egan looked puzzled. "The one who sent you the email, Egan — come on, keep up. What was the name of the kid who sent you the video you then helpfully sent to Emily's mother?"

Egan was silent.

"On your conscience, is it? Her suicide?"

"Fuck off, Martin."

"The name, Egan."

He looked up at her then, mumbling into his glass as he took another swig. "Kid was called Daniel Shepherd."

CHAPTER
FORTY-EIGHT

Thursday 25 May, 9.18 a.m.

Martin sat opposite Nick in the interview room. Jones was next to her, fiddling with the tape machine. Nick had asked for a lawyer, and she sat beside him, her hands folded in her lap, her Joseph suit too thick for the early heat of the day, yet she looked perfectly groomed, the ends of her sleek ponytail fringing her padded shoulders, pale-pink fingernails encasing her hands in a study of relaxed repose. Martin ran her fingers through her own unruly red hair. She had looked at herself in the mirror this morning, ignoring the other side of the bed, which remained unslept in. Jim had stayed in Newcastle the night before. With whom, she didn't know. She had tried to cover up the dark circles under her eyes and then given up, dashing out of the front door with no breakfast.

"We're just going to let you listen to this tape, if that's okay, Nick? And then we'll ask you some questions afterwards."

Nick glanced at his lawyer, who nodded. He looked back at Martin. "Fine," he said sullenly.

Jones turned on the tape, and Emily's voice bounced around the breeze-blocked walls of the small, hot room. Nick shuddered as he heard it, the Ghost of Christmas Past joining them at the table. Martin didn't take her eyes off him as Emily spoke.

"The night started well. It was really nice, you know? Everyone was in a good mood. Nick was being really sweet . . ."

Nick blinked slowly at this, his thumbs circling each other in a measured pace, a tiny red flush starting to creep across his cheeks from his ears. *He knows what Emily is going to say*, Martin thought.

"Anyway. It was fun to begin with. We had dinner. Some people started throwing food. It got a bit raucous. After we'd eaten, we went through to the bar while they changed things around in the dining room. The bar looked really pretty. They'd put decorations up, fairy lights."

"Were you drinking much?"

Nick exhaled loudly at this.

"I suppose so. I felt a bit — you know. Not too much. So then . . ."

"Then, what? Emily?"

"Then it all changed. We went back into the dining room. They'd set up the dance floor, there was a kind of DJ booth."

Nick shifted and recrossed his legs. His thumbs kept up their rhythmic circling. He looked down at his lap, his eyes hidden from Martin's stare.

"When we walked in, I felt, you know, the atmosphere had changed. People were staring at me, looking at me up and down. I felt . . ."

333

Sound of quiet sobbing.

"Here, Emily."

Sound of a nose being blown.

"Thanks. I felt, well, naked I suppose."

Nick sat up in his chair, ran his hands through his thick head of hair, still refusing to look at Martin, who eyeballed him mercilessly.

"What was it? Why did you feel this way?"

"I saw people looking down at their phones. They were laughing. Passing stuff around. I knew. It had happened before, I've told you." Pause. "I knew it was happening again. I went to Nick and asked him. Asked him why everyone was laughing."

"And what did he say?"

"Said I should chill out. That it was only a joke. He said . . ." sound of sniffing, ". . . that I shouldn't get all lesbian on him. If I couldn't take a joke then I shouldn't be with him."

Sound of a chair creaking.

"And what was the joke, Emily? What were you supposed to find so funny?"

Sound of crying.

"It was more photos of me. Me with Nick. Doing things with him."

The voices on the tape paused, although it carried on rolling, the sound like wind swishing through long grass. Martin continued to stare at Nick, whose crimson flush had now spread across his face, up to his hairline, where it met with beads of sweat. Martin leaned over the table and switched the tape off. She sat back in her

334

chair, bending one leg over the other in an expression of utter ease. She raised her eyebrows at Nick.

He said nothing.

"What did you do, Nick?" Martin asked after a while. "Get Emily on her knees, take a few happy snaps and then chuck 'em around your friends? *Again?*"

"There's no crime in passing around photos, as far as I'm aware," Nick's lawyer said. "Emily wasn't underage."

Martin shrugged. "Agreed. And no right to privacy, that's true. But what I'm interested in," she leaned forwards, "is a person who thinks that's okay. Thinks that's decent behaviour."

Nick laughed until his lawyer shot him a look. He rubbed his hand over his mouth, imprisoning further indiscretions. "What do you know about decency?" he muttered.

"I'm not even going to bother answering that," Martin said. "This is what I think happened. I think you and Emily got into a fight that night. She went home for Easter and you went off to — God knows where. And when you came back from the holidays . . ."

"What?" Nick sneered. "I'd festered about it for four weeks and then as soon as we got back, I dragged Emily off down to the weir and killed her? Give me a fucking break."

Martin scraped her chair back from the table in the interview room, the noise of it making Nick jump in his seat. "What time did you leave the party at the boathouse, Nick?" she asked rapidly.

"Uh, about 7.30 p.m. I think. I've told you that."

"We've got several witnesses who say that Emily left the boathouse at around the same time. And yet," she paused with a disbelieving smile, "weirdly, you didn't see each other." She waited with her arms folded. "I think you did see Emily, Nick. I think you're lying," she said at last.

Nick flushed red, cockiness seeping from him, a panicked boy left in its wake. "I didn't do it. I swear to you," he said, rubbing his face into his sleeve. Martin thought back to when they had first talked to him, outside the lecture theatre, bounding along the corridors; the epitome of chutzpah. Now he seemed shrunken and worn out. She softened her voice and spoke quickly before the lawyer could remind him he didn't need to answer her questions.

"I've been doing this a while, Nick, and do you know what I know?"

He looked up at her, his arm still resting on his forehead like a schoolboy.

"It's better to tell. That weight? The one you've got on you, all the time — pressing down on you like a ton of bricks? That'll go. It will be gone. And whatever comes next, whatever you have to face, it can't be worse than living like this, can it? With this pressure? Whatever you've done, Nick, we can sort it out, right? People make mistakes. Make them all the time. We can sort it out. I know . . ."

Tears rolled down Nick's face. He was deflated, shrivelling from the inside out, a rumpled mess of the boy who had swaggered so effectively before. He swallowed nervously, took a sip of water.

"I know you didn't mean to do it," Martin continued softly. "Talk to me. Tell me how it was. You did see Emily, didn't you? On Prebends Bridge?"

His lawyer changed positions in her chair and began to speak, but Nick held up his hand, preventing her. He nodded slowly. "She was just standing there. I couldn't tell who it was at first, it was getting dark, it was hard to see."

"This was when?"

"It must have been about 7.45p.m."

"And what happened? What did you say to her?"

"I went up to her. I was a bit pissed. I said I was sorry about everything that had happened before Easter. That things had got out of hand," Nick sniffed.

"Did you mean it? Or were you just on the pull?" Martin looked hard at him.

He half-smiled. "Sort of. I felt bad for her. When you spend time away from Durham, it gives you a bit of perspective, you know?"

She nodded. "Go on."

"Anyway," he sighed. "I didn't want there to be bad feeling between us. "'Specially not before the exams. We both had to do well." He looked up at Martin then in a vague alarm. "I've got to get a training contract with a magic circle firm next year."

Nick's lawyer shifted slightly at that, and Martin made a note on her pad. She had no idea what a magic circle firm was. "And how did Emily respond to this?"

"She was a bit drunk as well. At first, she told me to fuck off. She said she'd had enough of being treated like a slut."

"Was she? Treated like a slut, I mean?" she asked.

He shrugged. "It's just a game, you know? It's just the way it is. Girls and guys. They're just *different*. I liked Emily. I really did." Nick looked on the verge of tears again. "But, you know, I wouldn't have married her." He gave a short laugh. "Girls like that. She's too wild. Too strong. Not the marrying type," he mumbled.

"So," Martin said heavily. "You were happy to sleep with Emily. Post sexual photos of her online to get some kudos, get slaps on the back in the bar."

"I didn't post all of them." He wagged his finger at her, pausing. "Emily was always so on it, you know? She was . . ." he continued, waving his hands around as if searching for the right word. "She got it — what goes on here. She knew people judged her on her looks, her body. She didn't seem to mind. She used it to her advantage. I was surprised when she got so upset, I didn't get it. I mean, if you're going to get yourself photographed, why wouldn't you mind people seeing them?"

"But did she *get herself* photographed to begin with? As far as I understand it," Martin skimmed back through her notes, "the original photo at the Christmas Ball was a trick by you. And then you emailed round the video?"

"Yeah, that was a joke. I was a dick, all right?" Nick was pale under his tan. "But then it got out of hand. I see that. But she let it happen. It was just as much her as me."

She considered him, thinking. "She wasn't persuaded to take those photos by anyone else so far as you're aware?"

He shook his head.

338

"So, the night of the Regatta, you wanted to make it up with her. Carry on whatever it was you had with her."

"Yeah, I suppose," he answered, looking down.

"So what happened? Did Emily not like this proposed deal?"

He grimaced. "She slapped me," he said.

She paused slightly before speaking. "She slapped you," she repeated, "because she wasn't happy with you dumping her then picking her up again?"

"I suppose," he mumbled.

"And how did it make you feel? Being slapped by her?"

"It didn't make me feel anything."

"Really? It didn't make you feel angry? I'd feel angry if someone smacked me in the face and I didn't deserve it. You didn't deserve it, did you, Nick?"

"No. I mean — I didn't deserve it. But I didn't feel angry. I didn't feel anything."

"Did you go to Emily's memorial?" Martin asked suddenly. "I don't think I saw you there."

"No," Nick mumbled.

"Why not?" She looked at him intently. "She was your girlfriend. Why wouldn't you go?" She stopped and said softly, "Unless you were ashamed, perhaps?"

"You think I didn't go because I was ashamed?" Nick looked desolate, his voice cracked forlornly.

Martin was silent.

Nick stared at her, defeated. "It's not true. But what's the point, you're not going to believe me. I can't prove it. I . . ."

"What can't you prove?" she asked. "Why didn't you go to the memorial?"

"I *did* go to the fucking memorial!" Nick cried out. "You saw me! You chased me out of the fucking door and through the graveyard."

She paused, thinking, remembering the boy at the cathedral door, the chase through the gravestones. She'd thought that boy had been Daniel Shepherd.

Nick pushed his chair back and stood up. He walked towards one of the grey walls in the interview room, jiggling his arms as if trying to get the blood flowing. He flexed his fingers before putting them together and cracking his knuckles with a loud snap. "Look, are you going to believe me? I'm telling you everything."

"Yes."

"Are you?" he said desperately, his eyes shining with tears.

"Yes, I am," Martin nodded firmly. "Trust me."

Butterworth met Martin in the corridor as she left Nick a while later. "Rush and his dad will be here in an hour," he said, looking down at her.

She gave him a brief smile. "Thanks. I'm sorry we're playing musical chairs in the interview room."

Butterworth sighed. "Assistant Chief Constable Worthing's on the warpath, but I told him we'd have a result soon." He raised one eyebrow. "You swore it, after all."

Martin ignored the latent flirtation. "We've had a break at least. Nick Oliver admits he saw Emily on the bridge."

"And . . .?"

"Before she was killed. Says they had an argument, she slapped him, and then Nick stalked off and left her alone."

"Is that likely?"

"Is a spat enough? For the brutality of what was done to Emily?" Martin asked, her eyes growing distant, as if thinking out loud.

"People have murdered for less," Butterworth said.

"Yeah, I suppose." She rubbed her lips together. "But we need to ask Rush about the photo Emily had on her MacBook. That provides a concrete motive."

"Why did Emily take that photo?"

She sighed. "I think it's just what went on. There was an entire currency of swapping photos, videos. Everyone did it." She grimaced. "Does it."

"And the alibi given by Mason for Rush?"

She shrugged. "Enough for reasonable doubt? I don't think so, not once we put the evidence of the parties Rush was hosting and the interest Mason had in him on the table." She leaned back against the wall and gave another sigh.

"What is it?"

"This Daniel Shepherd. He keeps popping up: with the counsellor; online; even that journalist had been in contact with him. I just . . ." Butterworth waited, studying her face until she met his eyes. "I just don't get him," she finished lamely.

Well," Butterworth said, taking a step back. "See how you get on with Rush. If anyone can get something out of him, I'm sure it's you, Erica."

She smiled at him. "Thanks."

He turned to leave. "But don't take your eyes off Brabents," he said over his shoulder as he walked away. "The clock's ticking, don't forget."

She watched him go. The clock was ticking loudly. On everything.

CHAPTER
FORTY-NINE

Thursday 25 May, 11.11 a.m.

Martin and Jones looked at him through the grimy glass of the door to the interview room. Simon Rush was sitting on an orange bucket seat, leaning forwards, his elbows on his knees. His father was positioned next to him, a lone Sphinx guarding the tomb. Martin thought back to how he'd been in the last interview. Something had been triggered in him then, when he was pushed, when he was put under stress. Something frightening to witness. And yet — her lips moved as if talking to herself — the doctors had found no disorder, no condition suffered by Simon, other than some depression and anxiety.

The thought came impulsively to Martin that Simon's father knew nothing of the alibi Principal Mason had given the boy. Simon had been transferred to hospital on the same day and had almost immediately afterwards withdrawn his confession. There had been no chance to tell him about it. Mervyn was a bully, and Simon was afraid of him. *All right then.*

"You'll be watching upstairs?" she said to Jones, who nodded. "Give me about fifteen minutes. See how it's going. I'm going to push Simon a bit. When you see him getting stressed out, cause a diversion."

Jones looked at her, perplexed. "A diversion?"

"Anything, Jones," Martin said, exasperated. "Use your imagination."

Jones straightened and lifted her chin. "Yes, boss. I'm on it."

Martin smiled at her. "Good for you, Jones." She took a breath and pushed the door open. As she walked in, Rush turned his face to her and smirked briefly with cold eyes. She sat down with a relaxed expression. Mervyn Rush folded his arms pointedly.

She had turned on the tape, given the caution and was about to begin when Simon said, apropos nothing, in a statement which sounded as if it had been prepared, "I admit I was trolling Emily. But that's it. All the other stuff," he shook his head, closing his eyes tightly as if remembering a bad dream, "it was all lies. I was at breaking point. When I saw you in Principal Mason's office the morning that Emily was found, I saw my chance. I needed anything to get me out of here, out of Durham."

Martin considered this, taking a moment. *How to play it?* Simon's father was clearly letting him speak this time around. He had dealt the trolling card. Okay, then, she would match him. "Tell me about the trolling, Simon. What exactly do you mean by that?"

"Do you mind if I . . . ?" Simon gestured to the small window high up one of the walls in the interview room.

Martin shook her head, and he got up to stand underneath it, lifting his chin towards it as if to elongate himself, reach up and out to the sky. He turned to face her and a tunnel of sunlight appeared to zone downwards on to his head, dust particles floating above him like a halo. He swallowed before speaking. "With trolling, I mean I verbally insulted her online. I typed things on her profile, on the photos that had been posted of her." He raised his eyebrows and gave a small shrug. "I was despicable, Detective Inspector, I mean, really despicable."

"Give me an example. Of the things you said."

"*Slag. You are an ugly slut and the best you could do would be to kill yourself. Nobody would care anyway. You're so ugly, nobody would even want to rape you.*" Simon looked Martin dead in the eye. "See?"

Martin clasped her hands behind her neck. "But why, Simon? Why would you say such awful things? I know you had been hurt by Emily but you liked her, didn't you? It seems from what her friends say that you were quite keen on her, fancied her. Why would you want to hurt her like this?"

Simon shook his head, and tears sprang into his eyes. She studied his face carefully.

"I was under a great deal of stress," he said at last, taking his seat.

There's the opening, she thought. "Tell me about that stress, Simon." She spun a quick glance at Mervyn before looking back at the boy. "Was the stress to do with your relationship with Principal Mason?"

Simon made a sound at the back of his throat.

"What relationship?" Mervyn asked, frowning.

Martin gave him a puzzled look. "Ah, I'm sorry. I thought you were aware of the statement the principal of Joyce College gave subsequent to Simon's arrest." She turned her eyes to Simon, who had begun to breathe rapidly. She leaned back in her chair. "Simon, calm down, please. Have some water. We don't need any histrionics again. There's nothing wrong with you, so let's just keep it calm, okay?" She poured him a glass and he gulped at it, wiping his mouth after taking a drink.

Mervyn sat back in his seat and crossed his legs. His pen dangled in his fingers, tapping a rhythm on his knee. What are you talking about, Inspector? What statement?

"Aaah, let's see." Martin picked up the papers she had put on the desk in front of her. "Yes, here we are. What did he say again?" She looked up briefly at Simon before glancing back down. "That's it. He said that *He* — that's Simon — uh, *sexually excited me.*"

"Stop it," Simon said in a dull voice.

Martin thought fast, took a punt, hoping Jones would catch up from where she would be watching this with Butterworth. "And, ah yes, here we are," she pretended to read aloud, "*Simon would have parties, which I would attend.* When asked what would happen at those parties, the principal said, uh, *we would do private things. Things between men.*" She looked up, the dregs of a sad smile filtering away on her face. "Is that the stress you mean, Simon?" Simon had a sheen

346

of perspiration across his forehead. Mervyn's mouth gaped open unattractively. "I can't imagine how horrific that must have been for you," she said. "To be involved in something so . . ." She cleared her throat. "*Seedy.*"

"I don't know what you think you're playing at here," Mervyn said in anger, "but you'd better explain yourself. You're talking utter rubbish." His eyes glinted steel at his son. "Isn't she, Simon?"

Simon licked his lips and appeared to be unable to speak. *Come on, Jones,* Martin thought. *Come on.*

A knock came at the door, and Jones entered, slightly red in the face. "Your, uh, car's blocking the car park, boss. Sorry. You have to come now and, uh, move it now, if you don't mind."

Martin stood quickly and went to the door. "I'm sorry, Simon. I just have to deal with something. Won't be a minute." She ducked out of the room, leaving Simon and his father alone. "My car's blocking the car park?" she whispered to Jones outside, in a disbelieving tone. "That's the best you could come up with?"

Simon and his father sat in silence, next to each other, both staring straight ahead. After a moment, Mervyn bent his head self-consciously, darting a look to the corner of the room where the camera was, leaning in closer to Simon without looking at him. "What the *fuck?*" he whispered.

Simon said nothing, his eyes fixed on a point on the wall in front.

"Tell me you haven't been up to your old tricks, you little shit. Tell me." Mervyn spat the words hoarsely. His mouth curled down at the ends in disgust. "Have you been sticking your dick where it shouldn't go, Simon? Eh, you little queer?"

Martin and Jones watched them silently through the window in the door, hidden from sight. Rush and his father looked like statues, knees facing forwards, hands on the table. The only outward sign of rage was Mervyn's furious eyes and his mouth, twisting and turning like a fat slab of red, wet muscle. Simon, on the other hand, was still as stone and pale as marble. Martin waited, watching Mervyn's mouth, unable to hear the words but grasping the fury, knowing that the interview tape was still rolling inside. Eventually Mervyn stopped, his mouth hardened and flattened, and he moved his head back to centre. Simon still stared; his eyes were blank and cloudless spheres.

Martin opened the door loudly, marching in with Jones right behind her. "Sorry about that," she said briskly. "Now. Where were we? Jones?"

Jones smiled and introduced herself. "Maybe we could talk about last Sunday, Simon. Try and rectify the truth from your statement which you, uh, now say is untrue. Is that right?" She waited for Simon to respond, but nothing came. "Okay, then."

They waited for a few minutes as Simon continued to stare at the wall. His nostrils flared briefly.

"Simon?" Martin said gently after a time. "Simon? Can you hear me? You need to tell us what happened on Sunday. What happened down at the boathouse and on the bridge? It's okay, Simon. You can tell us now."

Simon blinked slowly and looked down into his lap. Martin waited, holding her breath. When he looked up, his face had changed. His eyes had darkened from blue to grey, and he put his head to one side, as if preferring the view from this angle; his chin was lifted a little higher. He removed his glasses and began to speak. His voice was different. It was softer and less well-spoken. He seemed now in a state of complete calm, his breathing steady, his hands resting idly on his jeans. He looked at Martin all the time as he talked, gazing right through her as if through a window. She let him go, let him speak without interruption, a cold shiver mounting steadily up her spine as she listened to his words.

"I love going to the weir. It's the one place I feel . . . *at home*," Simon said. "It was always there, you know? The waters rushing, the noise of it. It was peaceful," he sighed.

"It was a bright morning. I hadn't seen Emily since arriving back at Durham the week before. I couldn't bear to think of Easter. I'd pushed those weeks to the back of my mind. I was focused on running, on reading again and revising for the three exams I had to take at the end of the month. I had avoided Joyce, skirting round it on the routes of my runs. I stuck to the river, tracing its course around the island of the old part of the city. It's mouldy, don't you think? That mound of medieval architecture? Green and slimy, sinking into the water." He smiled briefly. "I always ended up at the weir, though. I could sit and watch the white water bubbling like a cold cauldron for an hour at a time."

Martin frowned. Simon was a changeling. Where he had been staccato, ranging from mute to monosyllabic, now he was articulate — talking in a strangely old-fashioned way, using words like beacons — lighting the way for Martin to see exactly what he was describing.

Simon smiled. "You know what a big deal the Regatta is in Durham. It was happening right then that day, downriver. I knew there would be a full-on day of partying with brass bands tooting, punnets of strawberries and cream, the colours of all the colleges flying in the wind, culminating in a big drunken free-for-all. But I was planning on seeing none of it. I had escaped up there, away from everyone, with my books and crib notes.

"I heard some voices then, coming along the path up to the bridge. I didn't want to see anyone so I ducked out of sight, into the bushes on the bank. It wouldn't be the last time I would do that before the day was out.

"The voices receded, and I emerged from my hiding place. It was past lunchtime, I guessed, although I wasn't wearing a watch. I found a patch of shady grass near to the water's edge but fairly out of the way and spread my waterproof jacket on the ground. I took out my notes and a textbook. The sun beat down on my back and on to my head. My eyelids kept dropping soporifically. The book must have fallen from my fingers, and I lay back on the ground and slept.

"I don't know how long I'd been asleep for but I was suddenly awake. It was much later, the sun was low. I sat up, rubbed my hands over my eyes and looked

350

down the riverbank towards the city centre. I decided to abandon my books for a while and take a stroll, see how the party was progressing.

"I walked slowly along the bank in the late-afternoon sun. I could hear the festivities before I saw them. There's a lazy corner of the river, just underneath some willow trees, where coxes give pep talks to their boats. That's where the Joyce boathouse is — and that day it was the castle of fun. Around it were stalls selling crepes and strawberries and jugs of Pimm's. People sprawled on the grass under the bunting, boats dripping with water discarded next to them. A loudspeaker droned above the noise, calling out race results. The competition was finished, and now it was time to get pissed in the evening light. Someone was half-heartedly blowing a trumpet, a sound which grated on my nerves, made me ill at ease.

"I wandered around the prone bodies on the grass. I didn't know why I was there. My sun-soaked sleep had shifted something in me, nudged the melancholy which I had successfully buried, so I thought. It emerged in me again, coming down on me like a shower, pin-pricks of misery obstructing me from the enjoyment I could see happening all around me. It wasn't fair. It was then that my mobile phone buzzed with a message. It was from Simon, saying he needed to see me and that he was heading to Palace Green."

"Sorry, Simon. Can I just interrupt you there?" Martin spoke, her heart hammering in her chest. "Did you just say that you received a text message *from Simon?*"

351

Simon's pupils slid over to her, his breathing steady. He nodded.

Martin's brow was furrowed, her mind racing. What was he talking about? A text message from himself?

"I went to meet him," Simon continued. "He was upset and frightened. I comforted him as best I could. Held him. After a while, he ran off. I stood there watching him, as the night began to draw in. He ran past the cathedral and down to the river through the graveyard. I wondered then if he would go to the boathouse. I could hear the sound of the voices there, trailing across the warm wind like the tail of a kite. I didn't know whether to go after him. In that state, he could have done anything. I made a decision. I turned to take the same path he'd just run down and followed him down to the weir . . ."

Simon paused, staring off into space, unseeing. Martin glanced over at Jones, who also appeared in a trance, so closely was she studying Simon. Only her fingers tapping her thighs in a rapid manner betrayed her confusion at what they were hearing. Mervyn Rush had turned his head to look at his son, an appalled expression on his face. He made to speak, but Martin cut him off. "Wait!" she said quickly. "Let him finish. Simon? Simon, it's okay. Keep going. Tell us what happened next."

Simon lethargically moved his face to Martin's and gave her a weak smile. He nodded before taking up his monologue again.

"The first person I saw as I got down to the river-bank was Emily. She left the throng of people at the boathouse and began to walk towards me along the course of the river. She looked miserable, I thought. The feelings I had for her — well, they'd never left me. Despite the trolling, despite everything that had happened before Easter and the awfulness of the holidays, I wanted to check that she would be okay.

"The light was waning, and clouds were rolling in with the rain. It was getting dark, so I don't think she saw me. Emily stumbled a bit as she left. I guessed she had been drinking. You'd have to be a nun not to do so in this environment. And Emily certainly wasn't that — ha!" Simon gave a short laugh before continuing. "I was sober, though. The idea of the gallons of Pimm's they'd all been drinking made my stomach sick. Emily put headphones in her ears, she was in a tipsy reverie, I could tell, listening to music as the sun went down, on her way back to Joyce, I presumed.

"Except that was when I saw him. He was standing on the middle of Prebends Bridge. Waiting. Waiting for Emily." He paused, licking his lips again.

"Who was standing on the bridge, Simon?"

Simon continued as if he hadn't heard Martin. "Emily carried on, stumbling a little up the bank towards the bridge, she was still listening to her music. The noise of that trumpet continued to blow from downriver, the melody cutting out on the wind like a bad internet connection. I didn't know what to do. I hadn't spoken to her since the night of the Formal. What could I say? She hated me, I thought. So I stood still in the shadows behind a fringe of trees. It was still light but at that moment where the darkness is about to hit. Everything seemed bathed in blue.

"She began to walk up the approach to the bridge, heading towards Nick." Martin felt Jones glance over at her. So far, Simon's story tallied with Nick's: he had been on the bridge with Emily. "He was standing quite still, he must have come back from the Regatta at the same time as me but along the other bank, for some reason. As she stepped on to the bridge, he pushed himself off the ramparts where he had been leaning. He moved towards Emily as she lifted her head and saw him for the first time. Underneath them both, the weir was dark with lights glinting through it. It looked like liquid liquorice.

"Then suddenly, as I'd thought he would be, I could see Simon watching them on the same side of the bridge as me. I didn't know what was going to happen but I edged in closer. It was dusky now, they didn't know I was there; I could only see their outlines. They looked like characters in a play. A sudden wail of that blasted trumpet and then it was quiet."

"I'm sorry, Simon, but I just want to get this clear," Martin said. "You were watching as Nick met Emily on the bridge? But *Simon* was also watching them, hidden in the bushes?" She narrowed her eyes, watching the boy's reaction. "You mean *you* were watching them, don't you?"

Simon ignored Martin, as if the question was an irrelevance and took a breath before beginning again. His voice lilted in the interview room, its timbre casting a spell over the other inhabitants, who stared at him as if stupefied, unable to believe what they were hearing. "I moved nearer to the bridge, wanting to know what

Nick and Emily were saying. There was a slight breeze rustling the surrounding trees, making it hard to hear things exactly. I got as close as I could without being seen, bent over almost on my knees, straining my neck to get my ears closer. I could hear Emily's voice; she sounded angry, talking nineteen to the dozen. Then I saw Nick take Emily by the arm. She tried to break free and managed to push him away so he fell back against the balustrade." Simon looked at Martin steadily, his shoulders sagging a little as if energy was leaking from his pores.

"And was that when you moved up on to the bridge, Simon? Were you trying to protect Emily?" Martin asked, her voice low, trying to keep him going.

"Nick ran off," he answered patiently. "Emily slapped him, and Nick ran away, like he *always* does," he said with disdain. "*That* was when Simon went on to the bridge."

"Simon, let me get this straight. *You* went on to the bridge after Nick had run off?" Martin repeated.

Something passed over Simon's face, a mild confusion. He seemed to focus again, his pupils dilating as he took in Martin, sitting on the edge of her seat in front of him, a fierce determination on her face.

"There's one thing I don't understand," he said in a puzzled way, shaking his head from side to side as if he had water in his ears.

"What don't you understand, Simon?" Martin asked softly. The question floated into the air, a weather balloon seeking out lightning.

Simon narrowed his eyes and jerked forwards quickly, unexpectedly, causing Martin to draw back in surprise. "Why do you keep calling me Simon?" he snarled. "You know that's not who I am."

Martin swallowed, looking him directly in the eye. The interview seemed to be hurtling towards some terrible, inevitable conclusion. "I'm sorry," she said, opening her palms in an attempt to calm him. "I've got it wrong." She paused for a second, taking a breath. Simon's eyes seemed to bore into her, into her very soul. She didn't falter, she held his gaze. "Who are you then? Tell me who you are."

She knew what the words would be before they left the boy's mouth. He smiled a charming smile, leaning back in his chair and crossing his legs. "Come, come. You know who I am," he laughed. "I'm Daniel Shepherd."

CHAPTER
FIFTY

Thursday 25 May, 12.13 p.m.

"What do you mean you're Daniel Shepherd?" Martin asked quietly.

Simon looked her, a smile playing on his lips. He shrugged. "What I say."

Martin stared at him. Mervyn and Jones were also transfixed, their eyes focused on Simon. He lifted his head in disdain.

Martin gave a low whistle. "Good lord, boy." She gave a short cough, flicking her eyes to the CCTV camera, a feeling of cold calm stealing through her, wondering what the team would be making of this. She would bluster, she thought with a start, feeling the fired-up energy of a result pulsing through her veins. She would brazen it out to the finish line.

"You're telling me that your name is not Simon Rush. But that you are actually called Daniel Shepherd. I just want to clarify this."

"I am Daniel Shepherd," Simon repeated.

Martin leaned forwards. "And yet, you say you saw Simon Rush on the bridge with Emily? It was *Simon* who was there on Sunday evening?"

"On the bridge," the boy repeated sullenly.

Martin cleared her throat. "All right. Let's talk about Stephanie Suleiman." She pulled at her earlobe, thinking fast. "Stephanie has a folder full of emails from Daniel Shepherd. Did you send those emails?"

Simon nodded.

"Why did you tell her you were called Daniel Shepherd?"

"I am Daniel Shepherd."

"Everything in those emails, all your descriptions of your friendship with Emily Brabents, your life here in Durham — that's all about you? You as Daniel Shepherd, not Simon Rush?"

Simon sneered. "How many times do I have to say it?"

Jones shifted uncomfortably, wondering when Martin was going to call the medical examiner. Something had gone terribly wrong with his assessment. How had they missed this? Rush appeared to be in the throes of some kind of blackout, the effects of a multiple personality disorder perhaps. He acted as if he were a different person, seeming entirely changed before their very eyes. She looked over at Martin — should she step in? Martin, though, was oblivious to anyone else in the room but Simon. She sat forwards on her chair; she looked like a wolf stretching on her hind legs, ready to pounce.

"Do you know a man called Sean Egan?" Martin asked.

Simon nodded again, blinking.

358

"Did you email him a sex video of Emily and Nick from an email account with the name of Daniel Shepherd?"

"Yes," Simon stifled a yawn and then giggled, putting a hand over his mouth.

Martin took a breath. "Let's take it back. When did you arrive in Durham?" She smiled at the boy. "Daniel."

"Boring," Simon said with scorn. "As I said, everything's in the emails to Stephanie. I started at Durham this year. You know I did."

"Simon, what are you talking about?" Mervyn Rush interrupted, bewildered.

Martin hurried on, ignoring Mervyn. "So, according to you, as you've detailed in the emails to Stephanie, you are not a third-year student but a Fresher at Nightingale College?"

Simon smiled at her.

"Is that when you met Simon? When you came up to Durham?" Martin continued.

"No, no, no. I've known Simon for years."

"Since when?"

Simon looked over at his father, who was white in the face. "Simon's daddy knows, doesn't he? Why don't you tell them, Mervyn?" He paused, watching Mervyn's bafflement. "No?" Simon turned his head back to Martin. "I met Simon on a little trip to the beach he took with his mummy. Ah, it was a sad day, wasn't it, Mervyn? Mummy running into the sea and never coming back. Poor old Simon. Standing on the beach in his little shorts, calling for her. And then he had to go home and see his daddy, who *didn't give a fuck*," he hissed. "Shunted him off to boarding school, didn't even have him back for Christmas. Oh, boo fucking hoo." Simon sniffed and straightened in his chair. "I kept in touch with Simon. Helped him through a few things. I was there for him. Unlike *some people*."

"Simon became friends with Daniel then? When he was a small boy?"

"Ten," Mervyn murmured. "He was ten when his mother died."

"That's what Simon always says you say!" Simon cried gleefully. "She didn't *die*. She *killed herself*. There's a big difference there, Mervyn."

Martin shook her head slightly. She knew Butterworth would already be frantically on the phone, trying to get hold of the psychiatric team. But that hadn't worked before. For some reason what was transpiring before their very eyes hadn't been picked up on, hadn't been diagnosed. This was a complete fuck-up. Martin felt the sheen of a cold sweat. Was she facing the end of her career?

She willed herself on, slapped herself in the face metaphorically. She was close — close to another confession to the murder, but this time in front of his father, a QC no less. She had to focus. To bring Simon or Daniel or whatever the fuck his name was to heel. Make him concentrate.

"How do you help Simon, Daniel? I mean, you do help him, don't you? Give him support?"

Simon nodded firmly. "Simon's under a lot of pressure," he said. "He has to do all these things he doesn't want."

"Like what?"

Simon shrugged. "Be the best. Get the grades. Be the president. Pander to Mason."

Martin waited.

"It's too much," Simon continued, shaking his head with tears in his eyes. "How can anyone expect him to cope with all of that? Especially when the girl he wants says no to him — *rejects* him. Especially when his dad's such a *cock*," he snarled, looking at Mervyn. "Simon tries his best. He drinks too much. Takes a little something here and there to help him." He looked sadly at Martin. "I don't agree with that, I've told him." He sighed. "But I do what I can. We go for coffee. We talk about books. We love talking about books. That makes him happy." Simon laughed. "He likes Greene, Inspector. Do you like Graham Greene, by any chance?"

Martin smiled easily at him despite the rushing of blood in her head. Something sparked in her then, a flame of a thought at the back of her brain. "I do," she answered. "Very much."

Simon nodded, pleased by this. "Yeah, well. So that's how I help him when he's stressed."

Martin inhaled quietly. "And Emily? Was Emily his friend?"

Simon frowned. "At first," he said quietly. "But then she went away from him. Got involved with all those dicks in college. Simon hated to see it. It wasn't fair."

He looked up without warning, with an expression of such pure innocence that Martin felt as if she had been smacked in the face. His body was stiff, a rigid conduit of ... something ... something Martin couldn't quantify, couldn't place. She continued to breathe quietly, observing him. What was it?

"Simon liked Emily, didn't he?" Martin asked gently. "Romantically, I mean?"

"I think so," Simon agreed. "I mean." He opened his hands, "I don't agree with everything he did. Pushing her to Nick," he scoffed, "was a pretty fucking stupid idea. And then getting Nick to show everyone the last set of photos. It just meant Emily ended up hating him." He halted and stared at the wall again, seeming confused. "She *hated* him . . ." he repeated softly.

Martin kept her eyes on Simon. Something was nagging at her. She couldn't put her finger on it. *What was it?* She thought again. The photos. The emails to Stephanie said that *Daniel* had got Nick to show off the photos. It didn't add up.

"But then again," Simon continued. "What sort of girl takes those kinds of photos unless she wants them to be seen? I couldn't understand it. It made me angry. She was allowed to go beyond the pale and get away with it. Something about that made me very angry. You see? I understand everything. It's not like I don't."

There it was again, Martin thought. Something wasn't right. *Push on*, she thought. *Keep it going*.

"So, Daniel," she said, causing him to focus back on her, "can you tell me what happened on the bridge on Sunday? Can you talk me through it?"

Simon put his head in his hands. "It's hard, you know?"

"I know it is," Martin said.

"After Easter, it was awful. I almost didn't come back to Durham."

"What had happened, Daniel?" Martin asked. "Why didn't you want to come back?"

He looked at her, confused. "Because Emily hated me. After the Epiphany Formal when everyone had seen the photos."

Martin said nothing, her mind whirring. She let Simon continue to speak, to carry on talking as if he were the boy called Daniel Shepherd.

"But I couldn't just run away. I had to face it. Who was I, if I couldn't do that? I went back up and tried to forget about everything. I studied for the exams. I ran a lot. I kept myself to myself. But then I saw Emily, one day, in the middle of town. She was just walking along the road by herself. Holding a carrier bag of shopping. She looked so — *at ease*. Everything melted away, all the anger and rage. I just wanted to be with her again. Just see her and talk to her and try and explain.

"So I left a note on her door. I asked her to meet me on Prebends Bridge on the day of the Regatta."

Martin remembered the jagged edge of a note stuck outside Emily's room. Simon must have come back later to rip off his message, to hide the evidence that he had arranged to meet her.

"And then I waited. I stood on the bridge, by myself, for an hour, getting colder and colder, knowing that she wasn't going to come. Then I was Kai in *The Snow*

Queen, and ice spread over my heart. I went to the boathouse, saw her lying on the grass with some people I didn't know. It was that I think. What I had known all along. I was *irrelevant*. I wanted to drill myself into the ground, be invisible; be buried in my grief."

Something was triggered in Martin again. "Your grief?" she asked quietly. "Or Simon's?"

Simon looked at her steadily. "Simon's." He paused. "He texted me and we met on the Palace Green. He was terribly upset." He shook his head sadly. "Emily had taken a photo of him with Mason. She'd told him about it down at the boathouse. He was terrified his father would see it." Simon swung his hand lazily towards Mervyn. "You can see why, right?

"I gave him a hug and told him to go home," Simon carried on speaking as Daniel, his voice flat but recognizably different from how he had spoken before. "Told him that everything would be okay. But he was distraught. He ran off, down towards the weir. That's when I followed him. I went to the boathouse, saw Emily come on to the bridge and meet Nick. They stood and talked. And then I saw her slap him.

"Just once. But it was hard. The sound carried into the trees. I felt a rush of excitement at that, I'm being honest with you. *Finally*, Emily had realized what a cock Nick was. She was going to show him he couldn't treat her like that. I was half-laughing to myself at the beauty of it, the fucking comeuppance he was getting. Seriously, the arrogance of him is quite astounding. Here he was, begging her to come back to him, and she was telling him to fuck off. I wanted to cheer and whoop. *The underdog was going to win!* It was like those films, *Rocky* or whatever, *The Champ*. I had watched them as a kid. The little guy, always beaten down, coming good and showing everyone what a supreme guy he *actually was*. That was me. I was going to show them. Emily had realized it, once and for all."

Martin's thoughts were racing through her brain, a jumble of competing ideas blaring at her through the drone of this voice that suggested another being, another person: Daniel Shepherd. Sentences jumped out at her as if white subliminal messages on a black screen: *Emily hated me, watched them as a kid* and *I was going to show them*.

" 'You can't just snap your fingers and expect me to jump,' I think I heard Emily say." Simon continued speaking as Daniel. "But I was so afraid of what might happen. That she would go back to him. Again and again I had watched her do it. *Why wouldn't she fucking learn?* She was wearing a purple Durham T-shirt. And she had on a kind of white tracksuit top. She looked so small next to Nick. That ponytail of hers, always swinging off her back. She was so cheery and good and wholesome. I couldn't bear what he'd done to her. What this place had done to her. Besmirched her. Made her into one of them. Now she was just a wax-work copy, entirely unoriginal. Where had my Emily gone?

"Nick ran away. I watched him go," he said in disbelief. "I mean, he *had* her, she would have done anything for him, even after the slap. I'm sure of it. But he tossed her away like a piece of dirt. Something rushed in me, the noise of the weir waters, spilling over stones, its current dragging against the bank. That devil in me, the one I thought I'd silenced, he came again. There he was, standing on the other side of the river, beating his wings, waiting to enfold me. I shook my head to try and rid myself of his image, but he leered into my face. In a flash, I was standing next to Emily. She turned to face me, a look of triumph on her face, which turned sour as soon as she saw it was me and not her *lover boy* back again.

"'Simon, what are you doing here?' Emily said, sounding frightened. I didn't want to scare her so I went to touch her arm, to comfort her. But she drew back quickly as if I'd burned her with my fingers. 'Stay away from me,' she cried.

"'Emily, I . . .' I stepped towards her, but she reared back."

As he spoke, Simon gestured and moved in his seat as if he were acting out the scene, taking on the different parts. Martin shuddered internally at the sight of it.

"I looked down at my feet. These feet which were mine. They took me over rocky grounds, up hills, to mountaintops, along beaches. *The things I'd seen.* Who was this girl to judge me? To judge whether I was good enough or not? I summoned it up in myself; that rage. I tried to make for Emily again. As I moved towards her, she stood taller, as if she too was calling up her strength. She lifted her chin and, oh God, it reminded me of her sitting on the train, that first day. How the light from that northern morning had hit her face, just for a second. How I had smiled at her as I took her suitcase and she had walked off the train in front of me. All that possibility then. Gone and smashed on the rocks of fucking mistakes and circumstance.

"She came at me then, as these thoughts doused me, she had one last fight in her. And as I grabbed her, all I could see were her eyes, like wet and glistening stones of mourning. I reached for her and then I had her with me. *With me*. I was holding her, cradling her head, cracking it, twisting it, bending her into me. I was holding her and she was mine."

Simon bent his head, breathing deeply.

"Afterwards, I carried her off the bridge and laid her on the bank. I took off her jacket, I don't know why. Then I saw the scars on her arms. I imagined her, alone and sitting in her bathroom, a razor blade in her hand. It broke my heart when I thought about it. That beautiful skin. Rivered with her blood. How could she do it — puncture herself? The strength, the strength she needed to do it. I was almost admiring. If I hadn't been so sad.

"I know it sounds crazy. But I didn't mourn for her then. I didn't believe it, really. I couldn't see it as real. There she was, lying beautifully in the moonlight. I could have sat there all night, stroking her hair. But then I heard a noise, footsteps; people coming back from the Regatta party. It burst the bubble of the last hour. The two of us: Emily and me. I stood up. I had won. I had conquered her.

"I looked westwards, into the mouth of the river, and, using the tip of my trainer, I prised Emily's shoulder up high enough, until the weight of gravity and the slope of the bank rolled her down into the weir."

CHAPTER
FIFTY-ONE

Thursday 25 May, 3.00 p.m.

Martin sat in the small canteen of the Durham police station, a cooling cup of coffee in front of her, a half-eaten KitKat in her hand. Mervyn Rush had asked for a break, and Martin had agreed, suspending the interview. She wanted to clear her head for a while in any event — whirring thoughts motoring inside her head, flapping ideas into sandstorms. She needed some calm to work it all out. She stared out of the window, looking on to the city.

The body of the cathedral rose up from its island in the distance. It was a visual illusion, as if the cathedral was actually poking up from the middle of the cluster of newer buildings around it. Martin wondered idly whether the modern town planners had intended this. The sunlit glassy surface of the River Wear circled round as ever. Not for the first time, Martin felt there to be something ominous in that. The river had a stranglehold on the island, it snaked it, tightening its grip with every whorl.

The canteen was quiet, most of the force were out in the city patrolling the streets, or downstairs in the bustle of the offices. The silence was oppressive. Martin jumped sharply at the noise of a plate being dropped into the sink in the kitchen. She looked at the rest of the KitKat but couldn't face it, pushed it away from her on the table.

"Boss?" Jones walked into the canteen and sat down opposite Martin.

"All along, throughout the past few days, I've been wondering to myself, who is Emily?" Martin said quietly. "It's the most interesting part about a case like this. Who is the victim? Why are they a victim?" She paused. "*Are they in fact a victim?* It's always puzzled me, that. Normal bright middle-class girl. Comes to university, just like she should. Gets here and has a crush on the captain of the hockey team. So far, so boring. But then," Martin wagged her finger at Jones, "*then*, she poses for some naked photographs to be put up online. Amazing." Martin turned sideways in her chair so she could cross her legs and lean on her knee. "I mean, it's just not what you'd expect from a girl like that, is it?"

Jones shook her head imperceptibly, unsure where Martin was going.

"But I was wrong, Jones. I was very, very wrong. The truth about this case wasn't Emily." She looked out of the window again. "No. It was Simon Rush."

"Or Daniel as he likes to be called," Jones said.

"Hmmm," Martin answered. She moved the rest of the KitKat towards Jones, who shook her head at it. "I've been thinking about those emails — the ones to Stephanie Suleiman."

Jones looked at her.

"There's something funny about the whole business."

"What do you mean?"

Martin rubbed her hands over her face and gave a small groan. "Ah, it's so fucked up. I can't get it straight." She lifted her head and met Jones' gaze. "Think about it: what's in those emails. Daniel's the loner, right? The outsider. He doesn't have any mates. He hangs around Emily like a bad smell. Fancies her, pushes her to Nick in the hope she'll see the error of her ways and come back to him. Good old ever-faithful Daniel."

"Yes," Jones said. "Simon was hoping she would come back to him but then he messed up by getting Nick to put the photos online, and Emily got mad at him. They had a big fight at Easter, and when he came back, he tried to shame her by selling the video to Egan and then snapped down at the weir when she showed him the photo she'd taken of him and Mason."

"Did Simon do all that? Or was it Daniel?"

Jones looked confused. "They're the same person, boss. We just saw it in the interview room. Before the break. He's got some multiple personality disorder. Whatever the psychs say. You saw it. He wasn't the same person."

Martin sat back in her seat and folded her arms. She said nothing but turned her head again to stare outside. A coxless scull was making its way lazily up the river, rounding the bend. Martin traced its course with her eyes as dark clouds scuttled across the sky.

"It's going to rain," she said.

* ★ *

"I just have a few more questions before we can end this," Martin said as she re-entered the interview room. Simon sat listlessly in his seat. Martin could see that Mervyn had pulled himself together; he was back in the legal zone, piecing together a way out of this for his son. The words *diminished responsibility* seemed to flash above them all in the room like a neon sign.

"I just want to check. I'm speaking to Daniel now, am I?" Martin asked.

Simon nodded.

"Daniel Shepherd is a construct of your imagination, brought on by the stress of witnessing your mother's suicide? Is that what you're saying?"

Simon looked confused. "What are you talking about? I am Daniel Shepherd."

"Yes, of course, sorry." Martin paused. "You'd do anything to protect Simon, wouldn't you, Daniel? I mean, that's the point of your whole existence, isn't it? To protect and help him. You arrive whenever he's in trouble. When he's overwrought, taken too much coke, or weed, when he can't sleep. I know about these things." She gave him a quick smile. "I studied it when I was at university actually. I know the premise."

Simon said nothing, merely looked at her calmly.

"Fugues, they call them. When life gets too painful, the brain splits. Another personality takes over, a personality more adapted to cope with a situation that the first person can't abide. Like today, for example. With Simon's father here. Simon couldn't cope with him hearing about his relationship with Principal

372

Mason. So Daniel arrives to help out. To calm everything down, reason with us all. Daniel's good at that, isn't he? He's articulate and intelligent. He can speak for Simon when Simon can't." She nodded encouragingly. "That's right isn't it?"

Simon shrugged. "I don't know. I only know who I am."

"And the other interesting thing about a condition of this type," Martin continued. "Is that it's incredibly hard to diagnose. It can take years. It's not something that any old doctor or counsellor would pick up on. Usually the initial diagnosis is one of anxiety. Or depression."

Simon said nothing. Mervyn Rush moved in his seat. "I think," he spoke carefully, "that we've said all we can say. We have a confession from Simon but clearly, in the circumstances . . ." His voice faded away. The air turned brittle as Martin's focus on Rush became hard as flint upon iron. Slamming into the ensuing silence, Martin began to clap her hands together loudly. Mervyn and Jones turned to her, amazement etched on to their faces. Simon narrowed his eyes.

"W-what are you doing, Inspector?" Mervyn stammered, rising from his seat. "Please . . ."

Martin carried on clapping. Jones struggled to keep a poker face. What *was* Martin doing?

"Round of applause, Simon. Really, you should get a standing ovation." Martin laughed, gesturing round the room, as Simon looked at her bemused. "You almost had me, I must say. A very clever idea indeed."

Mervyn got to his feet, but Martin waved him down. "Just give me a second, Mr Rush. Let me have my moment." She smiled at him. "So, Simon — sorry, Daniel — my mistake — here's the thing. The stuff you've said in interview, it just isn't adding up to me." Martin stood up herself and went to lean against the wall at the side of the room. She took a slow breath, focusing her thoughts, her eyes never leaving Simon's.

"Let's strip all this back. There've been a lot of smoke and mirrors in this room today. Any day you're in the room actually." She smiled again. "But let's get back to the very beginning. Make things nice and simple.

"Here's what I think happened. I think you — Simon — met Emily on the train coming up to Durham just as Daniel says in the emails. She was a Fresher, impressed by you as a third year — college president no less. She was a normal girl, Emily — as I've always thought. Nothing very special about her in all honesty. But I think she played you a bit. She liked being liked by boys, by you and others. She was pretty and bright, and it flattered her. You fancied her. You let yourself think about her, dream about her. You exposed yourself to her, didn't you? Let her see your vulnerable side.

"There's a lot going on inside your head, Simon. Your parents let you down, abandoned you, it seems. Life's pretty unfair isn't it? You, the massive over-achiever. Expected to get a double first. President of the college. Good-looking. Christ, even the principal fancies you. But Emily doesn't, does she? No. She fancies Nick."

A dank mist began to form over Simon's eyes, a fog which clouded their colour, made them cold.

374

"That rejection made you angry. There you were, having to be this person that you hated — with Mason, with everyone. And you couldn't even get the girl you wanted. That pretty girl who seemed to have it all, everything you thought you deserved. It burned you up, I think, watching her move around the university. And you did watch her, didn't you? You watched her like a hawk. You even went down to London," Martin smiled again, "although you hadn't been invited. You turned up at the place where her brother was doing a gig, tried to ingratiate yourself with her family — who completely ignored you; they didn't even remember your name.

"Emily thought it was funny. She spoke to Annabel about it. But there was no closeness between you. You weren't even friends. She was completely obsessed with Nick. Everything that Daniel says in his emails to Stephanie about his friendship, the intensity he had with Emily, Zack the loyal roommate, all of that is a lie. Fabricated by you, Simon." She paused as the words soaked into the hot, damp walls of the interview room.

"You began to hate Emily. She represented everything you loathed about Durham. The cliques, the subtle bullying. The pressure."

Simon was stone-faced.

"You started it all — her trolling. You — Simon Rush. You invented the character of Daniel Shepherd so that you could troll Emily, didn't you? Daniel's emails say that he joined in with it after his trip down to Brighton. But it started much earlier than that, didn't it? Sitting at different computers all over the university — so you couldn't be traced — tapping out your disgusting thoughts. You liked hurting Emily. It made you feel better. And she gave you good material to work with, after all. The photos and the video with Nick were a gift!" Martin gave a short laugh.

"I don't know why Emily did the video with Nick. I think she did it for the same reason as she posed for the photographs. Because she thought it was good to be seen. Even like that, it was better to be seen than to be ignored." Martin paused, thinking it through. "The irony of it. You *were* seen. You were known in the college. But that didn't make you happy did it — your notoriety? She'd got it in her head that notoriety was something to aim for. But you know it's better to hide in the shadows. To keep your desires secret."

Simon moved imperceptibly in his chair. Martin watched him; his hands were still. He sat like a reptile on a sun-baked rock, his eyes dry and hard.

"All of you here, at the university. You're all pretending to be something you're not, aren't you? Emily's pretending to be a slut to get herself noticed; Nick's pretending to be a stud and all-round sporting hero; Annabel's pretending to like everyone when she actually hates them; and you . . ." Martin pulled up short. "Then there's you."

Simon lifted his eyebrows at her. A challenge. She took it.

"You're pretending to be someone else entirely. Squirrelled away, behind your computer. You could be anyone you wanted to be there, couldn't you? Who would ever know? You could sit in the dark and pull the strings on all the puppets you'd put into place. And a trail would never lead to Simon Rush. It would only ever lead to Daniel Shepherd.

"Emily knew about the parties with Mason. She knew that he was slobbering all over you, that you couldn't escape from it. I suspect she probably knew that you hated it — Annabel said that she knew — but you got no sympathy from Emily. No. She saved it up as information. Like everyone seems to do in this place. Storing things to use against people. But, God forbid, anyone should ever complain it about, right? After all, *it's just a joke*. Isn't it?"

Simon didn't react, lifeless in his seat.

"But then everything changed. Emily took a photograph of you and Mason and told you she had it."

"What photograph?" Mervyn interjected. Martin watched as Simon gave a rapid blink.

"A photo of you and Mason in a — how shall we say — somewhat flirtatious moment?" Martin waited, but Simon managed to remain composed. "Now, that wasn't a joke at all. If that photo got put on the internet, your father might see it. Your father who you've done *everything* for, and who still doesn't give a toss about you." She smiled sadly at Simon. "The whole house of cards would come tumbling down. Everything you've been struggling to control, keep caged and hidden would be exposed. When Emily took that photo, she sealed her fate." Martin stopped, light as air, the realization that what she was saying was true embedding itself deep within her, even as the words danced out of her mouth.

"You had to get Emily's phone and delete that photograph. So you stuck a note on her door arranging to meet her. She ignored it, so you kept an eye on her at the Regatta and followed her when she left. But then Nick turned up. So you waited. And you watched. You saw Emily defend herself for once. That probably excited you." She shrugged with contempt. "I don't know. But you had to get the phone and so you did what you had to do. To injure Emily in the way you did, you would have had to get so close and use such violence . . . Well, she would have been able to see the whites of your eyes, Simon."

A stultified silence pulsed through the room.

"And then Emily was dead. You had to think fast. You chucked the phone in the river I'd guess. It's the obvious place. Oh, and we can dredge it to find out, don't worry about that." She nodded. "You ran back to Emily's room and ripped off the note arranging to meet her. I think that's when the idea first came to you. Someone to blame, Daniel Shepherd, the figment you'd been relying on for so long. I think it was more instinct than anything else, something done without really thinking: you added the impression of the letter *D* then." Martin nodded. "And then what? I can't imagine that night for you, Simon. Hard to come down from, I would think. That buzz, that feeling of power. The memory of Emily dying, scrabbling at her neck while you squeezed the breath out of it. You'd seen her eyes too, hadn't you? Staring into yours as the blood vessels burst and the spark of life was slowly turned off. I tell you what I'd do, if that was me, back in my room after doing that." Martin paused. "I'd start drinking."

Simon continued to stare coldly at her.

"I think you were still pissed when you walked into Principal Mason's office the following morning. There was a quality about you that I couldn't put my finger on. It's hard out of context isn't it?" Martin gave a nonchalant shrug. "I wouldn't have expected the college president to be drunk at seven in the morning. But I remember an aroma on you, and you had that kamikaze look, a burn. What had you got to lose? You walked into that office, saw the teacher who'd essentially been abusing you. You'd had no sleep, were filled up with booze and God knows what else, and you just told it like it was. You confessed."

Martin moved back to her seat and took it. She and Simon looked at each other over the table as if a current pulsed between them.

"It must have been an incredible relief." Martin rubbed the back of her neck with one hand. "You were exhausted after all. At that moment, all you wanted was to get the fuck out of Durham, escape everything — your dad, your life — leave this place that had become a living hell for you. And the best part of confessing was no one would ever need to know about the photograph. Your father would be brought up here to defend you — *look after you for once*. Because that's the only thing that makes sense of it." Martin looked over for a moment, at Mervyn Rush. "For the likes of him, murder seems preferable to the truth of his son living a homosexual life, voluntary or otherwise." She gave a short smile, shifting forwards in her seat. "So, you would be free of this place that's been killing you for the last three years. Everything else — the trolling, the parties with Mason — could all be swept under the carpet.

"But you underestimated your fear once you'd sobered up. How the thought of being locked up — most likely still here, in Durham Prison — made you sweat. You're a bright boy, Simon. A clever boy. And you realized, once you thought about it, that you already had something up your sleeve. Something that would help you get to hospital instead of prison. Your old friend, Daniel Shepherd." Martin gave a brief smile.

Simon shook his head wearily. "How many times do I have to say it? Mr Rush, please. Help me out here. Tell her that I am Daniel."

"A genius construction," Martin continued, as if he hadn't spoken. "Articulate, well-read Daniel, what a sensitive soul. All those things you couldn't be in your real life. How nice to be him for a while." She leaned forwards across the table so her head was parallel with Simon's. "But I know he's a lie," she whispered.

"You could kill a lot of birds with one stone by inventing Daniel, couldn't you?" Martin straightened and counted on her fingers. "Expose Mason and his appalling behaviour to the press by making contact with a journalist as Daniel. Expose Stephanie Suleiman for the croc she is by getting her to believe in a non-existent student. She'd let you down, hadn't she? Just like everyone else. You stopped going to see her, and she couldn't even be bothered to find out why."

She waited before extending her third finger. "And let's not forget the main thing: protecting your identity while trolling Emily within an inch of her life." She stopped.

"And then, of course, in the actual taking of her life, Daniel was your alter ego. But he also gave you the perfect alibi. Because if we all believed that *Daniel* had strangled Emily Brabents, then Simon Rush might not be considered responsible for it in a court of law."

Simon's eyes were lidded, his fingers curled motionless on his legs.

"You want us to believe that you were in a fugue. That the character of Daniel appears when Simon is under stress. That Daniel came on to the bridge. *That Daniel murdered Emily.*" Martin nodded. "Meaning Simon gets off scot-free. Daddy picks the pieces up by arguing you suffer from a multiple personality disorder. That would be enough to argue on balance that you were mentally impaired, that the charge of murder should be reduced to manslaughter due to diminished responsibility. And to think you've done all this thinking and working things out *after* you strangled the girl you say you loved. I'm almost admiring . . ." She smiled. "A very clever double bluff. Which very nearly worked."

Simon moved at last, blinking slowly before crossing one leg over another and crooking his arm over the back of his chair. Silence descended once more on the room. The wall clock hummed.

"Prove it," he said.

"Shut up," Mervyn Rush said quickly.

Martin sat back in her chair before shrugging. "I can't prove it," she said. "You know it as well as I do.

Even if the doctors say you don't have a multiple personality, the jury might still believe it. They might yet think that someone who behaves in the abhorrent way you have — well, they must have been out of control. Who would do as you've done otherwise?" She looked at him. "Unless they believe in evil, of course." She folded her arms, checking with a subtle movement of her eyes that the interview tape was still rolling. "But I can tell you how I know that what I've said is the truth.

"You fucked it up. Right here in this room. You'd been so clever, but it's easier on email, isn't it? Easier on the internet to rehearse your story, to hide away, pretend to be something you're not. Bit more difficult when you're face to face." *With me*, she might have said.

Simon raised his eyebrows. Martin spread her hands, gestured around the room. "Right here. This is where you let yourself down. You'd played it brilliantly up until then. Lured us in with your little playact on Monday. And then the *pièce de resistance* today — *I am Daniel Shepherd*." Martin laughed. "Genius." She turned to Jones. "Don't you think?"

Jones rubbed her lips together, feeling utterly baffled.

"Think about what you said, Simon. Think about what you said here today. Something just wasn't working for me. As I was listening to you, I kept wondering who was talking." She waved her hand. "Oh, yes — the ol' Simon/Daniel conundrum. But it wasn't that actually. It was something you said when you were talking about Emily posing for the photographs. You

382

said that it was *Simon* who had got Nick to show everyone the last set of photographs at the Epiphany Formal. And that Emily had hated him for it. But then . . ." Martin waited for a second, drawing it out, "you said after Easter, that you nearly hadn't come back to Durham because Emily hated *you* — Daniel. And that it made you angry — that *she was allowed to go beyond the pale and get away with it*. That phrase stuck in my head. And let's not forget Mr Greene." She sighed. "Graham Greene," she said again, relaxing with a smile on her face as if there was nothing left to prove. Simon stared at her quietly as Mervyn flicked rapidly through the notes he'd made on his pad.

"I don't get it . . ." Simon said eventually. "What's your point?"

"Who likes Graham Greene, Simon? You or Daniel?"

A ripple passed over Simon's face, a swell of fearful comprehension.

Martin picked up the papers on the table and waved them at him. "It's Daniel, isn't it? Daniel who reads *The Power and the Glory*. Daniel who retreats into books. But you said earlier — and it's all been recorded obviously — that it was *Simon* who liked Greene. You said it when you were talking as Daniel.

"There's more. You described the sequence on the bridge beautifully. How Emily had seen you. She said, *What are you doing, Simon?* And later, you asked — very pitifully, I'll give you that — *Where had my Emily gone?* She was *yours*, you said at the end. That *you* had won. You had conquered, I believe you said — over the two of you — Emily, and *me*.

"But there weren't two of you, were there? There were three. When you were talking like that, who were you being?" She waited a beat before whispering, "You fucked it up . . .

"All along, Daniel has talked about Simon. He's Daniel's friend, the person he's here to help. You mention him in your emails, you've talked about him right here in this very room." She shook her head, giving Jones a quick glance to check she was keeping up. "But it doesn't make sense. There are only two possible situations: either the personality of Daniel arrives when Simon blacks out in a fugue-like state, in which case, neither one would know that the other existed. Or," she raised her eyebrows, "Simon actively recognizes Daniel as another facet of his personality — a multiple of it, if you like. So . . . which is it?'

"What? What do you mean? I don't understand," Simon said.

"Which kind are you? The fugue or the multiple? Come on, Daniel." She put her head on one side. "Let's sort it out once and for all. Who killed Emily? Was it you . . . or was it Simon?"

Martin bit her lip. Adrenaline soared through her veins as she watched Simon's eyes darken before reflecting flashes of lightning. Martin remembered his eyes from that very first morning in Mason's office: fathomless green pools entangled with wet and heavy weeds.

"If the emails are right, and what you've told me today is true, then what you've said happened on the bridge doesn't make any sense."

"Why not?" Mervyn Rush interjected, looking utterly confounded.

Jones leaned forward excitedly. "Because Daniel has said that Simon was on the riverbank too, when Emily was killed. But then, when the murder actually takes place . . . there are only Emily and Daniel on the bridge. When he talked about the murder, he forgot that Simon was supposed to be there as well."

Martin flexed her fingers. "Correct, Jones. Look at everything you've said here today. And then look at the emails to Stephanie from Daniel Shepherd, which were sent well before he — or Simon, or whoever — thought about getting hold of Emily's phone because of that photo.

"Simon and Daniel go to a poetry reading together." She didn't even need to refer to her notes, the content of the emails was burned in her brain. "Daniel went to his room to party. And today, speaking as Daniel, you even describe Simon as sending you a text and meeting you on Palace Green. You said that Simon hid in the bushes and that you both watched Nick and Emily on the bridge before Nick ran off. But then Daniel goes on to the bridge and suddenly —" she inhaled softly — "Simon isn't there any more. Where is he? Where has he gone? He completely disappears from the scene, and it is Daniel who puts his hands around Emily neck; it is Daniel who commits the murder."

Simon's eyes moved hastily from Martin to his father. "He . . . he left . . ."

"They are two separate people," Mervyn interjected, his hand gripped tight on Simon's thigh. "Simon and

385

Daniel. Well, in Simon's head at least," he said with a frown.

Martin shook her head. "Of course they're not, Mr Rush. The truth is," she said, certainty carved into her features. "Daniel Shepherd does not exist."

"Yes, we know that," Mervyn said impatiently. "But Simon *thinks* he does. And so he can't be held responsible for his actions when Daniel takes him over. This is a waste of time, Martin. Let's get Simon the help he needs and wrap this case up."

"True, Simon would like us all to believe that that is the case," Martin said. "Because then he can be considered mentally unstable, or even — best-case scenario — unfit to stand trial. And all the better if *you* think he's got a split personality. Better you think him a loon, and crazy, than a boy who was shagging his university principal. You'd despise him for that, wouldn't you? Even though I'd describe their relationship more as a university professor preying on one of his charges than anything that would remotely be considered consensual."

Mervyn sagged in his seat, unwilling to meet Martin's stare.

"But I know it's a lie," she carried on. "And I will be doing everything in my power to ensure that Simon is charged with murder and that this little charade is seen as nothing more than that. Smoke and mirrors to disguise what he really is: an angry, jealous and violent boy who has no respect for the sanctity of life."

Simon began to blink rapidly. Martin focused in on him for the last time.

"The whole construct is a fake. All of those emails to poor old Stephanie. If Daniel was a split in Simon's personality, neither of them would know about the other, would they?" Martin stopped and folded her hands in her lap, her heart beating fast. "They wouldn't know the other one existed.

"I don't need to prove it, Simon. No matter what you say. That's the beauty of my job. We will be charging you with murder, and then it'll be up to you to defend yourself, somehow. I know you did it. And with the evidence of this interview and from what I'll say on the day, the court will know why it is I am certain that you, Simon Rush, murdered Emily." She stood up and rolled her shoulders. "And so, that's it, really."

"I am Daniel Shepherd," Simon said in vain, but Martin had already turned away to leave the room.

Martin left Jones to deal with the paperwork and headed down the corridor, pushing through the station entrance and stepping out into the transparent light of an afternoon before the rain comes, a sharp contrast to the studied quiet in which she had been contained for the previous few hours. Martin inhaled deeply and leaned against the metal railing of the station steps. Seagulls blared above her, those mysterious birds which constantly peppered the sky, although the sea was a good fifteen miles away eastwards. Time had been refracted since she'd been in that interview room. She felt outside of herself, looking down.

An elderly man stood in the doorway of the newsagent's on the opposite side of the street. She caught his eye, and he considered her for a while before waving his hand gently by his leg and retreating back into the shop.

Martin closed her eyes and breathed in the smell of the smoke and the car fumes and the dust of the pavements. So that was it. Whatever was to happen in the coming days, even if she had to battle for the CPS to make the charge stick, she knew the truth, what had happened to Emily Brabents. Emily, a girl who swam with her chin just up above the water, struggling to breathe, trying to become something more in her life, but choosing the wrong way, a way that led her to stir up rage and jealousy in others. Martin pushed herself off the railings. She had been wrong about Emily. She was not a normal girl. She was instead, maybe a girl born too early.

Feeling strangely empty, Martin turned round and jogged up the steps back into the police station.

CHAPTER
FIFTY-TWO

The last time Martin saw Simon Rush was at the reading of the verdict where he was found guilty of Emily Brabents' murder and sentenced to life imprisonment. Martin had looked up at the gallery to see an ashen Michael Brabents sink his head thankfully into his hands, his son next to him. As she left the court to a typically cold and grey Durham afternoon, Martin wondered whether Emily was predestined for this all along, whether, when it came down to it, Michael Brabents, judging by his fetish for photographs of Emily, would have ultimately been able to control himself with his daughter.

And Principal Mason too, she considered idly. Would he hear of the downfall of Rush — the boy he had abused and manipulated — wherever he had fled to after Egan's exposure of him a few months ago? He had been dismissed from the university under a cloud, that was true. But, Martin thought, was that enough of a punishment to stop him from preying on students again?

Martin stood at the top of the stone steps of the court building. She looked around, debating where to go to celebrate. Jim had moved back to Newcastle four months earlier. She knew it was for the best but she still missed him, missed his presence in the house.

As she switched on her mobile phone to check for messages, she felt someone come and stand next to her. "All right, Jones," she said with a grin. "I thought you were out ridding the Durham streets of crime."

Jones nodded. "I was," she said. "But the streets will be fine for an hour or so. I thought we could have a drink and celebrate."

Martin's phone beeped. She looked down and saw a message asking her to come to dinner. She gave a small smile. Sam could wait.

"Good for you, Jones." The women turned away from the court building. "Shall we cut through to The Oak down by the river?" Martin breathed in the air of the encroaching winter as they walked. She liked this place, she decided. She looked up at the sky, the grey sky with a corner of blue in it, those interminable seagulls screeching around in it, and then over and across the river, at the cathedral, looming in perpetuity over the flurry of the weir.

Acknowledgements

My first thank you is to the beautiful City and University of Durham itself.

Then, to all my remarkable friends in Singapore who have spent (too) much of their time reading numerous drafts of the novel. In no particular order: Fran Rittman, Andrew Stott, Magali Finet, Matthew Schnetter, Marion Kleinschmidt, Sarah Salmon, Sho' Asante and Christine Dawood.

Thank you to Christopher Wakling and Anna Davis for their excellent and invaluable advice and for all of their support in general.

To my incredible friends online and beyond for their insightful help and guidance on plot, names and much, much more. Particularly: Elin Daniels, Dawn Goodwin, Moyette Gibbons, Julietta Henderson, Alex Tyler, Jason Elliott, Rob Walsh, Heidi Perks and Catherine Bennetto.

Thank you to Neil Cramer, Melissa Nolan and Tim Wilson for giving up their valuable police time to read the novel and tell me exactly where I was going wrong. Any mistakes are, of course, my own doing.

To my spies in Durham for their help in reminding me of geography and place names: Jez Light, Sally Bell and Max Wurr.

I read a great deal of material before and during the writing of this book — non-fiction; blogs; and lots of newspaper articles. To the authors and academics who continue to inspire me with their incredible wisdom and philosophies: Ariel Levy (the origins of *liquor* in the book are directly inspired by the discussion of *lickerish* in *Female Chauvinist Pigs*), Naomi Wolf, Natasha Walter, Laura Bates, Caroline Criado-Perez, Hadley Freeman, Jessica Valenti and Nien Cheng.

Thank you to the wonderful Ariella Feiner at United Agents for believing in me, guiding me and having my back for the last couple of years. And for knowing here to buy awesome cinnamon buns.

Special thanks to Emad Akhtar, to whom I will be eternally grateful for loving the characters of *Bitter Fruits* as much as I do. I have been swept away on a tide of your enthusiasm and unstinting support and will be always thankful for your razor-sharp eyes and even sharper ideas.

To my parents, Avril and Malcolm, for their unending love and advice. And for reading the book more times than we can all care to remember. What a start in life you gave me. I hope this makes you proud.

Finally, to my heart outside itself — to Tom, Constance and India.

Other titles published by Ulverscroft:

MIDNIGHT IN DEATH
AND INTERLUDE IN DEATH

J. D. Robb

In *Midnight in Death*, Eve Dallas's name has made a Christmas list, but it's not for being naughty or nice — it's for putting a serial killer behind bars. Now he's escaped and has her in his sights . . . While in *Interlude in Death*, when respected Commander Skinner offers her a promotion if she'll give her husband Roarke up to custody, her reaction is furious. Roarke's Irish past is murky, but he's a changed man — so what is the commander after? With Eve and Skinner at one of Roarke's holiday resorts for a police convention, Skinner's thwarted vengeance soon brings death to their luxury surroundings.

TELL TALE

Mark Sennen

Five years ago, someone murdered DI Charlotte Savage's daughter and got away with it. Now Charlotte knows who was responsible — but the killer's father is a seemingly untouchable high-ranking official, and therefore his son is well protected. Before Charlotte can work out how to get her revenge, disturbing events start to unfold on Dartmoor: a woman's naked body is found near an isolated reservoir on the bleak winter moors. As the body count mounts, and the crimes are linked to mutilated animals and a sinister cult, Charlotte knows she must move fast. But in a police force tainted by corruption, her hunt for the killer won't be easy . . .